"I was thinking about you," David said.

Protectively, Callie's hand clutched her robe. "Me? Why?"

He shook his head. "You'll never know how much you mean to me, Callie. All you've done for us here. You're like a breath of spring after a long winter." A wry grin tugged at the corners of his mouth. "Pretty poetic for the middle of the night, huh?"

"But that's why you hired me. To help your daughter."

"But you've done more than that." He reached across the table and laid his hand on hers. "You've helped me, too. I feel alive again, like a man released from prison, his life restored."

Callie looked at his hand pressing against the back of hers. Though her initial thought was to recoil, she enjoyed the warm pressure against her skin. She wanted to touch his unshaven cheeks with her palms. Everything in her cried out to tell him her own secret, but she pushed the urge deep inside her.

Gail Gaymer Martin is a multi-award-winning novelist and writer of contemporary Christian fiction with fifty-five published novels and four million books sold. *CBS News* listed her among the four best writers in the Detroit area. Gail is a cofounder of American Christian Fiction Writers and a keynote speaker at women's events, and she presents workshops at writers' conferences. She lives in Michigan. Visit her at gailgaymermartin.com.

Virginia Carmichael was born near the Rocky Mountains, and although she has traveled around the world, the wilds of Colorado run in her veins. A big fan of the wide-open sky and all four seasons, she believes in embracing the small moments of everyday life. A home-schooling mom of six young children who rarely wear shoes, those moments usually involve a lot of noise, a lot of mess or a whole bunch of warm cookies. Virginia holds degrees in linguistics and religious studies from the University of Oregon. She lives with her habanero-eating husband, Crusberto, who is her polar opposite in all things except faith. They've learned to speak in shorthand code and look forward to the day they can actually finish a sentence. In the meantime, Virginia thanks God for the laughter and abundance of hugs that fill her day as she plots her next book.

Upon a Midnight Clear

Gail Gaymer Martin

&

Season of Joy

Virginia Carmichael

ISBN-13: 978-1-335-42501-0

Upon a Midnight Clear and Season of Joy

Upon a Midnight Clear
First published in 2000. This edition published in 2021.

Season of Joy
First published in 2012. This edition published in 2021.

This edition published by arrangement with Harlequin Books S.A.

For questions and comments about the quality of this book, please contact us at CustomerService@Harlequin.com.

Love Inspired
22 Adelaide St. West, 40th Floor
Toronto, Ontario M5H 4E3, Canada
www.LoveInspired.com

Printed in U.S.A.

CONTENTS

UPON A MIDNIGHT CLEAR

Gail Gaymer Martin

Dedicated to my sister, Jan,
who knows the sorrow of losing a child.
And in loving memory of her infant daughters,
Lisa Marie and Beth Ann, who live with Jesus.

Thanks to my husband, Bob, for his devotion,
support and hours of proofreading.
To Flo Stano for her nursing expertise,
and to the Bedford Chamber of Commerce
for their invaluable information.

Then you will call upon me and come
and pray to me, and I will listen to you.
And you will seek me and find me,
when you seek me with all your heart.
—*Jeremiah* 29:12–13

Chapter One

Callie Randolph scanned the employment ads of the *Indianapolis News.* Her eyes lit upon a Help Wanted entry: *Special child, aged five, needs professional caregiver. Live-in. Good wage. Contact David Hamilton. 812 area code.* Southern Indiana, she assumed. "Live-in" she wanted. But a child?

She raised her head from the ad and caught her mother, eyeing her.

"You've been quiet since you got home," Grace Randolph said, resting back in the kitchen chair. "Tell me about the funeral."

"It was nice, as funerals go. But sad, so close to the holidays." Ethel's death, coming as it did on the footsteps of Christmas, jolted Callie with the memories of a birth six Christmases earlier. Pushing away the invading thoughts, Callie shifted in her chair and focused on her mother. "More people than I would expect at the funeral for someone in her nineties, but I suppose most of the mourners were friends and business acquaintances of Ethel's children. The family has a name in the community."

"Ah yes, when we're old, people forget."

"No, it's not that they forget. When we're *that* old, many of our own friends and acquaintances have already died. Makes coming to a funeral difficult." Callie hoped to lighten Grace's negative mood. "It'll feel strange not taking care of Ethel. She had the faith of a saint and a smile right to the end. Always had a kind word." She raised her eyes, hoping her mother had heard her last statement.

Grace stared across the room as if lost in thought, and Callie's mind drifted to the funeral and the preacher's comforting words. *"Ethel lived a full and glorious life, loving her Lord and her family."* Callie pictured the wrinkled, loving face of her dying patient. Ethel's earthly years had definitely been full and glorious.

In contrast, Callie's nearly twenty-six years had been empty and dull. Her dreams had died that horrible March day that she tried to block from her memory. Her life seemed buried in its own tomb of guilt and sorrow.

"So, about the funeral—"

Callie slammed the door on her thoughts and focused on her mother.

"Tell me about the music. Any hymns?" Grace asked.

Callie eyed her, sensing an ulterior motive in her question. "Real nice, Mom. Organ music and hymns."

"Which hymns?"

Callie pulled her shoulders back, feeling the muscles tightening along the cords of her neck. "'Amazing Grace,' 'Softly and Tenderly.'"

"I can hear you singing that one. So beautiful."

Callie fought the desire to bolt from the room. She sensed an argument heading her way. Instead, she aimed her eyes at the newspaper clutched in her hands.

Grace leaned on an elbow. "So what will you do now?"

"Find a new job, I suppose." She hesitated, wondering what comment she'd receive about her newest resolve. "But I've made a decision." Callie met her mother's eyes. "I'm not going to give elderly care anymore. I'll find something else."

"Praise the Lord, you've come to your senses. Callie, you have a nursing degree, but you continue to waste your time with the deathwatch. You need to live and use the talent God gave you."

Deep creases furrowed Callie's forehead. "Please don't call it the deathwatch. Caring for older people has been a blessing. And I *do* use my talents." She shook her head, amazed at her mother's attitude. "Do you think it's easy to nurse someone who's dying? I use as many skills as I would in a regular hospital."

Grace fell back against the chair. "I'm sorry. I don't mean to belittle your work, but it's not a life for a young woman. Look at you. You're beautiful and intelligent, yet you spend your life sitting in silent rooms, listening to old people muttering away about nothing but useless memories. What about a husband…and children? Don't you want a life for yourself?"

She flinched at her mother's words. "Please, don't get on that topic, Mom. You know how I feel about that."

"I wish I knew when you got these odd ideas. They helped put your father in his grave. He had such hopes for you."

Callie stiffened as icy tendrils slithered through her. How many times was she reminded of how she had helped kill her father? After his death three years earlier, the doctor had said her dad had been a walking time bomb from fatty foods, cigarettes and a type-A personality. Though guilt poked at her, she knew she hadn't caused his death. Yet, she let her mother rile her.

Grace scowled with a piercing squint. "I think it began when you stopped singing," she said, releasing a lengthy, audible sigh. "Such a beautiful voice. Like a meadowlark."

"Stop. Stop, Mother." Callie slammed her hand on the tabletop. "Please, don't call me that."

Grace looked taken aback. "Well, I'm sorry. What's gotten into you?" She gaped at Callie. "You're as white as a sheet. I only called you a—"

"Please, don't say it again, Mother." Callie pressed her forehead into her hand.

"I don't know what's wrong with you." Grace sat for a moment before she began her litany. "I don't know, Callie. I could cry when I think of it. Everyone said you sang like an angel."

Callie stared at the newspaper, the black letters blurring. Her mother wouldn't stop until she'd made her point. Callie ached inside when she thought about the music she'd always loved. She struggled to keep her voice calm and controlled. "I lost my interest in music, that's all." Her fingernails dug into the flesh of her fisted hand.

"Your father had such hopes for you. He dreamed you'd pass your audition with the Jim McKee Singers. But his hopes were buried along with him in his grave."

Callie modulated her pitch, and her words came out in a monotone. "I didn't pass the audition. I told you."

"I can't believe that, Callie. You've said it, but everyone knew you could pass the audition. Either you didn't try or… I don't know. Being part of Paul Ivory's ministry would be any girl's dream. And the Jim McKee Singers traveled with him in the summer all over the country, so it wouldn't have interfered with your college studies. And then you just quit singing. I can't understand you."

"Mother, let's not argue about something that happened years ago."

"But it's not just that, Callie. I hate to bring it up, but since the baby, you've never been the same."

Unexpected tears welled in Callie's eyes, tears she usually fought. But today they sneaked in behind the emotions elicited by Ethel's death, and the memory of the baby's Christmas birth dragged them out of hiding.

Callie had never seen the daughter she bore six years earlier. The hospital had their unbending policy, and her parents had given her the same ultimatum. A girl placing a child for adoption should not see her baby.

She begged and pleaded with her parents to allow her to keep her daughter. But they would have no part of it. She struggled in her thoughts—longing to finish an argument that held weight. In the end, her parents were correct. A child needed a secure and loving home. Adoption was best for her baby daughter. But not for Callie. Against her wishes, Callie signed the papers releasing her baby for adoption.

Grace breathed a ragged sigh. "Maybe your father and I made a mistake. You were so young, a whole lifetime ahead of you. We thought you could get on with your life. If you'd only told us who the young man was—but you protected him. Any decent young man would have stood up and accepted his responsibilities. For all we knew, you never told him, either."

"We've gone over this before. It's in the past. It's

over. It's too late." She clutched the newspaper, crumpling the paper beneath her fingers.

"We meant well. Even your brother and sister begged you to tell us who the fellow was. You could have been married, at least. Given the baby a name, so we could hold our head up in public. But, no."

Callie folded the paper and clasped it in her trembling hand. She rose without comment. What could she say that she hadn't said a million times already? "I'm going to my room. I have a headache." As she passed through the doorway, she glanced over her shoulder and saw her mother's strained expression.

Before Grace could call after her, Callie rushed up the staircase to her second-floor bedroom and locked the door. She could no longer bear to hear her mother's sad-voiced recollections. No one but Callie knew the true story. She prayed that the vivid picture, too much like a horror movie, would leave her. Yet so many nights the ugly dream tore into her sleep, and again and again she relived the life-changing moments.

She plopped on the corner of the bed, massaging her neck. The newspaper ad appeared in her mind. *David Hamilton.* She grabbed a pen from her desk, reread the words, and jotted his name and telephone number on a scratch pad. She'd check with Christian Care Services tomorrow and see what they had available. At least she'd have the number handy if she wanted to give Mr. Hamilton a call later.

She tossed the pad on her dressing table and stretched out on the bed. A child? The thoughts of caring for a child frightened her. Would a child, especially a sick child, stir her longing?

She'd resolved to make a change in her life. Images

of caring for adults marched through her head—the thought no longer appealed to her. Nursing in a doctor's office or hospital held no interest for her: patients coming and going, a nurse with no involvement in their lives. She wanted to be part of a life, to make a difference.

She rolled on her side, dragging her fingers through the old-fashioned chenille spread. The room looked so much the way it had when she was a teenager. How long had her mother owned the antiquated bedspread?

Since college, her parents' home had been only a stop-off place between jobs. Live-in care was her preference—away from her parents' guarded eyes, as they tried to cover their sorrow and shame over all that had happened.

When she'd graduated from college, she had weighed all the issues. Geriatric care seemed to encompass all her aspirations. At that time, she could never have considered child care. Her wounds were too fresh.

Her gaze drifted to the telephone. The name *David Hamilton* entered her mind again. Looking at her wristwatch, she wondered if it was too late to call him. Eight in the evening seemed early enough. Curiosity galloped through her mind. What did the ad mean—a "special" child? Was the little one mentally or physically challenged? A boy or girl? Where did the family live? Questions spun in her head. What would calling hurt? She'd at least have her questions answered.

She swung her legs over the edge of the bed, rose, and grabbed the notepad. What specific information would she like to know? She organized her thoughts, then punched in the long-distance number.

A rich baritone voice filled the line, and when Callie

heard his commanding tone, she caught her breath. Job interviews and query telephone calls had never bothered her. Tonight her wavering emotions addled her. She drew in a lengthy, relaxing breath, then introduced herself and stated her business.

Hamilton's self-assured manner caught her off guard. "I'm looking for a professional, Ms. Randolph. What is your background?"

His tone intimidated her, and her responses to his questions sounded reticent in her ears. "It's *Miss* Randolph, and I'm a professional, licensed nurse." She paused to steady her nerves. "But I've preferred to work as a home caregiver rather than in a hospital.

"The past four years, I've had elderly patients, but I'm looking for a change."

"Change?"

His abruptness struck her as arrogant, and Callie could almost sense his arched eyebrow.

"Yes. I've been blessed working with the older patients, but I'd like to work with…a child."

"I see." A thoughtful silence hung in the air. "You're a religious woman, Miss Randolph?"

His question confounded her. Then she remembered she'd used the word *blessed.* Not sure what he expected, she answered honestly. "I'm a Christian, if that's what you're asking."

She waited for a response. Yet only silence filled the line. With no response forthcoming, she asked, "What do you mean by 'special,' Mr. Hamilton? In the ad, you mentioned you needed a caregiver for a 'special child.'"

He hesitated only a moment. "Natalie… Nattie's a bright child. She was always active, delightful—but since her mother's death two years ago, she's become… withdrawn." His voice faded.

"Withdrawn?"

"Difficult to explain in words. I'd rather the prospective caregiver meet her and see for herself what I mean. Nattie no longer speaks. She barely relates to anyone. She lives in her own world."

Callie's heart lurched at the thought of a child bearing such grief. "I see. I understand why you're worried." Still, panic crept over her like cold fingers inching along her spine. Her heart already ached for the child. Could she control her own feelings? Her mind spun with flashing red warning lights.

"I've scared you off, Miss Randolph." Apprehension resounded in his statement.

She cringed, then lied a little. "No, no. I was thinking."

"Thinking?" His tone softened. "I've been looking for someone for some time now, and I seem to scare people off with the facts…the details of Nattie's problem."

The image of a lonely, motherless child tugged at her compassion. What grief he had to bear. "I'm not frightened of the facts," Callie said, but in her heart, she was frightened of herself. "I have some personal concerns that came to mind." She fumbled for what to say next. "For example, I don't know where you live. Where are you located, sir?"

"We live in Bedford, not too far from Bloomington."

Bedford. The town was only a couple of hours from her mother's house. She paused a moment. "I have some personal matters I need to consider. I'll call you as soon as I know whether I'd like to be interviewed for the position. I hope that's okay with you."

"Certainly. That's fine. I understand." Discouragement sounded in his voice.

She bit the corner of her lip. "Thank you for your time."

After she hung up the telephone, Callie sat for a while without moving. She should have been honest. She'd already made her decision. A position like that wouldn't be wise at all. She was too vulnerable.

Besides, she wasn't sure she wanted to work for David Hamilton. His tone seemed stiff and arrogant. A child needed a warm, loving father, not onc who was bitter and inflexible. She would have no patience with a man like that.

David Hamilton leaned back in his chair, his hand still clasping the telephone. *Useless.* In two months, his ad had resulted in only three telephone calls. One courageous soul came for an interview, but with her first look at Nattie, David saw the answer in the woman's eyes.

He supposed, as well, the "live-in" situation might be an obstacle for some. With no response locally, he'd extended his ad farther away, as far as Indianapolis. But this Miss Randolph had been the only call so far.

He longed for another housekeeper like Miriam. Her overdue retirement left a hole nearly as big, though not as horrendous, as Sara's death. No one could replace Miriam.

A shudder filtered through him. *No one could replace Sara.*

Nothing seemed worse than a wife's death, but when it happened, he had learned the truth. Worse was a child losing her mother. Yet the elderly housekeeper had stepped in with all her love and wisdom and taken charge of the household, wrapping each of them in her motherly arms.

Remembering Miriam's expert care, David preferred to hire a more mature woman as a nanny. The voice he heard on the telephone tonight sounded too young, perhaps nearly a child herself. He mentally calculated her age. She'd mentioned working for four years. If she'd graduated from college when she was twenty-one, she'd be only twenty-five. What would a twenty-five-year-old know about healing his child? Despite his despair, he felt a pitying grin flicker on his lips. He was only thirty-two. What did he know about healing his child? Nothing.

David rose from the floral-print sofa and wandered to the fireplace. He stared into the dying embers. Photographs lined the mantel, memories of happier times—Sara smiling warmly with sprinkles of sunlight and shadow in her golden hair; Nattie with her heavenly blue eyes and bright smile posed in the gnarled peach tree on the hill; and then, the photograph of Sara and him on his parents' yacht.

He turned from the photographs, now like a sad monument conjuring sorrowful memories. David's gaze traversed the room, admiring the furnishings and decor. Sara's hand had left its mark everywhere in the house, but particularly in this room. Wandering to the bay window, he stood over the mahogany grand piano, his fingers caressing the rich, dark wood. How much longer would this magnificent instrument lie silent? Even at the sound of a single note, longing knifed through him.

This room was their family's favorite spot, where

they had spent quiet evenings talking about their plans and dreams. He could picture Sara and Nattie stretched out on the floor piecing together one of her thick cardboard puzzles.

An empty sigh rattled through him, and he shivered with loneliness. He pulled himself from his reveries and marched back to the fireplace, grabbing the poker and jamming it into the glowing ashes. Why should he even think, let alone worry, about the young woman's phone call? He'd never hear from her again, no matter what she promised. Her voice gave the telltale evidence. She had no intention of calling again.

Thinking of Nattie drew him to the hallway. He followed the wide, curved staircase to the floor above. In the lengthy hallway, he stepped quietly along the thick Persian carpet. Two doors from the end, he paused and listened. The room was silent, and he pushed the door open gently, stepping inside.

A soft night-light glowed a warm pink. Natalie's slender frame lay curled under a quilt, and the rise and fall of the delicate blanket marked her deep sleep. He moved lightly across the pink carpeting and stood, looking at her buttercup hair and her flushed, rosy cheeks. His heart lurched at the sight of his child—their child, fulfilling their hopes and completing their lives.

Or what had become their incomplete and short life together.

After the telephone call, Callie's mind filled with thoughts of David Hamilton and his young daughter. Her headache pounded worse than before, and she undressed and pulled down the blankets. Though the evening was still young, she tucked her legs beneath the warm covers.

The light shone brightly, and as thoughts drifted through her head, she nodded to herself, resolute she would not consider the job in Bedford. After turning off the light, she closed her eyes, waiting for sleep.

Her subconsciousness opened, drawing her into the darkness. The images rolled into her mind like thick fog along an inky ocean.

She was in a sparse waiting room. Her pale pink blouse, buttoned to the neck, matched the flush of excitement in her cheeks. The murky shadows swirled past her eyes: images, voices, the reverberating click *of a door. Fear rose within her. She tried to scream, to yell, but nothing came except black silence—*

Callie forced herself awake, her heart thundering. Perspiration ran from her hairline. She threw back the blankets and snapped on the light. Pulling her trembling legs from beneath the covers, she sat on the edge of the bed and gasped until her breathing returned to normal.

She rose on shaking legs and tiptoed into the hall to the bathroom. Though ice traveled through her veins, a clammy heat beaded on her body. Running cold tap water onto a washcloth, she covered her face and breathed in the icy dampness. *Please, Lord, release me from that terrible dream.*

She wet the cloth again and washed her face and neck, then hurried quietly back to her room, praying for a dreamless sleep.

Chapter Two

Christian Care Services filled the two-story office building on Woodward. Callie entered the lobby and took the elevator to the second floor. Usually she walked the stairs, but today she felt drained of energy.

Twenty-five minutes later, she left more discouraged than when she'd arrived. Not one live-in care situation. How could she tell the young woman she couldn't live at home, not because she didn't love her mother, but because she loved herself as much? The explanation seemed too personal and complicated.

Feeling discouraged, she trudged to her car. Live-in positions weren't very common, and she wondered how long she'd have to wait. If need be, she'd look on her own, praying that God would lead her to a position somewhere.

Standing beside her car, she searched through her shoulder bag for her keys and, with them, pulled out the slip of paper with David Hamilton's phone number. She didn't recall putting the number in her bag, and finding it gave her an uneasy feeling. She tossed the number back into her purse.

The winter air penetrated her heavy woolen coat, and she unlocked the car door and slid in. As thoughts butted through her head, she turned on the ignition and waited for the heat.

Money wasn't an immediate problem; residing with others, she'd been able to save a tidy sum. But she needed a place to live. If she stayed home, would she and her mother survive? God commanded children to honor their parents, but had God meant Callie's mother? A faint smile crossed her lips at the foolish thought. Callie knew her parents had always meant well, but meaning and reality didn't necessarily go hand in hand.

Indianapolis had a variety of hospitals. She could probably have her pick of positions in the metropolitan area, then get her own apartment or condo. But again the feeling of emptiness consumed her. She wasn't cut out for hospital nursing.

Warmth drifted from the car heater, and Callie moved the button to high. She felt chilled deep in her bones. Though the heat rose around her, icy sensations nipped at her heart. Her memory turned back to her telephone call the previous evening and to a little child who needed love and care.

She shook the thought from her head and pulled out of the parking lot. She'd give the agency a couple of weeks. If nothing became available, then she'd know Bedford was God's decision. By that time, the position might already be taken, and her dilemma would be resolved.

Callie glanced at David Hamilton's address again. Bedford was no metropolis, and she'd found the street easily.

Two weeks had passed and no live-in positions had become available, not even for an elderly patient. Her twenty-sixth birthday had plodded by a week earlier, and she felt like an old, jobless woman, staring at the girlish daisy wallpaper in her bedroom. Life had come to a standstill, going nowhere. Tired of sitting by the telephone waiting for a job call, she had called David Hamilton. Despite his lack of warmth, he had a child who needed someone to love her.

Keeping her eyes on the winding road lined with sprawling houses, she glanced at the slip of paper and reread the address. A mailbox caught her eye. The name *Hamilton* jumped from the shiny black receptacle in white letters. She looked between the fence pillars, and her gaze traveled up the winding driveway to the large home of oatmeal-colored limestone.

She aimed her car and followed the curved pathway to the house. Wide steps led to a deep, covered porch, and on one side of the home, a circular tower rose above the house topped by a conical roof.

Callie pulled in front, awed by the elegance and charm of the turn-of-the-century building. Sitting for a moment to collect her thoughts, she pressed her tired back against the seat cushion. Though an easy trip in the summer, the two-hour drive on winter roads was less than pleasant. She thanked God the highway was basically clear.

Closing her eyes, she prayed. Even thinking of Mr. Hamilton sent a shudder down her spine. His voice presented a formidable image in her mind, and now she would see him face-to-face.

She climbed from the car and made her way up the impressive steps to the wide porch. Standing on the expanse of cement, she had a closer view of the large tower rising along the side. *Like a castle,* she thought. She located the bell and pushed. Inside, a chime sounded, and she waited.

When the door swung open, she faced a plump, middle-aged woman who stared at her through the storm door. The housekeeper, Callie assumed. The woman pushed the door open slightly, giving a flicker of a smile. "Miss Randolph?"

"Yes," Callie answered.

The opening widened, and the woman stepped aside. "Mr. Hamilton is waiting for you in the family parlor. May I take your coat?"

Callie regarded her surroundings as she slid the coat from her shoulders. She stood in a wide hallway graced by a broad, curved staircase and a sparkling crystal chandelier. An oriental carpet covered the floor, stretching the length of the entry.

Two sets of double doors stood closed on the right, and on the left, three more sets of French doors hid the rooms' interiors, leaving Callie with a sense of foreboding. Were the doors holding something in? Or keeping something out? Only the door at the end of the hallway stood open, probably leading to the servants' quarters.

The woman disposed of Callie's coat and gestured for her to follow. The housekeeper moved to the left, rapped lightly on the first set of doors, and, when a muffled voice spoke, pushed the door open and stepped aside.

Callie moved forward and paused in the doorway. The room was lovely, filled with floral-print furnishings and a broad mantel displaying family photographs. Winter sunlight beamed through a wide bay window, casting French-pane patterns on the elegant mahogany grand piano. But what caught her off guard the most was the man.

David Hamilton stood before the fireplace, watching her. Their eyes met and locked in unspoken curiosity. A pair of gray woolen slacks and a burgundy sweater covered his tall, athletic frame. His broad shoulders looked like a swimmer's, and tapered to a trim waist.

He stepped toward her, extending his hand without a smile. "Miss Randolph."

She moved forward to meet him halfway. "Mr. Hamilton. You have a lovely home. Very gracious and charming."

"Thank you. Have a seat by the fire. Big, old homes sometimes hold a chill. The fireplace makes it more tolerable."

After glancing around, she made her way toward a chair near the hearth, then straightened her skirt as she eased into it. The man sat across from her, stretching his long legs toward the warmth of the fire. He was far more handsome than she had imagined, and she chided herself for creating an ogre, rather than this attractive tawny-haired man whose hazel eyes glinted sparks of green and brown as he observed her.

"So," he said. His deep, resonant voice filled the silence.

She pulled herself up straighter in the chair and acknowledged him. "I suppose you'd like to see my references?"

He sat unmoving. "Not really."

His abrupt comment threw her off balance a moment. "Oh? Then you'd like to know my qualifications?"

"No, I'd rather get to know *you*." His gaze penetrated hers, and she felt a prickling of nerves tingle up her arms and catch in her chest.

"You mean my life story? Why I became a nurse? Why I'd rather do home care?"

"Tell me about your interests. What amuses you?"

She looked directly into his eyes. "My interests? I love to read. In fact, I brought a small gift for Natalie, some children's books. I thought she might like them. I've always favored children's literature."

He stared at her with an amused grin on his lips.

"I guess I'm rattling. I'm nervous. I've cared for the elderly, but this is my first interview for a child."

David nodded. "You're not much beyond a child yourself."

Callie sat bolt upright. "I'm twenty-six, Mr. Hamilton. I believe I qualify as an adult. And I'm a registered nurse. I'm licensed to care for people of all ages."

He raised his hand, flexing his palm like a policeman halting traffic. "Whoa. I'm sorry, Miss Randolph. I didn't mean to insult you. You have a very youthful appearance. You told me your qualifications on the telephone. I know you're a nurse. If I didn't think you might be suited for this position, I wouldn't have wasted my time. Nor yours."

Callie's cheeks burned. "I'm sorry. I thought, you—"

"Don't apologize. I was abrupt. Please continue. How else do you spend your time?"

She thought for a moment. "As I said before, I love to read. I enjoy the theater. And the outdoors. I'm not interested in sports, but I enjoy a long walk on a spring morning or a hike through the woods in autumn— Do I sound boring?"

"No, not at all."

"And then I love..." She hesitated. *Music.* How could she tell him her feelings about music and singing? So much time had passed.

His eyes searched hers, and he waited.

The grandfather clock sitting across the room broke the heavy silence. *One. Two. Three.*

He glanced at his wristwatch. "And then you love..."

She glanced across the room at the silent piano. "Music."

Chapter Three

Callie waited for a comment, but David Hamilton only shifted his focus to the piano, then back to her face.

She didn't mention her singing. "I play the piano a little." She gestured toward the impressive instrument. "Do you play?"

David's face tightened, and a frown flickered on his brow. "Not really. Not anymore. Sara, my wife, played. She was the musician in the family."

Callie nodded. "I see." His eyes flooded with sorrow, and she understood. The thought of singing filled her with longing, too. They shared a similar ache, but hers was too personal, too horrible to even talk about. Her thought returned to the child. "And Natalie? Is your daughter musical?"

Grief shadowed his face again, and she was sorry she'd asked.

"I believe she is. She showed promise before her mother died. Nattie was four then and used to sing songs with us. Now she doesn't sing a note."

"I'm sorry. It must be difficult, losing a wife and in a sense your daughter." Callie drew in a deep breath.

"Someday, she'll sing again. I'm sure she will. When you love music, it has to come out. You can't keep it buried inside of..."

The truth of her words hit her. Music pushed against her heart daily. Would she ever be able to think of music without the awful memories surging through her? Her throat ached to sing, but then the black dreams rose like demons, just as Nattie's singing probably aroused sad thoughts of her mother.

David stared at her curiously, his head tilting to one side as he searched her face. She swallowed, feeling the heat of discomfort rise in her again.

"You have strong feelings about music." His words were not a question.

"Yes, I do. She'll sing. After her pain goes away." Callie's thoughts turned to a prayer. *Help me to sing again, Lord, when my hurt is gone.*

"Excuse me." David Hamilton rose. "I want to see if Agnes is bringing our tea." He stepped toward the door, then stopped. "Do you like tea?"

Callie nodded. "Yes, very much."

He turned and strode through the doorway. Callie drew in a calming breath. Why did she feel as if he were sitting in judgment of her, rather than interviewing her? She raised her eyebrows. Maybe he was.

In only a moment, David spoke to her from the parlor doorway. "Agnes is on her way." He left the door open, and before he had crossed the room, the woman she'd seen earlier entered with a tray.

"Right here, Agnes. On the coffee table is fine." He gestured to the low table that stretched between them. "Miss Randolph, this is Agnes, my housekeeper. She's caring for Nattie until I find someone."

"We met at the door. It's nice to know you, Agnes." The woman nodded and set the tray on the highly polished table.

"Agnes has been a godsend for us since we lost Miriam."

"Thank you, Mr. Hamilton," she said, glancing at him. "Would you like me to pour?"

"No, I'll get it. You have plenty to do." With a flicker of emotion, his eyes rose to meet the woman's. "By the way, have you checked on Nattie lately?"

"Yes, sir, she's coloring in her room."

"Coloring? That's good. I'll take Miss Randolph up to meet her a bit later."

Agnes nodded and left the room, closing the door behind her. David poured tea into the two china cups. "I'll let you add your own cream and sugar, if you take it," he said, indicating toward the pitcher and sugar bowl on the tray. "And please have a piece of Agnes's cake. It's lemon. And wonderful."

Callie glanced at him, astounded at the sudden congeniality in his voice. The interview had felt so ponderous, but now he sounded human. "Thanks. I take my tea black. And the cake looks wonderful." She sipped the strong tea, and then placed the cup on the tray and picked up a dessert plate of cake.

David eyed her as she slivered off a bite and forked it into her mouth. The tangy lemon burst with flavor on her tongue. "It's delicious."

He looked pleased. "I will say, Agnes is an excellent cook."

"Has she been with you long?"

He stared into the red glow of the firelight. "No—a half year, perhaps. Miriam, my past housekeeper, took Nattie—took all of us—under her wing when Sara died. She had been with my parents before their deaths. A longtime employee of the family. She retired. Illness and age finally caught up with her. Her loss has been difficult for us."

He raised his eyes from the mesmerizing flames. "I'm sorry, Miss Randolph. I'm sure you aren't interested in my family tree, nor my family's problems."

"Don't apologize, please. And call me Callie." She felt her face brighten to a shy grin. "Miss Randolph sounds like my maiden aunt."

For the first time, his tense lips relaxed and curved to a pleasant smile. "All right. It's Callie," he said, leaning back in the chair. "Is that short for something?"

"No, just plain Callie."

He nodded. "So, Callie, tell me how a young woman like you decided to care for the elderly. Why not a position in a hospital, regular hours so you could have fun with your friends?"

She raised her eyes to his and fought the frown that pulled at her forehead. Never had an interview caused her such stress. The man seemed to be probing at every nerve ending—searching for what, she didn't know. She grasped for the story she had lived with for so long.

"When I graduated from college, I had romantic dreams. Like Florence Nightingale, I suppose. A hospital didn't interest me. I wanted something more…absorbing. So I thought I'd try my hand at home care. The first job I had was a cancer patient, an elderly woman who needed constant attention. Because of that, I was asked to live in their home, which suited me nicely."

"You have no family, then?"

She swallowed. How could she explain her relationship with her mother. "Yes, my mother is living. My father died about three years ago. But my mother's in good health and active. She doesn't need me around. My siblings are older. My brother lives right outside Indianapolis. My sister and her husband live in California."

"No apartment or home of your own?"

"My mother's house is the most permanent residence I have. No, I have no other financial responsibilities, if that's what you're asking."

David grimaced. "I wasn't trying to pry. I wondered if a live-in situation meets your needs."

"Yes, but most important, I like the involvement, not only with the patient, but with the family. You know—dedication, commitment."

A sound between a snicker and harrumph escaped him. "A job here would certainly take dedication and commitment."

"That's what I want. I believe God has a purpose for everybody. I want to do something that has meaning. I want to know that I'm paying God back for—"

"Paying God back?" His brows lifted. "Like an atonement? What kind of atonement does a young woman like you have to make?"

Irritation flooded through her, and her pitch raised along with her volume. "I didn't say *atonement,* Mr. Hamilton. I said *purpose.* And you've mentioned my *young* age often since I've arrived. I assume my age bothers you."

The sensation that shot through Callie surprised even her. Why was she fighting for a job she wasn't sure she wanted? A job she wasn't sure she could handle? A sigh escaped her. Working with the child wasn't a problem. She had the skills.

But *Callie* was the problem. Already, she found herself emotionally caught in the child's plight, her own buried feelings struggling to rise from within. Her focus settled upon David Hamilton's startled face. How could she have raised her voice to this man? Even if she wanted the position, any hopes of a job here were now lost forever.

David was startled by the words of the irate young woman who stood before him. He dropped against the back of his chair, peering at her and flinching against her sudden anger. He reviewed what he'd said. Had he made a point of her age?

A flush rose to her face, and for some reason, she ruffled his curiosity. He sensed a depth in her, something that aroused him, something that dragged his own empathy from its hiding place. He'd felt sorry for himself and for Nattie for such a long time. Feeling grief for someone else seemed alien.

"To be honest, Miss Rand—Callie—I had thought to hire an older woman. Someone with experience who could nurture Nattie and bring her back to the sweet, happy child she was before her mother's death."

Callie's chin jutted upward. Obviously his words had riled her again.

"Was your wife an old woman, Mr. Hamilton?"

A rush of heat dashed to his cheeks. "What do you mean?"

"I mean, did your wife understand your child? Did she love her? Could she relate to her? Play with her? Sing with her? Give her love and care?"

David stared at her. "Wh-why, yes. Obviously." His pulse raced and pounded in his temples, not from anger but from astonishment. She seemed to be interviewing him, and he wasn't sure he liked it, at all.

"Then why does a nanny—a caregiver—have to be an elderly woman? Can't a woman my age—perhaps your wife's age when she died—love and care for your child? I don't understand."

Neither did he understand. He stared at her and closed his gaping mouth. Her words struck him like icy water. What she said was utterly true. Who was he protecting? Nattie? Or himself? He peered into her snapping eyes. *Spunky? Nervy?* No, *spirited* was the word.

He gazed at the glowing, animated face of the woman sitting across from him. Her trim body looked rigid, and she stared at him with eyes the color of the sky or flowers. Yes, delphiniums. Her honey-colored hair framed an oval face graced with sculptured cheekbones and full lips. She had fire, soul and vigor. Isn't that what Nattie needed?

Callie's voice softened. "I'm sorry, Mr. Hamilton. You're angry with me. I did speak to you disrespectfully, and I'm sorry. But I—"

"No. No, I'm not angry. You've made me think. I see no reason why Nattie should have an elderly nanny. A young woman might tempt her out of her shell. She needs to be around activity and laughter. She needs to play." He felt tears push against the back of his eyes, and he struggled. He refused to sit in front of this stranger and sob, bearing his soul like a blithering idiot. "She needs to have fun. Yes?"

"Yes." She shifted in her chair, seemingly embarrassed. "I'm glad you agree." Callie stared into her lap a moment. "How does she spend her day now?"

"Sitting. Staring into space. Sometimes she colors, like today. But often her pictures are covered in dark brown or purple. Or black."

"No school?"

David shook his head. "No. We registered her for kindergarten, but I couldn't follow through. I took her there and forced her from the car, rigid and silent. I couldn't do that to her. But next September is first grade. She must begin school then. I could get a tutor, but..." The memories of the first school day tore at his heart.

"But that won't solve the problem."

He lifted his eyes to hers. "Yes. A tutor won't solve a single problem."

"Well, you have seven or eight months before school begins. Was she examined by doctors? I assume she has nothing physically wrong with her."

"She's healthy. She eats well. But she's lethargic, prefers to be alone, sits for hours staring outside, sometimes at a book. Occasionally, she says something to me—a word, perhaps. That's all."

Callie was silent, then asked, "Psychological? Have you seen a therapist?"

"Yes, the physician brought in a psychiatrist as a consultant." He recalled that day vividly. "Since the problem was caused by a trauma, and given her age, they both felt her problem is temporary. Time will heal her. She can speak. She talked a blue streak before Sara's death. But now the problem is, she's unwilling to speak. Without talking, therapy probably couldn't help her."

Callie stared into the dying flames. "Something will bring her out. Sometimes people form habits they can't seem to break. They almost forget how it is to live without the behavior. Maybe Nattie's silence has become just that. Something has to happen to stimulate her, to make her want to speak and live like a normal child again."

"I pray you're right."

"Me, too."

He rose and wandered to the fireplace. Peering at the embers, he lifted the poker and thrust at the red glow. Nattie needed to be prodded. She needed stimulus to wake her from her sadness. The flames stirred and sparks sprinkled from the burned wood. Could this spirited woman be the one to do that?

"You mentioned you'd like me to meet your daughter," Callie said.

He swung around to face her, realizing he had been lost in reverie. "Certainly," he said, embarrassed by his distraction.

"I'd like that, when you're ready."

He glanced at the cup in her hand. "Are you finished with the tea?"

She took a final sip. "Yes, thanks. I have a two-hour drive home, and I'd like to get there before dark, if I can."

"I don't blame you. The winter roads can be treacherous."

He stood, and she rose and waited next to the chair, bathed in the warm glow of the fire. David studied her again. Her frame, though thin, rounded in an appealing manner and tugged at his memory. The straight skirt of her deep blue suit hit her modestly just below the knee. Covering a white blouse, the boxy jacket rested at the top of her hips. Her only jewelry was a gold lapel pin and earrings. She stepped to his side, and he calculated her height. Probably five foot five or six, he determined. He stood a head above her.

He stepped toward the doors, and she followed. In the foyer, he gestured to the staircase, and she moved ahead of him, gliding lightly up the steps, her skirt clinging momentarily to her shape as she took each step.

Awareness filled him. No wonder he'd wanted to hire an elderly woman. Ashamed of his own stirrings, he asked God for forgiveness. Instead of thinking of Nattie's needs, he'd struggled to protect his own vulnerability. He would learn to handle his emotions for his daughter's sake.

At the top of the stairs, he guided her down the hallway and paused outside a door. "Please don't expect much. She's not like the child God gave us."

His fingers grasped the knob, and Callie's soft, warm hand lowered and pressed against his.

"Please, don't worry," she said. "I understand hurt."

She raised her eyes to his, and a sense of fellowship like electricity charged through him, racing down to the extremity of his limbs. She lifted her hand, and he turned the knob.

He pushed the door open, and across the room, Nattie shifted her soft blue eyes toward them, then stared again at her knees.

Callie gaped, wide-eyed, at his child. Pulled into a tight knot, Nattie sat with her back braced against the bay enclosure, her feet resting on the window seat. The sun poured in through the pane and made flickering patterns on her pale skin. The same light filtered through her bright yellow hair.

Standing at Callie's side, David felt a shiver ripple through her body. He glimpsed at his child and then looked into the eyes of the virtual stranger, named Callie Randolph, whose face now flooded with compassion and love.

Chapter Four

Callie stared ahead of her at the frail vision on the window seat. She and David stood in Nattie's bedroom doorway for a moment, neither speaking. Finally he entered the room, approaching her like a father would a normal, happy child. "Nattie, this is Miss Randolph. She wants to meet you."

Callie moved as close to the silent child as she felt comfortable doing. "Hi, Nattie. I've heard nice things about you from your daddy. I brought you a present."

She detected a slight movement in the child's body at the word *present.* Hoping she'd piqued Nattie's interest, she opened her large shoulder bag and pulled out the books wrapped in colorful tissue and tied with a ribbon. "Here." She extended her hand holding the books.

Nattie didn't move, but sat with her arms bound to her knees.

Stepping forward, Callie placed the package by the child's feet and backed away. She glanced at David. His gaze was riveted to his daughter.

He took a step forward and rested his hand on his

daughter's shoulder. "Nattie, how about if you open the present?"

The child glanced at him, but made no move to respond.

David squeezed his large frame into the end of the window seat. He lifted the gift from the bench and raised it toward her.

She eyed the package momentarily, but then lowered her lids again, staring through the window as if they weren't there.

Frustration rose in Callie. The child's behavior startled her. A list of childhood illnesses raced through her mind. Then other thoughts took their place. How did Sara die? Was the child present at her death? Questions swirled in her thoughts. What might have happened in the past to trouble this silent child sitting rigidly on the window seat?

David relaxed and placed the package on his knees. "I'll open the gift for you, then, if you'd like." Tearing the paper from the gift, he lifted the books one by one, turning the colorful covers toward her. *"The Lost Lamb,"* he read, showing her the book.

Callie looked at the forlorn child and the book cover. If ever there were a lost lamb, it was Nattie. The next book he showed her was a child's New Testament in story form, and the last, children's poems. Nattie glanced at the book covers, a short-lived spark of interest on her face.

David placed the books again by her feet and rose, his face tormented. Callie glanced at him and gestured to the window seat. "Do you mind?"

He shook his head, and she wandered slowly to the vacated spot and nestled comfortably in the corner. "I think I'd like to read this one," Callie said, selecting *The Lost Lamb,* "if you don't mind." The child made no response. Callie searched David's face, but he seemed lost in thought.

Leaning back, Callie braced herself against the wall next to the window and opened the book. She glanced at Nattie, who eyed her without moving, and began to read. "'Oh my,' said Rebecca to her father, 'where is the new lamb?' Father looked into the pasture. The baby lamb was not in sight."

Callie directed the bright picture toward Nattie, who scanned the page, then returned her attention to her shoes. Callie continued. Nattie glimpsed at each picture without reaction. But the child's minimal interest gave Callie hope. Patience, perseverance, attention, love—Callie would need all of those attributes if she were to work with this lost lamb.

Glancing from the book, she caught David easing quietly through the doorway. The story gained momentum, as Rebecca and her father searched the barnyard and the wooded hills for the stray. When they found the lamb, who had stumbled into a deep hole, Nattie's eyes finally stayed attentive to the page. When the lamb was again in Rebecca's arms, Callie heard a soft breath escape the child at her side. Nattie had, at least, listened to the story. A first success.

"That was a wonderful story, wasn't it? Sometimes when we feel so alone or afraid, we can remember that Jesus is always by our side to protect us, just like Rebecca protected the lamb. I love stories like that one, don't you?" Callie rose. "Well, I have to go now, Nattie. But I hope to be back soon to read more stories with you."

She lay the book next to Nattie and gently caressed

the child's jonquil-colored hair. Nattie's gaze lifted for a heartbeat, but this time when she lowered her eyes, she fastened her attention on the book.

Callie swallowed her building emotions and hurried from the room. She made her way down the stairs, and at the bottom, filled her lungs with refreshing air. When she released the healing breath, her body trembled.

"Thank you."

Callie's hand flew to her chest, she gasped and swung to her left. "Oh, you scared me."

David stood in the doorway across from the parlor where they had met. "You did a beautiful thing."

"She's a beautiful child, Mr. Hamilton. She breaks my heart, so I can only imagine how she breaks yours."

"Call me David, please. If we're going to live in the same house, 'Callie' and 'David' will sound less formal."

She faltered, her hand still knotted at her chest. *If we're going to live in the same house.* The meaning of his words registered, and she closed her eyes. He was asking her to stay. Could she? Would the experience break her heart once more? But suddenly, her own pain didn't matter. Her only thought was for the child sitting alone in an upstairs room.

Callie stepped toward him. "Yes, if we're going to live in the same house, I suppose you're right… David. The 'David' will take some doing," she admitted with a faint grin.

He extended his hand. "I pray you'll make a difference in Nattie's life. In our lives, really. I see already you're a compassionate woman. I can ask for no more."

Callie accepted his hand in a firm clasp. "I hope you'll continue to feel like that." She eyed him, a knowing expression creeping on her face. "You've already seen me with my dander up, as they say." Her hand remained in his.

"Then we have nothing to worry about. I survived."

"Yes, you did. And quite admirably. Thank you for trusting in my...*youthful* abilities."

His hazel eyes captured hers and held her suspended until his words broke the spell. "It's my pleasure."

Callie gazed around her childhood bedroom, facing a new and frightening chapter in her life. Five times she had packed, heading for a patient's home. But tomorrow was different.

Nattie appeared in her mind, the child's face as empty of feeling as Callie's would be when she stepped into David Hamilton's home in Bedford. He was the last person she wanted to have know the fear that writhed inside her. She would step through the doorway with a charade of confidence. She had announced with no uncertainty that she could provide professional, compassionate care for Nattie. And she would.

The sound of Grace's unhappy voice echoed in Callie's head. *"Bedford is too far away. Why must you be a live-in nurse? What if I need you? Dr. Swanson, right here in town, still needs an office nurse."*

She'd heard the same questions and comments since she chose home-care. Tomorrow, another day—a new beginning.

Though she hadn't finished packing, Callie's thoughts dragged through her, sapping her energy. A good night's sleep would refresh her, she thought. With that notion, she crawled into bed.

But Callie couldn't escape her dream. It soon rose in her slumber, shrouded in darkness and mist.

* * *

In a foggy blur, his stare toyed with her, sweeping her body from head to toe, and her flush of excitement deepened to embarrassment. His smooth voice like a distant whisper echoed in her head. "Callie. That's a lovely, lovely name. Nearly pretty as you are, sweetheart."

An uneasy sensation rose in her, unexpected and unnatural. Why was he teasing her with his eyes? She felt self-conscious.

In the swirling darkness, he flashed his broad, charming smile, and his hushed voice touched her ear again. "You're nervous. No need to be nervous." He turned the bolt on the door.

The *click* of the lock cut through her sleep. Callie wrested herself from the blackness of her dream to the darkness of her room.

"Bedford's only a couple hours away, Mom. I told you already, I can get back here if you need me." Packing the last suitcase the next morning, Callie glanced over her shoulder at Grace. "I don't understand why you're worried. You've never needed me yet."

Grace leaned against the door frame. "Well, I get older every year. You never know." Grace's pinched expression gave witness to her unhappiness.

Callie bit back the words that could easily have sailed from her lips: *Only the good die young.* Her mother was well-meaning, she knew that, but Callie found a chip growing on her shoulder when she spent too much time with Grace. She needed to keep that situation in her prayers—only God could work a miracle.

Callie chuckled out loud. "We have the same problem, Mom. I seem to get older every year myself. Any idea how we can fix that?"

Grace's compressed features gave way to a grin. "Can't do much, I suppose. I just worry. Your sister lives thousands of miles away. Kenneth is useless. Sons don't care much about their mothers."

"If you need Ken, he can be here in a minute. But you have to call him and let him know. Men just aren't as attentive as women." Guilt swept over her. She hadn't been very attentive, either. And Grace was right—though she wasn't ready for the grave, they had celebrated her sixty-fifth birthday. And no one was getting any younger.

A sudden feeling of tenderness swept over her. She was her parents' "surprise" baby. At the age of forty, Grace had her "babies" raised. Patricia was fourteen, and Ken, eleven. Then came Callie, who was soon deemed the "little princess." All her parents' unfulfilled hopes and dreams were bundled into her. She had let them down with a bang.

A heavy silence hung in the room as Callie placed the last few items in her luggage. When she snapped the locks, she turned and faced her mother. "Well, I guess that's it. I may need a few other things, but I'm not that far away. And at this point, I'm not sure how long I'll be needed."

The words caught in her throat. Already, the face of Nattie loomed in her mind. Her greatest fear was beginning to take shape. This child would continue to linger in her thoughts when her job was completed in Bedford. And could she walk away from another child? She prayed she could handle it.

Grace stood at the doorway, her hands knotted in front of her. "You'll be coming back occasionally? So I'll see you once in a while, then?"

"Well, sure. I'm not chained to the house. At least, I don't think so." She grinned at Grace, trying to keep her parting light. Most of her previous patients had lived in the area. Living in Bedford would make trips home a bit more complicated.

Grace heaved a sigh and lifted her smaller bag. Callie grabbed the larger piece of luggage and followed her mother down the stairs and out the door.

As Callie loaded her car, she shuddered, thinking of her dream the night before. She drew the chilled, winter air through her lungs, clearing her thoughts. She stood for a moment, staring at the house where her parents had lived for most of her life, remembering…

When she returned inside, Grace had lunch waiting on the table. Seeing the food as another attempt to delay her, Callie wanted to say "no, thank you," but she had to eat somewhere. Noting her mother's forlorn expression, she sat at the table.

"Thanks, this will save time. I should arrive in Bedford in the mid-afternoon, if the weather cooperates. I'll have a chance to get settled before dinner." She bit into her sandwich.

Grace raised the tuna salad to her lips, then lowered it. "Are you sure you're safe with this man, Callie? He saw your references, but did you see his?"

Callie understood her mother's concern. "I think seeing his daughter is reference enough. He's not an outgoing, friendly man. I saw so much sadness in his eyes. Anyway, he has a full-time housekeeper who lives in. She looked comfortable enough. Though once I'm there, I imagine she'll enjoy having the opportunity to go home." Callie sipped her tea.

"You mean you have to keep house, too?"

Callie choked on her sip of tea. She quickly grabbed up her napkin to cover her mouth. "No, Mother. Agnes is from the community. She'll be able to go home and visit her family. Since I'm there, she won't have the responsibility to be the nanny. That's all. He says I'll have my own suite of bedrooms—room, private bath and a little sitting room. And I'll have dinner with the family. Now, don't worry. I'll be fine."

Grace raised an eyebrow. "What kind of business is this man in to afford such a big home and all this help?"

"Limestone quarries and mills. They've been in the family for generations. His grandfather opened a quarry in the middle eighteen-hundreds, I think. Eventually his father took over."

"Family business, hmm? Must be a good one to keep generations at it."

"It is. I was really amazed. I picked up some brochures at the Chamber of Commerce office on my way out of town. So many famous buildings were made with Indiana limestone—the Pentagon, the Empire State Building, lots of buildings in Washington, D.C. So I'd say the family has enough money to get by."

Grace grinned. "To get by? I'd say. One of those aristocratic families…with money to throw away."

"Not really. It's a beautiful house, but David seems down to earth."

"David? What's this 'David' business?"

"Mother." Callie rolled her eyes, yet heat rose up her neck at her mother's scrutiny. "Since we're living in the same house, I suppose he thought 'Miss Randolph' and 'Mr. Hamilton' sounded too formal."

"A little formality never hurt anybody."

"I'm an employee, Mom. And he has no interest in me. The man's not over the death of his wife."

"Accident?"

Callie's brows knitted. "I don't know. He didn't say, and I didn't ask. I'd already asked too many questions for someone who was supposed to be the person interviewed."

"Never hurts to ask questions."

"I'm sure I'll find out one of these days. And I don't expect to be with him much. Mainly dinner. He'll be gone some of the time, traveling for his business. I'm there to be with Natalie. Nattie, they call her. She's a beautiful child."

"Just keep your eyes focused on the child, hear me?"

Callie shook her head. "Yes, Mother. I think I've learned to take care of myself."

She caught a flicker of reminiscence in Grace's expression, and froze, praying she wouldn't stir up the past. Grace bit her tongue, and Callie changed the subject.

"The area is lovely there, all covered with snow. And imagine spring. The trees and wildflowers. And autumn. The colored leaves—elms, maples, birches."

An uneasy feeling rippled down her back. Would she see the autumn colors? Nattie needed to be ready for school. If the child was back to normal by then, her job would be finished.

"It's snowing," Grace said, pulling Callie from her thoughts. "And hard."

"Then, I'd better get moving." Callie gulped down her last bite and drained the teacup.

Without fanfare, she slipped on her coat and said goodbye. She needed to be on her way before she was snowbound. Time was fleeting, and so was her sanity.

Chapter Five

David sat with his face in his hands, his elbows resting on his large cherrywood desk. The day pressed in from all sides. Callie should arrive any time now. He'd expected her earlier, yet the uncooperative weather had apparently slowed her travel.

The day of her interview lingered in his memory. Though Nattie had responded minimally to Callie's ministrations, David was grateful for the most insignificant flicker of interest from his daughter these days. Callie had brought about that infinitesimal moment.

The major concern that lodged in his gut was himself. He feared Callie. She stirred in him remembrances he didn't want to face and emotions he had avoided for two years. His only solution was to avoid her—keep his distance.

Though often quiet, Sara had had her moments of liveliness and laughter. He recalled their spring walks on the hill and a warm, sunny day filled with play when she dubbed him "Sir Knight" with a daisy chain she'd made. Wonderful moments rose in his mind of Sara playing pat-a-cake with Nattie or singing children's songs.

If he let Callie's smiles and exuberance get under his skin, he might find himself emotionally tangled. Until Nattie was well, and he dealt with his personal sorrow, he had no interest in any kind of relationship—and he would live with that decision. But he wished wisdom had been his gatekeeper when he'd extended her the job with such enthusiasm.

On top of it all, today they would celebrate Nattie's sixth birthday. Tension caught between his shoulder blades when he pictured the occasion: a cake with candles she wouldn't blow out, gifts she wouldn't open, and joy she wouldn't feel.

David was reminded of the day Sara had surprised him for his birthday with tickets to see Shakespeare's darkest, direst play, *King Lear.* Yet, he'd accompanied her, looking pleased and interested so as not to hurt the woman he loved so deeply.

But Nattie would not look interested to please him. She wouldn't say "thank you" or force a smile. The lack of response for the gift was not what hurt. She appeared to feel nothing, and that tore at his very fiber.

His wife's death had been no surprise; Nattie's living death was.

Rising from his chair, David wandered to the window and pulled back the draperies. The snow piled against the hedges and mounded against the edge of the driveway. Lovely, pure white at this moment, the snow would soon become drab and monotonous like his life.

A flash of headlights caught the mounds of crystal flakes and glowed with diamond-like sparkles. David's heart surged, and for a heartbeat, he held his breath.

Dropping the edge of the drapery, he spun toward the doorway. She would need help bringing in her luggage. He could, at least, do that.

Callie climbed the snow-covered stairs with care and rang the bell. When the door opened, her stomach somersaulted. Her focus fell upon David Hamilton, rather than Agnes. "Oh," she said, knowing her face registered surprise, "I expected Agnes." Her amazement was not so much at seeing him at the door as feeling her stomach's unexpected acrobatics.

"I was keeping an eye out for you, concerned about the weather." His face appeared drawn and serious.

"Thank you. The drive was a bit tense."

He stepped back and held the door open for her.

She glanced at his darkened face. "I hope nothing is wrong. You look…" Immediately she was sorry she had spoken. Perhaps his stressed appearance had to do with *her*—hiring someone "so young," as he had continually reminded her.

"I'm fine," he said, looking past her toward the automobile. "Let me get my jacket, and we can bring in your luggage."

He darted to the entrance closet, and in a brief moment, joined her.

Heading down the slippery porch stairs, Callie's eyes filled with his Titan stature. In her preoccupation, her foot missed the center of the step and skidded out from under her. She crumpled backward, reaching out to break her fall.

David flung his hand behind her and caught her in the crook of his arm, while the other hand swung around to hold her secure. "Careful," he cautioned.

Captured in his arms, his gaze locked with hers, she

wavered at the sensation that charged through her. She marveled at his vibrant hazel eyes in the dusky light.

"Be careful. You could get hurt," he repeated, setting her on her feet.

She found her voice and mumbled a "thank you."

Capturing her elbow, he helped her down the next two steps. When she opened the trunk, he scanned its contents.

"I'll help you in with the luggage," he said, "and I'll come back for the rest."

She nodded. Hearing his commanding voice, she couldn't disagree. He handed her the smallest case, taking the larger himself, and they climbed the steps with care.

Once inside, David set down the larger case and addressed Agnes, who was waiting in the foyer. "Show Callie her rooms, please. I'll carry in the boxes and bring them up."

Agnes nodded and grabbed the larger case. But when David stepped outside, Callie took the case from her. "Please, let me carry this one. It's terribly heavy."

Agnes didn't argue and grasped the smaller case, then headed up the stairs. At the top, the housekeeper walked down the hallway and stopped at a door to the left, across from Nattie's room. She turned the knob and stepped aside.

As Callie entered, her heart skipped a beat. She stood in the tower she had admired from outside. The sitting room was fitted with a floral chintz love seat and matching chair of vibrant pinks and soft greens, with a lamp table separating the grouping. A small oak desk sat along one curved wall, and oak bookshelves rose nearby. A woman's touch was evident in the lovely decor.

Callie dropped her luggage and darted to the center window, pulling back the sheer white curtains framed by moss-colored draperies. She gazed outside at the scene. A light snow floated past the window, and below, David pulled the last carton from the trunk and closed the lid. He hefted the box into the air, then disappeared beneath the porch roof.

Agnes remained by the door, and when Callie turned back and faced the room, the housekeeper gestured through the doorway to the bedroom. Callie lifted her luggage and followed her inside. The modest bedroom, too, illustrated a feminine hand. Delicate pastel flowers sprinkled the wallpaper that ended at the chair-molding. Below, the color of palest blue met a deeper blue carpet.

"Agnes, this is beautiful." She wanted to ply the woman with questions about Sara and how she used the charming rooms.

"Mr. Hamilton hoped you'd like it."

"How could I not? It's lovely. So dainty and feminine."

Agnes nodded and directed her to a door that opened to a walk-in closet; across the room, another door led to a pristine private bathroom, graced by a claw-foot bathtub.

As she spun around to take in the room once again, David came through the doorway with the box.

"Bricks?" he asked.

"Nearly. Books and things."

"Ah, I should have guessed. Then you'd like this in the sitting room."

"Please." Callie followed him through the doorway.

David placed the box between the desk and the bookshelves. "I'll be right back with the other. Much lighter, I'm happy to say."

Callie grinned. "No books."

He left the room, and she returned to Agnes, who hovered in the doorway.

"Miss Randolph, did you want me to help unpack your things?"

"Oh, no, Agnes, I can get it. And please call me Callie. The 'Miss' stuff makes me nervous." She gave the woman a pleasant look, but received only a nod in return.

"Then I'll get back to the kitchen," Agnes said as she edged her way to the door.

"Yes, thank you."

Agnes missed David by a hairbreadth as he came through the doorway with the last box. He held it and glanced at Callie.

"Bedroom," Callie said, before he asked, and she gestured to the adjoining room.

David turned with his burden and vanished through the doorway. Before she could follow, he returned.

"So, I hope you'll be comfortable here. I still want to get a television for you. But you do have a radio."

Callie's focus followed the direction of his hand. A small clock radio sat on the desk. "The rooms are lovely. Just beautiful. Did your wif—Sara decorate them? They have a woman's touch."

"Yes," he said, nodding his head at the sitting room. "She used this as her reading room, and she slept here if she worried about Nattie's health. The bedroom was the baby's nursery then."

"I couldn't ask for a nicer place to stay. Thank you."

He glanced around him, edging backward toward the door, his hands moving nervously at his sides. "Then I'll let you get unpacked and settled. Dinner will be at six. We're celebrating this evening. We have a couple of guests for Nattie's birthday."

"Really? I'm glad I'm here for the celebration. And pleased I brought along a couple of small presents. I'd be embarrassed to attend her birthday party empty-handed." She kept her voice level and free of the irritation that prickled her. Why hadn't he thought to tell her about the birthday?

"I'm sorry. I should have mentioned it." A frown flashed over his face, yet faded as if another thought crossed his mind. He stepped toward the door. "I'll see you at dinner."

He vanished through the doorway before Callie could respond. She stared into the empty space, wondering what had driven him so quickly from the room.

Glancing at her wristwatch, the time read four-thirty. She had an hour-and-a-half before dinner. She needed time to dress appropriately if they were celebrating Nattie's birthday.

The word *birthday* took her back. Nattie was six today, so close in age to her own child, who had turned six on Christmas Day. Her chest tightened as the fingers of memory squeezed her heart. Could she protect herself from loving this child too deeply? And why did Natalie have to be six? Eight, four…any other age might not have bothered her as much.

She dropped on the edge of the bed and stared at the carpet. With an inner ache, she asked God to give her compassion and patience. Compassion for Nattie, and patience with herself.

As he waited for Callie's entrance, David prepared his guests for her introduction. Reverend John Spier listened attentively, and his sister Mary Beth bobbed her head, as if eager to meet someone new in the small town of Bedford.

"How nice," Mary Beth said, lowering her eyelids shyly at David. "Since I've come to help John in the parsonage, I've not met too many young unmarried women. Most people my age have already settled down. I look forward to our meeting."

"Yes, I hoped Callie might enjoy meeting you, too."

"Although once John finds a proper bride, I assume I'll go back to Cleveland…unless God has other plans."

David cringed inwardly, noticing the young woman's hopeful look, and wondered if he'd made a mistake inviting the pastor and his younger sister to the birthday dinner. The evening could prove to be difficult enough, depending on Nattie's disposition.

Looking toward the doorway, David saw Callie descending the staircase. "Here's Callie, now. Excuse me." David made for the doorway.

By the time Callie had reached the first floor, he was at the foot of the staircase. Caught off guard by her attractiveness, David gazed at her burgundy wool dress adorned with a simple string of pearls at her neck. The deep red of her gown emphasized the flush in her cheeks and highlighted the golden tinges of her honey-colored hair. As he focused his gaze, their eyes met, and her blush heightened.

"I see the party has already begun," she said. "I heard your voices as I came down the stairs."

"Now that you've joined us, everyone's here but the guest of honor." A sigh escaped him before he could harness it. "I invited our new pastor and his sister. I thought you might like to meet some of the younger people in town." He motioned for her to precede him. "We're in the living room."

She stepped around him, and he followed, watching the fullness of the skirt swish around her legs as she walked. The movement entranced him. Passing through the doorway at her side, he pulled his attention from her shapely legs to his guests.

As she entered the room, John's face brightened, and he rose, meeting her with his outstretched hand. "You're Callie."

"Yes, and you're David's pastor."

"John Spier," he said, then turned with a flourish. "And this is my sister, Mary Beth Spier."

"It's nice to meet you," Callie said, glancing at them both.

The young woman shot Callie an effusive grin. "And I'm certainly pleased to meet you. Being new in town myself, I've been eager to meet some young women who—"

"Have a seat, Callie." David gestured to the love seat. Interrupting Mary Beth was rude, but he couldn't bear to hear her announce again that she was one of the few single women in town. David chided himself. He should have used more sense than to invite a young woman to dinner who apparently saw him as a possible husband.

When he joined Callie on the love seat, she shifted closer to the arm and gracefully crossed her legs. His attention shifted to her slim ankles, then to her fashionable gray-and-burgundy brushed-leather pumps.

John leaned back in his chair and beamed. "I hope we'll see you at church on Sundays. We're a small congregation, but loaded with spirit. Although we could use a benefactor to help us with some much-needed repairs." His glance shot toward David.

David struggled with the grimace that crept to his face, resulting, he was sure, in a pained smile. "Agnes will announce dinner shortly. Then I'll go up and see if I can convince Nattie to join us. I never know how she'll respond." He eyed them, wondering if they understood. "I've had a difficult time here since Sara... Well, let's not get into that."

He wished he would learn to tuck his sorrow somewhere other than his shirtsleeve. He turned his attention to Callie. "Would you care for some mulled cider?"

She agreed, and he poured a mug of the warm brew. He regarded her full, rosy lips as she took a sip. She pulled away from the rim and nodded her approval.

His mind raced, inventing conversation. Tonight he felt tired, and wished he could retire to his study and spend the evening alone.

When Pastor John spoke, David felt himself relax.

"So where do you hail from, Callie?"

Without hesitation, she related a short personal history. Soon, Mary Beth joined in. David listened, pressing himself against the cushions rather than participating.

To his relief, Agnes announced dinner.

"Well, finally," David said, embarrassed at his obvious relief. David climbed the stairs to find Nattie, as Callie and the guests proceeded toward the dining room.

Callie held back and followed David's ascent with her eyes. He was clearly uncomfortable. She wondered if it was his concern for Nattie or the obvious flirtations of Mary Beth.

In the dining room, Agnes indicated David's seating arrangement. Mary Beth's focus darted from Callie to Agnes; she was apparently wondering if the housekeeper had made an error. She was not seated next to David.

When he arrived back with Nattie clinging to his side, he surveyed the table without comment. Except for a glance at Callie, the child kept her eyes downcast. David pulled out her chair, and Nattie slid onto it, focusing on the folded napkin on her plate, her hands below the table. David sat and asked Pastor John to offer the blessing.

Callie lowered her eyes, but in her peripheral vision she studied Nattie's reaction to the scene around her. Until David said "Amen," Nattie's eyes remained closed, but when she raised her lids, she glimpsed around the table almost without moving her head.

When her focus settled on Callie, their gazes locked.

In that moment, something special happened. Would she call the fleeting glimmer—hope, premonition or fact? Callie wasn't sure. But a sweet tingle rose from the base of her spine to the tips of her fingers. Never before had she felt such a sensation.

Chapter Six

After dinner, Nattie withdrew, staring into space and mentally recoiling from those who addressed her. David blew the lit candles on her cake as they sang "Happy Birthday" and excused her before the gifts were opened, saying she needed to rest. The wrapped packages stood ignored like eager young ladies dressed in their finery for the cotillion, but never asked to dance.

Callie longed to go with the child to the second floor, but refrained from suggesting it. Tonight was her first evening in the house, so she was still a stranger. And Nattie needed her father.

After they left the room, Callie sat uneasily with the Spiers, lost in her own thoughts.

"Such a shame about the little girl," John said, looking toward the doorway. "Has she always been so withdrawn?"

With effort, Callie returned to the conversation.

"Since her mother died a couple of years ago. I'm sure she'll be herself in time."

Mary Beth sighed and murmured. "Such a shame. And poor David having to carry the burden all alone."

John turned sharply to his sister, his words a reprimand. "Mary Beth, we're never alone. God is always with us."

"Oh, John, I know the Lord is with us. I meant, he has no wife." Her look pleaded for forgiveness, and she lowered her eyes.

Callie didn't miss Mary Beth's less-than-subtle meaning. "I don't think you need to worry about David. He'll come through this a stronger person, I'm sure. And don't forget, Mary Beth..."

The young woman looked curiously at Callie. "Don't forget...?"

"David's not alone anymore. I'm here to help him."

Mary Beth paled, and a flush rose to Callie's cheeks. Callie raised her hand nonchalantly to her face, feeling the heat. Her comment astounded her. She sounded like a woman fighting for her man.

When David returned to the parlor, the guests rose to leave, and Callie took advantage of their departure to say goodnight and head for her room. Confusion drove her up the stairs. She felt protective and possessive of this family—not only of Nattie, but of David. In less than a day, the situation already tangled in her heart.

Callie woke with the morning light dancing on the flowered wallpaper. She looked around the room, confused for a moment, and wondered where she was. Then she remembered. She slid her legs over the edge of the bed and sat, collecting her thoughts. How should she begin? What could she do to help this child, now bound in a cocoon, to blossom like a lovely butterfly?

One thing she knew. The process would take time. She stepped down to the soft, lush carpet and padded to the bathroom. A shower would awaken her body and her mind, she hoped.

When she finished dressing, she steadied herself, knowing what she had to do wouldn't be easy. She bowed her head, asking for God's wisdom and guidance, then left her room to face her first day.

Across the hall, Nattie's door stood open. Callie glimpsed inside. The child again sat on the window seat, but this time was looking at one of the books Callie had given her. Suddenly, she lifted her head and connected with Callie's gaze.

With her eyes focused on Nattie, Callie breathed deeply and strode purposefully to the doorway. "Well, good morning. Look at the wonderful sunshine."

Nattie followed her movement, but her face registered no response.

"When I woke, I saw the sun dance on my walls. I bet you did, too."

Nattie's attention darted to her wallpaper and back again to Callie. Was it tension or curiosity Callie saw settling there? She longed for a cup of coffee, but she'd made her move, and she'd stick it out. When she ambled toward the window seat, Nattie recoiled slightly. Callie only leaned over and glanced out the window. Nattie calmed.

"Did you look outside? The sun has turned the snow into a world of sparkling diamonds. And I've been told 'diamonds are a girl's best friend.'" She giggled lightheartedly, hoping Nattie would relax. "That's pretty silly, isn't it. I think the *snow* is a girl's best friend. Maybe we could take a walk outside today. We might even make a snowman."

Callie saw Nattie turn toward the window and scan

the fresh, glistening snow. She had piqued the child's interest.

"Nattie, I imagine you had breakfast already." She looked for some kind of response. None. "I'll go down and have a bite to eat. If you'd like to go outside, you can put on some warm stockings before I return. How's that?" Callie swung through the doorway with a wave and headed toward the stairs.

Would the child have the stockings on when she returned? If Nattie didn't want to talk, Callie would find another way to communicate until the child trusted her. Callie's thoughts thundered with questions. But mainly, she wanted to learn about Sara's death.

Silence filled the lower level of the house. She followed the aroma of breakfast and entered the dining room, where a lone table setting waited for her. She filled a plate with scrambled eggs and bacon from a small chafing dish, and poured a cup of coffee. This morning she didn't feel like eating alone. Looking for company, she carried the plate and cup through the door leading to the kitchen.

She found herself inside a butler's pantry, but through an arch, she spotted a stove and counter. Sounds emanated from that direction, and she headed through the doorway.

Agnes spun around, flinging her hand to her heart.

"Sorry, Agnes. I scared you."

The housekeeper's wide eyes returned to normal. "I didn't expect anyone, that's all. Can I get you something? I left your breakfast in the—" Her gaze lowered. "Oh, I see you have your plate."

Callie placed her dish and cup on the broad oak table.

"Do you mind if I eat in here with you, Agnes? I don't feel like eating alone this morning."

Agnes appeared flustered. She rushed forward with a damp cloth to wipe the already spotless table.

"I'm not trying to make work for you. The table's fine. I just thought you and I could get to know each other a little better. We're both employees here, and I'm sure familiarity can make our days more pleasant."

Agnes eyed her for a moment, then her face relaxed. "I sort of keep my place around here. Behind the scenes. You're more involved with Mr. Hamilton and Natalie. Except recently, while Mr. Hamilton looked for someone. But I'm at a loss. I never quite knew what to do for the child." She took a deep breath.

"Do you have a moment to join me in a cup of coffee?" Callie motioned to the empty chair across from her.

Agnes glanced at the chair, then at Callie. "Why, I don't mind if I do." She poured herself a mug of coffee from the warming pot and slipped onto the chair. "Black," she said, raising the mug. "I drink it black."

"Never could drink coffee black, myself. I like a little milk. I say 'cream,' but I prefer milk really." Callie smiled, and for the first time received a sincere smile in return. "So you've been here only a half year, if I remember correctly."

"Yes, about seven months now."

"I suppose following in Miriam's shadow was difficult."

Agnes nodded vigorously. "Oh yes, very hard. Miriam was part of this family forever. She's a wonderful woman. I knew her from church—Mr. Hamilton's church. That's how he knew me. When Miriam had to retire, he asked if I might be interested in the job. I'd been working for a family that had recently moved. Sort of destined, I suppose."

"Do you like working here?" In Callie's view, Agnes seemed to tiptoe around the house. The image didn't imply comfortable working conditions.

"Mr. Hamilton pays me well, and I'm always treated with respect."

Callie eyed her. "But you don't like working here."

Agnes fidgeted for a moment. "It's not that I don't like it here. The place isn't really homey, if you know what I mean. Mr. Hamilton has his moods. He's quiet and so is the child. Like the house is filled with shadows. He travels a lot, and I struggle to relate to the poor little thing upstairs. Yet whether he's here or not, she doesn't seem to notice one way or the other." She paused, drawing in a deep breath. "Now I don't mean Mr. Hamilton doesn't love his child. I'm sure he does."

"Don't apologize, Agnes. I know what you mean. Sometimes he seems as withdrawn as Nattie. Once in a while, I sense a chink in his wall, but he mends it as quickly as it appears."

Agnes's head bobbed again. "You do understand."

Callie nibbled on a piece of bacon. She was filled with curiosity. "Did you know Mrs. Hamilton?"

"So lovely. Yes, she played the church organ."

"The church organ? Well, that explains some things." Callie recalled David's comment about music.

"Such a sad thing, when she died."

Callie's pulse skipped through her veins. "You know how she died, then? I wasn't told."

"She was sick for a time. Cancer. They weren't married very long...maybe six or seven years. Such a shame."

Callie shook her head at the thought of someone dying so young. "I wonder what caused Nattie to withdraw so badly. All children are close to their mothers, but her behavior seems so unusual. Odd, really."

"Wondered that myself. I didn't know the family real well. Just Sundays, that's all, and being a small town, you hear about troubles. They were a happy family until the missus got sick."

"I'll ask Mr. Hamilton sometime, but I don't want to sound nosy. If I had a clue to Nattie's problem, I'd have someplace to begin with her."

Callie rose and placed her empty plate and cup in the sink. "Mr. Hamilton is at work, I suppose."

"Yes, he left early this morning. Probably relieved you were here."

"I'm hoping to coax Nattie outside. She's in her room too much. She needs fresh air."

"That'd be nice. I hope she goes out with you."

"Me, too," Callie said, wondering what to do if her plan didn't work.

When she returned to the second floor, she found Nattie on the floor with a puzzle. Her feet were tucked beneath her, so Callie couldn't see her stockings. She scanned the room and saw a pair lying discarded on the floor. Her stomach flip-flopped. Had the child put on the thick ones?

"I'm back," Callie called as she made her entrance.

Nattie glanced at her, then turned her attention to the odd-shaped puzzle pieces spread out on the floor. Callie wandered in and sat next to her on the carpet. The child withdrew her hand for a moment, glancing at Callie with a slight frown, then changed her mind and continued to locate the pieces.

Callie didn't speak, but searched until she found a piece, then placed it in the correct spot. They continued until the last piece remained. Callie waited, letting Nattie fit in the last of the puzzle.

"That's wonderful, Nattie, and you got to put in the last piece. I love to find the last piece." She tittered, hoping to gain some reaction from the child.

Instead, Nattie slid the puzzle aside and pulled her feet out in front of her.

Relief spilled over Callie. The child had donned thicker stockings. "Good. I see you want to go outside. Now, it's my turn to get ready. Would you like to come with me to my room?" Callie rose, but Nattie remained where she was. "Okay, then, you wait here, and I'll be back in a minute. You'll need a sweater, too, to wear under your coat."

She slipped quickly from the room to collect her warm coat and gloves, and hoped she could find Nattie's coat, boots and gloves somewhere. She'd ask Agnes.

David pulled down the driveway as dusk settled. Once again, he'd put in a long workday. The sky had faded to a grayish purple, and the ripples of glistening snow he had admired early in the morning now looked dull and shadowed. As he neared the house, he felt a twinge at his nerve endings, and he applied the brake and peered at the snow-covered lawn.

Sets of footprints had trampled through the snow. He shifted into park and opened his door, intrigued by the sight of the boot marks. The woman's print would have meant little, but beside the larger indentions, he saw the smaller footprint of his daughter.

In a trancelike state, he followed the prints that wove

through the evergreens and around the elms. In an open area, he paused. On the ground, he stared at imprints of angels. Heads, wings and bodies pressed into the snow. But, sadly, all adult angels. No seraphim or cherubim. No Nattie. Only the impression of the household's newest employee stamped a design into the fresh snow.

Yet a bright thought pierced his disappointment. Though Nattie had not made an angel, she had been outside and had walked in the snow—more progress in one day than he had seen in months. He should be grateful for each small gift.

He looked again at the fanned angel impressions at his feet. He counted three, four. He pictured the young woman, flinging herself to the ground, flailing her arms and legs to amuse his silent child. Callie's laughter rang in his mind. Angel? Yes, perhaps God had sent a human angel to watch over his daughter.

He dashed to the car and drove the short distance to the house. His eager feet carried him up the steps, and when he opened the front door, the house had come alive. In place of the usual silence, music played softly from a radio or television program in the parlor, and with anticipation he glanced into the room before hanging his coat. Callie sat curled on the sofa with her feet tucked beneath her, a book in her hand.

She heard him, for she raised her eye from the book, and a playful look covered her face. "Hello. You're home late this evening."

From the doorway, he stared at her in the firelight, his coat still clutched in his hand. "Too often, I'm afraid."

"Let me take your coat, Mr. Hamilton."

David jumped slightly and turned apologetically to Agnes. "Oh, thanks." After he released his coat to her care, he strode into the parlor, his eyes riveted to the firelight glinting on Callie's golden-brown hair.

He fell into the chair across from her. "I noticed a slight miracle outside when I came up the driveway."

Her lips parted in an easy smile. "The angels?"

Watching the animation on her face, he nodded.

"Only mine, I'm afraid. I tried." She lifted a bookmark, slid it between the pages and closed the volume.

"Oh, don't feel discouraged. Nattie went outside with you. We haven't been able to move her beyond these doors. In one day, you've worked wonders. I'm amazed."

Her eyes brightened. "I'm pleased then. I thought I was a minimal failure."

"Not at all." A scent of beef and onions drifted through the doorway and his stomach growled. "You've eaten?"

"No." She shook her head, and her hair glistened in the light. "I waited for you."

"That's nice."

"But Nattie ate, I'm afraid."

"Let me run up and see her, and I'll hurry right down." He rose and dashed up the stairway.

Callie watched him hurry away and filled with sadness, thinking of his excitement over something as simple as his child's walk in the snow. Her attention fell to her lap and the book that lay there.

Then his words rang in her head, and she raised her hand to her chest to calm the fluttering from within. "That's nice," he'd said, when she told him she'd waited for supper. Callie closed her eyes. Why did she care what he said? She was an employee doing her job. That was all.

His footsteps left the oriental carpet and hit the shiny

wood floor at the entrance to the parlor, and she looked toward the doorway.

"Agnes says dinner is ready," he said.

She rose, and as they neared the dining room, the aroma stirred her hunger. A low rumble from her stomach echoed in the hallway. She glanced at him apologetically.

"Don't feel bad. My stomach isn't complaining loudly, but I'm starving. You shouldn't have waited, but I'm glad you did."

A flush of excitement rose in her, until she heard his next sentence.

"I'm anxious to hear about your day with Nattie."

I'm being foolish. Lord, keep my mind focused on my purpose in this home. Not on silly thoughts. Her flush deepened in her embarrassment, and she hoped he might not notice in the softened light of the dining room doorway.

As they stepped into the room, Agnes came through the kitchen entrance with a steaming platter. She placed it on the table, then hit the switch as she exited, brightening the lights above the table.

David pulled out a chair for Callie, and she sat, waiting for him to be seated. The platter, sitting before them, aroused her senses. A mound of dark roasted beef was surrounded by sauteed onions, browned potatoes and carrots. She bowed her head to murmur a silent prayer, but before she asked God's blessing, David's warm voice split the silence.

He offered thanks for the food and the day, then he thanked God for Callie's presence in the house. A heated blush rose again to her cheeks. Now in the brightened room, when David looked up from his prayer, she knew her pink cheeks glowed.

"Sorry," Callie said, touching her cheeks, "I'm not used to being blessed along with a roast."

An unexpected burst of laughter rolled from David's chest. Agnes halted in the doorway, balancing a gravy boat and a salad bowl in apparent surprise. She looked from David to Callie, then added a smile to her face as she approached the table.

"This roast looks and smells wonderful, Agnes," David said, the merriment still lingering in his tone.

"Why, thank you, Mr. Hamilton." She placed the items on the table and scurried from the room with a final wide-eyed glance over her shoulder.

"Poor Agnes hasn't heard much laughter in the house since she came. I think I've surprised her." His hazel eyes crinkled at the edges as he looked at Callie.

"Then it's about time," Callie said lightly, trying to ignore the beating pulse in her temples. "'Laughter is good for all that ails you,' my father used to say."

"He was right. Laughter is music everyone can sing."

The word *music* seemed to catch them both off guard, and they each bent over their plates, concentrating on filling their stomachs. They ate quietly, keeping their eyes directed at the meat and potatoes. Callie searched her mind for something to draw him out again and distract her own thoughts.

"I borrowed a book from the library. What a lovely room. And so many wonderful books." She pictured the room next to the library. She'd turned the knob, but the door had been locked. Though curious what the room was, she didn't ask. "I hope you don't mind about the book."

"No, not at all. You're welcome to read every one."

"I'd have to live here forever to do that."

He lifted his eyes to hers. "Yes, I suppose you would."

Silence lingered again, until David asked about Nattie. The rest of the meal was filled with tales of Callie's day with the child. They both were comfortable with the topic, and the conversation flowed easily until the meal ended.

When they reentered the foyer, she said goodnight and climbed the stairs. But the *click* of a door lock startled her, and she spun around. David slipped quietly into the room at the bottom of the stairs. Another faint *click* told her he had locked himself in. The sound bolted her to the floor, as her dreams rose up to haunt her. She stood a moment until she gained composure, then continued up the stairs.

Chapter Seven

After breakfast, Callie knocked on Nattie's door. Since the day in the snow, two weeks had passed with no new breakthrough.

Today, Nattie sat staring out the window with a doll in her lap. Pieces of doll clothing lay at her side, and Callie sensed she had stopped in mid-play. The doll wore a diaper and dress, with the shoes and bonnet waiting in a pile.

Nattie glanced at Callie, but turned her attention to the doll.

Callie ambled to the window seat and sat for a moment before she spoke. "What a pretty baby you have there. But the poor child is only half dressed. What about her shoes and bonnet?"

Nattie ignored Callie, though occasionally she looked curiously at her and then lowered her eyes again.

Callie wondered what would make a difference. How could she get through to the lonely little girl. "Would you like to color? Or maybe we could draw some pictures?" Nothing. Whatever she encouraged Nattie to do, Callie would first do it alone. That much she had learned. She shifted to the floor and pulled out one of Nattie's puzzles. Tumbling the pieces onto the floor, she turned them so all the picture pieces were facing up.

Nattie glanced at her, swiveling so her legs dangled over the window seat. She lay the doll to the side and watched.

Callie began forming the outer rim of the puzzle. When the frame was nearly complete, Nattie slid from the bench and joined her. She peered at the pieces to see if the fit matched, and often they did. Each time the child joined her, Callie felt they had made some progress.

Callie hummed a tune as she worked the puzzle. The sound surprised her. Humming, like singing, had vanished from her life. Today she felt like murmuring the simple melody, and best of all, Nattie eyed her more than usual. The child seemed comforted by the droning sound. Certainly her mother had hummed to her, too. Perhaps the memory soothed her.

Eventually, Callie rose and stared outside. The past days had seemed lonely. David had gone to Atlanta on a business trip, and except for an occasional conversation with Agnes, her world was as silent as Nattie's.

March would be along shortly, and she longed for warmer weather when she and Nattie could go for walks and run in the fresh air. Maybe then the child would warm the same way the summer sun would heat the soil, encouraging new shoots to sprout. Nattie, too, might come alive again.

As David finished his breakfast, Callie entered the dining room. Each time she appeared, a deep longing filled him.

"Good morning," she said brightly, and turned to the buffet.

David returned her greeting and watched as she took a plate and scooped up a serving spoonful of scrambled eggs. With toast and sausage on her plate, she sat on David's left. "How was your trip?"

"Fine. Too long actually, but that's business."

They hadn't talked much recently. All he'd learned was that nothing dramatic had occurred as yet with regard to Nattie. Though his hopes remained high, the process seemed to be taking forever.

"I wouldn't know much about business. I've always been a nurse. Whole different career. Though, we notice how quiet it is when you're away." She lowered her eyes, focusing on her plate and scooping egg onto her fork.

David knew exactly what she meant. Before she had come, the house had seemed a tomb. He sipped his coffee, hating to tell her he would be gone again that evening.

"I have a dinner invitation this evening, so I won't be home. I suppose you can endure one more night without my tantalizing conversation."

As he spoke, her face faded to disappointment. "One more night, huh? When I took the job I didn't have any guarantees of dinner entertainment, so I suppose I can handle it." She put a smile on her face, but David had learned enough about Callie to know the smile was to appease him.

He folded his napkin and laid it next to his plate. "To be honest, I'd rather stay home."

"Business dinner?"

"Probably, but on the pretense of a social evening at the parsonage."

Callie's face gave way to a wry grin. "Ah, an invitation from Mary Beth, no doubt."

A sigh escaped him before he could control it. "No doubt." He eyed his wristwatch and rose, longing to stay and talk. He had forgotten how comfortable it was to sit after a meal and chat. He and Sara had often lingered at the table long after the meal was finished. He could easily do the same with Callie. But his business waited him. "I'd better be on my way."

"I'm sure you'll have fun." Callie tilted her face toward him, and her words sounded to David as if they wavered between sarcasm and wit.

"How about a wager?"

"Sorry, kind sir, I don't make bets. It's sinful, you know."

Her smile sent a tingle through him, and he glanced at his face as he passed a mirror in the entry to see if the unexpected sensation showed.

"I suppose we should have been polite and invited Callie to join us," Mary Beth gushed, after they settled into the cozy living room after dinner. "I don't know where my mind was."

I do, David thought as he gallantly tried to smile at her comment. "I'm sure she understands." Thinking of Callie's wry smile, he realized she understood Mary Beth Spier was looking for a husband—but in the wrong direction.

"Perhaps next time," John said. "We should enjoy each other's company more often. Other than Sundays, I might add."

David enjoyed his private joke. If John were to be perfectly honest, he might also add that he didn't see

David on many Sundays, either. David waited, wondering where John was going from there.

"Speaking of Sundays," John said, "we certainly miss having an organ for worship. Looking back at the records, I see your wife was the organist for a couple of years."

David gathered his wits, keeping his face unemotional. "Yes, she was. I believe a lady named Ruta Dryer filled in for my wife while she was ill…and after Sara died."

"Yes, I noticed that, too. But then the organ needed some work, and I'm afraid financially we haven't been able to make those repairs."

"I see," David said, waiting for the pitch.

"I wonder if you'd considered helping out with that little project. I imagine we could find an organist—but first, we need the instrument."

David bit his lip, struggling to control his emotions. "Sara's death was a tremendous loss for my daughter and me, as you can imagine. I haven't given much thought to the organ since then. I've been concerned about my child, and to be honest, thoughts of the organ music fill me with some raw spots yet. You'll have to let me think about it."

"Oh, certainly, I wasn't suggesting that—"

"I may seem self-indulgent, but the congregation has adjusted to the piano. And I need to deal with my own problems—and my daughter's—before I deal with someone else's."

"Yes. Do take your time. I suppose I should have been more considerate in my request."

"Don't worry about it. How would you know what goes on in my head?"

Mary Beth leaned across the table and latched onto

David's arm. "I wish I could help. I'm sure life isn't complete without…well, being alone and with your daughter, too. Hiring a woman to fill in for Nattie's mother is all right, but—"

"Callie is far more than a fill-in. She's a professional nurse, well-trained. I'm very hopeful that her influence with Nattie will bring her out of her cocoon. Callie's full of spirit and a delightful…" He looked at their astounded faces and realized he had gone overboard in Callie's defense.

Mary Beth stared at him wide-eyed. "Oh, I didn't mean she isn't capable. I'm sure she is. I mean your daughter has needs, but so do—"

"David knows what you meant, Mary Beth," John sputtered. "We shouldn't dwell on the subject. Would you care to play a game of Chinese checkers, David?"

Better than the Chinese water torture you're putting me through. David nearly laughed aloud at his thought.

On the first Sunday in March, late in the afternoon, Callie sat curled on the sofa in the library, reading Jane Austen's *Mansfield Park.* She'd read the author's other novels, enjoying the wit and social commentary on the lives of women in the early eighteen-hundreds.

Sometimes, she felt her own life was tangled in social principles.

Today for the first time since her arrival, Callie had gone to church. She had chosen to worship at a new, larger church on Washington Avenue, one with a large vibrant pipe organ. She longed to hear something uplifting, something to take the ache from her heart and give her patience and courage.

Even in church, for the past few years, she had

avoided singing. But today she raised her voice, and her spirit lifted with the music. *Sweet hour of prayer, sweet hour of prayer.* Prayer? Had she prayed as she ought to have done? Or had she leaned on her own humble abilities, forgetting God's miracles?

The pastor's voice shot through her mind, like an answer to her question, with the Scripture reading. *"Then you will call upon Me and go and pray to Me, and I will listen to you. And you will seek Me and find Me, when you search for Me, with all your heart."* The morning's message settled into her thoughts. Pray, she must.

Now, as the sun lowered in the sky, Callie snapped on the light. Doing so, a shadow fell across her page. She glanced up to see David standing a distance from her, observing her silently.

He slid into a chair across from her. "Disappointed?"

"Disappointed?"

"With Nattie. I suppose you imagined by now she'd be playing like any six-year-old?" His face told his own story.

"I'm optimistic again. But you're disappointed, I think."

He lowered his head, studying his entwined fingers laying in his lap. "Oh, a little, I suppose. I don't know what to expect, really."

"You can't expect more from her than you do from yourself."

His head shot upward, and Callie swallowed, wondering why she had been so blunt.

"What do you mean?" His brows knit tightly, and his eyes squinted in the artificial light.

Well, here goes. Callie took a deep breath. "You can't hide behind these walls, totally. Not with your business.

But look at you. You aren't living, either. Just marking days off the calendar."

"That's what you think, huh?"

"I suppose I'm too forward."

"I expect nothing less."

His eyes, despite the abrupt comment, crinkled in amusement.

"I should be angry at you, but I imagine you're telling the truth."

"That's what I see. Maybe you have another side, but here, everything is shut off. The doors are closed as if you want nothing to escape. Or is it, nothing to enter? You build walls around yourself…or lock yourself in your secret room."

His face pinched again. "Secret room?"

Callie tilted her head forward. "Yes, the room next door. The locked door."

He released a quiet chuckle. "That's my study. I suppose I've gotten into the habit of keeping it locked. All my business secrets are in that room." He rose. "Come. I'll show you."

Callie felt her cheeks grow hot. "No, I didn't mean—"

"Up, up." He reached down and took her hand, pulling her to her feet. "I don't want you to think I have bodies locked away in there or skeletons hiding in the closets."

"I'm sorry. Really."

But her pleading did no good. David wrapped his arm around her shoulder and marched her to the hallway. He turned the handle, and the door opened without a key. He glanced at her with a playful, smug look and pushed open the door.

Though she felt foolish being led in as if she were a

naughty child, she savored the warmth of his arm embracing her. She longed to be in his sturdy arms, feeling safe and secure. But as she stepped into the room, he raised his hands to her shoulders and pivoted her in one direction, then the other, showing her the room.

"See. Not one body."

His voice rippled through her. She turned toward him, her eyes begging forgiveness. "I wasn't suggesting you had something bad in here. I meant, you lock yourself away. There's a difference."

He looked deeply into her eyes, and her heart stopped momentarily, dragging her breath from her. When the beat returned, its rhythm galloped through her like a horse and rider traversing rocky ground. Faster. Slower. Faltering. She struggled for control.

"You're right, I suppose," he said.

His words unlocked their gaze. But in the lengthy silence, Callie became flustered. "I'm right?"

"Yes, about locking myself away from the world."

He moved into the room. "Since you're here, come in. As you see, your sitting room is directly above this one. It's the tower room."

The tower intrigued her, and she moved voluntarily into the depth of the uniquely shaped room. The heavy wooden paneling darkened his study in comparison to her sunny room. Centered on one wall, his vast desk faced the outer hall. Tall shelves and a row of file cabinets stood nearby. A leather sofa and chair sat in the center of the room on an elegant Persian carpet.

"All man. No woman's touch here," she said.

A fleeting grin dashed across his face. "This room is mine, remember." His right hand gestured toward the tower room, and she wandered through the archway.

Only two windows lit the circular room, smaller than hers above. As she turned, her eyes were drawn to another piano, a console, against an inner wall.

She stepped forward, noticing manuscript paper spread along the stand. She turned to him in surprise. "You write music?"

"Not really."

She felt him withdraw, swiftly rebuilding the wall he had opened when he let her enter his sanctuary. "But this is an unfinished manuscript." Her eyes sought his.

"I used to write music. I haven't touched that in a long time. I haven't played in a long time."

She nodded. Neither had she. She'd let the music in her life die the way part of her had died that terrible day. Yet, today, truth rose from the solemn moment. David would never live again until he lived fully. And neither would she.

A sound caused them to turn toward the foyer. Agnes stood in the doorway of the study.

"Dinner's ready when you are, Mr. Hamilton."

"Fine, we're coming now."

Callie pulled herself from the room. "I'll get Nattie," she said, hurrying into the hallway. She climbed the stairs, trembling over her second revelation of the day. Earlier, she'd considered the importance of prayer. Now, she knew she could ask no one else to join the living unless she lived herself.

After breakfast two weeks later, Callie and Nattie lay together, coloring on the parlor floor. David stepped into the room wearing his overcoat, his briefcase in his hand. He leaned down and kissed Nattie's head. "Goodbye, Nat."

Callie tilted her head and looked at him standing above her.

"We'll see you later."

"Yes, I shouldn't be too late. By the way, this Friday I have a meeting in Indianapolis. I don't know if you need to make a trip home, but you're welcome to ride along. The meeting should run only a couple of hours. Perhaps you'd like to visit with your mother."

Callie rose from the floor, surprised at his offer. "Yes, I'd like that. I know my mother would enjoy the visit, and I have a few things I can pick up while I'm there." Retrieving her lightweight clothing excited her more than did visiting with her mother, but she kept that to herself. Most of all she'd enjoy the private time with David. "I'd love to go, if you don't mind."

"Not at all, I'd enjoy the company. And Agnes said she'd be happy to keep an eye on Nattie."

Their gazes connected, and Callie sought the flashing green specks that glinted in his eyes. A flush rose to her neck, and she looked away from him. "I'll call my mother then, so she'll be expecting me."

He nodded and took a step backward toward the door. "Good." He spun around, and she heard the front door close.

Nattie paused momentarily, almost as if she would speak, but instead, she lowered her head and concentrated on her picture. Recently, her dark-toned coloring had given way to brighter shades, one success Callie had noticed. Nattie used a yellow crayon to color the sun, then traded for a medium green to fill in the grass. Big progress in Callie's view.

She stretched out on the floor again next to the child and turned back to her picture: red tulips, green leaves, yellow daffodils. It reminded her that spring lay on their doorstep. Then, without direction, her thoughts jumped to the changing colors in David's eyes. In the morning light that streamed through the window, the colors had shifted and altered, creating earthy, vibrant hues. Her heart skipped at the vision, and the image hummed within her.

Humming. Callie eased back on her elbows and held her breath. She hadn't been humming, but a sweet lilting melody rose to her ears. Without moving, she listened. Softly, Nattie hummed as she concentrated on the coloring book, her silence finally broken.

Callie's pulse raced, and her joy lifted as high as the prayer of thanks she whispered in her mind for the wondrous gift.

Chapter Eight

With David at the wheel, Callie leaned back and enjoyed the passing scenery. Though spring was yet a few days away, a fresh green hue brightened the landscape, and a new warmth promised things to come.

David, too, seemed to sense Nattie's own promise of things to come. Since hearing of her latest progress, David smiled more often. He referred to Callie as another miracle worker, though she reminded him more than once that God worked miracles, she didn't.

David glanced at the dashboard clock. "I figure we'll arrive about eleven. I'll drop you off and still have time to get to the meeting." He shot her a glance. "I should only be a couple of hours."

"Just come when you're finished. I'll be ready I'm sure." She'd probably be ready sooner. Yet she had to admit, she and her mother had plenty to talk about. She had spoken to Grace only briefly since arriving in Bedford.

"Are you sure? Maybe I should call."

Callie opened her shoulder bag and jotted down the telephone number. "Here you go."

"Slip it in my pocket so I remember to take it with me."

She leaned across the space between them, slipping the note into his nearest suit coat pocket. Her fingers tingled at the touch of the soft cashmere wool, and she warmed at his nearness. *Don't get carried away,* she chided herself.

Romantic fantasies had long disappeared from her dreams. She had never known a man before or after the experience of her child's conception. The thought of intimacy with any man frightened her.

As a teen, she had dreamed of the special day when she would dress in a white gown and float down the aisle as a bride, giving herself to a loving man, exploring and learning about love and passion. The dream had vanished as quickly as her virginity, and in its place, shame and guilt festered like an infected wound.

"You're so quiet," David said.

"Sorry. Just thinking."

"I hope they're nice thoughts."

She closed her eyes and avoided the truth. "Yes, they're very nice." She couldn't tell him the private things that filled her mind. No one would ever hear those thoughts. Another reason she could never fall in love.

After a short distance, the outskirts of Indianapolis spread along the horizon, and David soon left her at Grace's front door. She raised her hand as he pulled away, then she entered the house. She expected her mother to be hanging out the window, waiting for her, but instead the rooms were silent.

"Mom," she called. She wandered to the kitchen, where dishes lay piled on the countertop. Very unlike her mother.

"Mother." She listened and heard a noise above her.

"Callie?"

"You're upstairs, I take it." Callie climbed the steps, and saw her mother standing in the hallway, still in her bathrobe. Concern prickled her. Grace never slept late. "What's up with you?"

"I don't know," Grace answered, seeming confused. "I didn't feel well this morning."

"Or last night," Callie added.

"What do you mean?" Grace shuffled down the hallway.

Callie stood by the stairs, transfixed. "The dishes. You didn't clean up after dinner last night. That's not like you at all. Something's wrong. You need to see a doctor."

Grace swished the air with her hand as if erasing her words. "I don't need a doctor. Probably just a little spring cold. You know how they can be."

She studied her mother's face. Grace's mouth was pulled to the side in a faint grimace. Dark circles ringed her eyes, raccoonlike against her pale skin. "I don't know, Mom."

"You go down and make us some coffee, and I'll get dressed. I'll look much better when I wash my face and comb my hair."

Callie moved to her mother's side, giving her a brief hug. "Okay, but we'll talk about this when you come down."

When she returned to the kitchen, she put on a pot of coffee and rinsed last night's dishes, then loaded the dishwasher. It hadn't been run for a couple of days. Callie's concern was not the untouched dishes or her mother's appearance. Grace loved to play the martyr. Yet today, she denied valiantly that something was wrong. Callie knew something was *very* wrong.

She started the dishwasher, then looked into the refrigerator. "Old Mother Hubbard's cupboard," she said aloud to herself. Inside, she found three eggs and the end of a bread loaf. When the eggs were scrambled and in the frying pan, Callie popped the bread into the toaster. Her mind worked over the problem. No question. Grace wasn't herself. Living two hours away, she'd have to depend on Ken to keep an eye on their mother. She'd call him after breakfast.

Grace entered the kitchen as the toast popped.

"Perfect timing, Mom. I made us some breakfast." Though Callie had eaten, she joined her mother at the table. She heaped the egg on Grace's plate, giving herself only a tablespoon full.

"Now, I'm not going to leave you without knowing what happened. When did you get sick?"

"Please, Callie, I'm fine. Wait until you're an old woman. Then you'll understand about being tired... and confused once in a while." She nibbled the toast.

"I'm tired and confused now, Mom. Age has nothing to do with it. I think you need to see a doctor. You're not ninety. You're only in your mid-sixties. I'll call Ken before I go."

"I felt fine until yesterday afternoon. I got a terrible headache. Sort of achy in my left arm. I think it scared me. I laid down for a while, and it seemed to pass."

Callie pictured the dishes piled on the counter. The problem hadn't passed as fast as Grace wanted her to believe. Rather than press her mother, she allowed Grace to change the subject, and filled her in on Bedford, her progress with Nattie, and a description of the lovely house.

As the time approached to leave, Callie made a doctor's appointment for Grace and phoned Ken. "I know you're busy, but could you please see Mom gets to the doctor?"

"Are you that worried?" Ken asked, sounding as if he thought she was being foolish.

"Look, Ken, she said her arm ached, and she had a bad headache. We can't play around with symptoms. Let's let a doctor tell her it's nothing."

"I suppose you're right."

"And you really should check with her every day or so, at least until she's feeling better."

"Easy for you. You go off and let me do the work, huh?"

"For a change, it won't hurt you. The thought of leaving her here alone bothers me."

"Where's our dear sister Patricia, when we need her?"

Callie sighed at her brother's complaining. "In California, where she's always been. Quit trying to wheedle out of this. Just check on her once in a while. Can you do that?"

"Okay, I give."

Though his voice was teasing, Ken left Callie less than confident, but there was little else she could do. Before she walked away from the telephone, David called to say he'd be later than expected.

When he finally arrived, Callie hurried out to his car. "Would you mind coming in a minute? Mom insists upon meeting you."

David turned off the ignition and stepped out into the

afternoon sunshine, a knowing look etching his face. "We have to make mothers happy."

Callie led him up the porch steps. "I'm worried about her, actually." She glanced at him over her shoulder and grasped the doorknob.

He paused. "Something wrong?"

"Yes, but I'm not sure what. She seems ill, but she denies it."

David's brows furrowed as Callie led him inside. As they came into the living room, Grace eyed him.

"Mother," Callie said, "this is my employer, David Hamilton. David, my mother, Grace Randolph."

David reached forward as if to shake hands, but Grace's arms remained folded against her chest. Unabashed, he retraced his hand and tucked it into his pocket. "I'm sorry to hear you're not feeling well, Mrs. Randolph."

"I'm fine. My daughter lives so far away she's forgotten what I look like."

"Mother," Callie said, controlling her irritation, "you are not fine. I've called Ken, and I want you to promise to call me after you see the doctor."

"It's nothing. You're making a mountain out of nothing."

Callie rested her hand on her mother's shoulder. "Let the doctor tell me that, okay?"

Grace snorted her protest.

"Promise you'll call," Callie said.

After a lengthy pause, Grace nodded her head.

Callie bent and brushed a kiss on her cheek. "We have to go, Mom. Please do as I say."

Callie gave David a desperate look and stepped backward. David proceeded ahead of her and held the door open while Callie gave her mother a final wave, then stepped outside.

When they had settled in the car, Callie rubbed her temples. "She won't call. I'll have to call Ken. I pray he knows something. Sometimes brothers are useless when it comes to asking questions."

David glanced at her. "Do you want to drive up and take her yourself?"

Callie sighed. "I don't know. Ken should be able to handle it. I'll call him when we get home. Maybe I'll feel better."

"That's fine, but if you need to come here, Agnes can keep an eye on Nattie for the day."

"Thanks." She caught his image in the rearview mirror. His concern touched her.

Callie leaned her head against the headrest, and they drove in silence until they passed the city limits of Indianapolis. A few miles beyond the Franklin exit, she straightened in her seat. "Sorry. I'm not good company."

"No problem. Did you get a little rest?"

"Yes, I think I drifted off for a minute. I've spent my life in silent battles with my mother, and now that something's wrong, I'm dealing with some guilt. And a lot of worry."

"That's part of life." David drew his shoulders upward in a deep sigh. "I think we all do that, Callie. It's so easy to take things for granted. Complain and grumble. Then when we're gripped by worry, we have all the 'I wishes' and 'I should haves' thrashing around inside us."

"I want to resolve some of those things with my mom before anything happens. I guess this scare reminded me of that."

"Good. Look at the positive side. And speaking of positive thoughts, how's your stomach? Mine's empty. They only gave us coffee and pastries at the meeting. No good wholesome food. Did you eat at your mother's?"

"I made her breakfast, but I only nibbled."

"Then we'll stop for dinner. We should reach Columbus about five o'clock. I think Weinantz opens about then. The food is excellent. I called Agnes and warned her not to cook for us."

A strange shyness filled her. David had planned ahead for their dinner together. She'd chased such thoughts from her foolish dreams, and now he was making her hopes come true. She could deal with fantasy, but reality made her vulnerable. *The boss is taking his employee to dinner. Nothing more.* She repeated the words over and over in her mind until they reached Columbus.

The town proved to be a surprise. In the middle of small, turn-of-the-century communities, Columbus rose like a contemporary misfit. Buildings of modern design filled the city center; buses carried tourists through the streets to view the renowned architecture. The restaurant lived up to David's praise, and after their meal, Callie relaxed over coffee, the worries of the day softening.

David studied her concerned face, as she sipped from the steaming cup. For the first time since they had left her mother's, a slight smile touched her rosy lips. "You look more relaxed."

"I feel better. The meal was wonderful," Callie said.

Her smile warmed him. "I'm glad. I know what worry can do. And I've had the same guilty thoughts myself. I look at Nattie's situation and blame myself. After Sara's death, I wasn't there for her. Such a little girl, and I crept away like a wounded animal. I feel terrible about that."

"I think it's more than that, David. Something happened. Something more than Sara's death. I don't know exactly what I mean, but her silence seems deeper than normal grief. You know, children are usually known for bouncing back."

"They do." Her comment pushed him deeper into thought. "I don't know. I've always blamed myself." Was she right? What could have happened? Sara's death was no surprise. And still, it hit him harder than he would ever have imagined. Then, what about Nattie? Could something else have happened?

He gazed into Callie's perplexed-looking eyes, and felt his chest tighten. Bluer than the sky. Rich, deep and filled with her own secrets. What dark moments hid behind those lovely eyes?

"What you've been able to do for Nattie makes me so grateful," he said. "You've already made a difference in her life." In *my* life, he thought, feeling his pulse waver as he regarded her. "Nattie leaves her room now...and the humming. Something more will happen. I sense it."

Callie's face tensed. She lowered her eyes, then raised them shyly. "Could we talk a little? About things that might bother you?"

A knot of foreboding formed in his stomach. "Like what?"

"Tell me about Sara's death. You've never said anything, and like I said, I suspect something more happened to Nattie than losing a mother. Was Nattie with Sara when it happened? Would she feel to blame for some reason?"

"To blame? No, how could she?" He closed his eyes

for a moment, the awful memories rippling through him. "Sara had cancer. Leukemia. Nattie couldn't feel responsible for that. Anyway, she was only four."

"I know, but children overhear things that they don't understand. They fill in the blanks, make up their own stories, and things get out of context. I just wondered if that might be possible."

"No, I'm sure that didn't happen." Though he said no, thoughts galloped through his mind as he wondered if something had been said to make Nattie feel Sara's death was her fault.

"If she misunderstood something, anything, it might explain her silence," Callie repeated. "I suppose I'm grasping for it all to make sense."

"I've done the same. Wondered. Worried."

"When did you learn your wife had cancer?"

An overwhelming sorrow washed over him, and the answer stuck in his throat. Callie's question disturbed thoughts he'd tucked away. Now they came crashing into his memory. Without knowing, she was treading on raw nerve endings and deep painful wounds that had yet to heal.

Her drawn face overflowed with tenderness. "I'm sorry," she said. "I guess I'm dredging up hurtful memories. I just thought, the more I understand, the more I'll know what to look for."

He reached across the table and touched her hand clasped in a tense fist. At first, she flinched at his touch, but in a heartbeat her hand relaxed.

"You're right. On both counts." He drew his hand away, balling it, too, into a fist. "Sara had leukemia before we married…but we were hopeful. Like all young, idealistic couples, we thought love could solve every problem—even cancer."

"Oh, David, I'm so sorry. I had no idea. And then when she got pregnant..." Callie tossed herself back against the cushion with a lengthy sigh. "Never mind, I understand."

He grimaced. "Thanks." But she didn't really understand. Not everything. He was not ready to open all the wounds. He hid behind her misconceptions in safety. What would she think of him if she knew the whole story? He leaned against the seat and folded his arms across his chest. He had told her enough.

Chapter Nine

The following week Callie stayed in the parlor after dinner, trying to concentrate on her book. Concern dogged her as she assessed Ken's surprise telephone call.

"Dr. Sanders thinks Mom may have had a minor stroke."

"Minor stroke? How bad is that? Major. Minor. The thought scares me, Ken."

"He'll know more after he gets the results of the MRI test. It's scheduled for next week. Apparently, it takes some kind of picture of the brain."

"MRI. Yes, it's magnetic resonance imaging."

"Thank you, Florence."

"Florence? Oh, Nightingale." She snickered. "Poor Florence wouldn't know anything about an MRI. Anyway, how's Mom doing? Do you think I should come up there?"

"She's good. I don't notice a difference."

Callie rolled her eyes. "Do you really think you'd notice?"

"Thanks, sister dear."

"You're welcome. You'll call me as soon as you hear something."

"Don't worry. She's okay…really."

When Callie hung up the receiver, she had a tremendous urge to get in her car and go to Indianapolis. At dinner, she told David. Again, he encouraged her to go if she would feel better, but wisdom stepped in. She'd wait to hear the test results.

After the meal, David went to his study to work, and she relaxed on the sofa, her legs stretched on the cushion and her feet over the edge. Staring at the book propped in her hand, she saw only a blur, as her thoughts twisted and turned. Nattie had carried storybooks down with her before dinner, and she lay on the floor nearby, flipping through the pages.

When David stepped into the room, she and Nattie glanced up.

"Hmm? All the ladies have their noses buried in a book, I see." He walked to Nattie and stroked her hair with his fingers.

Callie watched her raise the book toward her father, and her heart stood still when she heard the child's soft, sweet voice.

"Read to me, Daddy."

"Nattie," David gasped. His eyes widened and his face paled momentarily, then brightened with happiness. "I sure will, sweetheart." He scooped her up in his arms and carried her to the chair.

Callie's heart skipped and hammered in wild rhythm. She fixed on Nattie's face, witnessing the special moment of her first full sentence since her mother's death. Where one sentence lived, there were two. Then three. It was only a matter of time.

Glowing with rapture, David read two storybooks without stopping, holding the child in his arms. She hugged him tightly when he finished, and for the first time, Callie witnessed Nattie showing affection. Callie and David shared the special moment with quiet looks of elation, not wanting to break the spell.

After Nattie had gone to bed, David returned, bounding into the room like a man saved from a firing squad. Callie rose at his exuberant entrance, feeling her own joy. In a flash, he closed the distance between them, grasping her in his arms and pulling her to his chest.

"Thank you. Thank you," he whispered into her hair.

His warmth surrounded her, and the heat of surprise rose to her face.

"What you've brought into our lives has been like a miracle. Two years I've waited and longed for a single sentence, and tonight—" he looked into her eyes "—my prayer was answered."

A gasp escaped her, and David stepped back abruptly as if embarrassed.

"I'm sorry," he said. "I didn't mean to frighten you."

"Surprised me was all. Not frightened." Though she said the words, the truth was that she was shaken by his actions. She hadn't been that close to a man since… She remembered her father's arms comforting her, but that had been so long ago.

"No, I scared you. I saw the look in your face. I'm sorry. But I didn't think. Tonight's been so wonderful."

"Oh, David, it is wonderful." Though thrilled with the moment, her reaction concerned her. Had she truly been frightened? In her daydreams, she imagined herself in his arms. She had never expected the fantasy to come true. "I guess I didn't expect—"

"Don't apologize. Any apology should come from me."

But she didn't hear one. And she didn't want one. Looking into his eyes, she saw a hint of mischief. "Perhaps," Callie teased, "but I don't hear you apologizing."

A wry grin lightened his face. "And you probably won't. It was my way of saying thank you."

She grinned. "And much less expensive than a raise."

While Callie lay in bed that night, thoughts of the evening filtered over her like warm sunshine. Nattie's words, *"Read to me, Daddy,"* sang in Callie's mind like a melody. David's smile and his joy rushed through her, jostling her pulse to a maddening pace. *Stop. I'll never go to sleep.*

Though Callie cautioned herself, she didn't heed her own warning. Again, her thoughts stirred, and she remembered his strong, eager arms embracing her. But with that image, her dreams ended, and her nightmare began.

She stiffened at the thought. What could she do with herself? Frustration dampened her lovely memories, and she threw the pillow over her head, fumbling in her self-inflicted darkness to turn off the lamp.

Her black dreams had lain dormant for weeks. Tonight, like a rolling mist, the nightmare crept silently into her sleep.

As she moved through a fog, a click *resounded in her ears. Then, she saw the lock. He flashed his broad, charming smile. "You're nervous enough, I'm sure. We don't want anyone popping in and making things worse, do we?"*

Her chest tightened, anxiety growing inside her. She nodded, afraid to speak.

His fingers ran over the keys in flourished arpeggios, *and she lifted her voice, following his fingers, up and down the scales. Her tone sounded pinched in her ears. She wished she could relax so he could hear her natural quality. Suddenly her singing turned to a silent scream.*

In the pulsing silence, Callie's eyes opened to blackness. She raised her hand and wiped the perspiration from her hairline. Again she fumbled in the deep darkness for the light switch. The flash of brightness hurt her eyes, and she squinted.

"I can't bear this anymore," she said aloud. "Please, go away and let me live." Her shoulders lifted in a shivered sigh. She pulled her flannel robe over her trembling body and slid her feet into her slippers. Milk? Tea? Something to wash away the dreams.

She dragged herself into the bathroom and rinsed her face. Her image in the mirror frightened her, her skin pale as a gray shroud. She turned from the glass and wandered through her rooms to the hallway. Quietly she edged her way down the stairs. The whole house slept, and falling down a dark staircase would add not only grief to her terrible night, but also chaos to everyone else's rest.

At the bottom of the stairs, the moon shining through the fanlight above the door guided her path around the newel post toward the kitchen. Deeper in the wide foyer, darkness closed in, but she kept the carpet beneath her feet, knowing the door would be straight ahead at the end.

With her hand in front of her, she touched the knob and swung open the door. A light coming from the kitchen surprised her. She hesitated. Having a middle-of-the-night conversation with Agnes didn't appeal to her, but despite the thought, the choice seemed better than turning back.

As she stepped into the kitchen, she halted. It wasn't Agnes, but David, who sat at the table, sipping from a thick mug. When their eyes met, he looked as surprised as she must have. "Well," she said. "I thought I'd be the only nightwalker wandering the house. Am I intruding on your solace?"

"No, to be honest, you're a pleasant sight."

She thought of her ashen face and disheveled hair and grinned. "I beg to differ, but beauty is in the 'beholder's eye,' they say."

His gaze swept hers, and warm tenderness brushed her heart.

"Beauty is," he agreed, and took another drink. He held the cup poised in the air. "How about some hot chocolate?"

The aroma reached her senses. "Sounds wonderful."

"I made more than I wanted. Sit, and I'll get it for you."

He rose and pulled a mug from the cabinet. Callie slid into a chair, running her fingers through her hair and thinking how perfectly terrible she must look.

He poured the cocoa and placed the hot beverage in front of her. "There." He sat again, then regarded her. "So what brings you out of a warm bed in the depths of the night?"

"A mind that won't stop, it seems." She avoided the truth.

"I know what that means. Nattie's in my mind… among other things."

"Business?" she asked, looking into the milk-chocolate liquid. Rays from the overhead light glinted in splayed patterns on the surface of her drink. When she experienced his silence, she looked up. His eyes met hers.

"No, not business. I was thinking about you, to be honest."

Protectively, her hand clutched her robe. "Me? Why?"

He shook his head. "You'll never know how much you mean to me, Callie. All you've done for us here. You're like a breath of spring after a long winter." A grin tugged at the corners of his mouth. "Pretty poetic for the middle of the night, huh?"

She couldn't speak. She struggled to keep her eyes from widening any more than they already had. "But that's why you hired me. To help Nattie."

"But you've done more than that." He reached across the table and laid his hand on hers. "You've helped me, too. I feel alive again, like a man released from prison, his life restored."

Callie looked at his hand pressing against the back of hers. Though her initial thought was to recoil, she joyed in feeling the warm pressure against her skin.

His gaze traced the line of her face. "I wish you'd tell me what troubles you. You know so much about me. I know so little about your life."

She drew her hand from under his and tucked it in her lap. "What troubles me? Nothing really. Old problems crop up once in a while. Nothing you can do about them."

"But…sometimes you seem frightened. Is it me? Are you afraid of me? Callie, I'd never hurt you. If you think—"

Lifting her hand, she pressed her finger on his lips to quiet him. "Please, it's me. Not you."

He raised his hand, capturing her finger against his lips. A kiss as gentle as a fluttering breeze brushed across her skin. Her heart stopped, and she drew in a quick breath. He wrapped her fingers in his and lowered his hand. "I pray someday you can tell me. Whatever it is."

She withdrew her hand a second time. He tilted his head, his face filled with emotion. She wanted to touch his unshaven cheeks with her palms and kiss the worry from his eyes. A worry that she knew was for her, not for himself. Everything in her cried out to tell him, but she pushed the urge deep inside her, praying this time the pangs would stay there.

Patches of sunlight glinted through the sprouting foliage. Callie glanced over her shoulder at Nattie running behind her, looking like any happy child. A rosy glow lit her cheeks, and her eyes sparkled in the brightness of the afternoon.

"Can't keep up with me, can you?" Callie called as she neared the crest of the hill.

Nattie stumbled along, her young, inactive legs not used to the rigors of dashing up a hillside. When Callie reached the top, she fell to the grass, laughing and breathless. Nattie reached her, puffing, and plopped down near her.

Though the hillside was sprinkled with trees, the landscape offered a view of a smattering of houses and distant barns. The new grass and tree leaves, sporting their pale green colors, sent a charge of rebirth and excitement through Callie.

Like spring bursting on the scene, so Nattie's blossoming was another new gift. Nattie had opened her silent world a little more, and brief sentences popped from her like the unexpected surprise of a new Jack-in-the-box. Neither David nor Callie knew at what moment the child might add another sentence to those they had already tallied with joy.

With her heart full of the abounding changes around her, she began with a hum, and before she realized she had risen, as if the trees were her audience, and had opened her mouth in song—*"Beautiful Savior, King of Creation."* She began timidly as a lilting murmur. She hadn't sung in such a long time. But by the third verse, her voice soared into the sky.

Nattie blinked, then widened her curious eyes. A glimmer of awareness covered her face. Callie studied her. Had her mother sung to her in this spot? Or was it the song? Something in the child's look gave Callie a sense of connection. Could music be a catalyst to help the child heal from her terrible hurt?

The sunlight shimmered through Nattie's hair, creating a golden halo around her face. Callie's heart tugged at the lovely picture. Lost forever was the sight of her own child. Since arriving in Bedford, she had locked her own sorrow in her heart's prison. How could she help Nattie if she spent all her energies grieving over something that could never be?

But today, the sorrow gushed from her like a geyser pent up in the earth. Did her child have dark hair like her father, or honey-toned tresses like hers? Were her eyes blue or brown? Was she happy? Or was she sad the way Nattie had been? All the questions that she had stuffed away rose, pouring over her.

She let the questions flow, then, with new conviction, forced them away. In her silence, the only sounds were the chirping birds and a distant mooing cow. Then Nattie tilted her head, and a grin pulled at the corners of her bowed mouth. "Sing more."

Hearing the child's voice, Callie's heart skipped a beat. Her voice little more than a whisper, she asked, "Do you have a favorite?"

Nattie shook her head.

"No favorite?" With a chuckle, Callie leaned down and tickled her neck. "I won't know what to sing for you, then." She sank to the ground as near to Nattie as she dared. "Maybe someday you'll want to sing with me."

Callie began humming softly. A favorite hymn tangled in her memory. As the words unscrambled in her mind, her heart lifted like the melody of the song. *"What wondrous love is this, oh my soul."* The years that her voice had been silenced by her battered memories seemed forgotten. *"That caused the Lord of life to bear the heavy cross."* The child only listened, staring at the ground with an occasional glimpse toward Callie's face. She too bore some secret "heavy cross."

A deep sorrow filled the child's eyes, and when the line of the verse had ended, Callie stopped her song. Music had definitely touched the child's heart. But with *sadness.* Callie longed to tell David her discovery.

Chapter Ten

David was out of town again, and Callie felt antsy for adult conversation. With a short grocery list tucked in her shoulder bag, she drove into town. Agnes usually shopped, but today Callie needed fresh air and a distraction, and the housekeeper had graciously agreed to keep an eye on Nattie.

Outside, spring worked its magic on her spirit. She wanted to run and play in the bright, new grass, not be bound to the quiet, closed-in house. She longed to leave her worries and sadness behind.

Through the trees, she caught a glimpse of the steeple of John Spier's church, and an unexplained urge tugged at her. She pulled the car into the empty parking lot, stepped out onto the gravel and looked around. The young pastor's car was parked in the parsonage driveway. She headed for the door, wondering if Pastor John might be working inside.

At the entrance, she pushed the handle on one of the big double doors, and it opened. The bright sunshine spread inside along the worn carpet in the small foyer.

She stepped inside, pulling the weighty door closed.

Standing still, she waited for her eyes to adjust to the gloom. She listened for a sound, but heard nothing. With hesitant steps, she wandered down the aisle, which was lit by the daylight shining through the deep-toned stained glass. Above the dark walnut altar hung a large wooden cross. But the image that caught in her eye was the piano.

She moved as if drawn to the fruitwood console, which was flanked by chairs for a small choir. A trembling melancholy clung to her as she edged forward. Her gaze caressed the keys, and she slid onto the bench, an old desire surging within her.

A hymnbook lay open on the music stand, and her hands trembled as she placed them on the keyboard. As she followed the music, her fingers felt stiff and uncertain on the keys. Though the grand piano sat in silence at the house, she hadn't been moved to play, perhaps knowing the piano was Sara's.

When the hymn ended, she turned the pages to another, then another. Before she realized it, her voice was lifted in song. *"There's a quiet understanding when we're gathered in the spirit."* She had often sung that song in her church in Indianapolis. Longing tugged at her heart. She had not sung in church for the past seven years, and today, with no congregation, she sang for God alone. When the song ended, she bowed her head.

"That was wonderful."

Callie jumped, her head pivoting at the sound of a familiar voice. "Oh, you scared me."

Pastor John halted. "I'm sorry. I didn't mean to."

"How long were you there?"

Smiling, he shrugged. "About two hymns, I'd say. I didn't want to stop you. You play and sing beautifully."

Her hands slid from the keyboard to her lap. "Thanks. I, um, don't sing much anymore."

"But you should." He leaned toward her, his elbows resting on top of the piano. "You have a real gift. It's a shame not to use it."

Callie's shoulders tensed; she felt cornered. "I… I did years ago."

"We could use a soloist in church some Sundays." He raised his eyebrows in question.

Callie lowered her lids, then raised them. "Yes, well, I've been giving thought to singing again."

"And?"

"And I guess I'm not quite ready."

"Not stage fright? You seem so confidant, I can't imagine your being intimidated by an audience."

His tone pushed her for an explanation. "I don't have stage fright. I had a bad experience a few years ago."

"I'm sorry."

She shifted uncomfortably. "Wounds heal eventually."

"Well, I'll keep your…wound in my prayers."

Callie whispered her thanks, relieved to end the conversation.

John lifted a chair from the choir area and swung it next to the piano. He sat, and a need to escape gripped her. Not wanting to be rude, she struggled against the urge.

He leaned toward her. "Have you ever thought about directing a choir?"

She sputtered a laugh. "Direct? No. Never in my life. I take it you need a choir director."

"Pam Ingram, our pianist, is doing her best, but playing and directing is difficult, especially for someone with limited training."

"Yes, it is." Callie's heart thudded, as she wondered how to escape without being utterly rude. "I really should get going. Agnes is waiting for the groceries." A nervous titter broke from her lips. "Today wasn't the best day to stop, but I've never been here, and… I was curious."

"You're a member somewhere else?"

"No, I've been going to, um, New Hope over on Washington."

John nodded. "Ah, the new church. We have a terrible time keeping members here. They have so much. Including an organ."

Callie's attention was drawn to the small balcony and the line of pipes. "The organ needs work, you mentioned."

"Yes, a few thousand dollars. We don't have it. I'd sort of hoped since Sara Hamilton had been the organist—and David directed the choir—he might make a donation."

Callie's stomach somersaulted. "David was the choir director here?"

His eyebrows shot upward. "Yes, I've been reading all kinds of things to learn the church's history. I was surprised. And so are you, I see."

Callie felt defensive. "He's never mentioned it, but why would he? He's still healing."

"That's what he said."

"So you asked him?"

John rose, stepped to the console, then spun around. "Yes, I mentioned it."

Wounds heal. She prayed they would. Music was the

way to reach Nattie. Might David refuse to let her try? Time and patience, that's what they both needed. "Give him time. Things will get better, I'm sure."

A grin curled his lips. "And you? Should I give you time, too, to consider my offer?"

"Your offer?"

"To sing for us? Or help with a choir?"

"Yes, time. It's something we all need." She rose abruptly and stepped to the center aisle before turning around. "I'd better be on my way."

She surveyed the surroundings again as she headed for the door, then stopped halfway down the aisle. "Your church has charm, you know," she said, turning toward him. "New Hope doesn't have charm at all. You should stress that. A lot of people still enjoy the 'old-time religion.'" She waved and rushed up the aisle before he asked her any more questions—or favors.

Though David had returned from his trip, he kept himself closed up in his study. Callie was disappointed. She missed him and hoped to talk to him about the questions that filled her mind regarding Nattie. Sitting in the parlor, she looked through the foyer to the closed door across the way.

Since Nattie had already gone to bed for the night, Callie's responsibilities for the day were over. She rose and marched across the hall, but when she reached the door, she halted. Filling her lungs with air, she released a stream of anxiety from her body, then knocked.

Seconds ticked by. A near-eternity passed before she heard David's response.

"Yes?"

She closed her eyes, prayed, and turned the knob.

David sat at his desk across from the door. "Callie, come in," he said.

She stood shyly near the door. "I'm sorry to disturb you."

"Is something wrong?"

"No, I… I wondered if you have a minute to talk."

"Sure, have a seat." After shuffling the papers in front of him, he rose, motioning for her to sit. "I'm sorry to be hidden away again. I've been preoccupied with a ton of paperwork and some big decisions since I came back from the trip."

"I understand, but I've had a lot on my mind, too." She sank into an overstuffed chair. "And…and I wanted to get your opinion."

David joined her, choosing one of the comfortable chairs across from her. He leaned over with his elbows on his knees, his hands folded in front of him, as he listened to her story of Nattie's day on the hillside. His eyes brightened when he heard about the child's interest in Callie's singing. Yet, as always, sadness followed when he learned of her retreat into silence again.

"But I know music is the key," Callie said. "I believe if I encourage that interest, we'll get somewhere. But since it's a sensitive issue, I wanted to check first. I don't want to do anything that might hurt either of you."

David stared at his shoe, moving the toe along the pattern in the oriental carpet. "I appreciate your concern."

She waited.

In time, he lifted his gaze to hers. "I've been selfish in many ways, protecting myself more than thinking of Nattie." Stress tugged at the corners of his mouth. "I'd like to think I've made some progress. So as they say, you're the nurse. I'll trust your judgment to do what's needed. Anything that will make Nattie a happy child again is fine with me."

Callie relaxed. "Thanks for your confidence."

"You're welcome."

His eyes connected with hers again, and a twinge shot through her chest. The connection sparked liked wires charged with unbound electricity. Finally, she found her voice. "What are you thinking?"

He lowered his gaze. "Nothing. I'm sorry."

She longed to know his thoughts. But she had more to ask, and struggled to organize her musings. "Did Nattie have a particular song she liked to sing with you and Sara?"

David leaned his head back for a moment and then tilted it forward. "Oh, some of the children's songs, I suppose. 'Jesus Loves Me,' for one. Something else about 'two little eyes.'"

"Yes, I know them both. I'll see if she'll sing them with me. I'm grasping for anything."

"Yes, even the slightest progress."

Callie knew she should say goodnight, but she longed to be with him, to talk…about anything.

He drifted away in thought. She sensed she should go and leave him with his own reveries, but a playful look glinted in his eyes. "Have you gotten into mischief since I've been gone?"

"Just a little." She grinned. "On the way to town the other day, I stopped by the church. *Your* church, I should say. I talked a bit with Pastor Spier."

"I suppose he's asking you to join the coalition to pry a donation from me."

"No, but he did mention that he'd asked you." She

glanced down at her fingers and realized they were tapping the edge of the chair. "He told me you were once the choir director at First Community Church. Is that right?"

David closed his eyes, and lifted his shoulders in a heavy sigh. "Wish I could get my hands on those church records." He peered at her. "Yes, I'm guilty as charged. I did it to help Sara. Playing and directing is difficult. She could do it, but having a director made things easier."

"I just wondered. Was surprised, naturally. But I suppose you have a lot of surprises hidden away that I don't know about."

He flinched. "Only a few. And you seem to pry them out of me daily."

"Good for me." She shifted in her chair. "So, are you thinking about helping with the organ repairs?"

"Should I throw you out on your ear now? Or later?"

A pleasant expression hovered on his face, so she continued. "He paid me good money to pry this information out of you." She rose with a grin. "I'd better leave before you follow through on your threat." She headed for the door. "Good night."

David rose and stepped toward her. "How's your mother?"

She spun around, meeting his questioning eyes. "Mom seems to be fine, but she did have a minor stroke, according to the MRI test. The doctor has her on some new medication. Now all I can do is pray she takes care of herself."

"I'm glad to hear it was minor. God gives us warnings sometimes, a little reminder to take care of ourselves. Problem is, we have to listen."

Callie grinned as she turned the doorknob. "And

listening is definitely one of Mom's serious problems." She glided through the door and closed it before he could respond.

Climbing the stairs, she hummed a simple children's hymn. The tune brought back old questions. Did her own child, living somewhere in the world, know the song? Had Christian parents adopted her tiny little girl? A heavy ache weighted her heart. Drawn by her emotions, or perhaps more by her loneliness, Callie opened Nattie's bedroom door and tiptoed inside.

The child lay curled in a tiny ball on the edge of her bed. The rosy night-light sent a wash of pink over her face, her cheeks glowing with the warm hue. Callie had fought her instincts so often to lavish her affection on Nattie, knowing it might not be good for the child when she had to leave, and positive it would not be good for her own throbbing hurt.

But tonight, she leaned over, brushed the child's hair from her cheek with her finger, and lay her lips against Nattie's warm, soft skin. Tears filled her eyes as she backed away and turned to the door. Taking one more glimpse, she stepped into the hallway—and into David's arms.

Chapter Eleven

Callie gasped as David held her in his arms outside Nattie's room. Her body trembled in fear as she pulled away from his grasp and closed the bedroom door.

"I didn't mean to frighten you," he said. Pausing, he searched her face, then raised his fingers to capture her chin. "Why do you have tears in your eyes? Is something wrong?"

"Nothing. Nothing's wrong with Nattie, if that's what you mean." Callie released a trembling sigh and pulled herself together.

"But why are you crying?" he whispered, sounding concerned.

"I'm not crying." She kept her eyes lowered, praying the evidence of her tears would vanish. When she raised her eyes to his, he held her riveted.

David lifted his hand and brushed his fingers across her lashes. "Your eyes are still wet. Please tell me what's wrong."

Callie grasped for something to tell him. "I'm worried about my mother, I suppose. Looking down at Nattie reminds me how my mother hovered over me when

I was a child. I keep praying for my mother, but fears still creep into my thoughts."

He drew a clean handkerchief from his back pocket and daubed her eyes. "You know, Callie, if you need to go home for a few days, I can manage without you. Not that I want to—but Agnes will take care of Nattie. Please, go home. You'll feel better."

Callie's lie had gotten out of control. She remembered her mother's words that a lie spoken becomes a web of deceit that grows bigger and bigger. "No, really. A good night's sleep is all I need. But thanks for the offer. Maybe one of these days I'll visit her for a weekend."

He rested one hand on her shoulder and tilted her face with the other. "If you're sure?"

His eyes again bound her, and her breath quivered through her body. "I'm sure," she whispered.

His fingers touched her cheek in a tender caress before he pulled his hand away and turned toward his own room.

Callie darted into her bedroom across the hall. Overwhelmed, she shut the door and leaned against the jamb. Her cheek tingled where his fingers had touched, and she raised her own hand and pressed her burning skin.

Her mind raced. Was she a fool? Was his touch only kindness, or had his feelings grown? If he cared about her, she should leave now while she still could. She leaned her head back, pressing her eyelids closed. She could offer him nothing. But how could she walk away from Nattie now that the child had begun to leave her shell.

Foolish. Foolish. Her thoughts were nothing but nonsense. She rushed to the bathroom and turned the shower on to a full, heavy stream, stripping her clothes from her shaking body. She stepped into the tub and let the water rush over her, feeling its calming warmth. She scrubbed herself until her thoughts, like the soapy bubbles, washed down the drain.

No man would love her once he knew the truth. She could offer a man like David nothing but her less-than-perfect self. He deserved a lovely, unsullied woman. She dried herself, rubbing the nubby towel over her body until she glowed bright pink. As she brushed her hair with heavy strokes, she stared at herself in the mirror. No one wanted a used, sinful wife.

Callie tossed the hairbrush on her vanity table and crawled into bed, praying sleep would come quickly. In the darkness, her mind drifted, and, as on so many nights, the mist rolled in. His voice came from the shadows.

"Why, Callie, that's a lovely, lovely name. Nearly pretty as you are, sweetheart."

A flush of excitement deepened to embarrassment. He pulled the door closed behind her, and she stepped inside the room, moving toward the black, gleaming grand piano.

He flashed his broad, charming smile. "You're nervous enough, I'm sure. We don't want anyone popping in and making things worse, do we?" The lock clicked.

Her chest tightened, anxiety growing inside her as his fingers touched the keys. She wished she could relax, so he could hear her natural quality.

He winked, then eyed her hand resting on the piano edge. He stopped playing and placed his hot, sweaty fingers on hers. "You just relax there. I can hear you have a pretty voice."

Callie filled her diaphragm with air, and her voice soared from her, natural and strong.

He looked at her with admiration, swaying and moving on the bench as she sang. "Why you're a little meadowlark, aren't you."

Callie's eyes shot open in the darkness, as the name pierced the night like a knife, *Meadowlark, Meadowlark.*

A gentle breeze drifted through the open parlor windows. Callie leaned her head against the sofa back, her attention drawn to Nattie. With an array of crayons and a coloring book, Nattie concentrated on her artwork, her golden curls hiding her face. The afternoon sun glinted through the windows, and rays danced on the child's hair like a sprinkle of fairy dust.

Each time Callie allowed herself to think about the little girl, her heart ached. No matter how hard she tried to avoid the inevitable, her heartstrings tangled more and more around Nattie.

Daily, she prayed for Nattie's healing, yet the reality sent a sad shiver through her. Nattie, healthy and happy, would start school in September, and Callie would have completed her task. She would have to leave Bedford. How could she ever say goodbye?

As if the child knew she filled Callie's thoughts, she sat up, tearing the picture carefully from the book.

She rose, glancing with lowered lids toward Callie, then carried the picture to her side.

"How beautiful," Callie said, holding the paper in

front of her. "You color so well, Nattie. Everything's inside the lines. And such pretty colors, too. I love it."

Nattie's timid grin brightened her face. "It's for you."

Her pulse skipped a beat, and she clutched the paper to her chest. "Thank you. This is one of the nicest presents I've ever had."

Nattie slid onto the sofa and nestled by her side. Callie pulled herself together, reviewing the event as if it occurred in slow motion. With caution, she slid her arm around the child's shoulders. Nattie leaned into her arm without hesitation. Longing, delight, amazement swirled through her in one rolling surge.

"Oh, Nattie, you are a gem," Callie said.

Nattie tilted her face upward, her brows knit together.

"You don't know what a gem is?"

Nattie shook her head.

"I didn't say a 'germ,' did I?" The moisture in her eyes belied her mirth. "I said a gem. Like a diamond. You know what a diamond is?"

"Uh-huh," Nattie said, her face glowing.

"You're *my* diamond, Nattie."

Nattie snuggled more closely to her side. Callie savored the moment, wishing and longing for miracles, thoughts she couldn't speak for fear of losing them.

The magic moment evaporated when Agnes called them to lunch, but Callie's mind replayed the scene over and over. Nattie had already made a giant stride forward, though Callie had yet to put her plan into effect to use music to draw her out more completely.

The thought filled her mind, and she decided to begin after lunch. When they had settled back in the parlor, Callie wandered to the piano and lifted the bench lid. Inside, she found music books of all kinds. She ruffled through them, pulling out a bound selection of well-known classics. She lowered the lid and adjusted the bench. Nattie watched her with curiosity.

Sliding onto the bench, Callie propped the music on the stand, and glanced through the pages and found a favorite. Her hands rested on the keys covered with the dust of disuse. She made a mental note to clean the ivory with witch hazel. But for now, she allowed her fingers to arch and press the first notes of the sonata.

The rich, vibrant tone of the piano filled the room. Like a tonal magnet, Nattie rose, drawn to the instrument. She stood at Callie's side, her sight riveted to Callie's experienced fingers moving over the keys. The music held the child transfixed, and Callie continued, her emotions caught in the rhythm and tones of the masterpiece.

When she finished the selection, she sought Nattie's eyes. The child's face seemed awed by the experience.

"Would you like to sit next to me?" Callie held her breath.

Nattie tried to scoot onto the bench, and Callie put her arm around the girl's slender shoulders, giving her a boost.

"There, now you can see much better. How about another song?"

Nattie nodded, and Callie selected a shorter piece, hoping to keep the child's interest. The Bach étude resounded in a bright lilting melody, and when she finished, she turned to Nattie. "Okay, now it's your turn. Would you like to play?"

Nattie's eyes widened, and a small grin curved her lips.

"Good. I'll show you a simple song. And later, I'll

pick up a beginner's book for you. We can surprise your daddy."

Again, Nattie's quiet voice broke her silence. "Okay."

Though her word was a near whisper, to Callie the sound was a magnificent symphony.

Callie slid the beginner's book into the piano bench when she brought it home from the music store. In her excitement, she wanted to share the moments with David, but she wondered if the fact would stir up sad memories. And she'd only asked him about singing, not piano lessons. Waiting seemed to be the better option. Yet already, Nattie's natural talent blossomed.

She and Nattie had made a pact to keep her lessons a secret. When Nattie felt ready to play for her father, they would hold a surprise concert. Like true comrades, their secret bonded them.

With the music book stowed in its hiding place, Callie returned to her room. Tonight she wanted to give Nattie and David time alone. Each day the child's progress seemed more evident. With more than three months before the beginning of school, Nattie would be ready for first grade.

Bored with television, she turned the clock-radio dial on her desk. A familiar hymn drifted from the speakers, and the music wrapped around her like a loving arm. She settled into her favorite recliner and leaned back, closing her eyes.

John Spier's request glided into her thoughts. Years had passed since she'd sung in church. But like Nattie, she'd begun to heal. For so long, her throat had knotted when she opened her mouth to sing. Now her voice lifted often in praise to God and in her love of music.

Music completed her and made her whole again. At least, almost whole.

Maybe she should consider Pastor John's request. She could praise God all she wanted on the hillside and in private, but singing in church was a loving testimony. Hymns drifted through her mind, favorites she had not sung forever, it seemed.

Woven into the radio's musical offering, Callie heard a rhythmic sound. She lowered the radio's volume. The tap came again. She grinned to herself. The door—someone had knocked. She strode across the room and pulled it open.

David stood outside, a sheepish expression on his face. "We missed you."

Callie stepped backward. "Missed me?"

He scanned her face, then his eyes focused behind her.

Callie turned around and glanced into her sitting room, trying to figure out what he wanted. "Did you want to come in?"

He shifted from one foot to the other. "If you don't mind—I just tucked Nattie in for the night, and I felt lonely."

Callie teetered backward, opening the door for him to enter. He had never come to visit, and the situation caused her a strange uneasiness. "Have a seat." She motioned to the recliner, but instead, he pulled out a smaller chair from the desk and straddled the seat, resting his hands on the back.

"You're welcome to sit here," she repeated, but he ignored her offer and remained seated. "So." She glanced around her. "I don't have anything to offer you, except tap water." Her nervous titter sounded ridiculous in her ears.

David shook his head. "I didn't come for refreshments. I just wondered why you made yourself so scarce this evening."

"Oh." Callie relaxed. Now she understood. "Well, I thought since Nattie and I spend a lot of quality time together, you and she deserved a night alone. Sometimes, it's nice for the two of you to be together…without me. I'm a distraction."

Again his gaze traced her face. "But a pleasant one," he finally said.

She felt a rush of heat rise to her face, a blush she couldn't hide. "You embarrass me. I don't know how to handle comments like that."

"I suppose that's one of the reasons I find you so lovely."

Her blush deepened. "See, you're doing it again." She covered her face with her hands, feeling like an utter fool.

"You're beautiful when you blush, Callie. You remind me of a butterfly locked in its chamber, then suddenly released." He rested his chin on his arms. "Sorry, my poetry's running wild again."

Her gaze sought his. "But it sounded lovely. Really."

"I can never pay you for the joy you've brought back to my life. Every day I see Nattie grow more open, like the little child she was before her mother died. If it was Sara's death alone or something else that made her so withdrawn, I don't know. But whatever it was, you're bringing her out of it. And I…love you for it. I'm sorry if I've embarrassed you again, but I have to tell you."

Callie's feelings tumbled into words. "I see the same

progress. Each day I watch her open up a little more, and I'm happier than I can tell you. But I have to be honest with you.

"It makes me sad, too."

He studied her. "Sad?"

"When she's herself again, I'm out of a job. Joyful for her. Sad for me. Do you see the paradox? I long to see her bubbling with happiness like children her age—but then I have to say goodbye. And…she's stolen a piece of my heart." Callie lowered her lids, the tears building along her lashes.

David rose, moving to her side in one giant stride. In a flash, he knelt before her and grasped her hand. "No, not goodbye. Nattie needs you…and *will* need you. You're the one who's making her strong again. You can't just up and leave her. Even when she begins school, she'll need support and someone who loves her…a woman who loves her. Little girls need a mother's nurturing, not a father who bungles his way along. Don't even think of leaving us. Please."

Callie heard his words, but what he said knotted in her thoughts. *A mother's nurturing.* By delaying her departure, she would only hurt herself more. Could she bear it? "I appreciate the nice things you're saying. But, David, I have to look after my own well-being, too. Time will tell what I can handle emotionally. I can't make any promises."

"I'm not asking for promises, just understanding that we need you."

Words left her mouth that she didn't bite back fast enough. "What you need, David, is a wife. That's who should be nurturing Nattie, not me. You need to live again, too. I'm sure somewhere in the community is a fine, single woman just waiting to be someone's wife."

To Callie's astonishment, David laughed.

"Please don't laugh at me, David. I'm speaking from my heart."

Again, he touched her hand. "I'm not laughing at you, Callie. Please, don't even think such a thing. I forgot to tell you about our invitation."

"Our invitation?" Her forehead wrinkled to a frown.

"Pastor John called earlier this evening. He asked to speak to you about accompanying him to the church picnic. I told him you had already retired for the evening. Then, Mary Beth latched onto the telephone and invited me."

Callie's stomach flip-flopped with his words. "Pastor John asked me to the picnic?" What she really wanted to say was *"Mary Beth asked* you *to the picnic?"*

David nodded his head. "Yes, I told him to call you tomorrow. But I couldn't come up with an excuse quick enough, so I had to accept Mary Beth's offer. Please accept John's invitation. At least we can be a buffer for each other. You'll save me from a fate worse than… well, from a trying experience."

Though an unexpected jealousy raged inside her, she contemplated his poignant pleading. A protective camaraderie bound them together. "But accepting the invitation isn't kind, David—not if we're making fun of them."

"I don't mean to make fun. I suppose both of them would be a good—how should I put it—catch. But I'm not ready to be caught, and Mary Beth's efforts are so obvious. I'll have to be honest with her. Somehow."

"Honesty is the best thing."

“Then let me be honest. Make my day worthwhile and accept John’s invitation. I can bear it if you’re there. And Nattie will want to be with you, too. Please.”

She lowered her eyes, and when she raised them, her heart fluttered like the wings of the butterfly David had just compared her to. She nodded.

“Thank you from the bottom of my heart.” He rose and stepped back. “I suppose I should let you get back to…whatever you were doing.” He turned toward the door.

“David,” she said, stopping him in mid-stride. “Could you stay a minute? I’d like to talk.”

Chapter Twelve

David faltered when Callie spoke his name. Turning, he faced her, his heart galloping at the sound of her voice. His eyes feasted on her tonight, sitting near him as if she belonged in the house forever. Not an employee, but a woman. A woman who loved his child and who, he prayed, could learn to love him. Startled by his own longings, he shivered.

"I hope I didn't startle you. This has been on my mind for some time now."

He tensed, considering the serious expression on her face. "Is something wrong?"

"No. When I visited the church a while back, Pastor John asked me if I would sing for a Sunday service." She grinned.

"He also asked me to direct the choir, but I'll leave that talent to you."

David halted her with a gesture. "Forget that." He wondered if Pastor John had put her up to the comment.

"Well, anyway, I'm thinking about singing, and I wanted to warn you."

"Warn me? You have a lovely voice, Callie. You should sing."

She halted and searched his face. When she spoke, her voice sounded controlled and thoughtful. "How do you know I have a lovely voice?" Her eyes lit with a questioning brightness, as if she'd learned the answer to a secret.

He'd spoken without thinking. "I've heard you sing with Nattie. The children's songs. I have ears."

"And you? Do you sing, David?"

"I sang long ago. Nothing like you."

She squinted as if weighing his response, then continued. "I just wanted to tell you that I'm accepting your pastor's invitation to sing."

"If you're singing—" He faltered over the words. "I'd like to hear you. I'll attend worship that Sunday."

Her eyes widened. "You don't attend worship?"

"I've felt very lonely at First Community. Too many memories." He thought of his promise to Sara. "Since Nattie's doing better, I'm taking her to Sunday School, but I usually drop her off and wait."

"You wait for her." Her eyes widened even more. "David, you'll never get *less* lonely unless you work at it."

But it was more than lonely. Much more. "I'm angry, too, I suppose…at God." The words escaped his control.

"Angry? At God?" Her face bent to a scowl. "Because of Sara's death? But you said you knew she had cancer."

"You've asked a whole parcel of questions. Which do you want me to answer?" Despite the tension edging inside him, a quirky grin flickered on his mouth.

Callie eyed him. "It's wrong, you know, to be angry at God."

"I know." He wandered back to the chair he had left a few minutes earlier and again straddled the seat, leaning on the back. "But as I said before, I had tremendous faith that our love would heal Sara's cancer. A young lover's error. But I had faith. When Sara died, I felt betrayed."

The scowl retreated, and her face overflowed with empathy.

Surprised, he felt his eyes mist at his admission. "And when Nattie reacted like she did, I felt devastated. God took my wife, and then my daughter. I couldn't accept that."

"Oh, David, I understand. We shouldn't, I know, but I've been angry at God, myself. When I stopped singing, I wasn't only punishing my parents, but I probably thought I was hurting God, too."

Her own vulnerability wrapped around his thoughts. Questions that he'd tucked back in his mind surged forward. "And why were you punishing your parents, Callie? What secret hides behind your lovely face?"

She paled, squeezing her saddened eyes closed for a heartbeat. When she opened them, fear clouded her face. "Please don't ask. Don't we all have things in our lives we don't want to talk about to anyone?" She lowered her eyes to her hands knotted in her lap, then raised them and focused on him. "At least, not yet."

David nodded, yet his heart tugged inside; he wanted to know what caused her such pain. What stopped her from sharing her grief with him? What scared her when he touched her? Who had hurt her so badly?

"Thanks for understanding," she added. Her eyes softened as she gazed at him. "I'm pleased Nattie's going to Sunday School."

If he were honest, he couldn't even take credit for that. "I promised Sara I'd raise Nattie to know Jesus.

I'm keeping that promise. I take her to Sunday School. But church…my heart hasn't been in it."

"I know you pray, David. Maybe at dinner it's for Nattie, but you do say prayers." Her gaze searched his. "Let's pray for each other, David. Prayers can work miracles. We both need help."

Her eyes glowed with her request as she looked at him. *Prayer.* Such a simple gift he could give her…and himself. "A deal," he said, and rose. "I'll pray for you, and you pray for me. How's that?"

She peered into his eyes. "Not quite what I meant."

Her look penetrated his soul. The guilt he'd hidden under layers of self-pity peeled away, one by one.

"I said, let's pray for each other. 'Where *two* or *three* are gathered,' the Bible says. We need to pray for our *own* needs, too. Still a deal?" Her hand jutted toward him.

He stepped forward and clasped her tiny fingers in his. Their eyes locked as firmly as their handshake, and heat radiated through him like a match flame touched to gasoline, searing his frayed emotions.

He needed her—wanted her in his arms nestled against him. Yet her fear permeated his thoughts. Moving with caution and tenderness, he drew her to his chest. Her body trembled against him. His voice caught in his throat, and his "thank you" was only a murmur. When he'd corralled his emotions, he gently released her and left the room, feeling as if he had left a piece of his heart behind.

David woke in the morning and looked out the window. The weather couldn't have been better for the church picnic. The sky shone a bright blue, with no hint of rain.

If he hadn't accepted Mary Beth's invitation, he

might have looked forward to the occasion, but instead, he glowered as he drove to the parsonage with Callie and Nattie belted in the back seat. He wanted, with all his heart, to seat Callie in the front, but protocol determined the spot belonged to Mary Beth.

When their tedious journey to the park ended, John helped tote their gear, and they found a table beneath a large elm tree.

Nattie clung to Callie's side, her timidity obvious in the crowd of gathering church members. Though distressed at Nattie's discomfort, David found pleasure in watching her relationship with Callie. As soon as she opened a folding chair and sat, Nattie slid onto her lap. The love, evident between them, warmed his heart.

Mary Beth unfolded a chair. "Nattie, aren't you too big to be sitting on your nanny's lap?" Mary Beth asked as she eyed the child. "I think it would be nice if you sat on your own chair here by me." She opened another chair. "I'd like to get to know you better."

Nattie shook her head and Mary Beth's mouth dropped in an awkward gape.

"My, my, aren't we a temperamental child." She plopped into a chair and glowered at Callie, whose protective hand cupped Nattie's shoulder.

"Nattie's shy, Mary Beth," David countered. "Give her time to adjust." He wanted to shake the woman for her comment.

Mary Beth beamed at him with a smile as false as her long, well-polished fingernails. "You're right, David. I wasn't thinking. Let's go for a little walk. What do you say?" She rose without waiting for his response.

David glanced at Callie in desperation, hoping she would intervene. But she only looked at him with an arched eyebrow, and he slumped off, not knowing how to avoid Mary Beth without being rude.

"What did you have in mind?" he asked her, as they moved away from the safe circle of chairs. He realized too late that his question might be misconstrued.

"I'm sorry?" Her pitch elevated.

"I meant, where did you want to walk?"

She let out a minute sigh, her fingers playing with the collar of her blouse. "Nowhere in particular. I thought we might enjoy some privacy."

She had thought wrong, but he allowed her to lead him through the trees and up a grassy knoll. His mind wandered, envisioning Callie and Nattie sitting back under the elm tree.

Mary Beth squeezed his arm. "My, you are quiet today."

Her comment amused him. "Obviously, you don't know me very well. I'm not a live wire, I'm afraid."

His words didn't ruffle her confidence. "You see, then, our little walk is important. We'll get to know each other better."

He shrugged off her statement and uttered a thought of his own. "When are you returning home, Mary Beth?" His blatant question dropped in the air like a cement brick.

His weighted words seemed to squelch her enthusiasm. "I haven't made plans yet. I've considered staying in Bedford for a while. I had hoped to…develop some lasting friendships here."

"I see." *Coward*, David yelled inside his head. How could he tell her with finesse that he didn't want to be one of her lasting friendships. The only friendship he wanted at the moment was Callie. But in her case, he wanted more than friendship.

He tried with discretion to uncurl her fingers from his arm and step away. "I'm sure your brother enjoys your company. And if I recall, the congregation has a number of young women…and men eager for a new friendship. You have a particular young man in mind?"

Her look sought his, sadly pleading, and he wished he could retract his foolish statement, throwing in the white flag. Obviously, she had a man in mind—not a young man, perhaps, but a man. *Him.* "I'm sorry, Mary Beth, my question was much too personal."

She averted her eyes, staring back toward the groups of parishioners gathering under the trees near the pavilion. "I had hoped you already knew the young man I find so attractive."

He pressed his lips together, wondering how to worm his way out of the pitiful situation he'd created. "Sometimes, I'm thick-headed, Mary Beth. My wife's death was two years ago, but I haven't quite thought of myself as single. I've been preoccupied with my daughter's problems. But thanks for your compliment."

Glowing red splotches appeared on her cheeks, and she turned toward their picnic spot beneath the trees off in the distance. "I doubt if anyone will attract your attention until the nanny leaves your employ. You seem to have eyes only for her."

"I beg your pardon?" David might have been less surprised by a kick in the shin. "I don't have a relationship with Callie." *But I want one.* His own realization brought a rush of heat to his neck.

"Your heart does, I think." She turned and headed back toward the picnic tables.

Flustered by her reaction, he followed her. Was his heart that obvious? He could no longer deny his feelings to himself—nor, apparently, to the rest of the world. Perhaps he needed to let Callie in on the news. Or did she know already?

When David walked away with Mary Beth, Callie wished she were the woman on his arm. He had squeezed into her thoughts and into her heart, and she had no way of protecting herself.

A romantic relationship frightened her, even one with David. His innocent touch excited her, yet a prickling of fear crept through her at the thought of intimacy. She had prayed, but had she really given her fear to God?

Callie observed Nattie. The child's gaze, too, followed her father and Mary Beth across the grass. Callie's hand rested lovingly on Nattie's arm, and she brushed the girl's cool, soft skin with her fingers. Her heart swelled, feeling Nattie's body nestled against hers. As David had said, the young girl needed a mother's love, and Callie had so much love to give.

When Callie looked away from Nattie, Pastor John was studying her. Did he see how much she loved the child snuggled in her arm?

"Are you enjoying your life here in Bedford?" he asked. His query sounded innocent, but Callie sensed more behind it.

"Yes, very much."

He nodded with a subtle reflex toward Nattie. "I notice you have other things holding you here, too."

Callie glanced down at the quiet child and back at him. "Pretty obvious, huh?"

"I worry about you. You need to take care of yourself. One day things will change, and you'll be the one left empty-handed. And empty-hearted."

His words washed over her like ice water. "Yes, I know."

"I didn't mean to offend you. I just wish your days could be a little more pleasant for *you*...personally. I'd like to see you if you're willing."

She gave him a blank stare. Obviously, he wasn't referring to church services. Why hadn't she seen this coming? "Well, I've decided to take you up on your Sunday morning offer. I'll be happy to sing occasionally for the worship service."

"Great. I'm pleased to hear that. But...that's not exactly what I had in mind."

"I know, and I'm sorry. For now, let's begin there. I'm not sure how settled I want to get in Bedford. I have family in Indianapolis, and...well, I suppose you understand."

He fixed his eyes to the ground. "For now, then, I'll just enjoy having you sing with us." He lifted his gaze and a half-hearted smile rose to his lips.

"Daddy."

Callie glanced at Nattie, her word a whisper. She looked up to see Mary Beth charging toward them, David following her with a look of helplessness.

Mary Beth shot Callie a glance and plopped into the folding chair. It lurched, giving a precarious bounce to one side. If it hadn't been for John, she might have ended up sitting on the ground.

"Careful," John said, eyeing her and then David. "You could have fallen flat on your face."

She raised her eyes, scanning her audience. "I already have," she sputtered.

Chapter Thirteen

Callie awakened early, knowing this morning she was singing in church. Feeling jittery, she rushed through breakfast and dashed to church before service for a final rehearsal.

Waiting for her solo, she sat in the front row. When the sermon ended, Pastor John gave a faint nod, and she rose and joined the pianist. As the musical introduction to "The Gift of Love" rippled from the keys, Callie faced the congregation.

Already the words of I Corinthians 13 filled her thoughts, *"Faith, hope, and love abide, these three; and the greatest of these is love."* Awareness jolted her. Much of her life had been loveless. Not her childhood, perhaps, but her later years—empty, punishing years of feeling unloved by others, by herself and by God.

As she sang, lifting the words in song, her gaze swept over the congregation. Her stomach tightened. David and Nattie sat conspicuously among them. Two pairs of eyes met hers, and like strands of a fragile cord, woven and bound together, she felt strengthened by their presence. The song touched her heart. What was life without love—both human and divine?

When the service ended, Callie rose and turned to where David and Nattie had been seated, but they were gone. Her pleasure turned to disappointment, and she edged her way to the exit.

As Pastor John greeted the worshipers, he caught Callie's hand before she slipped away and asked her to stay until he was free. She hung in the background, waiting. When the last parishioner had left, he joined her.

"Thanks so much for sharing your wonderful voice with us. And I see you persuaded David to worship with us this morning." He eyed her with a wry smile.

"No, I was as surprised as you."

"Then you've been a good influence without trying."

He made her uneasy. "Perhaps," she said, avoiding his eyes.

"I hope you'll sing again soon."

"Sure. I'll be happy to sing once in a while."

He offered a pleasant nod and rocked back on his heels. "And, by the way," he said, his hand sweeping the breadth of the sanctuary, "we had a few more people here today. Your idea seems to have worked."

She sent her mind back, but came up empty. "My idea?"

"The church with charm, remember? You suggested we advertise we're an old-fashioned church. We hung a few posters in the local supermarkets, and I put an ad in *The Bedford Bulletin.* I've already noticed a difference."

"That's great. I'm glad." She sensed he was stalling.

"Well, thanks for the idea." He dug his hands into

his navy blue suit pockets. "And have you given any thought to *my* idea?"

She felt her brows knit again. "Your idea?"

"That you have dinner with me."

The floor sank beneath her. She kept her eyes connected to his and swallowed. What could she say? *I'm falling in love with my employer.*

He shuffled his feet and pulled his hands from his pockets. His eyes never wavered.

"You know I can't get away easily. Nattie still needs a lot of—"

"You have a day off? An evening when David's home?"

She bit the corner of her lip and released it immediately. *Trapped.* "Why don't you call, and I'll check my schedule."

He contemplated her words for a moment. "All right, I'll do that." He touched her arm. "Thanks for singing today."

"You're welcome, John… Pastor John."

"Call me John, Callie."

Callie stepped backward toward the door. "John, then." She lifted her hand in a wave and hurried through the door.

When Callie arrived home, David was nowhere in sight. She climbed the stairs to slip out of her Sunday clothes. As she approached her room, she noticed Nattie's door ajar. Listening outside, she heard Nattie singing softly to herself. *"Jesus loves me; this I know."* Her murmured tone was sweet and wispy.

Callie stood still. What might Nattie do if she stepped inside the room? Her heart soared with each note of the song, perfectly in tune. When the melody ceased, she pushed open the door and stood at the threshold.

"Did I hear you singing?" she asked.

Nattie's face sprouted a tiny grin, and she nodded.

"You sing very pretty." Callie took a step forward. "Just like your mom, I would guess."

"Like you," Nattie said.

The child's words danced in her heart. "Thank you." She eyed the scene for a moment. "What are you doing?"

Nattie tilted her head the way David often did. "Playing."

"Playing, huh?" She moved into the room and slid onto the window seat. "I saw you in church. Did you see me?"

Nattie giggled and nodded.

"What's this head nodding? Cat got your tongue?"

Nattie gave another titter, but this time she opened her mouth wide and wiggled her tongue. When she closed her mouth, she added, "You're silly."

"Well, I guess I am."

In one motion, Nattie scurried up from the floor into Callie's arms. Her heart pounding, Callie hugged the child. "Well, what do I owe such a wonderful greeting?"

The child lifted her soft blue eyes to meet hers. "You sang pretty in church."

Air escaped Callie in a fluttered breath. "Thank you, sweetheart. You sounded pretty, too, just now."

The child wrapped her arms around Callie's neck, and Callie drew her to the window seat, keeping her arm around the girl's shoulders. Nattie cuddled to her and laid her head against Callie's side.

"I have an idea. Sometime we can sing together.

Maybe on our next walk on the hillside." She glimpsed down at the bright eyes looking up at her. "Okay?"

Nattie nodded, her eyes drooping sleepily.

Callie swung Nattie's legs up on the window seat, and the child rested her head in Callie's lap. With pure joy, Callie caressed the child's cheek and arm as she hummed a lullaby she remembered from her childhood. As the words rose in her mind, she sang them gently, and Nattie's breathing grew deep and steady as she sank into a restful sleep.

She smiled down at the little girl, and when she raised her eyes, David stood in the doorway watching her. Her pulse galloped like a frisky colt in a spring meadow. She longed to rush to his arms.

But then he vanished, and, not wanting to disturb Nattie, Callie eased herself back, leaning her head against the wall. He would have to wait if he'd wanted to talk to her. She was busy being a…mother. The word moved through her like an angel's song, lifting the hairs on her arms.

Later that evening, Callie found a gift-wrapped package next to her dinner plate. She flushed, wondering if John had sent something over in the hopes she would accept his dinner invitation. As she turned the small box over in her hand, David entered the dining room and eased into his chair.

"I wonder where this came from?" Then she saw the look on his face, and knew.

"Just a small token."

A tenderness that filled his eyes caught on her heartstrings and, like a kite, tugged and pulled until she let the string go, her love lifting to the sky. "For what?"

"Do you have to ask? I picked it up the other day, and was waiting for the right moment. I saw the perfect moment today. You, with Nattie sleeping on your lap."

"Sorry to ruin the lovely picture, but I don't think Nattie feels well. When I tried to get her ready for dinner, she said she didn't want anything to eat. Her cheeks are a little flushed, too. I'll take her some soup later."

"You can't wiggle out of it, Callie. I saw you holding her in your arms. Please accept my little gift."

She studied the box again, turning it over in her hand.

"Thank you. May I open it?"

"Sure, what do you think I'm waiting for?"

She grinned and pulled the tissue from the box. When she lifted the lid, a delicate rosebud lapel pin lay on a cushion of blue velvet. A rosy shade of gold shaped the bud, and the leaves and stem contrasted in the traditional golden hue. "It's beautiful. I've never seen anything like it."

"The clerk told me the pin was designed in one of the Dakotas. Apparently, they're known for three shades of gold. Sorry, this only has two."

She raised her eyes from the lovely brooch, heat flushing her cheeks. "I do feel deprived. Only two shades of gold, huh?"

"I promise. Your next gift will be three." He locked her in his gaze.

Your next gift. She raised her trembling hand to her heated flesh. "I believe I have two-toned cheeks at the moment."

"I seem to embarrass you, don't I?"

Embarrass? He thrilled her. Her voice bunched in her

throat. If she spoke, only a sob would escape. Regaining control of herself, she murmured a simple “thank you.”

David rose, and in one stride, stood at her side. He lifted the brooch from the box, unlatched it and pinned it to the wide lapel of Callie’s simple summer blouse. “There, now we can eat.”

When he sat again, he reached toward her. She glanced at his hand in confusion. But when she saw his bowed head, she lay her icy hand in his, and he asked the blessing. The warmth of his fingers and of his prayer radiated a comforting quiet through her. She whispered her “Amen” with his, then concentrated on dinner, afraid if she thought about anything else, the sentiments of the day might overwhelm her.

As she sat on the wide porch, Callie raised her head from her book at the sound of a car motor. Her stomach tumbled, as Mary Beth stepped from her automobile and crossed to the walk.

“Good morning,” she called. “I was passing by and noticed you on the porch. I hope you don’t mind that I stopped by.”

Callie rose. “No, not at all.” If God had wanted to punish her, he could have zapped her with a bolt of lightning for her lie. Of all the people in the world Callie *didn’t* want to see, Mary Beth topped the list.

“Beautiful summer day, isn’t it?” Mary Beth commented, flouncing up the porch stairs.

Callie cringed. The woman brought out the worst in her. She summoned her Christian manners. “May I get you some lemonade?”

Mary Beth stood uneasily on the top porch stair. “That would be nice.”

"Have a seat," Callie said, pointing to a chair near hers, "and I'll be right back."

She dashed into the house, raced up the stairs, pulled a comb through her hair, smeared lipstick across her lips, then flew down the stairs to the kitchen. Holding her chest, she gasped to Agnes, "A glass of lemonade, please."

Agnes stared at her wide-eyed. "Something wrong?"

"No—yes. Mary Beth Spier dropped by for a visit."

Agnes didn't seem to understand, but filled a glass with ice cubes and lemonade. "Here you go," she said, handing it to her.

Callie stood a moment to regain her composure, then turned and did her best to saunter back to the porch. Pushing open the screen door, she glued a smile to her face and handed the drink to Mary Beth. Nattie, playing in the yard, glanced at them, but kept her distance.

"The child seems more adjusted now than when I first came to Bedford," Mary Beth said as she eyed Nattie.

"Yes, she is. We thank God every day."

Mary Beth stared at her lemonade, then turned to Callie. "So then, what will you do with yourself?"

"Pardon me?" Callie got the drift of her remark, but she wasn't going to admit a thing.

"I mean, you're a nurse. If the patient is well, the nurse usually finds a new patient, right?" Her eyes widened, and when Callie didn't respond, she blinked. "Wrong?"

"No, for a physical illness, you're right. Nattie's problem is more psychological. Healing is different."

"So you're planning to stay, then?" Her face puckered.

"For a while." Seeing the woman's face caused her

to wonder about her own. She struggled to display what she hoped was a pleasant expression. “I’ll leave eventually,” she added, not wanting to utter the words. “Why do you ask?” Callie already suspected why, but she wanted to hear the woman’s explanation.

“Well, uh, I suppose I should be out-and-out honest with you.” Her shoulders raised, and she gave a deep, disgruntled sigh. “David is an attractive man, and available. Nattie needs a mother. Someone to give her love and affection. I realize right now that you’re providing for her care, but David needs…well—I don’t know why I’m explaining this to you.”

Callie stared at her in amazement. “I’m not sure why you are, either.”

Mary Beth rose, fists clenched at her side. “As long as you’re here, David isn’t going to realize he needs a wife and a mother for Nattie. I would make him a good companion. You’re hired help, Callie. He certainly can’t marry his child’s nanny, now can he?”

Her words smacked Callie across the face. Struggling for composure, Callie concentrated on keeping her voice level. “I don’t think you or I have any business deciding who David should marry.” Mary Beth’s hand clutched her chest, but Callie continued. “Am I to understand you want me to leave so David will come to his senses and marry you?”

“I didn’t say it quite that way. I said, as long as you’re here taking care of—”

“Of Nattie. That’s what I do here.” Callie raised her hand and fondled the two-tone gold rosebud pinned to her summer sweater.

“Well, I wasn’t suggesting… I find it very difficult to talk to you.”

"If you're waiting for me to leave, I have a piece of advice for you. Don't hold your breath."

Mary Beth's face reddened, and she bolted from her chair. "That's what I get for being honest. If you cared at all for that little girl and her father, you'd feel differently. I'm sorry you don't understand."

She swung on her heel and rushed down the stairs. When she reached the sidewalk, she turned and faced Callie again. "And thank you for the lemonade. It was very good." With that, she spun around and dashed to her car.

Chapter Fourteen

Nattie had made wonderful progress on the piano for a six-year-old. She'd begun her second book in only a few weeks, and Callie listened in awe to her obvious talent. The lessons continued to be their secret, so Nattie practiced during the day when David was at work.

While she practiced, Callie sat nearby, her mind filled with Mary Beth's words. Despite her irritation with the woman, Mary Beth had pinpointed the truth. As long as Callie lived in the house, David wouldn't look for a wife and mother for Nattie.

The image of David falling in love with someone else seeped like poison through Callie's thoughts, making her sick at heart. An inexpressible loneliness surged through her. If she had nothing to offer David, she would be kind to leave. Maybe Mary Beth wasn't the woman for him—but somewhere in the world a lovely young woman waited for a man like David and a beautiful child like Nattie.

Callie pulled herself from her doldrums and eased her way across to the piano, as Nattie finished her piece.

"Was that good?" Her shy eyes sought Callie's.

She rested her hand on Nattie's shoulder. "That was wonderful. Your daddy is going to be so proud of you."

Nattie turned on the bench and faced Callie. "I'm tired of practicing."

"You can stop if you want. You practiced a long time."

She placed her hand in Callie's. "Can we go outside now?"

"Sounds good to me. But first, let's go see what Agnes is doing. I think I smelled cookies earlier."

The child's eyes brightened, and she dragged her tongue across her upper lip. "Yummy. Cookies."

Callie pulled her by the hand. "Let's go see if we can have a sample."

Like two conspirators, they marched toward the kitchen. Agnes, apparently hearing their giggles, waited for them as they came through the door. She placed a plate of cookies on the table, then headed for the cabinet and pulled out two glasses. "Milk goes good with cookies, don't you think?"

"I think you're right, Agnes," Callie said, sliding into a chair next to Nattie.

Before Callie could reach for a cookie, Nattie had one half eaten. Agnes put the glasses of milk on the table, and they munched on cookies and sipped milk until the plate was empty.

"Good thing I only put out a few," Agnes said with a grin, shaking her finger at them. "You wouldn't have left any for the man of the house."

"My daddy's the man of the house," Nattie announced.

"None other," Callie agreed, tousling her hair. "Thanks, Agnes. They were delicious."

"Thanks, Agnes," Nattie echoed. They rose and headed for the side entrance.

Callie halted at the screen door. "We're going for a walk up on the hill, Agnes. Tell David we'll be back in a while, if he gets home before we do."

The housekeeper nodded, and the screen slammed as they made their way down the steps.

Nattie skipped on ahead, and as she watched from behind, Callie marveled at the change in her. Only months ago, Nattie had been silent and withdrawn. Today she behaved like any six-year-old. Only on occasion did she slip into a deep, thoughtful reverie that filled her young face with dark shadows of sadness. Callie thanked God those times grew fewer and farther apart.

But today, the child skipped on ahead, and only when she reached the highway did she stop and look over her shoulder, waiting for Callie to catch up with her.

Hand in hand, they crossed the street, then raced up the hill and through the trees to their favorite spot, the spot where Nattie had spoken her first words to Callie. Now the fields were overgrown with wildflowers, and wild raspberry bushes bunched together along an unshaded path. Nattie plucked a black-eyed Susan as she twirled through the field, holding it out in front of her to show Callie.

They plopped down to rest under the shade of an elm, where the leaves and sun left speckled patterns on the green grass.

"Can I pick some more flowers? For Daddy."

"You can, but wait until just before we leave, okay? Wildflowers need water. We don't want them to get limp and die before we get them home."

Nattie agreed, then flopped back onto the grass and

raised her hand over her head, staring into the cloudy sky. "I can see pictures in the clouds, Callie."

"You can?"

"Uh-huh." She pointed to a large fluffy cumulus.

Callie stretched out on her back next to Nattie, and together they pointed out dragons and elephants and ladies with long hair. The sun spread a warmth over her body, but not as completely as did the glow of her precious moment with Nattie.

As she lay there, Callie's mind filled with old, old songs she remembered her father singing when she was a child. "Buttermilk Sky." "Blue Skies." Then a hymn came to mind, and she sat up cross-legged, humming the tune.

Nattie rolled over on her side and listened for a while in silence, until she touched Callie's leg and said, "Sing."

Callie closed her eyes, and the song filled the air. *"For the beauty of the earth, for the beauty of the skies, for the love which from our birth…"* As Callie sang, Nattie's face glowed. The soft blue of her eyes sparkled with dots of sunshine. If ever in her life Callie had felt fulfilled, today was the day.

Somewhere in the reaches of her mind, the words to the song tumbled out. On the third verse, she rose, lifting her hands to the sky, and Nattie followed her, twirling among the wildflowers.

"For the joy of ear and eye, for the heart and mind's delight."

Then she heard a voice in the distance singing with her, drawing closer. *"For the mystic harmony, linking sense to sound and sight."*

Nattie said the words first. "It's Daddy." She raced

from the spot and darted into the grove of trees. Callie stood transfixed for a moment, then thought better and hurried after Nattie. But she had taken only a few steps, when David came through the elms with Nattie in his arms.

A smile filled his face, and as he neared Callie, his rich, resonant baritone voice finished the verse. *"Christ, our Lord to You we raise this our sacrifice of praise."*

When he finished, Nattie giggled in his arms, hugging his neck. "I knew that was you, Daddy."

Callie stood in a daze. "But I didn't."

He unwound Nattie from his arms and slid her to the ground. Then he sank onto a grassy patch, stretching his legs out in front of him. "This is the life."

Callie, still astounded, sank next to him. "You should sing more, David. You talk about me? You have a tremendous voice."

"Not great. Adequate. I can carry a tune."

Callie looked at him and rolled her eyes. "And I gave Sara all the credit for Nattie's talent."

David checked her statement. "We should give God the credit."

Callie stopped in mid-thought. She turned slowly toward him. "You're right." Since the day David had told her about his anger with God, Callie had worried. But his words today eased her mind. And she leaned back on her elbows and breathed in the fresh, sun-warmed air.

David had surprised himself with his comment. But what he said was true. Neither he nor Sara could take credit for Nattie's talent. He'd given the glory to God. He eyed the child, her face glowing and her golden hair curling around her head like a bright halo.

He had an idea, and with a chuckle, he clapped his

hands together. "Nattie, pick some daisies for me. With long stems. I'll make something for you."

She dashed off, bringing back a flower on a long spindly stem. "Is this a daisy?"

"That'll do. It's a black-eyed Susan." He pointed to the patch of white flowers nearby. "Those are daisies over there."

She darted away, then hurried back with a couple of the milky-colored blossoms with yellow centers. He sat and wound the stems together, fashioning a daisy chain. Sara had often created flower garlands, but today, as if God had given him another gift, the thought of her didn't press on his heart. Instead, he longed to make a wreath of flowers for Nattie's hair.

As his fingers worked the stems binding the flowers together, he eyed Callie and saw a look of wonderment on her face.

Amazement trickled through him, too, as he pictured himself immersed in blossoms. "I suppose you never thought you'd see the day that I'd sit and make flower garlands, huh?"

She laughed. "No, you're right. Maybe in a hospital for mental therapy—but not sitting here on the grass. Couldn't have imagined it in a million years."

"See, you just never know."

Nattie darted back and dropped a few more flowers in his lap, and then headed off again.

"Look at that child, Callie. Can you believe it? I hoped for so long, but I had dark moments when I thought she'd never come out of it. Now here she is—like new."

"I know. Watching her lifts my spirits higher than anything."

He raised his eyes to hers. "I'll tell you what lifts my spirits."

She sensed what he would say, and her chest tightened in anticipation.

"You. I believe Nattie came around because you've given her the tender love she needs. Not her mother, maybe. But you're soft and gentle like Sara. You're fair, blond hair, blue eyes."

"Spitting image?"

David shook his head. "Not spitting," he said, giving her an amused grin. "Only a faint resemblance. And you're a whole different person. Sara was quiet, sometimes too thoughtful. Even before her illness, she concentrated too much on things. She had fun, but… you're full of life and laughter."

Her face filled with surprise, and for the first time, he realized Callie had no idea how lovely she was.

"When I first met you, the word *spunky* came to mind."

"Spunky? I always thought I was a bit drab and boring."

"You?" David stared at her, amazed. Never in his life would he think of her as drab and boring. Lively, unpredictable, perhaps a little irritating at times—but never dull and lifeless.

"So what's the grand pause for? You're thinking bad things about me, aren't you?"

Pleasure tumbled through him. "I plead the fifth."

"Swell." She gazed down at the grass and plucked at a blade with her fingers.

"You'll only blush if I tell you what I was thinking. Except for the part about 'irritating.'"

Her head shot upward. "Irritating?" Her brows

squeezed together, and she peered at him. "What do you mean 'irritating'?"

"Occasionally."

She arched an eyebrow.

"Once in a while."

She leaned closer, squinting into his teasing eyes.

His heart thundered at their play. "Rarely. Hardly ever. Once in a blue moon." He shrugged. "Okay, never."

She flashed him a bright smile. "See, I knew it."

He felt as if he were sailing into the clouds. He watched Nattie picking daisies, and Callie smiling at him with her glinting, delphinium-blue eyes. He wondered if he'd ever been so content.

When Nattie returned, he rested the daisy chain on her hair and kissed her.

"Am I pretty, Daddy?" She twirled around the way she and Callie had done earlier.

"You're absolutely beautiful."

Her eyes widened. "Like Callie?"

His heart lurched with awareness. "Yes," he murmured, glancing over at the woman who brought unimagined joy to his life. "Just like Callie." He allowed his gaze to sweep over her before he turned back to Nattie. "But we aren't finished here, Nattie. We have another lady who needs a crown."

Nattie regarded Callie with excitement and ran off again, as David's fingers manipulated the stems in his lap.

After a few concentrated minutes, he rested a laurel of flowers on Callie's head, too. Then he rose. "And now, my two princesses, I think we'd better get home. Looking at my sundial, I see Agnes is probably wondering how to keep our dinner warm."

He reached down, extending his hands to Callie. She looked up and took his hands. With one slight pull, she rose as easily as if she were a feather pillow. David smiled at the two most important women in his life, each with sun-speckled hair adorned with a flowered garland.

That night when Callie went to her room, her thoughts drifted back to the three of them in the meadow earlier that day. Each memory brought a warmth to her heart, as she witnessed Nattie stretching herself back into a normal life. But most of all, Callie pictured David, sitting on the grass, weaving flowers into crowns for their hair. She chuckled to herself, remembering the day they had met and his stern, pinched face.

Yet her joy changed to apprehension when she thought about the future. For them, she saw no hope of a life together. Mary Beth had planted a seed in her mind that continued to grow. When September came, whether she wanted to or not, she must leave.

Going home would be the best for David and for Callie. Though she'd warned herself many times, she had done the unthinkable. She had fallen in love with him.

At first, she wondered if her love for Nattie had made her think fondly of David. Yet the more time she spent with him, the more she was sure that wasn't true. She loved him as a man, not as Nattie's father. He excited her. His touch thrilled her.

Yet her old fears crept into her mind when she least wanted them to. Like her haunting dreams, they covered her with empty, hopeless thoughts.

She rose and turned on the lamp in her bedroom. A shower would relax her, and maybe she could sleep.

She turned the nozzle on full blast and stepped into the steaming water, letting it wash over her and soothe her tightened muscles. Afterwards, when dry, she massaged her skin with the vanilla-and-spice-scented cream that reminded her of Agnes's cookies. Her stomach growled, and she chuckled to herself.

Slipping her feet beneath the blankets, Callie fluffed her pillow and snapped off the light. Behind her eyelids, she saw again the afternoon sky filled with puffy white clouds: animals, people and wonderful imaginary shapes.

Then David appeared, lifting a garland of flowers and resting it on her head. In her imagination, his hands touched her face tenderly and his arms reached out, pulling her to him.

But then as sleep descended, the clouds, too, lowered, turning to a gray, swirling mist, and Callie heard the *click* of a lock. The black dream enveloped her, and David's handsome face changed into the face leering from the shadows.

He winked and placed his hot hand on hers. "You just relax there. I can hear you have a pretty voice. Take a nice deep breath. Throw out your chest and fill those lungs."

She drew a deep breath, her blouse buttons pulling against the cloth as her lungs expanded and her diaphragm stretched.

"That's better." He smiled, gazing at her with admiration.

But when she saw his eyes resting on the gaping buttons, the air shot from her.

His fingers moved across the keys, his body sway-

ing on the bench, as she sang. When he played the final chord, his hands rose immediately into applause. "Why, you're a little meadowlark, aren't you?"

He rose and beckoned her with a finger to a sofa across the room. "Have a seat here so we can talk." She froze in place, his leering eyes riveting her to the floor, and as he reached toward her, a soundless scream rose in her throat.

Callie opened her eyes, her body trembling as she stared into the darkness. *It's only the dream. I'm dreaming.* She wiped the perspiration from her brow and rolled over on her side. Someday the dream would fade. It had to.

Chapter Fifteen

"Well, what do you think?" Callie asked, as Nattie grinned from the piano bench. "Is tonight our surprise concert?"

Her golden curls bounced in the sunlight streaming through the windows. "Uh-huh," she said, giving a nod, "and we'll really surprise him, too."

"We sure will. You play so well already, Nat. I'm proud of you." She rose from the chair and gave the child a squeeze. "Right after dinner, we'll tell him to come into the parlor. Then, I'll be the announcer, and you stand up and take a bow."

Nattie giggled, as Callie described the scene. Filled with their conspiracy, they tiptoed from the parlor and raced up the stairs to wait for David to come home.

They filled their time with puzzles and a storybook, until a car door slam alerted them.

"Daddy's home," Nattie said, peering out the window and turning to Callie with her hand over her mouth to suppress her giggle.

"I heard, but don't forget, we can't let on about the secret."

"Okay," she said, a mischievous twinkle in her eye.

Shortly, his footsteps reverberated on the stairs, and Nattie jumped up and raced to the doorway. "Daddy." She lurched into his arms.

As she did daily, Callie watched their reunion. Since Nattie's return from her quiet world, their day had established a few pleasant routines. At the sound of David's arrival, Nattie dropped whatever she was doing to greet him. Best of all, David's love, once shrouded by his own knotted emotions, had opened as widely as his arms now stretching toward his daughter.

With Nattie captured in his embrace, he looked at Callie over her shoulder. "So what have the two of you been up to, today?"

Nattie let out a giggle and glanced at Callie.

Without giving away their secret, Callie shushed her with a look, then said to David, "Just our usual fun-filled day. Nothing special—puzzles, storybooks, the usual." She figured "the usual" covered the piano practice.

David eased Nattie to the floor. "Well, I think I'll change. Agnes said dinner's in a half-hour."

"We'll see you there," Callie said, grasping Nattie's hand and pulling her back into her room before she burst with the news.

Callie tempered Nattie's excitement at dinner. But as the evening progressed, the child's gaze lingered on her, beseeching her to conclude the meal so the surprise concert could begin.

David, for a change, filled the time with talk about some new business opportunities. Rarely did he bring his work to the table, but tonight Callie listened with appreciation, knowing that the chatter distracted Nattie from blurting their after-dinner plans.

"I have an idea," Callie suggested. "Let's have dessert in the parlor a little later. Agnes made homemade peach pie, and I suspect we all need to rest our stomachs before dessert."

"Sounds good to me," David said, folding his napkin and dropping it alongside his plate. He slid back his chair and rose. "How about you, Nat? Willing to wait for dessert?"

She eyed Callie before she commented. "Yes, because I want to show you something now."

"Show me something? Hmm? What could it be? A picture?"

Nattie jumped from her chair. "Nope. Come on, Daddy, and I'll show you our surprise."

David glanced at Callie. She only shrugged innocently. But when he turned his back, she gave Nattie a wink. The child giggled and skipped off to the parlor.

Callie expected to find Nattie seated at the piano when they caught up with her, but she had remembered their plan and now waited in a chair, her hands folded in her lap. Callie delighted in the heartwarming picture.

"So where's my surprise?" David asked as he entered the room.

"Don't rush us," Callie cautioned. "You sit down right there." She pointed to the chair in good view of the piano. "Are you ready?"

He looked at her, a confused frown knitting his brows. "As ready as I'll ever be."

"Okay, then, let me introduce our entertainment for the evening. Da-da-da-dum!" Callie imitated a drumroll. "Give a warm welcome to Nattie Hamilton, who will perform for us on the grand piano." She began the applause.

David gaped and looked at Nattie, who rose from her chair, bowed and scurried to the piano.

She grinned at her father, then slid a book from under the seat and propped it on the music stand. Easing onto the bench, she adjusted the music book, arched her fingers over the keys and began the song she had prepared: Bach's étude, "Minuet." Her small fingers struck the keys, sending the spirited melody dancing across the room.

With his mouth hanging open like a Venus flytrap, David's attention was riveted on his daughter. When she struck the final note, his quick look at Callie's amused expression prompted him to snap his mouth closed with embarrassment.

Callie burst into applause, praying that David wasn't angry. But in a heartbeat, his surprised expression turned to joy, and he leaped from the chair in a thundering ovation and a cry of "Bravo!"

Nattie slipped from the piano bench, pulled out her pant legs as if she wore a skirt, and took a deep bow.

He bolted to her side and knelt to embrace her. "Oh, Nat, I'm so proud of you. Just like your mom." Turning, his eyes focused on Callie, who was standing in the distance and observing the scene. "And I know I have you to thank for her lessons."

She lowered her lids to hide the tender tears that rose in her eyes. "You're welcome."

"Nat, this is the best concert I've ever heard. You are my personal star."

Nattie grinned and wrapped her arms around his neck. "I'm your star."

"You sure are. Best gift in the whole world." He

rose, taking one of her hands. "So when have you been practicing?"

"Every day," Nattie told him. "After you go to work. But we couldn't practice on Saturdays or Sundays. Otherwise, you'd hear me. I'm on my third book already."

David turned to Callie. "You've been buying her music books?"

She nodded.

"You are a gem, Callie. A real gem."

"She's a diamond, just like me." Nattie's voice burst with excitement. "Callie told me I was her gem. Did you know that means a 'diamond,' Daddy?"

David raised his hand quickly and wiped what Callie guessed was a tear that had escaped his eye. "I do. You're both my diamonds."

Nattie ran to Callie's side, hugging her waist. "We're Daddy's diamonds, Callie."

She looked down at the child's beaming face. "I heard. That makes us both pretty special."

"Yep," she said, her head resting against Callie's hip.

Callie looked at David. "Before our throats are too knotted to enjoy dessert, I should probably ask Agnes to bring in the pie. What do you say?"

He grinned, his eyes glistening with moisture. "I say, you're not only a diamond, but a very wise woman."

When John Spier called, Callie could think of no excuse. She agreed to attend a jazz concert at the historic Opera House in Mitchell. When she accepted the invitation, he suggested dinner, as well.

A whole evening with John didn't excite her. But she'd told him to call, and he'd done what she asked.

Telling David was difficult. She had no idea whether

he cared or not, but *she* cared. And she took forever to harness her courage.

"Tonight?" David asked.

"Yes." She wanted to tell him she'd rather stay home and sit in the parlor with him, but her truthfulness would only embarrass her, and lead nowhere. "But if it's a problem, I'll call him and explain. I didn't give you much notice."

"No, that's fine, Callie. I, ah… I have no plans for the evening."

Disappointment filled her. She wished, at least, that he looked upset or inconvenienced.

He peered at his shoes. "You need a private life. You devote a lot of time to us."

"All right, if you don't mind." She had so much more to say—but if he didn't care, why should she? "I'll go, then. Thank you."

"You're welcome," he said, glancing at her. "Have a nice time."

Suddenly her disappointment turned to irritation. "I'm sure I will," she said, her voice picking up a spark. "I'll go."

"Good."

This time his tone sounded edgy. She turned and left the study. Nattie stood in the hallway, peering at her, as Callie came from the room. She had more than two hours to get ready, but she wasn't going to sit there and feel sorry for herself. She had a date, and she'd enjoy herself if it killed her.

With a final look at David through the doorway, she charged up the stairs and into her room. Plopping on the edge of her bed, she stared into her open closet. What should she wear? Hardly anything she owned seemed appropriate for a date. She needed to go on a shopping spree—but where around here? Shopping meant a trip to Indianapolis. More guilt rose as she thought of her mother.

Though they talked on the telephone, Callie hadn't been home to visit Grace in a while. She should arrange a trip. *Trip?* In September, she would be leaving Bedford altogether. Bleak dread raked through her. But it was a cold, hard fact.

She rose and maneuvered her outfits along the wooden rod, glancing at skirts, blouses, dresses. The Opera House. Was it dressy? She was positive she didn't have anything appropriate. Taking care of Nattie didn't require fancy dress, only casual. She searched through the clothing again, but stopped when she heard a noise at the hall door.

She turned and saw Nattie peering in from the sitting room. "Come in, Nat."

Nattie rarely came to Callie's room, and today she edged through the door.

"Did you need something?"

Nattie shook her head, her eyes focused on the closet. "Are you going away?" she asked.

"Uh-huh," Callie said, peering at a summery dress she held in front of her on the hanger.

"Please, don't go away." Nattie's voice quivered with emotion.

Callie spun around and faced her. Nattie's lower lip trembled, leaving Callie confused. "What's wrong? Don't you feel well?"

She shook her head. "I don't want you to leave. Who will take care of me?"

Callie crossed to her and knelt to hold her. "No, I'm

not leaving for good. Just for tonight, Nat. Your daddy's home, and Agnes. They'll be here. I'll be back later."

Nattie's misty eyes widened. "Oh… I thought you were going away."

"What would make you say that? Heaven forbid. I wouldn't leave you." Nattie lay her head on Callie's shoulder, and the unintended lie she had uttered, like a boomerang, spun back, whacking her conscience. Hadn't she just decided she would leave Bedford in September?

She gazed into the child's sad face and couldn't bring herself to say any more. Instead, she held Nattie tightly to her chest until she felt her relax, then tickled her under the chin. "So, you thought I was leaving you. You silly. Wouldn't I tell you if I were going away for good?"

"But you and Daddy hollered. I thought—"

"No, we were just talking loudly. There's a difference. And don't you worry about that, anyway. I'm not going anywhere, except out to dinner and to a concert with Pastor John."

Nattie tilted her head, staring directly into her eyes. "Why don't you go with Daddy?"

The child's look of sincerity tugged at Callie's heartstrings. Yet, the words made her smile. Sometimes she wondered the same thing. What might it be like to spend an evening with David—on a real date? She took a minute to find her voice. "I suppose because your daddy didn't ask me—"

"Didn't ask you what?"

Her head shot upward, and she felt a flush spill over her face like a can of rose-colored paint. "I didn't hear you."

David stepped into the room. "Yes, I know. So what didn't I ask you?"

"You didn't ask Callie to go to dinner," Nattie offered, still hugging Callie's neck.

"And why would I do that?" He glowered at Callie.

She unleashed Nattie's arms, then rose. "You shouldn't. She's upset because she thought I was leaving—for good. I explained I was going out with John."

"Ah," David said. "She thought that because you were yelling at me."

Callie lifted her chin. "*I* yelled at *you?*"

"Yes. And now she wants to know why I don't take you to dinner and the concert?"

Nattie shook her head, her eyes wide, certainly not understanding all the innuendos.

Callie glared at him. "Yes, that's what she asked." She waited for his arrogant, stinging response.

"I guess," he said, kneeling down to Nattie, "that I didn't think of it first."

Callie's mouth dropped open wider than David's had days earlier at Nattie's concert. Her pulsed raced like an *arpeggio.*

He raised his soft, apologizing eyes to hers, and she faltered backward, grasping the dresser to steady her trembling legs. "You've caught me off guard."

His full, parted lips flickered to a smile. "Yes, I see that. You can close your mouth now." He scooped Nattie into his arms, as she let out a squeal. "We'd better let Miss Randolph get herself decked out for her *date,* Nattie."

"Who's Miss Randolph?" Nattie asked, as he carried her, giggling, toward the door.

He glanced at Callie over his shoulder. "I'm not sure myself, Nattie. I have to figure that one out."

Chapter Sixteen

When Callie arrived home from her evening with John, David's study light glowed through the tower room window. She said goodnight to John and hurried inside. Stopping outside the study door, she paused. She longed to talk to him, but couldn't bolster her courage, so instead she headed upstairs to her room.

The evening had been a strange one. She wondered if, instead of being interested in her, after all, he hoped she could be a liaison between David and the church. Though John said how much he enjoyed her company, the conversation continued to backtrack to the church, the broken organ, and a variety of other congregational concerns.

Callie had decided a pastor's life must be a difficult one, and her heart softened a little as she'd listened to him. She knew the pianist was leaving, and he needed a replacement or, at least, a substitute until a new pianist could be found. Callie sat beside him feeling guilty. He knew she played the piano, and by the end of the evening, she suggested that she might consider helping out "in a pinch."

As well as addressing John's concerns, Callie had her own. She couldn't get Nattie's question out of her mind: *"Are you going away?"* Thinking of the situation, she ached. It was no-win. If she stayed with Nattie, David would eventually fall in love and find a wife. She didn't know if she could bear it.

Still, she knew David's feelings for her had grown. At the thought, her heart soared—until reality smacked her in the face and her feelings nosedived to the ground. How many times did she have to tell herself she had nothing to offer him? She could never allow him to fall in love with her—nor she with him.

With her mind in a turmoil, she climbed into bed. She lay for a long time, her thoughts pacing back and forth like someone waiting for a last meal. She knew she was a loser no matter how she looked at it—and was suffering because her actions would also hurt Nattie.

Finally her eyes grew heavy, and she drifted to a near sleep, awakened again, then succumbed. And as her mind glided into sleep, so the shadows rose from her subconscious.

With his hot hand on hers, she heard him. "You just relax there, little lady. I can hear you have a pretty voice. Take a nice deep breath. Throw out your chest and fill those lungs."

She drew a deep breath, her blouse buttons pulling against the cloth, and she saw his eyes resting on the gaping buttons.

"That's better." He smiled. "Let's try a song.

"We'll do one you know." He handed her some sheet music. "Pick something you know well."

She made her selection and handed him the music.

She heard the introduction clearly and filled her diaphragm with air. She opened her mouth, and her pure, natural voice, filled with strength and joy, soared from her.

He gazed at her with admiration, swaying on the bench, as she sang. When he played the final cord, his hands rose immediately into applause. "Why you're a little meadowlark, aren't you."

He rose, beckoning her to follow him across the room to the sofa. "Have a seat, my little Meadowlark, so we can talk business." Her heart raced at first, then the hammering began. He settled next to her, placing his hand on hers. "Are you more comfortable now?"

"Yes," she said, trying to extract her hand. "A little nervous, I guess."

"How old are you?"

"Just turned nineteen. I'm a sophomore at the University of Indiana."

"You'd really like to sing with our group, wouldn't you? Travel with us in the summer? I'm sure you'd be grateful for a place in our choir."

"Oh, I would. Yes, my father thinks you're wonderful."

"And you? Am I wonderful, Meadowlark?"

His hand slid across her knee, and she grabbed it, holding him back. But his strength overpowered her.

"You want to make your daddy proud, don't you? If you want your daddy to be proud, you have to please me a little. How about a kiss?"

His face loomed above her. Her chest hammered, thundered inside her, and she opened her mouth to scream, but she had no voice. Instead, she couldn't breathe, she was sinking into some deep swirling ocean of icy black water. She heard her blouse tearing and felt her skirt rising on her thighs, and she died beneath the blackness.

When Callie woke, her hands clasped the blankets and her arms ached from fighting off the monster in her dream. She had kept her secret from everyone. No one knew why she had stopped singing. No one knew what had happened—only she and Jim McKee.

She rolled on her side and snapped on the light, squinting at the brightness. Why had she not pulled herself from the dream sooner? Lately, she'd been able to stop the dream before the end, but tonight the horrible memory wrenched through her. All the filth and pain she had felt these past years lay on her shoulders.

Callie rose from her bed and went into the bathroom, ran cool tap water over her face and arms. She returned to the bedroom and eased herself to the edge of the bed, noticing the clock. Only twenty-five minutes had passed since she'd crawled under the sheets. She needed to talk to David, to do something to make the terrible thoughts go away. But if she talked tonight, she might regret it. The burden she had carried so many years struggled for release.

She leaned back again on the pillow and dimmed the bulb to a soft glow. As she folded her hands behind her head, her mind wandered, and while it strayed, she heard faintly, a soft, lilting melody drift through the room. Her radio? Had she accidentally set the clock-radio alarm?

She rose and strode to the sitting room. The sound was stronger there, louder than in her bedroom. Television? A recording? She listened more closely. A piano coming from below. Was David playing the piano? She had never heard him play. The music rose through the walls, poignant and beautiful.

She slipped into sweatpants and shirt, and opened her sitting room door. The hallway was empty. No light glowed beneath the second-floor doorways. She followed the stairs down to the dimly lit foyer. A light still shone beneath David's study door, and from outside, she heard the lovely, haunting melody.

Whether wise or not, she turned the knob and eased the door open. Barefoot, she tiptoed into the room, following the music coming from the piano. As she reached the archway, she stood back and watched David's shadow dip and bend as his body moved with the rapture of the music. Her heart soared, yet wept at the haunting sound.

When the last strain died away, he sat with his head bowed, then, as if he sensed her presence, he turned. She stepped through the opening, and his gaze lifted to her face, caressing her, his eyes glistening with emotion.

"Callie, I thought you were sleeping." He rose and moved toward her. "Is something wrong? Did I wake you?"

"No. A dream woke me." She closed the distance between them. "David, the song was beautiful. What is it?" She glanced toward the piano and saw his manuscript spread out on the music stand. "You wrote that, David?" Callie dashed to the paper and lifted the music. "You wrote this." She swung to face him.

He rested his hands on her shoulders. "Yes, I wrote it. It's been playing in my mind for months, but I hadn't written in so long, not since…since Sara died. I didn't think I'd write again. But I couldn't make the music stop roaring in my head until I put it on paper."

Swirling emotion drew her eyes to his, and in them, she searched for an answer. His words promised a release for her. He couldn't make the music stop until he put it on paper. Would her dreams stop if she said them aloud?

She struggled with her thoughts. The truth lay in his heart and in hers. If he knew, could he love her? If she told him, would she be released from her self-made prison? Could she take the chance? She slid the music back on the stand.

"Callie, I could no more fight the music in my head than I can fight the feelings inside me. You should know that I love you. I've been falling in love with you ever since the day we met."

"Oh, please, David, don't say anything that will hurt us."

"Hurt you? Never. My feelings are far too powerful to hide any longer. I've tried to sense how you feel about me. I'd hoped you were learning to love me, too."

"There are too many things you don't know about me, David. Awful things. If you knew them, you wouldn't say you loved me. I've struggled with them in my dreams, but not aloud. They hurt too bad. Please, don't say you love me."

David looked into her eyes, trying to fathom what terrible things she could mean. Her eyes glowed, but with fear. He felt her trepidation in the tension of her shoulders. He drew her to him and wrapped his arms around her.

"Please, Callie, tell me. Do you love me? If you love

me, I can handle anything. Whatever you need to tell me. I promise."

She clung rigidly to his arms, and he sensed her panic.

"Don't promise anything until you know the truth," she pleaded. "I couldn't bear to have you reject me."

"Then you do love me? Say it, please."

"I've tried not to love you. For a long time, I told myself I only loved Nattie, but I can't lie. Yes, I do love you, but I can never marry you…or anyone. Never."

He caught her face in his hands and lowered his lips to hers. Her mouth yielded to his, but just as quickly, she pulled away. Instead, he kissed her cheeks and her eyes, tasting the saltiness of the tears that clung to her lashes.

"Callie, if you love me, you'll tell me what's wrong. Let me know what's hurt you so badly. Maybe I can help you."

"Please, let me think about it, David. Play your music for me again. I'd love to hear your song once more. I'll sit right here." She backed up and lowered herself into a chair.

"Promise you'll tell me?"

"I promise I'll think about it."

"Promise you'll tell me, Callie."

"Play for me, David, and I'll try."

David looked with longing into her eyes, and didn't argue, but wandered to the piano and slid onto the bench, shifting the music on the stand. He glanced at her, then lifted his eyes to the music. He played, and the love he'd felt for these past months rose from the keys and drifted through the room.

He sensed her watching him, and he trembled at the thought. As his attention drifted to the last phrase of music, she rose and moved across the floor to stand behind him, her hands resting on his shoulders. He felt the warmth of her hands on his arms, and his fingers tingled with the fire burning in his heart.

On the last chord, he turned to her, and tears ran down her cheeks. Her eyes were focused on the sheet of music resting on the stand. Almost imperceptibly, he heard her whisper, "'Callie's Song.' You named it for me."

He swiveled on the bench. "The music is you, Callie. All the longing and joy, fear, confusion, wonder you brought into our lives here. Nattie, you, me, everything."

She stared at him in disbelief. "Thank you," she whispered.

He stood and placed his hands on her arms. "Thanks to you, Callie." He took her hand and led her toward the door. "Let's sit in the parlor. It's more comfortable there. We need to talk. I'll make us a cup of tea. How does that sound?"

She nodded and followed him, his arm guiding her. When they reached the foyer, he kissed her cheek, aiming her into the parlor as he turned toward the kitchen.

Callie wandered through the doorway, wondering what she would do now. Where could she begin? She had so much she should tell him, yet so little she wanted to admit. He loved her. And she had finally told him the truth: she loved him with all her heart. And Nattie, too. But…

She eased herself onto the sofa, her gaze sweeping the room. The grand piano stood in silence in the bay window, and she thought about the wonderful day, not long ago, when Nattie had played her concert. What happiness she had felt that day. But tonight, though

David's song touched her with tenderness, her pulse tripped in fear at the story David wanted her to tell.

Hearing his steps in the foyer, she looked toward the doorway. He came into the room carrying two mugs, and sending a steamy, fragrant mist into the air. Handing one mug to her, he sat by her side, stretching his legs in front of him. "Be careful. This stuff's really hot."

She blew on the beverage before taking a cautious sip, and curled her legs underneath her.

David studied her. "So. Where do we begin?"

She stared at her hands folded in her lap. "I was trying to decide while you were getting the tea. This is very difficult for me. Harder than you can ever imagine. If I get through this, David, you should know you're the only person in the whole world I've told this to."

"I know. You've suffered far too long for whatever this is about. I'm honored to be the one you trust enough to tell."

A sigh tore through her, and an unbelievable desperation raged inside. A sob escaped from her throat. She swallowed it back, choking on the emotion.

He took her hand in his and brushed her skin with his fingertips without speaking.

Another sigh rattled from her. With a gentle touch, David caressed her hand. Then she began, slowly at first.

"Seven years ago I sang in church, in college—anywhere an audience would listen. I studied music in college. Even thought I might like a career as a musician or singer. But my father longed for me to audition for the Jim McKee Singers. It was made up of college-age students who traveled in the summer. My father was a powerful Christian, and his greatest joy was for me to sing with them during one of their summer tours."

Callie closed her eyes, wondering how far she could get before she lost control. David shifted his fingers to her arm, caressing her the way a father calms his child.

"I arranged for a tryout and waited in an office set up near the college for the local auditions. I felt more and more nervous as each person went in and left. Soon, I was alone. He came to the door and called me in."

"Who, Callie? Who was he?"

She swallowed, struggling to speak his name. "The director… J-Jim McKee." Her lips stammered the name.

"So what happened?"

She felt David tense, almost as if he could guess what she was going to say, but his eyes only emanated tenderness.

She returned to the story beginning with the *click* of the lock. "'You're nervous enough, I'm sure,' he said to me as he bolted the door. 'We don't want anyone popping in and making things worse, do we?'"

As if marching through her dream, she led David through the audition. "Then Jim McKee led me to the couch, and kept calling me his 'little meadowlark.' My poor mother called me that a few months ago, and I panicked. I can't hear that word without remembering."

David leaned over to kiss her cheek. "It's okay, Callie. I love you."

"How can you love me, David? You already know what happened." The sobs broke from her throat, and she buried her face in her hands. "I was a virgin. And he took the most precious gift I longed to share with a husband someday. He raped me, David."

Chapter Seventeen

David drew her into his arms, holding her as she wept and rocked her as he would a child. "It wasn't your fault, Callie. You didn't make it happen. It wasn't your fault."

Seven years of pain and sorrow flooded from her in a torrent of hot tears. His murmured words lulled her. When she gathered her strength, she lifted her head, fearing to look in his eyes, but there, she saw only his gentle understanding.

"I've kept that a secret so long, David."

"Why? That's what I don't understand. Why? How many other young women's lives did that demon destroy?"

"I didn't have the courage to tell my parents. My father idolized the man. He wouldn't have accepted that Jim McKee would do something like that." She searched his face for his understanding. "I thought my dad would blame me, think I had been so awed that I was a willing partner. I don't know. I thought I could wash it away with soap and water and prayers."

"Callie, my love, you suffered too long."

"I read in the paper a few years ago that he died

suddenly from a heart attack. *David, I was happy.* I'm ashamed of myself, but I was happy he died."

David buried his face in her hair. She didn't know what he felt. But his eyes had said he understood, and that's what mattered.

She filled her lungs with healing air and released a ragged sigh. "You know, deep inside I've felt so much guilt. I've wondered if I *did* do something to make him think I wanted him." She sighed. "Do you know what sticks in my mind?"

He shook his head.

"I remember my deep breath and the buttons gaping on my blouse. I kept asking myself, did I tempt him? Did he think I did it on purpose, that it was a come-on?"

David closed his eyes and shuddered. "Callie, how many women in the world take deep breaths and their buttons pull on their blouses? Do you think it's their announcement to the world that they want to be raped? I can't believe you've worried all these years about that."

"I was barely a woman then, naive and so innocent… until that terrible day."

Helplessness washed over her again as she recalled the day she realized she was pregnant. How could she tell her parents then about the horrible event she'd kept from them? That was the moment she decided to let them think the baby growing inside her was fathered by a college student. Why destroy everything they believed? She let them accept her lie.

And now, how could she tell David? He and Sara had chanced everything, even Sara's life, to have a child, and Callie walked away from hers. Maybe the rape wasn't her fault. But losing her child was.

An abortion had been out of the question. God would

never forgive her for taking the life of an innocent child. Despite her supposed wisdom, she'd never forgive herself for agreeing to the adoption. How could she tell David?

The silence lingered, and David held her close in his arms.

"David?" she murmured.

"Yes." He pulled his face from her hair and looked into her eyes, questioning.

"Do you understand why I'm afraid? I don't know if I can ever love a man fully without those memories filling my mind. Even your innocent touch scares me sometimes."

"I sensed your fear, Callie, and I didn't understand. I thought it was *me*."

"Oh, no, it isn't you."

"I know that now. And now that I understand, we can work on it, Callie. We'll take it slow. One step at a time. You can learn that being loved is a gentle, powerful experience. *Love,* Callie—love is a gift from God. A wonderful, pure gift."

Tears rose in David's eyes, and for the first time, Callie saw them spill down his cheeks. Her stomach knotted when she saw his sorrow—sorrow he had hidden for so long.

"You're crying." Callie reached up to wipe away the tears from his cheeks. She kissed his moist eyes and buried her face in his neck.

David's heart reeled at her tenderness. She was not alone in bearing shame for so many years. "I'm crying for both of us. We've both carried secrets longer than we should."

"Secrets? You mean Sara's pregnancy and—"

"Yes, I went against God's wishes and demanded

an abortion. I didn't want her to die, and I knew if she carried the baby, she couldn't have the treatment she needed. But Sara refused, and we waited too long. God punished me for my selfishness."

Callie looked at him, her face filled with confusion. "She was too far in her pregnancy for an abortion?"

He didn't comment, leaving her to accept his silence as his answer. Sara had wanted a baby so badly. He remembered the anger he had felt shortly before she died, how he blamed her pregnancy for her short life. Shaking his fist at God for their losses.

David pulled himself from his sad musings. "Callie, we both have some issues to deal with, but doing it together will give us strength. Love is a mighty healer."

He saw in her face understanding and acceptance. He lowered his lips to hers, and this time, she didn't recoil, but raised her mouth to meet his. Gently their lips joined, and she offered him the love that had lain buried inside her.

When they parted, he held her close, praying that the healing for both of them had already begun.

Callie leaped from bed the next morning. The clock read ten. She'd not slept that late in years. What about Nattie? She threw on her robe and darted across the hall. Nattie was not there. Her bed was unmade, her pajamas in a pile on the floor.

Callie hurried back to her room, completed the most rudimentary cleansing ritual and threw on a pair of slacks and a top. As she dashed down the staircase, she saw David and Nattie at breakfast. Embarrassed at her lateness, she slowed her pace and worked at regaining her composure.

At the bottom of the stairs, a bouquet of fresh flowers sat on the foyer table. At its base lay a card with her name scrawled on the envelope. David caught her eye as she stood in the foyer, and she nodded, touched that he had sent her flowers already, so early in the morning.

But the biggest surprise occurred when she opened the card. The flowers were from John. She flushed, knowing she had to call him immediately after breakfast, to thank him and give him some kind of explanation as to why she couldn't go out with him again.

She hurried into the dining room.

"Callie." Nattie giggled. "You didn't wake me up. Daddy said you overslept."

"Good morning." David eyed her with a searching look. "I believe you overslept."

"I did, didn't I. And why aren't you at work?"

He grinned. "Guilty as charged. And the flowers?"

"You got flowers," Nattie chimed.

Callie nodded. "From John." She wrinkled her nose. "I guess I owe him a telephone call."

"I guess," David said with a hint of jealousy. "What would make him send you a bouquet, I wonder?"

"Guilt? Payola?"

"Blackmail?" His grin grew. "Whatever. Call him, please."

"I will. I promise. By the way, I agreed to fill in as the pianist. Pam Ingram is leaving. She's expecting a baby and doesn't have time to handle the piano and choir right now."

"Pianist and choir director?"

"No. You heard me. *Pianist.* You're the choir director."

"Was."

"We'll see."

"I repeat, *was*."

She gave him a grin, not saying another word. They enjoyed breakfast together, then David hurried off to work. Later in the afternoon, Agnes called Callie to the front door. She descended the stairs with Nattie on her heels and halted in surprise halfway down.

"More flowers?" she asked, gaping at a deliveryman holding a huge package wrapped in floral paper.

"Must be a special occasion," he said. "This is the second bouquet I've delivered here."

She swallowed. "Not really. Just a coincidence." She took the bouquet from him and closed the screen door.

Nattie skipped around her in excitement. "More flowers?"

"Looks like it, doesn't it?"

Callie pulled the protective paper from the magnificent arrangement of mixed flowers: lilies, orchids, roses. John's simple vase looked sad by comparison. She didn't need to open the card to know the source. A grin crept to her lips.

"Who are they from, Callie?"

"Your daddy, I think." Callie pulled the card from the envelope. *I love you. Never forget. David.* She laughed, seeing the sense of competition John's bouquet had aroused. Then her stomach churned as she recalled her promise: she needed to march to the telephone without delay and talk to John.

Callie thanked John by telephone for the flowers and made arrangements to practice on the church piano. Though two pianos were available at the house, her "practice" was an excuse to see him. She reviewed a variety of ways she might tell him about David and her, but nothing felt comfortable.

A cooling air washed over her as she entered the church. The stained-glass windows held the sun's scorching rays at bay. She headed down the aisle, and by the time she reached the piano, John was coming through a side door. But to her dismay, Mary Beth followed behind him.

His sister wore a bright smile painted on her lips, and the look gave Callie an eerie feeling. In a flash, she knew what Mary Beth was thinking. If Callie was dating John, David was "available." She had bad news for both of them.

John stepped to her side. "I appreciate your willingness to fill in here. I'm looking for a regular pianist, I promise, but it may take some time. We don't have too many accomplished musicians hanging around Bedford."

"As long as you know this is temporary," she reminded him.

Mary Beth fanned her face with her hand. "Whew, you saved me, Callie. I play a little, and John was trying to coerce me."

Callie bit her tongue. If she had had any idea Mary Beth played, she wouldn't have volunteered—but it was too late now. "Well, I'm glad to hear you can play, Mary Beth. I do plan to visit my mom in Indianapolis. I haven't seen her in a while, and I'm feeling guilty."

Mary Beth raised her hand to her throat with a titter. "Oh, my, I guess I shouldn't have spoken."

She leaned intimately toward Callie. "And how are things with you? I understand you had a nice evening.

And flowers. He sent you flowers." Her voice lilted with feigned enthusiasm.

"Yes, we had a nice time, but I didn't expect flowers."

Mary Beth took a step backward. "I suppose I should leave and let the two of you talk privately."

She needed to act now or never. "No, Mary Beth, don't go. I have something to tell both of you."

John's face brightened, then faded when he looked at her expression. Mary Beth had a similar reaction.

Callie cleared her throat. "I don't want to mislead you. I had a lovely time. The food was excellent, and I enjoyed the concert. But I'm afraid I can't accept any more invitations."

"You can't?" John asked.

Mary Beth's head pivoted from one to the other.

"That evening, David and I came to…an understanding."

Mary Beth gasped. "An understanding?"

"Yes, we realize that we've grown to…care very deeply for each other, and we—we've fallen in love."

"Fallen in love." The words escaped them in unison like the chorus of a Greek tragedy.

Callie looked at them. "I hope you can be happy for us."

"Happy?" John looked bemused, then his brows unfurrowed. "Happy, yes. I'm happy for you."

She watched him struggle to maintain a neutral expression. Mary Beth's face registered pure frustration.

"Well, I hope under the circumstances," Mary Beth said, her face pinched, "that you don't plan to continue living together in the same house."

Callie's heart dropped. The thought hadn't occurred to her. But she had to live here. How would she and

David know if they could work through their problems? Yet how could she explain the situation to others—once Mary Beth spread the news?

Callie leveled her stare at Mary Beth. "We don't live in the house alone, as you know. Agnes and Nattie are both there. I don't believe in premarital relationships, Mary Beth, if that's what you're insinuating." She almost became catty, wanting to add the words, *"Perhaps you do."* But God intervened and removed the words from her lips.

"I'm not insinuating anything. I just wouldn't want others to think differently."

John pressed his sister's arm. "I don't see how others will think anything, Mary Beth. No one knows this, except you and me. And we won't spread idle gossip, will we?"

Mary Beth grasped the neck of her blouse for a second time. "Why…no. I certainly wouldn't spread gossip."

"Then I don't believe we have a problem at all."

Callie wanted to hug him, but instead, she extended her hand. "Thank you, John, for understanding." Mary Beth hovered as if waiting to receive her thank you, but Callie sat at the piano to practice.

Chapter Eighteen

No matter what John had said to make things better, Callie couldn't forget his sister's words. Was it wrong for her to stay at the house now that she and David had admitted their love for each other? Wonderful, fulfilled days passed by, and though they said nothing to Nattie, the child seemed to understand changes had occurred. And her joy had grown as much as theirs.

September was nearly on their doorstep, and Nattie would soon begin school. With her debut into the world of education, Callie faced a decision. What reason did she have to stay in Bedford? The time had come to talk honestly with David.

But Callie's procrastination had blossomed into avoidance. Today she set a deadline. One week. Within the week, she had to broach the subject of leaving. She couldn't stay in the house under the circumstances, no matter what her heart said.

Callie descended the staircase to a flutter of activity. Yesterday David had announced he'd invited their old housekeeper, Miriam, to dinner. With improved health, she had come to Bedford to visit her sister.

At the bottom of the stairs, Nattie clung to the banister, staring at the door and awaiting Miriam's arrival. At the sound of an automobile, Nattie raced to the door and tugged it open.

As soon as Callie saw her, she understood why Miriam held a special place in their hearts. Stepping from the car was a woman who fulfilled everyone's dream of a roundish, warm, lovable fairy godmother. Her face glimmered with animation and love as she threw her ample arms around Nattie and David.

Callie waited inside, allowing their welcome to be unburdened by introductions. David helped Miriam through the door, and Callie met her in the foyer.

The elderly woman moved cautiously forward, a cane in her left hand, and Callie joined her in welcome. "I'm so happy to meet you. I've heard nothing but wonderful things about you."

Miriam's eyes twinkled. "And I've heard nothing but wonderful things about you." She wrapped one arm around Callie's shoulders, giving her a warm hug.

"Come into the parlor, Miriam. We'll sit until dinner's ready." There, David guided her to a comfortable chair. Nattie clung to her side and leaned against the chair arm, as Miriam settled herself.

"I'd hold you on my lap, precious, but I'm not sure my old legs will bear the weight. You've grown so big since I last saw you. It seems years, rather than months."

Nattie stood straight as if pulled by a string. "I forgot. Agnes said I could help set the table." She skipped from the room, as the others chuckled at her enthusiasm.

"David, what a joy to see her so well." Miriam turned toward Callie. "I know we have this young lady to thank."

Callie murmured a thank you, as Miriam continued.

"When I left, my heart was nearly broken, seeing

Nattie so distraught. David had already gone through enough without that burden."

"I've enjoyed every moment I've spent with Nattie," Callie said. "I've had the rare pleasure of watching her blossom. It's like a special gift from God."

"I'm sure it is," she said. "And now, David, what's happening with you?"

"Seeing Nattie get better has been amazing. And I might add, meeting Callie has been a blessing for me, too."

A healthy grin curved Miriam's mouth, and her eyes twinkled. "Am I to understand you two have—how should I put it—an understanding?"

Callie glanced at David with a shy grin.

He nodded. "Yes, you could call it that. Callie has brought me back to life as much as she has Nat."

Miriam turned to Callie. "Then, I thank you. You've made an old woman feel very happy."

Callie laughed. "Thanks. We're a pretty happy bunch."

"And we'll be even happier when we eat. Let me check on dinner." David jumped up and left the room.

Miriam checked the doorway, then faced Callie. "While he's gone, I want to thank you privately. I love this family like my own, and my heart was heavy with all the sadness in this house. But today, I feel love—and best of all, promise."

"Thank you. When I first came, I thought David was a grouchy, unloving, hard-nosed man. At times he was, but I soon found the real David underneath all that cover-up."

"David hardened himself. He blamed himself for Sara's death, I know. Letting her get pregnant, and then losing the baby. But when they got Nattie, what joy! She was the answer to their prayers."

"Losing the baby? You mean Sara had a miscarriage. I didn't know that." Callie's stomach knotted. David's words echoed in her mind, *"God punished me for my selfishness."* Is that what he'd meant?

"Oh, yes, such sadness that day."

"I can imagine their joy when Nattie arrived."

"Yes, but short-lived." Miriam's old grief resurfaced in her voice.

"Only four years, I understand."

Miriam lowered her eyes and a look of disapproval swept over her. "Yes, Sara was a lovely woman… David knew she had cancer when they married."

Callie nodded. "Yes, he told me." Obviously, Miriam had stronger feelings than she allowed herself to say.

The older woman regrouped. "But the four years with Nattie were wonderful years for them both. Right up to the end."

David's footsteps signaled his return. He came through the doorway with his hands outstretched. "Dinnertime. Have you ever heard sweeter words?"

Callie helped Miriam from the chair and whispered in her ear, "I always thought the sweetest words were 'I love you'—but you know men."

The two women chuckled, and David raised an eyebrow at them.

They lingered over a dinner of good food, reminiscences and laughter—until the telephone rang.

Agnes summoned Callie.

It was Ken. "It's Mom," he said. "She had another stroke. More serious this time."

"Oh, no, Ken. I've been meaning to visit, but I haven't. I feel so terrible. I'll leave right away."

"You can wait if you'd rather. I'll keep you posted. No sense in rushing here tonight."

Callie clenched the receiver. "No, I want to come now. I'll feel better. I won't sleep a wink if I stay here."

"Okay. Give me a call when you arrive. If I'm not home, I'll be here at the hospital."

"It'll take me three hours or so, Ken. It'll be late. Nine-thirty or ten, maybe. So don't worry."

"Callie, drive carefully."

She placed the receiver in the cradle and turned toward the dining room. She hated to put a damper on the visit.

As she entered the room, David rose. "Is something wrong?"

When the words stumbled from her tongue, she fought back her tears. "My mom's had a bad stroke. I have to go home tonight."

"Get ready, Callie, and I'll drive you," David said. "I don't want you to go alone."

"No, I need my car while I'm there. I'm fine, please. You go ahead and enjoy your visit. I'll run up and pack. As soon as I know something, I'll call."

When Callie arrived, she went directly to the hospital. Grace lay sleeping, connected to a machine that hummed and flashed numbers measuring her vital signs. Ken stepped from the bedside and wrapped his arm around Callie.

"She's about the same. She seems to be out of danger, but you can see the stroke has affected her this time."

Callie leaned over the bed and saw her mother's mouth twisted to one side. "So how much damage? Can they tell yet?"

"No. They'll run some tests in the morning. The doctor said her speech will be affected, at least for a while." He motioned to the chair. "Sit here for a few minutes. I'll take a walk and stretch my legs."

Callie nodded and eased herself into the chair. Pushing her arm through the bed's protective bars, she patted her mother's hand. Tears rose in her eyes, and she felt angry at herself for not having taken the time to come up for a visit.

She rested her head against the high chair back, and her mind filled with prayers. As her thoughts turned to God, she remembered her quandary—whether to stay in Bedford or come home. Maybe this was God's way of intervening. Perhaps her decision would be made for her.

Ken returned, bringing her a cup of coffee. They stayed by their mother's side until their eyelids drooped, then agreed that sitting there all night was foolish. Grace was out of danger, and they needed their rest.

Walking into the night air, Callie looked up into the sky, wondering if indeed God was directing her. If her mother needed her here, she would move back to Indianapolis. She had little choice.

In the morning, Callie called the nurse's station. Grace had rested during the night, and remained the same. Before leaving for the hospital, Callie called David and promised to phone later when she knew more.

By the time she reached the hospital, Ken had not arrived, and Callie stood alone in the doorway of Grace's room. Her mother's eyes were closed, but as Callie neared the bed, Grace opened them with a look of confusion.

"Everything's fine, Mom. You're in the hospital."

Grace opened her mouth, but the muddled words filled her eyes with fear.

"Don't try to talk, Mom. Just rest. The doctor will be in soon, and we'll know more then." Callie adjusted the chair and sat beside her. "If you need me, I'm right here."

She took her mother's hand and gave it a squeeze. And to her relief, Grace exerted a faint answering pressure. Callie clasped her mother's hand, thanking God.

Grace drifted into a fitful sleep, and Callie waited, speaking with nurses as they came in and out to check machines and the IVs, but they said little about her mother's condition.

Ken arrived, and two doctors followed on his heels, then conferred outside the room. Callie rose and met them in the hallway, while Ken stood beside Grace. When they entered, Ken kissed his mother's cheek and joined Callie.

"They suggested we go down for coffee while they examine her. He'll catch us later. Okay?" Callie asked.

Ken agreed, and they hurried to the cafeteria and moved quickly along the food line. Balancing her tray, Callie found a table near an outside window. They ate in silence, until Callie could gather her thoughts.

"I'm trying to decide what to do, Ken. Nattie has improved so much. She'll be starting school in a couple more weeks, and I suppose I should come back home and stay with Mom."

"I thought the last time I talked to you things were going well with you and David. Didn't you say a little romance was cooking?" Ken lifted his coffee cup and drank.

"That's another issue. I'm not sure if I should stay at the house under the circumstances. What will people say?" She leaned back against her chair, her fork poised in her hand. "But if I'm not there, we have little hope for a relationship, either. A two-hour drive each way doesn't encourage a budding romance."

"It's your call, sis."

"I know. But I'm so confused." She placed the fork on her plate and rubbed her temples.

"Well, don't try to make decisions now. Let's see what the doctors say. Mom may be in better shape than we think."

"I don't know if that really solves my dilemma. I still think I should come home." Her hands knotted on the table.

He placed his hand on hers. "Don't ruin your life, Callie. You overthink things sometimes. Try to be patient. Let's take one problem at a time. We're worried about Mom right now."

When they finished eating, they returned to Grace's room and met the doctor outside her door.

"So what do you think, Dr. Sanders?" Callie asked. "Any idea yet what happened?"

"Let me use layman's terms."

"Thanks. But I might mention I'm a nurse."

"Good. That could be helpful. Your mother apparently had an embolism. A blood clot broke loose from somewhere in her body, perhaps the heart. It often travels through the arterial stream into the cerebral cortex. When the clot lodges somewhere along its path, it can stop the flow of blood to the brain. In your mother's case, it did, and the stroke resulted."

Ken's face tensed. "So what happens now? Do you know how bad it is?"

"We'll run more tests, but we know she has some paralysis. She'll need physical therapy, and we'll begin that as soon as she's strong enough. Speech therapy will begin as soon as she's alert. Sometimes we have to wait two or three months before we see if she'll have permanent damage."

Ken's eyes widened. "Two or three months? You mean, we just have to sit and wait?"

"We'll do what we can." He looked at Callie. "And

you might be able to speed up the process if you're willing to handle additional physical therapy at home."

Helping with Mom's treatment meant staying in Indianapolis. Nattie's face rose in Callie's mind, and a lonely feeling engulfed her.

"Good. Right now, your mother has IVs, but later she'll be on a variety of medications. An anticoagulant to keep her blood from clotting, and a vasodilator to keep the arteries open. If she has a narrowing or blockage in the carotid artery, she'll need surgery. Right now, your guess is as good as mine. The test will answer a lot of questions."

Ken glanced at Callie.

She shrugged. "We'll wait, then, until you have more information."

The doctor nodded. "You're welcome to visit for a while, but I suggest you let your mother rest as much as possible. Later today, we'll run the tests. Why not stay for a few more minutes, and then go on home? Come back this evening, if you like, and by tomorrow we should have some answers."

Ken nodded. "How about it, Callie?"

She heaved a sigh. "Not much we can do now, I suppose." She looked at the physician. "And we should follow doctor's orders."

With a gentle grin, the doctor rested his hand on her arm. "I only hope your mother's as good at following orders as you are."

According to the test reports, Grace's prognosis gave Callie hope. The week passed during which she was scheduled for daily therapy. Another week or so in the hospital, Dr. Sanders said, and her mother could go home.

The news still lay unsettled in Callie's mind. She sat in her mother's house, staring at the telephone. She had promised to call David, but she had delayed for a full week, wanting to clarify her decision.

David had sent flowers to Grace at the hospital, and another lovely bouquet sat on a nearby table. The brilliant colors should have brightened Callie's evening, but they didn't. Her thoughts were too muddled. She missed David and Nattie. But when Grace was released, she'd need help. Callie knew she had to provide it.

She raised the receiver and punched in the numbers. David's voice echoed across the line.

"How are you two?" she asked.

"We miss you. How are things there?"

"Better. Mom started therapy, and I'm happy to say, she's doing pretty well. Her speech is slurred, but I can understand her. And she forgets words once in a while."

David chuckled. "I do that without a stroke. How about movement?"

"She can't walk by herself yet. But things are promising. It'll take time. She'll have to continue therapy when she gets home."

He sighed. "So that means…?"

"So that means, I'll be coming to Bedford for my things."

Silence.

David finally spoke. "Then you'll go back for a while. I understand. Your mother needs you."

Callie closed her eyes to catch the tears that formed. "Not for a while, David. I'm coming back for good."

Chapter Nineteen

David hovered in her doorway, the blood in his veins as frozen as if he were an ice sculpture. Callie stood at the closet, packing. His wonderful new life was melting away; where his hopes and dreams had been, he saw only empty space.

"Callie, can't you listen to reason?"

"You mean *your reason,* David, not mine."

He strode across the room to her side. "I know your mother needs you now, but not forever. Please, we can't manage here without you, and I don't mean taking care of Nattie. We both love you. You're part of our lives."

She swung to face him. "Please, don't make this harder than it is. I love you, too, David, but we're both dealing with issues from the past. I'm not sure this relationship can go anywhere. Especially now, since someone made me think." Her eyes closed for a heartbeat. "I can't ruin your reputation or mine."

"What are you talking about? 'Ruin your reputation or mine'? That doesn't make sense."

"Yes, it does. Nat's fine now. She doesn't need me. So what purpose do I have living here? I'm a paid...what?

You tell me." She grasped his arms. "I'm a pretty expensive babysitter, wouldn't you say?"

Tears spilled from her eyes and ran down her cheeks.

"Oh, Callie, what do you think you are—a kept woman?" David slid his arms around her back. "God knows that we need you here. I don't care what others might say. And why would they? Who would say anything?"

Callie shook her head without answering.

"Everyone knows about Nattie's problems. For you to walk in and out of our lives when you mean so much to her is unthinkable. She lost her mother, and now you—someone she's grown to love. Who would put such crazy thoughts in your head?"

David's mind swam. *Pastor John? Agnes?* None of it made sense. "You're a Christian. You serve the church. No one would think wrong of you for being here. And what about Nattie?"

"But she's well, David. She doesn't *need* me anymore."

He dropped his arms to his sides and spun away. "No? You think she doesn't need you. Do you know where she is right now?" He whirled around to face her. "She's crying in her room. Nattie loves you. When you came, I didn't think about her loving you. All I thought was that I needed someone to make her better. I never thought I would hurt her."

Callie covered her face with her hands, and remorse spilled over him for the sorrow he had created by his words. "I'm not trying to make you feel guilty. I'm only trying to help you understand how much we love you."

"I'm sorry, David. I've given this a lot of thought. I pray I'm doing the right thing. If I'm wrong, I hope God will help me make it right. That's all I can say. I spent my life bearing a secret anger toward my parents. My mom is the only parent I have left to whom I can make retribution for my feelings. I have to do this."

David closed his eyes and filled his lungs with air. Why did she feel anger toward her parents? He didn't understand her cryptic comment. "I know you want to be with your mother, Callie. And Indianapolis is only two hours away. We'll work things out. Remember our 'deal' a while ago? We agreed to pray for each other. Like Jesus said, 'Where two or three are gathered in my name, I am with them.' We'll leave it in God's hands."

He moved to her side again and held her close. Her heart pounded against his chest, answering his own thudding rhythm. "I love you, Callie." He tilted her face to his. "I have faith in us." His lips touched hers lightly, then he backed away and left, knowing his life would soon be as lonely as the room she was vacating.

Callie struggled to see the road through her tears on her return to Indianapolis. Signing adoption papers had been the hardest thing she'd ever done. Saying good-bye to Nattie was the second. And saying goodbye to David… Callie had no words for the way she felt. She loved them both, but too many things stood in their way. Mary Beth's words hammered in her mind. David still struggled with Sara's death, and Callie had yet to heal from the rape and the adoption. Like someone who carries baskets of bricks up a hill, she carried the weight of Jim McKee's sin on her shoulders.

So often when she looked at Nattie, she imagined her own child. Did her daughter have a halo of blond curls? Was she loved? Was she learning about Jesus? Callie couldn't bear to think the worst. She longed to know—her heart ached. And all the love she had denied herself for years had risen like a wonderful gift and showered down on Nattie. And again Callie was letting a child go. Callie longed for a release. Would telling David about her own child help to heal the wounds? Now she would never know.

Since the telephone call, her thoughts had been filled with worry about her mother. But as she left Bedford, her talk with Miriam drifted into her mind. David hadn't told her Sara had miscarried. Yet he'd told her about wanting the abortion. Callie's head spun with disjointed bits of information, spilled out like pieces of one of Nattie's puzzles. Why didn't David feel God's forgiveness when Nattie was born? Why did he cling to his anger? God had given him a second chance—Nattie.

Finally, she turned her concerns to her present problem—Grace. Would Mom listen to her—as her nurse, and not as her daughter? What might that do to their relationship, which she had hoped to heal? Her head ached with wondering.

The next days flew past with preparations for Grace's return: a hospital bed, therapy training, treatment scheduling, grocery shopping. Yet keeping busy didn't help Callie feel less sad or lonely.

David persisted. He phoned, sent flowers and wrote notes on Missing You cards, but Callie clung to her decision. She believed God's hand had guided her.

Grace's day of homecoming arrived, and Callie stood beside her hospital bed packing her belongings. "Anxious to get home, Mom?"

Grace nodded as she had begun to do, avoiding her distorted voice.

"Talk, Mom. No head-nods. The more you talk, the quicker you'll have your old voice back."

Grace clamped her lips together like a disobedient child.

"Very adult of you, Mom." Callie shook her head in frustration. She had watched hospital films and talked to the psychologist for tips on helping Grace and being supportive. She already felt like a failure.

As she finished packing, Dr. Sanders appeared at the doorway. "So today's the big day? How are you feeling?"

Grace shrugged, then struggled to get out a thick-sounding "Fine."

"Good. I have your prescriptions written out for you. And you're a lucky woman to have a daughter who's a nurse."

"I'm not sure that will go over too well," Callie said. "She's going to resent me."

Dr. Sanders patted Callie's hand. "She'll be fine." He turned to Grace. "Now, you'll listen to your daughter, right? She's trained to help you, and you'll have to mind her. If not, you'll end up back here. I know you don't want that."

Grace's eyes widened, but she kept her lips pressed together.

Dr. Sanders pointed to her mouth. "And you have to speak, Grace. You'll never talk if you don't practice."

He turned to Callie. "We'll send the speech therapist out three times a week, and then count on you to do the rest."

"That's fine. I've had instructions, and I can handle the therapy—if she'll listen." She directed her last words to Grace.

He spoke for a moment with Grace, and when he left, Callie gathered up the overnight bag and parcels and headed to her car.

Grace was wheeled outside and eased into the car. The trip home was silent, except for Callie's own running monologue. And she breathed a relieved sigh when Ken's car pulled into the driveway behind them.

"Glad you're here," she said, sliding from the car. She closed her door. "I didn't know if I could get Mom in alone. Besides, I need a little moral support."

"You look beat already," Ken said, standing at the trunk, as they unloaded the wheelchair.

She looked at him, shaking her head. "I'm afraid this'll be the undoing of Mother and me. I hoped, coming home, we could smooth out our differences, but she's being terribly belligerent. Like a child."

Ken rolled his eyes. "We'll just have to be patient. She'll come around."

She rested her hand on his shoulder. "And don't forget, I'll need a break once in a while. I can't do this alone or I'll end up in a hospital…and it won't be *medical* hospital."

Ken slammed the trunk. "No one would ever notice."

"Thanks." She poked his arm.

He rolled the wheelchair to the car door, and with his strong arms settled Grace into the seat. Together, they hoisted Grace up the porch stairs into the house and into the hospital bed, as the patient grunted and pointed.

Hands on her hips, Callie stood beside them. "Make her talk, Ken." She scowled at her mother. "We'll have no grunting or pointing in this house."

Grace glowered back as much as her face would allow, and Callie covered a snicker. Her heart broke for her mother, but she knew she'd better learn to laugh if they were to survive.

When Grace was settled, Callie invited Ken into the kitchen for a sandwich. He stretched his legs in front of him, twiddling his thumbs, as Callie buttered the bread. "Do you think you can do this?" he asked.

"Oh, they say God never gives us more than we can handle." She turned to face him. "But I think He's pushing it this time."

Ken threw his head back and laughed. "I was thinking the same thing. Hang in there, and I'll do what I can to help."

"Great, but I won't hold my breath."

David sent two more bouquets the following week—one for her, and the other for Grace. Callie missed him more than she could say. The situation hadn't eased. Grace fought her at every turn, and her nerves pulsed like wired dynamite.

One day, Callie was sitting in the kitchen, nibbling a sandwich that she could barely swallow, when the telephone rang. When she heard David's voice, her hand shook. She longed to tell him how awful things were, but instead she inquired about him, avoiding what was in her heart.

Finally she asked, "How's Nat?"

"Lonesome." A heavy silence hung on the line. "So am I, Callie. Nothing seems worth much anymore."

She refused to respond. She'd say far more than was safe to admit. "How's Nat's school? Is she doing okay?"

She waited. A chill ruffled through her. "Is something wrong, David?"

"I don't want to burden you. You have enough problems."

She stiffened. "Don't leave me hanging, David. What's wrong?" Her voice sounded strained to her ears. "I'm sorry, David, but you've upset me. Is something wrong with Nattie?"

"She's…beginning to withdraw again. Not like before, but she's not herself. I know she misses you. It'll pass with time. Her teacher was concerned, but I explained that…well, I didn't want to get into a lengthy discussion. I said her mother had died recently. I figured that would explain it."

If she'd felt stress before, she felt a thousand times worse hearing his words. "I don't know what to say. Even if I wanted to come back, I can't. Mom needs too much right now, and Ken works full time. He gives me a break once in a while, but I'm it, David. I'm the caregiver here."

He sighed. "I know. I know. I'm trying to think of something."

When she hung up, she covered her face and wept. She felt pity for everyone: Grace, David, Nattie and herself. When her tears ended, she splashed water on her eyes and planted a smile on her lips. Her wristwatch signaled Grace's therapy—and if Callie didn't smile, she'd scream.

"Look at you, Mom," Ken said, as Grace shuffled her feet across the floor while leaning heavily on her walker.

A twisted grin covered Grace's face; she looked as pleased as a toddler learning to take her first steps.

Callie stood nearby, watchful for any problems, but

Grace moved steadily along. "Mom's worked hard," she said to Ken. "It makes it worthwhile, doesn't it, Mom? At least, you can get up and move around a little."

Grace grunted a "yes." Her speech had improved, too, turning their hope to reality.

Callie kept her eyes focused on Grace. "See if you can make it to the living room, Mom. You can sit in there for a change."

Grace heaved her shoulders upward as she moved the walker. When she was seated, Callie made a pot of tea and brought out some freshly baked cookies for a celebration. As difficult as it had been, she could see that Grace was mending.

As they talked, the telephone rang, and Callie left the living room to answer it in the kitchen. Something inside her told her the caller was David.

"Don't say a word, Callie, but Nattie and I are coming to Indianapolis to see you."

"Please, David, no. I'm still miserable. I don't think I could bear to see you...and not Nattie. I'll cry for sure."

"Good. Tears soften the heart, Callie, my love. You might as well give up. I'm coming. Nattie will be terribly disappointed if I tell her you don't want us to come."

"Oh, David. Don't say that. Come, then. I'll be here...forever."

"Maybe not. I think I have a solution."

Chapter Twenty

Callie's heart did cartwheels when she saw Nattie through the window. The child darted up the porch before David could catch her. Callie flung open the door and knelt to embrace her; Nattie flew into her arms and buried her face in Callie's neck.

Her small, muffled voice sounded on Callie's cheek. "I miss you."

"I miss you, too, Nat. Terribly." Callie raised her eyes toward David. "I miss all of you."

"Aren't you coming home?" Nattie asked.

The word *home* tore through her. Bedford was more home to her than her mother's house. The answer caught in her throat. She swallowed, and avoided a direct answer. "My mom is sick right now, Nat, and I have to take care of her."

Nattie tilted her head back and searched Callie's face. "Is she going to die?"

"No, she's getting better. But you know what? She won't talk much at all. Do you remember someone who didn't want to talk much a while ago?"

Nattie hung her head shyly and nodded. But her head popped up with her next words. "Is your mommy sad?"

Callie grinned. "No, not sad." She glanced up at David. "More like 'mad.' As mad as a wet hen, in fact."

Nattie giggled at the old saying.

"Well, let's not stand in the doorway. Come in." Callie rose, took Nattie by the hand, and moved so David could enter.

He stepped inside and slipped his arm cautiously around her waist, as Nattie eyed them. "How are you?"

Callie lowered her eyes. "Miserable. And you?"

"Terribly miserable."

Nattie pushed her shoulders forward, squeezing her hands between her knees, and chuckled. "I'm miserable, too."

Her words made them smile. Callie gave her another hug.

"Well, that's good, then. We're all miserable together." She gestured them into the living room. "Have you eaten? Anyone starving?"

"No, we had some breakfast on the way."

"We stopped at Burger Boy," Nattie added.

"Burger Boy, huh?" Callie gave David a disapproving look.

He wiggled his eyebrows. "They have biscuit breakfasts."

"Ah. Well, then, how about something to drink and maybe a cookie or two?"

They agreed, and while they waited in the living room, Callie gathered the drinks and cookies, taking deep breaths to control her wavering emotions. She loved them both, and seeing them today, though wonderful, felt painful, as well.

"Here we go," she said, carrying a tray into the living room and putting the cookies closest to Nattie.

Sinking into a chair, Callie studied David's face. His usual bright, teasing eyes looked shadowed. She gazed at Nattie, longing to speak privately to David. Then an idea struck.

"David, would you and Nat like to say hello to Mom?"

"Sure, if she's up to it."

"Nat, you've never met my mother. I might have a book around here somewhere, and you could show her the pictures and tell her a story. Would you like that? She gets pretty lonely in her room."

Nattie nodded, and Callie hurried to her room. On her bookshelf, she'd kept some favorite children's books. She shuffled through them and located a book of well-known tales and stories illustrated with colorful pictures. Before she returned to the living room, she popped into Grace's room to announce visitors, then left without giving Grace a chance to say no.

In the living room, she handed Nattie the book. "When I was young, this book was one of my favorites."

As soon as Nattie held the book, she flipped through the pages. "I know this story, and this one," she said.

"Good, then let's go in to see my mom."

She took Nattie by the hand, with David following, and headed down the hallway. Grace was staring at the doorway as they entered, looking stressed, probably over Callie's announcement. But when her gaze lit upon Nattie, her face softened. Only the slight tug of paralysis distorted her usual expression.

"Mom, here's David. And Nattie. You've never met her."

David stepped forward, extending his hand. "It's good to see you, Grace. Callie says you're doing great. A little more time, and you'll be back to normal, huh?"

"Oh, I don't know," Grace said, her speech thick and halting.

Nattie stared at Grace and then glanced at Callie. "I thought your mommy didn't talk."

Callie snickered. "Maybe she just doesn't talk to *me,* Nattie." She peered at Grace. Her mother averted her eyes. Instead, she watched Nattie.

"When I was younger, I didn't want to talk," Nattie said, leaning her folded arms on Grace's bed.

"No?" Grace said, not taking her eyes from the child.

"I was too sad."

"Happy now?" Grace laid her hand on Nattie's arms.

"Uh-huh, except Callie went away to take care of you." Nattie glanced at Callie over her shoulder. "I miss her."

Grace's skewed face formed an angled smile. "You do, huh?"

"Yep." Nattie leaned forward and whispered at Grace. "But we came for a visit to tell her to come home."

Grace raised her eyes toward Callie. "Home?" She reached out and drew her hand over Nattie's blond hair, then nodded. "Yes, I suppose that is her home."

Tears burned behind Callie's eyes, and she quickly changed the topic. "Mom, Nattie wants to show you a picture book. You want to get up in a chair, or would you rather have her up there on the bed with you?"

Grace patted the coverlet beside her, and David boosted the child to the edge of the bed.

"You can get up for lunch, okay? We'll be in the

other room for a few minutes. Can you get down by yourself, Nat?"

"I think so." She stared down at the floor.

"If not, give a call, and I'll come running," David said, patting her cheek with his fingers.

Callie and David walked out of the room, leaving Nattie to entertain Grace.

"I think Nat could work wonders with Mother. I haven't seen her so talkative since the stroke. She buttons up when I'm the one she has to talk to."

"But you're the nurse. No one likes nurses. They're too mean, and they make you take medicine and do things you don't want to do."

She returned his tease, rolling her eyes. "Thanks."

"And they always say, 'It's time to take *our* bath.' Have you ever seen a nurse—other than yourself, that is—take a bath?"

She listened to David's chatter, but inside, her stomach dipped on a roller-coaster ride. What would happen now that they were alone? David answered her question. He slid his arm around her waist, drawing her against him. His hand ran up her arm to her face, and he touched her cheek, drawing his fingers along her heating skin to trace her lips.

Her knees wanted to buckle beneath her, and a sensation, beginning as a tingle, grew to an uncontrollable tremor, as his face neared hers. She thought of pulling away, but her desire overpowered her intentions. She met his lips with hers, eagerly savoring the sweetness, and a moan escaped his throat, sending a deepening shudder through her body as her own sigh joined his.

Out of breath, she eased away and gazed into his

heavy-lidded eyes. "David, you can't kiss me like this. I can't handle it."

"Good. Let *me* handle things. I refuse to leave this house without knowing you'll come back to us."

"How can I do that? Tell me." She raised her voice overwhelmed by a sense of futility. She longed to be with them in Bedford. No matter what others thought, she loved them and belonged with them.

"Let's sit, and I'll tell you how. I've figured it out. Come." He took her hand and guided her into the living room, and together they sank onto the sofa in each other's arms.

Her first thought was Nattie. What if she saw David's arms around her? "What if Nattie see us?"

"I told her I love you, Callie. And guess what she said."

She could only shake her head.

"She loves you, too. That was her response. And she needs you. She's been so quiet. But as soon as she saw you today, she opened again. Look at her with Grace. She's good for Grace, too."

Callie couldn't deny that. Grace hadn't been so receptive to anyone. Maybe a child's exuberance would bring her out of her self-pitying mode. She thought of her own situation. Nattie had worked a miracle, making her a whole person again.

"So," Callie asked. "What's your plan?"

"Bring your mother to Bedford."

"What?" She scanned his eager face. "I can't do that."

"Why not? Bring her to the house. We have tons of room."

"But it doesn't make sense…does it?"

"It makes all the sense in the world. I've already made arrangements. We'll set the library up as her room. She'll have an easy chair, television, books if she likes to read. There's a telephone there. A bathroom nearby."

"You're overwhelming me." She shook her head in confusion.

"I realized there's no shower on the first floor, except in Agnes's quarters. She said, 'Great, no problem.' So that's solved."

"What about her doctors and medication?"

"Once she's able to get around more, you can bring Grace here for her appointments. And her prescriptions can be filled in Bedford or here. That's not a problem."

Callie stared at him, dazed. "You've thought of everything, I take it."

"Please, don't get upset with me."

"I'm not upset, really. I'm stunned, David. I made a decision that staying in Bedford was the wrong thing to do, and now you're organizing and arranging my life."

"I'm sorry. That was selfish of me to assume that—"

"No, no, I'm not angry. I love you for it, because it means you love me. But I need to think things through."

"I understand, and you'll want to wait until the doctor says it's okay for Grace to travel. But, Callie, we can handle things if we know you're coming home."

"Home?" she said.

"Yes, home." He turned her face to his, and their lips met.

Past fears of intimacy rose inside her, and she tensed for a flickering moment. Then, as quickly, she relaxed her shoulders. With David, she experienced what God meant by loving…giving herself to a special someone and feeling complete.

With his kiss still warm on her lips, Callie rested her head against his shoulder. "David, I can't do anything without Mom's approval. I don't know if she'll be willing to come to Bedford."

"I've prayed." He ran his hand across the back of his neck. "I've prayed, and I believe God heard my prayers. I think Grace will come, Callie. Give her time, but I think she'll come."

She closed her eyes, adding her prayer to David's. Life was nothing without him and Nattie. That's where she belonged. But in all the confusion, she had yet to accomplish what she had set out to do: resolve the hurt that affected her relationship with Grace. She had to forgive and be forgiven.

Forgiving and being forgiven. Such complicated concepts.

She hadn't been totally honest with David, either. Would he forgive her when he learned about her child and the adoption? If only she knew her daughter was happy, maybe she could forgive herself.

But God had given her another child: Nattie. Was this her second chance to make things right?

Chapter Twenty-One

David checked the library for the fifth time. The room looked comfortable. Bed, bedside table, small dresser, all hauled down from an upstairs bedroom. He'd added a television set, and today, a bouquet of fresh flowers had been delivered. He wanted Grace to feel welcome.

The move had been difficult. Callie had been met with resistance from her mother, but finally, Grace had a change of heart. He didn't question the cause, but Callie said it followed on the footsteps of Nattie's second visit to Indianapolis. Nattie had latched onto Grace as she had the first time and had remained at her side. One evening, they sat together in the living room. As David and Callie talked, they grinned, overhearing Grace's and Nattie's conversation from the sofa.

"Tell me about school," Grace said, her speech clearer than it had been on their first visit.

Nattie tilted her head and thought. "Well, the teacher said I'm a good reader for first grade. And I can print my name and some other words..." She paused and raced across the room to Callie. "Do you have paper and a pencil? I want to show your mommy how I can print."

"Sure, I do," Callie said, and pulled a pad of paper and pencil from a lamp table drawer. "Here, you go."

Nattie returned to Grace, nestled at her side and proceeded to demonstrate her printing talents. David listened to Grace's encouraging comments and then returned to his own conversation.

"Any progress with Grace?" David asked in a near whisper, knowing his plans for them to move to Bedford had not set well.

"She's stubborn, David. I suppose I understand. But I haven't given up."

"She seems to be doing well."

"She is. She's using her own bed now, and she walks with the cane, though one leg still isn't cooperating totally."

"I'd hoped once she got around a little on her own, she might think of Bedford as a vacation," he said.

Callie rolled her eyes. "There's where you made your second mistake. Mom isn't crazy about vacations. She's a homebody."

He glanced at Grace and Nattie, the weight of hopelessness on his chest. His life had been empty and futureless without Callie. Though Nattie had withdrawn after she left, their visit two weeks earlier had seemed to work a miracle. All he could think about was his prayer that Callie would come back to Bedford.

Muddled in his thoughts, Nattie's words pulled him back to the present.

"Could you be my grandma?" she asked, looking into Grace's attentive eyes.

David's heart kicked into second gear. He glanced at Callie and saw that she had heard. He waited for Grace's response, his heartbeat suspended.

She lifted her gnarled hand and patted Nattie's leg, which was snuggled close to her own. "I'd like that, Nattie. You can call me Grandma Grace." Her eyes hadn't shifted from the child's face.

"Could I just call you Grandma?"

Grace's face twisted to a gentle smile. "Whatever makes you happy, child."

"Good," Nattie said, and lifted herself to kiss Grace's cheek.

David's heart melted at the sight, and when he turned to Callie, she was wiping tears from her eyes.

"Sentimental, huh?" she asked.

"Just plain beautiful," David responded.

That day had replayed itself over in his mind for the past two weeks. A week after their last visit, Callie had called to say Grace was becoming more receptive to a trip to Bedford. Today, his dream would become a reality.

Now, glancing out the window once again, David grinned, as he saw Nattie gallop through the autumn leaves gathered in mounds under the elms. She was as anxious as he.

Tired of waiting inside, David tossed on his windbreaker and joined Nattie in the yard. Seeing him, she giggled and filled her arms with leaves, tossing them into the air. As the burnished leaves settled to earth, Callie's car came up the winding driveway. Nattie let out a squeal and ran toward him. Together, they followed the car until it stopped in front of the wide porch.

"Grandma. Callie," Nattie called, racing to the car door.

Callie climbed out and gave Nattie a hug. David opened the passenger door and helped Grace from the car.

He longed to take Callie in his arms, but Grace leaned

heavily on him, so he controlled himself. Later, when they were alone, he could welcome her as he longed to do. He eased Grace up the wide steps and across the porch. Agnes greeted them at the door and held it open so Grace had easy access.

"My, now this is what I call a foyer," Grace said, looking wide-eyed around the vast entrance. "Callie didn't quite prepare me for something this elegant."

Nattie jigged around her, encouraging her to follow. "Look, Grandma, here's your bedroom. It's the lib'ary, but now it's your room."

"David didn't want you to climb the stairs," Callie explained. "He has extra bedrooms upstairs. When you're up to it, we can move your things up there, if you'd like."

Grace concentrated on her steps, but shifted her focus for a moment from the floor to Callie's face. "When I can climb those steps, I'll be ready to go back home." She grinned at David. "And you'll probably be ready to kick me out."

Nattie spun around, hearing her words. "We won't kick you out, Grandma. You can stay with me forever."

With a knowing eye, she glanced at Nattie. "Thank you, child. That's the sweetest thing I've ever heard."

Callie leaned close to David's ear. "That's because she doesn't listen to me. Believe it or not, I have said some pretty sweet things."

David winked at her. "I'm sure you have."

Grace raised her head and looked at the two of them. "I may have had a stroke, but I'm not deaf. So quit talking about me."

Nattie grasped her hand. "We have to be nice to Grandma. She's sick."

David and Callie burst into laughter, with Grace's snicker not far behind. Nattie looked at the three of them, then tucked her hands between her knees and joined them with her own giggle.

Callie hung up the telephone and turned to David. "I gather you told Pastor John I was coming back."

He nodded. "Why? Was it supposed to be a secret?"

"No, but he just called to ask me to sing on Sunday. And he told me about the organ, David. I'm really pleased."

"Give thanks to God, not me. He brought me to my senses."

"What do you mean?"

David took her hands in his and kissed them. "My anger was focused in the wrong direction. I've been angry at God for taking Sara and for Nat's problems, instead of being angry at myself. We knew Sara had cancer, but I expected God to work a miracle."

She nodded. "We can't expect miracles."

"No, we can't expect anything, but we need to have faith. It's the faith that works the miracles. And God hasn't let me down, even when I was being bullheaded. I wanted instant gratification. But sometimes, we have to do a bit of soul-searching before we can appreciate God's will."

"So after some soul-searching, you decided to donate to the organ-repair fund."

"Paid for the repair. I can afford it, and the congregation enjoys the organ music as much as I do."

"It's nice for everyone. I'm glad, David. Oh, and Pastor John mentioned the new organist…with much enthusiasm, I might add." She suspected John valued the organist for more than her musical contributions on Sunday mornings.

"Wait until you see her. She's cute and single. And the right age."

Teasing, Callie arched an eyebrow. "The right age for whom?"

"For Pastor John." He caressed her cheek with the back of his fingers. "*Whom* else?" He gave her a wink.

"Well, I'm glad." She sat next to him on the sofa. "She doesn't happen to have a brother Mary Beth's age, does she?"

"Jealous, are you?" He clasped her hand.

"Should I be?"

"No, but I forgot to tell you what happened while you were gone."

Callie raised both eyebrows this time. "Ah, true confessions?" She curled her legs beneath her and faced him.

"Not quite." His words were accompanied by a chuckle. "But this is about Mary Beth."

Callie's eyes glinted in jest.

"And?"

"A day or two after you left, she called, inviting me to dinner."

"And you accepted, I'm sure."

"Anticipating her motive, yes. I wanted to clear up the issue once and for all…and for no other reason."

"I'm certain." Callie batted her eyelashes at him. David grinned.

"Anyway, to get back to the subject—as I intended—"

"Ah, as you intended."

"Yes, as I intended, she let me know she was interested in making my lonely life less lonely."

"Beautifully said."

"Thank you."

Callie draped an arm around his neck. "And what did you say to that?"

"I thanked her graciously, but declined her offer." He filled his lungs. "Actually, I felt terrible for her. She was embarrassed and flustered. She wasn't quite as blunt as I made her out to be, but she did let me know how she felt."

"I hope you were nice when you rejected her."

"As nice as a rejection can be. I said I was in love with you—but that if I weren't, she'd be a likely second." He tilted his head, giving her a coy look.

"Now that's a rejection."

"I didn't really add the last part." He chucked her beneath the chin. "And I told her I planned to do all I could to bring you back to Bedford."

"You did? Really?"

"I did. She handled it quite well, I'd say."

"No weeping or gnashing of teeth?"

"Only a little."

"Good. She can probably handle it better than I can. With weeping, I'm skilled, but gnashing…?" She gave him a silly grin.

After church on Sunday morning, Callie slipped into her casual clothes and went outside. More leaves had fallen overnight, and winter's chill had put a coating of hoarfrost on everything. She drew in a deep breath of frigid air.

In less than a month Thanksgiving would arrive, then Christmas. On Christmas Day her child would be seven, and little more than a month later, Nat would celebrate her seventh birthday. All the love Callie had kept bundled inside for her own child, she lavished on Nattie. Still, she clung to her secret. And until she had the courage to tell David and Grace, the secret was a barrier between them.

Without question, Nattie had wrought a change in her mother. Grace's critical martyrdom had faded, and in its place, she seemed to have found a joy in living. She would have made Callie's child a wonderful grandmother, after all.

No wedding had been mentioned, but Callie was sure marriage was David's intention. They had settled, without words, into a warm, committed relationship.

But marriage was built on honesty. She wanted to start the new year with the truth. And the longer she waited, the more difficult it would become. The last time she'd set a deadline for herself, she had sensed that God worked to bring it about sooner. Now, she set a second deadline. She would summon her courage, and by the first of January she would tell David about her baby.

Chapter Twenty-Two

Callie and Grace sat in the parlor, a fire glowing in the fireplace. Thanksgiving was still a week away, but the first snow had fallen early and muted the world outside. With David at work and Nattie in school, the house was also quiet.

Callie studied her mother, seated cozily in front of the fire reading a magazine. A year earlier, she would never have believed that her feelings for Grace would change so radically, but they had. And with a renewed fondness welling inside her, she knew the right moment had arrived.

"Mom, could we talk?"

Grace glanced up from the magazine, a look of tenderness etching her face. "I've been wanting to talk to you, too."

"You have?" For the first time in years, she saw her mother with clearer eyes. Grace had always loved her, but her love had seemed doled out in controlled portions, as if she were afraid she might give it all away at one time and have nothing left. Today she seemed different.

Grace tossed the magazine to the floor and leaned back in the chair. "I didn't want to come here at first. You knew that, of course. And I suppose you saw what changed my mind. That wonderful child. I can understand why you wanted to come back here, Callie, not only because of David, but for Nattie."

"I know. She stole my heart."

"And I think David has, as well. He's a loving man. Kind and generous. You couldn't find a better husband." She peered into Callie's eyes. "I pray that's what the two of you have in mind."

"I pray so, too, Mom. And I'm glad you like him."

"I do. But God gave both of us a gift in Nattie. I look at her, Callie, and all I can think is somewhere in this world there's another little girl just like her. Nattie's so much like you, Callie." Her lips trembled, and she paused, her voice hindered by emotion. "I can imagine what your own little girl is like right now."

Tears stung Callie's eyes. "That's what I want to talk about, Mom. Part is a confession—a terrible secret I kept from you for so many years. Part is to help you understand my hurt and anger toward you and Dad."

"What are you talking about?" Grace's face paled, her eyes narrowed.

"I kept things hidden from you, and I've done the same with David. He doesn't know that I had a child. But I'm going to tell him. He and Sara wanted a child so badly that they took life-threatening chances to have a baby. Sara couldn't continue her radiation or chemotherapy without harming the baby, and without it, she endangered her own life. How could I tell him I had one that I gave away?"

"Oh, Callie, that was a whole different matter. You can't compare the two situations."

"But I can. What would he think of me? I've worried that I'll disillusion him. He expects more of me. I always thought that you and Daddy felt that way, and I couldn't endure that rejection again from someone else I love so much."

Grace threw her hand to her mouth, and her eyes brimmed with tears. "Not rejection, Callie. Your dad and I were so hurt for you. We were irritated that you protected the young man. That's the part that upset us. And naturally, we were disappointed."

"And that's the part that hurt me so much, Mom."

"We had such dreams for you—with all your talents and gifts from God. And your refusal to sing. We felt you were punishing us because we forced the adoption. But we always loved you and thought we were doing the right thing about the baby."

"I know. And my anger at you wasn't fair. Because I never told you the whole story."

Grace's body stiffened. "The whole story?"

"I couldn't tell you the truth, because I knew both of you would be crushed. And to be honest, I wondered if you'd believe me, because I felt guilty thinking I might be partly to blame for what happened." Pressure pushed against her chest and constricted her throat.

"Callie, you're talking in circles. Please, tell me what you mean. You're scaring me."

Strangling on the words, Callie whispered, "The baby's father wasn't a college boy, Mother."

"Not a—" She faltered and clung to the chair. "Then, who?"

"I was raped." The word spilled out of her along

with a torrent of blinding tears. Her body shook with the knotted, bitter hurt that had bound her for so many years. Telling David had been difficult, but telling her mother was devastating.

Grace rose with more speed than Callie could have imagined possible, and made her way to the sofa. She wrapped her arms around Callie and held her with every bit of strength she had. She asked no questions, but she held her daughter with the love only a mother could have for her child.

When Callie had regained control, she told Grace the story, in all its horror. Her mother listened, stroking and calming her until the awful truth was out. A ragged sigh raked through her shaking body.

Tears rolled down Grace's cheeks. No words were needed—Callie understood her mother's grief as well as she knew her own. They talked through the afternoon in a way they had never talked before. Their tears, like a cleansing flood, purified them, purged their past hurt and anger, and united them in love.

Ken joined them for Thanksgiving, and Grace had been content until then. But as Christmas approached, she urged Callie to take her home.

"Look how well I'm doing. My bedroom's upstairs now. I'm getting around. The cane is only a prop—see?" She lifted the cane and took a few steps. "I miss my house. And my things."

"That's why I don't have things, Mom. I've learned to live everywhere without a bunch of trappings."

"That's because all your trappings are with my things—at the house."

She chuckled at the truth. "I'll tell you what, Mom.

Christmas is less than three weeks away. Why not stay here through the holidays, and then we'll take you home. You'll have nearly three weeks to get stronger."

"No sense in spending Christmas alone, is there?" David asked.

Grace eyed them both. "You promise? If I shut my mouth, you'll take me home after the holidays?"

"Promise," Callie said. "And think of what a nice Christmas you'll have this year with Nattie around. Christmas is always special with children."

Grace's face softened. "It has been a long time, hasn't it. You were my last baby."

David folded the paper and dropped it beside the chair. "And she's sure not a baby anymore." He winked at Grace.

"Me?" Nattie asked from the doorway, her brow puckered. "I'm not a baby anymore."

David opened his arms to her. "You sure aren't, Nat. But no, we were talking about Callie. She's no baby, either."

Nattie laughed. "I wish we had a baby."

Callie looked from Nattie to David, wondering what his response would be.

"First, we need a husband and wife. Then babies can come."

Nattie glanced at Callie. "You can marry Callie, Daddy. Then you'll be a husband and wife."

David gave her a giant hug. "My girl. She's making all the arrangements." His amused eyes sought Callie's. "We'll have to see about that, won't we?"

"Okay," Nattie said, and dropped the matter without another comment.

But Callie's heart pounded. Marriage seemed the

next step for them, but the words were yet to be spoken. And Callie couldn't answer yes—not yet.

"I have an idea," Callie said.

Three pairs of eyes turned toward her. Surprise lit Grace's face. Callie grinned to herself—did Grace think Callie was about to propose? "Let's go out and buy a Christmas tree."

"Goody," Nattie said, jumping in place at David's side. Her enthusiasm was contagious.

"Before this child knocks me out with her exuberance, I suppose we ought to do just that. A Christmas tree, it is," David said.

For Callie, many years had passed since she'd decorated a house. But this year, she joined in the excitement. The tree stood in the family parlor, covered in lights and bulbs. The house smelled of ginger and vanilla, and every day Callie and Nattie tiptoed into the kitchen to snatch a cookie or two from Agnes's baking.

Four days before Christmas, to Callie's dismay, David had to squeeze in a two-day business trip, returning Christmas Eve.

With David's absence, Callie felt lonely. The house was silent, and she opened her door and glanced across the hallway. Nattie seemed too quiet, and she wondered if the child missed David, too, or if something else bothered her.

She tiptoed across the hall and peeked through the doorway. Nattie was curled on the bed with a book on her lap. She looked up when Callie came into the room.

"So, how are you doing?" Callie asked, sitting on the edge of her bed.

"Okay."

"Just okay? And with Christmas coming so soon? I thought you'd be all excited."

She looked at Nattie's face and saw a question in her eyes.

"Is something wrong, Nat?"

Nattie snuggled down into her bed, turning her head on the pillow. "If you marry my daddy, would you have a baby?"

Callie's pulse skipped a beat. "Only God can answer that, Nattie. Would you like a new baby?"

She nodded yet her eyes blinked as if a fearful thought hung in her mind.

"What are you worried about, sweetie?" Did she wonder if Callie and David had enough love to share?

Nattie lowered her eyelids. "Would you die if you had a baby?"

A ragged sigh shivered through Callie, and she slid her legs onto the bed and curled up next to Nattie. "No, Nattie, I wouldn't die. Are you thinking of your mom?"

Her head moved against the pillow, nodding. "When my mommy was sick, Daddy said he was sorry that I was born, because it made Mommy die."

Callie struggled to contain her gasp. "Oh, Nattie, your daddy wouldn't say that. He loves you so much. Your parents wanted you so badly, and Miriam said that you gave your mom and dad so much happiness. No, no, you couldn't have heard your daddy say that. Maybe you misunderstood."

"Because my mommy was having a baby, she couldn't get her medicine, and she died. So I made her die, didn't I?"

"Is that what's made you sad all this time, Nattie?"

Nattie didn't have to speak. Her face reflected the

answer. Callie understood now—Nattie's silence for so long, her burden of guilt that she had caused her mother's death.

She wrapped Nattie in her arms and held her tightly against her chest. Looking at the little girl's blue eyes, nearly the color of her own, she knew this would be what she'd feel for her own child. She couldn't love her own flesh any more than she had grown to love Nattie. And Nattie's hurt was her own.

"Whatever you heard, Nattie, I think, you didn't understand. Your mom had a bad disease for a long time. God was so good to her and gave her four years to spend with you before she went to heaven. Do you remember how much she loved you?"

"Uh-huh," Nattie whispered. "She hugged me like you do." Her small arms wound more tightly around Callie's neck.

"Callie?" Her voice was a whisper.

"What, sweetheart?"

"Could you be my mommy?"

"I think I am already, Nattie. I love you as if you were my own daughter. I couldn't love you more." The words caught in her throat. "And your daddy thinks you're the greatest in the whole wide world.

"So does Grandma Grace."

Nattie nodded. "Grandma loves me. She told me."

"She did, huh? You go to sleep. Your daddy'll be home tomorrow." She nestled Nattie in her arms, singing softly in her ear.

What could Nattie have heard? When David returned, Callie would know.

Chapter Twenty-Three

David stepped into the foyer loaded with packages, and Callie rushed into his arms, suppressing her questions. He lowered the bags, and, despite the snow that clung to his coat, he pulled her to him and pressed his icy lips against her warm, eager mouth. "What a greeting. I should go away more often."

"Don't you dare." She dodged from his damp, chilled arms.

"So where's my favorite daughter?"

He heard a giggle, and Nattie leaped through the parlor doorway into his arms and planted a loud kiss on his cheek.

"You're freezing, Daddy."

"And you're snuggly warm, Nattie."

She wiggled until he released her.

David slid off his coat, and Callie took it from him as he retrieved his packages.

"What have you got there?" she asked, eyeing the parcels.

"Wouldn't *you* like to know?"

"Yes, I would."

"Me, too," Nattie added. "Did you buy me a present?"

"Both of you are nosy. Yes, they're all Christmas surprises, so you'll have to wait. And before I let you two bury your noses in the bags, I'm taking them upstairs right now."

Callie and Nattie pretended to pout, but David ignored them and scooted up the stairs, carrying the bulging shopping bags.

He tossed them into his closet, then changed into his khaki slacks and a rust-and-green pullover. Before closing the door, he glanced with an anxious grin at the packages.

While in Bloomington, he had wandered through a jewelry store, finally selecting a gold locket for Nattie as delicate and lovely as she was.

His heart tripped when he thought of Callie's gift. As well as a gold chain with pearl and garnet beads, David had selected an engagement ring. Christmas Day, he would propose.

After he dressed, David returned to the first floor, admiring the holiday decor. For two years his Christmas spirit had lain dormant. Today, with Callie at his side, he felt complete.

As he neared the bottom of the stairs, Callie beckoned him through the library door, a strange look on her face.

"Something wrong?"

"Push the door closed, would you?" she asked. "I want to make sure we're alone before we talk."

Feeling his pulse quicken, he gave the door a push.

Her face told him she was terribly concerned. "What is it?"

"Something happened while you were gone, and I've been anxious to talk to you." She glanced over her shoulder at a chair. "Let's sit, okay?"

"Sure," he said, folding his tense body into a nearby recliner. "I see you're upset."

"It's something Nattie said. I think I know what's been bothering her all this time."

His pulse throbbed in his temples. "What is it?"

Callie blurted her story. Confusion and worry tangled in her words, and as he listened, he forced his mind back nearly three years, trying to decipher what Nattie might have heard.

"Callie, I don't know. I can't imagine what she heard. We never talked in front of her. Sara and I were very open about her illness and about her ill-fated pregnancy, but not with Nattie around. I was so angry and guilty when Sara had the miscarriage. But that was a year before Natalie—"

"Could she have overheard you talking when Sara was…really bad. Near the end?"

"If Nattie was listening, I didn't know. Yes, I was terribly upset. I knew Sara's pregnancy was a mistake. Stopping her treatment risked her life, and then we lost the baby, anyway. Oh, Callie, I probably yelled at her, telling her how foolish we were to try and have a child. I was a maniac right before she died."

"If Nattie heard it, she blamed herself."

"But she wasn't to blame. And Nattie should know that. She couldn't have been to blame."

Callie's eyes questioned him, her forehead furrowing in confusion. "Why, David? Sara couldn't have treatment during either pregnancy. Why *wouldn't* Nattie feel to blame?"

David's world crumbled around him. Words he hadn't said since Sara died rose to his lips. Nattie had been told, but she had been young. Maybe she'd forgotten. They had to raise her to know the truth.

"Answer me, David. Why?"

He struggled to say the words. "When Sara lost the baby, we knew that was our last chance. Nattie isn't my biological child, Callie. She was adopted."

Callie stopped as if struck by a sniper's bullet. Blood drained from her face. Trembling uncontrollably, she raised her hand to her chest. "Adopted?" She rose, her legs quaking. "Adopted?" she whispered. "And you never told me."

"Oh Callie, to me, Nattie was our own. I rarely think about—" He stopped speaking. Callie had dashed from the room and up the stairs.

Weakness overcame her. Callie stood in her room, holding her face in her hands, disbelieving. Why had David lied to her? But…he hadn't lied. He hadn't told her, that was all. A wave of sorrow washed over her. Neither had she told *him* the whole truth.

Adoption. Had David not spoken of it for a reason? Was he ashamed? Her chest tightened, restricting her breathing. She closed her bedroom door and locked it, then threw herself across the bed. Callie's own sorrow tore through her. *Nattie.* This beautiful child, like her own daughter, had been signed away—placed in someone else's home. And somewhere, another mother wondered about *her* lost child. The paradox knifed her. *Why Lord? Why should mothers feel such pain?*

She needed to calm down and reason. Callie closed her eyes, whispering a long-needed prayer to God. Compassion, wisdom, understanding. She needed so much.

Yet, so often she wore herself out trying to solve every problem on her own. God had guided her to this house. Was this His purpose?

She loved Nattie as her own, and the child almost could be hers: they had the same coloring and talents. But she knew in her heart, Nattie wasn't. She belonged to someone else.

She curled on her side and prayed aloud. *"Lord, please help me to understand. You tell us to seek You and You'll hear us. With all my heart Lord, I need to find peace and comfort. I want to understand."*

A light rap sounded on the door. *David.* She ignored his knock and his hushed voice, calling her name. For now, she had to think on her own. She could apologize for her behavior and explain her strange reaction later.

Finally, she rose and washed her face, staring at the pale image in the mirror that gaped back at her. Tonight was Christmas Eve, and Ken would arrive soon. This was not the moment for confessions and confusion. Now she needed to look presentable.

She retouched her makeup and tossed a teal-blue dress over her head, cinching the belt around her waist. The rosebud brooch from David lay on her dresser, and she pinned it to her shoulder. *Better? Yes, I look better.* She unlocked the door and descended the stairs.

Ken had already arrived, and called to her from the bottom landing. "Merry Christmas, Callie."

"Merry Christmas, Ken," she echoed.

David watched from behind her brother. Though handsome in his navy suit, tension ridged David's face, and he looked less than merry. She gave her brother a kiss on the cheek, then spoke to David. "I see you're ready for church."

"Yes. You look lovely, Callie." He gave her brother a friendly pat on the shoulder. "Go ahead, Ken. Let's sit in the parlor with the Christmas tree."

Ken went ahead, joining Nattie and Grace, and David leaned close to her ear as they followed him. "We need to talk."

"Later, David, please. I owe you an explanation."

He nodded, but she felt his arm tense. Tenderly, she pressed his forearm, hoping he understood and forgave her. A faint movement flickered at the corner of his mouth, and she relaxed, believing that he did understand.

With conversations flowing in many directions, the time passed, and Agnes soon announced their early dinner. The children's Christmas program began at seven-thirty, and Nattie had to arrive by seven.

At the church, they sat near the front. Beginning with "Oh, Come Little Children," the youngsters proceeded down the aisle, dressed as shepherds, wise men, Mary, Joseph and the angels.

Nattie's halo bounced as she marched past the rows in her white flowing robe and sparkling angel wings. When she saw the family, she raised her hand in a tiny wave.

The children took their places, and families beamed as the little actors spoke with practiced precision. When the angels chorused, "Peace on earth; goodwill to men," Nattie's voice rose above the rest, every word clear and distinct.

At the end of the program, they descended the stairs to the Sunday School rooms, while the children stripped off their costumes.

Nattie dashed to them when they hit the landing. "Was I good? I knew all my lines."

David crouched down and gave her a hug. "We were all very proud of you."

Callie's heart twisted, watching him with Nattie. So much love and devotion for his daughter. Natural or adopted, she was his child.

When David retreated to locate Nattie's coat, a familiar voice sailed toward Callie.

"Well, Merry Christmas."

Turning, Callie cranked her facial muscles into a smile. "Hello, Mary Beth. Merry Christmas."

A man was attached to her arm, and she batted her eyes toward her escort. "Callie, do you know Charles Robinson?"

"Not formally, but I know you from church. It's nice to meet you. And this is my brother, Ken." They shook hands. Saving further conversation, David returned just then with Nattie, now buttoned into her coat. After final amenities, they headed toward the door.

Once home, as they entered the foyer, the parlor clock chimed ten, and eager for Christmas Day, Nattie headed for bed with David's promise to tuck her in. Callie longed to talk with David but she had to join the others for Agnes's homemade cookies and coffee.

The conversation flowed until Callie yawned, followed by David. Finally, they agreed it was time to turn in.

David rose first. "I'd better call it a night. I still have a few 'Santa' things to do for tomorrow morning."

Ken followed and helped Grace up the stairs. As they made their way, Callie turned to David. "Can we talk now?"

He hesitated. "Let me get this stuff set up, so I won't feel hurried. I'll knock on your door when I'm finished."

Disappointment needled her, but he was right. They didn't need to be rushed. Their talk would be important, and she wanted to be emotionally ready. "Okay. I'll be waiting."

Upstairs, Callie paused outside Nattie's room. In the glow of the pink night-light, the child lay in a soft flush of color. Callie stood over her, her hand stroking the golden curls fanned out on the pillow. Nattie slept soundly.

Callie leaned over, brushing Nattie's cheek with her lips, then whispered, "I love you, Nattie." Her heart stirred with loving awareness. It didn't matter whose child she was—Nattie was loved and cherished. God had guided the baby to this house and to a Christian family who loved her.

Brushing the tears from her cheeks, Callie crossed the hall and slipped into a caftan, then waited. Her nerves pitched at each creak of the house, wondering if it was David. Tonight she would tell him about her daughter. How would he feel? And how did she feel? *Peace and understanding, Lord.* Her prayer lifted again. She pushed her door ajar and moved her chair so she could see David approach.

When he appeared, he passed her room and crossed to Nattie's. Surprised, Callie rose, padding softly to the doorway, but he only peeked in and then turned.

"You're waiting. I'm sorry it took so long. You know how it is assembling toys."

A knot tightened in her stomach. No, she didn't know.

"Let's sit," David said, drawing the desk chair beside her recliner. "We have lots to talk about."

Callie sank into the cushion. "I'm sorry, David. I was shocked. I—"

"First, let me explain, please. I wasn't hiding Nattie's adoption. When you first came, the thought entered my mind. But I didn't know you and wanted you to treat her as my own. Then, you grew to love her as I do, and the thought faded. She is my daughter. I love her no differently than I would a natural child."

"Please, David. My shock is more complex than you can imagine. Yes, I was startled when you told me. And then I wondered if you were ashamed of her adoption, and—"

"Ashamed? How could I be? Sara and I chose her. She was ours from her first days on earth. We nurtured her, loved her, cared for her. How could I be ashamed? I thank God for my beautiful daughter, Callie."

Her tears flowed, dripping to her hands knotted in her lap. She raised them to cover her face.

David rose and knelt at her feet. "Don't cry. Please. I don't understand what's happened."

"David, I didn't know how I was going to tell you this. I was so worried you'd hate me or wonder what kind of person I am."

David pulled her hands from her face. "Whatever it is, just tell me." He held her hands captive in his.

She closed her eyes, tears dripping from her chin. "After I was raped, I found out I was pregnant."

"Pregnant—oh, Callie, my love." Tears rimmed his eyes.

"My parents thought the father was a college boy,

and I let them believe it. I had a baby girl, David, born on Christmas Day. I placed her up for adoption."

"My love, how could I hate you? You were blameless. And hurt far more than I ever knew."

"But you did so much to have a baby—taking horrible chances. And I didn't fight to keep my child. I haven't forgiven myself. Every day I ask God why it happened—and if she's okay. Is she happy? Do her parents love her?"

David rose, lifted her from the chair, and cradled her in his arms. "Oh, my dear, look around you. Look at the beautiful child that gave Sara and me such joy. Wouldn't God do the same for your child? Trust in the Lord, Callie. You have strong faith in so many things. Believe that God placed your daughter in a home as filled with love as this one."

"I want to believe that." Music stirred in Callie's mind. She paused. The sad song that played within her heart faded, and a new melody filled her—a sense of peace and understanding. And love. "I went to Nattie's room when I came up and looked at her sweet face." The music lifted at the memory. "I couldn't love my own child more, David. I almost feel as if God has given me another chance."

"He has, my love, He has. And He's given us another chance. You've brought such joy to our lives. Nattie and I were shadows when you came, but you breathed new life into us—just as you gave life to your little daughter years ago."

The grandfather clock in the parlor began to chime. *One. Two. Three…* They paused, listening for the last. "It's midnight. Christmas Day." She didn't say what else lay in her heart. His eyes told her he knew.

"Doubt is part of life, Callie. When we first brought Nattie home, I wondered if I could love her. *Really* love her—like a true father. And—"

"You don't have to say it. If anyone was ever a true and loving father, it's you."

"And if anyone was ever a true and loving mother, it's you."

Callie looked into his face, and saw love glowing in his eyes. Her heart felt as if it would burst, and joy danced through her body. "A mother. It's a beautiful thought."

"A mother." Trancelike, David repeated her words and kissed her hair. He tilted her chin upward until their eyes met. "Callie, this is perfect. I planned this for tomorrow, but wait. Wait. Don't move."

He darted from the room, and in a moment returned to drop to his knees in front of her for the second time that night. "I've loved you for so long. You've brought happiness and completeness into our empty world, and, praise God, you've given me a healthy daughter. Nattie loves you so much and so do I. We would like to marry you, Callie. Will you be my wife? And Nattie's mother?"

Tears rolled down his cheeks as he handed her the blue velvet box. Callie knew what was inside, and without hesitating, she whispered her answer. "You know, I love you both with all my heart. Please forgive me for my foolish doubts and fears. I'm so filled with happiness—"

"And?"

She looked into his loving eyes. "And yes, I'll marry you."

His face brightened; the tension melted away. "Open the box, Callie." He turned it in her hand to face her.

She lifted the lid. Inside, a roping of three shades of gold entwined three sparkling diamonds. She raised her eyes. "Three shades of gold. And three diamonds. One for each of us."

"One for each of us. And we can always add a fourth."

His eyes glowed, and with quivering fingers, he took the ring from her and slipped it on her finger. "Perfect." His gaze caressed her face. "Yes, perfect."

She opened her mouth to speak, but he quieted her with his warm, tender lips. Captured in his arms, Callie's fears and shame were gone. Her black dreams could hurt no more. She nestled securely against David's chest, finally whole and at peace.

When their lips parted, they tiptoed, hand in hand, across the hall to gaze at their beautiful child, sleeping peacefully in a rosy glow of light.

Epilogue

On Christmas Day, a month before Nattie's ninth birthday, the family gathered in church. Even Callie's sister, Patricia, and her husband had come from California for the holiday. They arrived, eager to see Randolph David Hamilton, who'd been born in early November.

Grace held the baby in her arms, with Nattie nestled as close as she could without sitting on Grace's lap.

David and Callie stood at the front, their faces glowing with wide, proud grins. David's gaze drifted with admiration to his wife, almost as trim again as she had been before her nine months of "ballooning," as they'd called it. He couldn't take his eyes from her.

"What?" Callie whispered. "Why are you staring at me?"

"Because you're beautiful, and I'm the happiest man alive." He squeezed her arm and tilted his head toward the children, sitting in the third pew.

She teased him with the nudge of her hip. "Well, you'd better focus on the music. We have to sing in a minute."

The organ music voluntary ended, and the ushers

brought the offering plates to the front. As they retreated down the aisle, the organist played the introductory notes to the duet.

The opening strains began, and Callie's mind soared back to a Christmas midnight two years earlier—to the moment her past vanished and God's purpose became clear. On that day, a new life began.

Her gaze drifted to Nattie, growing lovelier each day, now looking at her with pure, joyous love. Somewhere on this Christmas night, another young girl celebrated Jesus's birth and her own birthday. Assurance filled Callie, as she trusted that God had guided her own baby daughter to a loving, Christian family.

Callie wiped away an invading tear. Today, with happiness, she looked at her son, the image of his handsome father. Raising her eyes to David's, she felt complete and wonderful. His smile captivated her, and she sighed.

As the last note of the introduction sounded, they each drew in a deep breath, then lifted their voices in the familiar words of an old carol that now rang with new meaning. *"It came upon a midnight clear, that glorious song of old..."*

* * * * *

SEASON OF JOY

Virginia Carmichael

This book would not exist if not for the support of many different people, old and young, near and far. Thank you to my daughters Isabel and Ana for being my beta readers. I'm sorry for the smooching. It just had to be in there somewhere. For Jacob, Sam, Edward and Elias, thank you for every time I asked for one more minute to write and you ignored me. Cruz, I want to say Marisol's food terms came from Google. Really. Thank you to my sister Susan who never reads this kind of book but was willing to put in serious time proofreading and giving comments. If I could write a good ghost story, I would, but that gene was passed to you alone. Thank you to my brother Dennis for making time to read and comment on all sorts of things, giving tech advice, big business advice and keeping a sense of humor through it all. For my brother Sam, who always keeps a clear view of what's important in life, sort of like Grant. For my parents, Murphy Carmichael and Bonnie Reinke, thank you for raising me in a house with more books than our local library. Bibliophiles unite!

Most of all, thank you to the fine ladies over at Seekerville who started this ball rolling in the first place. Your constant encouragement and advice is invaluable.

I have other sheep that do not belong to this fold.
These also I must lead, and they will hear my voice,
and there will be one flock, and one shepherd.

—*John* 10:16

Chapter One

A dark tidal wave of fear swept through Calista Sheffield as she paused at the door of the Downtown Denver Mission. She took a deep breath and wiped damp palms on the legs of her jeans. Her image was reflected in the glass door as clearly as in a mirror, the bright Rocky Mountain sunshine as backlighting. Giving her casual outfit a quick scan, she tucked a strand of honey-blond hair behind her ear and tugged at the hem of her black cashmere sweater. She prayed no one in the shelter would be able to tell the difference between Donna Karan and a knockoff, because she wasn't here to impress anyone. She was here to volunteer.

Her reflection showed a pair of large green eyes shadowed with anxiety. Calista squinted, hating her own weakness. There was no reason to be afraid when she ran a multimillion-dollar company. She gripped the handle and swung it open, striding inside before the heat escaped.

The exterior of the five-story mission was a bit worse for wear, but the inside seemed clean and welcoming. In the center of the enormous lobby, a tall pine tree bowed under the weight of handmade ornaments and twinkling lights. Calista's gaze darted toward a group of men clustered near the double doors at the far end. Probably the cafeteria. Maybe she was just in time to help serve a turkey dinner with trimmings. A vision of handing a plate piled high with steaming mashed potatoes and gravy to some desperate soul passed through her mind's eye. This was going to be great.

No, this was going to be more than great; the start to a whole new life. Not like the lonely existence she had right now with only her passive-aggressive Siamese cat for company. No more pretending she had somewhere to go on Thanksgiving, then suffering through everyone else's happy chatter after the holiday. It was her own fault for letting work take over her life, but that was all in the past.

This Christmas would be different.

Calista scanned the lobby for a secretary. The long, curving desk spanned the area between the elevator and far wall, but it was empty. An oversize wooden cross took center stage on a staggered section of ceiling that connected the lobby to the upper level. A small smile tugged at her lips, thinking of how that sight would have made her cringe just a few months ago.

A young man with the mission staff uniform and close-cropped dark hair exited the double doors, papers in hand. Calista stepped forward into his path.

"Excuse me, I need to see Grant Monohan," she said, in the tone she reserved for secretaries and assistants. Her eyes flicked from his deep brown eyes to the ID badge pinned to his shirt to the solid pattern of colorful tattoos that covered both of his arms from biceps to wrist.

He paused, frowned a little, glanced back at the empty desk.

"The director," Calista added, hoping she wasn't speaking the wrong language. His dark coppery skin and angular features made her think of paintings she'd seen of the Mayans.

"Just let me drop these papers in the office and I'll tell him you're here," he said, waving the stack of papers at her. He started off again without waiting for a response and punched in a series of numbers at the keypad by the far door.

The brown patterned couches were arranged in groups of three but none of them were occupied, except the very last one, near the large windows that faced the street. An older woman sat hunched in the corner, rocking and murmuring to herself. Her brown shawl slipped off one shoulder and pooled at her feet like a stain. Dark tangles framed a wrinkled, but somehow expressionless, face. Calista swallowed a sudden wave of anxiety.

A door swung open to her right and a wheelchair-bound woman rolled to a stop behind the desk. Her short gray hair was spiked on top and touched with violet. She maneuvered to the middle of the desk just as the phone rang.

"Downtown Denver Mission, this is Lana. How may I help you?" she responded in a cheerful tone.

None of this should have made her feel queasy, but the combination of the rocking elderly woman, the young man's tattoos and the purple-haired handicapped woman had Calista struggling with her resolve. She wandered toward the windows and gazed out at the snowy sidewalk, taking deep breaths. Life isn't pretty, she should know that. But after ten years of clawing her way to the top of the business world, Calista had buried any memories she had of imperfection. Memories of her own rough childhood in a place where there were worse things than purple hair and tattoos.

"Ma'am?" She snapped into the present at the word spoken quietly behind her. The young man was back. "The director is just finishing up but he can see you for a few minutes before his next appointment. Go ahead and have a seat."

Calista nodded and smiled brightly. "Thank you," she chirped, hoping she oozed positivity and enthusiasm. They wouldn't want unhappy people around here. She was sure they had enough of those already.

Grant Monohan checked the balance-sheet numbers for the third time. He knew better than to get upset at the decreasing number in black and the increasing number in red. The shelter scraped by most of the year until they got to the season of giving, or the "season of guilting," as Jose called it. God had provided every day of the past seventy-five years, so he wasn't going to start worrying now.

A light knock at the door and Jose popped his head in. "We got another one."

Grant wanted to roll his eyes but he nodded instead.

"Actress?" Aspen's popularity had been great for them, even all the way out here in Denver. The mega-rich had started to settle in the area a decade ago and it showed right around the holiday season. Every year, right when the store windows changed to sparkly decorations and Santas, the famous faces started appearing. Most were dragged in by agents or managers, but a few came on their own. They would spend a few days, sign some autographs and go away feeling good about themselves. He wasn't one to turn away help, especially when it came with good publicity and a donation, but it got real old, real fast. Last year they had a blonde starlet stumble in with a twenty-person entourage. Most of them were as high as she was. He cringed inside, remembering the scene that erupted as he informed them of the "no alcohol, no drugs" policy.

"Not sure. She's pretty enough but she came alone." Jose shrugged. Grant wished he would come all the way in, or open the door wider, but Jose always seemed to be in constant motion. It was all the kid could do to hold still for a few minutes.

"Why didn't Lana call back here?"

He shrugged again. "The lady just came up to me and said she had to see the director."

Grant frowned, wondering if it was worse to have a volunteer who demanded special treatment, or a volunteer who ignored the disabled secretary. He stood up and stretched the kinks from his back. Maybe he'd look into a better chair after the crazy holiday rush was over. The ratty hand-me-down was obviously not made for a six-footer like himself. Or maybe turning thirty was the start of a long, slow slide into back trouble.

"Tell her I'll be right out." Jose's head disappeared from the doorway. Grant crossed the small office space and absently checked his reflection in the mirror near the door. He was looking more and more like his father every year. Women told him what a heartthrob he was, like a classic movie star. They never knew how close they were to the truth. But what he saw—instead of the dark wavy hair, strong jaw and broad shoulders—was the man who walked away from his mother when he was just a kid. Grant shook his head to clear it. *All things are made new in You, Lord.* He had a heavenly father who would never run away and he needed to remember that.

Grant pushed open the heavy metal door and stepped into the lobby, letting the door close with a thud behind him. It wasn't hard to pick out the new volunteer. It wouldn't have been hard to spot her in a crowd at the Oscars, she was that pretty. She had the California party-girl look with an added healthy glow, but had wisely left the party clothes at home.

At least she was dressed conservatively. If you could call cashmere and designer jeans conservative. He sighed. Rich people could be so clueless. He watched her for a few moments as she stood near the window, arms wrapped around her middle. She sure didn't have the confidence of a professional actress. Unless the whole nervous attitude was an act.

She turned suddenly and looked straight into his eyes as if he had called her name across the lobby. Grant felt heat creep up his neck. He must look like a stalker, standing there silently. He strode forward, forcing a welcoming expression.

"Grant Monohan," he said, extending his hand. She took it, and he was surprised by the steadiness of her grip.

"Calista Sheffield," she answered. "Wonderful to meet you." The name sounded familiar. Her smile was a bit too wide, as if she was worried about making the wrong impression. Or maybe she was turning on the star power. As if that sort of thing worked on him.

"Jose told me you wanted to see me. Would you like to sit down?"

She frowned down at the couch and said, "You don't meet with anyone in your office?"

"Actually, I don't. We have meeting rooms for groups, and we have a reception area. There's another building at the south end of the block that we use for most of our administration needs."

There was a pause as she tilted her head and regarded him steadily. He could see her processing that information. "Is it a shelter policy?"

She was quick, this one. "It is. To protect the residents and myself from accusations or suspicion. We have plans drawn up for a new office that will have glass partitions but that's still a few years away." He motioned toward the long lobby desk. "So, for now we have Lana get pertinent information on visitors first."

She surprised him with a grin, green eyes crinkling at the corners. "That's usually the way it's done, isn't it?"

Grant hesitated, adjusting her age upward. Not for the laugh lines but for the gentle ribbing. He'd been told before he was slightly intimidating but she seemed able to hold her own.

"There was no one at the desk when I came in, so I just asked Jose."

He gave another tally mark, this time for remembering Jose's name. She might not be a total loss after all. He wasn't such a fool to think she'd stay more than a few days, but maybe she could do more than sign photos.

Grant motioned to the clean but worn couch behind her. "Let's sit down and you can tell me why you're here."

She settled on the edge, hands clutched together. Her

anxiety was palpable. “I’d like to volunteer on a weekly basis. Not just for Thanksgiving or Christmas.”

He plopped into the corner of the couch angled toward hers, putting a good three feet of space between him and those green eyes. “Why?”

She opened her mouth, but then closed it again. He raised an eyebrow and waited patiently. She looked down at her hands, then up at him again, emotions flitting across her face. Confusion, sadness, yearning.

Grant wanted to wrap his arms around her and tell her it was going to be okay. Shocked at how fast he’d forgotten his professional role, Grant frowned, eyes narrowing. She was good at playing the little lost girl, that was clear.

“Miss…” He struggled to remember anything more than those eyes trained on him.

“Sheffield,” she whispered.

“Miss Sheffield, let me tell you a little about the mission. We welcome any and all support. Seventy-five years of serving the community of downtown Denver has made our organization one of the most respected in the country. We provide shelter, addiction counseling, parenting classes, transport for schoolchildren and job training. There are five separate buildings and almost a hundred staff members.” He paused, making sure she was following him. “But everything we do here is aimed at one goal, meeting the deep spiritual needs of all people. We want to be the Gospel in action, be His hands and feet in this world.”

Usually at this point in his speech, the new recruit’s eyes glazed over. They nodded and smiled, waiting for him to finish. She leaned forward, eyes bright.

“So, you mean to say that you provide for the physical needs but the spiritual needs of the person are just as important?"

"Just as or more. If it makes you uncomfortable, there is also the Seventh Street Mission a few miles away. They are a very respected shelter that doesn't adhere to any spiritual principles."

"No, it doesn't bother me at all," she said, her whole face softening. Grant struggled to reclaim his train of thought. Maybe he needed a vacation, had been working too hard. He felt as if he was a knot with a loop missing and that smile was tugging him undone.

"Good," he said, eyes traveling toward the plain cross on the balcony overhang. "That's the only reason we're here. The only reason *I'm* here." He sure wasn't in it for the money. He paused for a moment, trying to get the conversation back on track. "Did you have anything specific in mind?"

"What about the cafeteria?"

A vision passed before him of men, young and old, lined up for limp broccoli served by a stunning blonde, while the regular servers stood abandoned, lasagna pans growing cold. "How about intake or administration? You would be working with Lana to get the paperwork in order and maybe interview new visitors or assign sleeping places."

She blinked and then nodded. "That sounds fine."

"We'll need to get some basic information and do a background check for security reasons. But you can start today, helping out in the cafeteria. We've got a lot of prep work for Thanksgiving."

"Of course."

"Lana can help with the details." He stood, offering his hand once more. "It was a pleasure to meet you and

I'm grateful for your willingness to serve the disadvantaged in our community."

She stood, gripped his hand and whispered, "Thank you."

Grant's heart flipped in his chest as their hands met and he looked into her eyes. Her heart-shaped face shone with hope and her bright green eyes glittered with unshed tears. There was more going on here than a rich person's guilty conscience.

But there was no way he was going to try to find out what. He had enough trouble keeping the mission afloat without adding a woman to the mix. Even a beautiful woman who reminded him that he might need something more than this place. Plus, with the secret he was carrying around, no woman in her right mind would want to get anywhere close.

Calista stood up, gripping the director's hand, his movie-star good looks bearing down on her full force. The man should have a warning sign: Caution: Brain Meltdown Ahead. She could just see him in a promotional brochure, that slightly stern expression tempered by the concern in his eyes. He reminded her of someone, somehow.

But her heart was reacting to more than his wide shoulders or deep baritone. The man had sincere convictions, he had substance and faith. There was nothing more attractive, especially in her job, where image was everything. She wanted to have a purpose in her life beyond making money and losing friends. She wanted to wake up in the morning with more to look forward to than fighting with her board of directors and coming home to a cat who hated her guts.

She met his steady gaze and felt, to her horror, tears welling in her eyes. She tried to smile and thank him for the chance to work at the mission, but the words could barely squeeze past the large lump in her throat. Heat rose in her cheeks as she saw his look of confusion, then concern. He probably thought she was completely unstable, crying over a volunteer gig.

She dropped his hand and immediately wished she could take it back. His hand was warm and comforting, but electrifying at the same time. A short list of things she hadn't felt in a very long time.

"Let's go get those papers from Lana, all right?" His voice had lost its brusque tone somewhat, as if he was afraid of causing her any more distress.

Calista cleared her throat and said, "Lead the way." She blinked furiously and turned toward the desk, hoping he couldn't see her expression. If only he hadn't sounded so sympathetic. If only he was pleasantly distant, the way a CEO is with employees. But he wasn't like that; he wasn't like her.

Grant introduced them quickly. Lana was ready with a stack of papers and handed them to Calista. She could see why the mission had a purple-haired secretary. The woman was efficient and friendly.

"Tell me when you need me and I can adjust my schedule pretty easily." Calista bent over to fill out the papers. One of the perks of being CEO was she could take time off when she wanted some personal time. Not that she ever had before.

Grant's eyebrows went up a bit. "We're short staffed right now and we could really use some help in the mornings. Maybe Wednesdays?"

"Sure, I can be here at seven." As soon as the words

left her mouth, she wondered if that was too early. Maybe the staff didn't get here until nine. But Grant only nodded, the corners of his mouth lifting the smallest amount. She wondered for just a moment what he looked like when he laughed…

Calista's cheeks felt hot as she dropped her gaze to the papers. Grant turned away to speak to a slim young man who was waiting behind them and Lana took the papers, glancing over them. Her eyes stopped at the employment section. "You're head of VitaWow Beverages? I could use someone with a knowledge of grant writing."

"I've written a few grant applications but they weren't for nonprofits. And it's been a while."

"It was worth a shot," Lana said, shrugging and stacking the papers together.

"But I'm sure I could work on whatever you need," Calista said quickly.

Lana looked up, and Calista saw genuine warmth in the woman's eyes. "That's the spirit," she said. "We have a grant-writing team that meets on Thursday evenings. There are only two of them right now because it's the holiday season and everybody's busy. It would be great to get some of these applications turned in before the January deadlines. Is that a good day for you? They might change the meeting time if you can't come then."

"That's fine. Thursday's fine," Calista said. Any evening was fine. Five years ago she'd been busy with the dinner-and-drinks merry-go-round. Once she was promoted to CEO, she cut out almost all the dinners. Of course, after she'd done so, Calista realized her schedule was completely empty. She was friendless and alone.

"Grant is on the team, too. He can fill you in."

"Does the director usually work in the evenings?"

Lana laughed, a lighthearted chuckle. "You don't know the man. It's all about the mission, all the time." The smile slowly faded from her face. "I know he feels at home here, and we could never survive without him, but I wish..."

Calista waited for the end of the sentence, but Lana seemed to have thought better about what she was going to say. She regarded Grant, deep in conversation with the young man, and a line appeared between her brows.

"You're afraid he'll wake up one day and wished he'd put more time into his own life, something apart from the mission?"

"Exactly." She appraised Calista with a steady eye. "You're good at reading people."

"I suppose I know what that feels like. And you're right, it's no fun." Calista dropped her eyes to the desk, wondering what it was about this place that made her feel she could be honest. She wasn't the CEO here; she was just a woman who had lost her place in the world.

She turned back to her paperwork and said, "I can find my way to the cafeteria—"

The end of her sentence was lost in the explosion of noise that accompanied a horde of children entering the lobby. They seemed to all be talking at once, the polished lobby floor magnifying the sounds of their voices to astounding levels. Just when Calista decided there was no one in charge of the swirling group of small people, two young women came through the entryway. One was short and very young, with a thick braid over her shoulder. The other was a powerfully built middle-aged woman with a wide face and large pale eyes. They were both wearing the mission's khaki pants and red polos under their open coats. They were laughing about something, not concerned in the least that their charges were heading straight for the director.

"Mr. Monohan!" A small girl with bright pink sunglasses yelled out the greeting as she raced across the remaining lobby space. She didn't slow down until she made contact with his leg, wrapping her arms around it like she was drowning. He didn't even teeter under the full impact of the flying body, just reached down and laid a large hand on the girl's messy curls.

A huge smile creased his face and Calista's mouth fell open at the transformation. He was a good-looking man, but add in a dash of pure joy and he was breathtaking. She tore her gaze away and met Lana's laughing eyes behind the desk. Of course, the secretary would think it was hilarious how women fell all over themselves in his presence. Calista gathered up the papers with a snap, when she realized she was surrounded. A sea of waist-high kids had engulfed them, with the two women slowly bringing up the rear.

She sidled a glance at Grant, hoping he would tell them to clear out and let her through. But he was busy greeting one child after another. How he could tell them apart enough to learn their names was really beyond her. They just seemed an endless mass of noise and motion, a whirl of coats and bright mittens.

"Miss Sheffield, this is Lissa Handy and Michelle Guzman. They take the preschoolers down the block to the city park for an hour every day." He was still mobbed by coats and children calling his name, but his voice cut through the babble.

Calista raised one hand in greeting, trapped against the desk, but only Michelle waved back. Lissa seemed to be sizing up the new girl.

She stood with her arms folded over her chest, unmoving. But Michelle reached out and touched her on the shoulder. "It's wonderful to have new volunteers," she said, her voice warm and raspy, as if she spent too much time trying to get the kids' attention. She smelled like fresh air and snow, and Calista smiled back. Her clear blue eyes reminded her of Mrs. Allen, her third-grade teacher. That kindhearted woman had given her confidence a boost when she was just like these little people.

"I don't know how you keep them all from escaping. It must be like herding squirrels."

Michelle laughed, a full-throated sound that came from deep inside. "You're right. The key is to give them some incentive. They head to the park okay, and then I tell them we're coming back, but Mr. Monohan will be here. Easy as pie."

Calista glanced back at Grant, his wide shoulders hunched over a little girl who was excitedly describing something that needed lots of hand waving. He was nodding, his face the picture of rapt attention.

"He seems really good with the kids. Does he have any of his own?" She suddenly wished she could snatch the words back out of the air, especially since it was followed by a snort from Lissa.

Michelle ignored her partner's nonverbal comment. "No, he's never been married. I keep telling him he needs to find someone special and settle down. He was one of the youngest directors the mission had ever had when he started here, but this place can take over your life if you let it."

"But that's what he wants, so don't stick your nose in." So, Lissa did have a voice. A young, snarky voice, coming from a sullen face. She flipped her dark braid off her shoulder and stuck her hands in her pockets. Calista wondered how old Lissa was, probably not more than nineteen. Just the age when a girl might fall in love for the first time.

"You'll understand when you're older, Lissa. But there's more to life than work, even if your work is filled with people like ours is here," Michelle said.

Lissa's face turned dark and threatening, like a storm cloud. "You always say stuff like that. I don't think my age has anything to do with my brain."

Spoken like a true teenager. Calista tried to smooth ruffled feathers. "Michelle's right that everyone needs a family or friends separate from work." Lissa's face twisted like she was ready to pour on the attitude. Calista hurried to finish her thought. "But not everybody is happiest being married, with a family. Like me. I don't think it would be fair to have a boyfriend when my work takes up so much of my time."

Lissa's eyebrows came up a little and she shrugged.

"But I could always use more friends." That last part was a gamble, but Lissa seemed to accept it at face value. She relaxed a bit, the smile creeping back into her eyes.

"Don't know why you'd be looking for friends at this place, though."

Michelle gave Lissa a squeeze around the shoulders. "Come on, you found me here, right?" Lissa responded with an eye roll, but Calista could tell the young woman appreciated the hug and being called a friend.

"Fine, but we got enough pretty people in here slumming it for the holidays. We don't need any more."

"I can wear a bag over my face, if that helps."

Lissa let out a surprised laugh. "Yeah, you do that. Maybe you'll start a trend."

"Maybe so." Calista took one more glance back and started to laugh. Grant had a pair of bright pink sunglasses on his face and the kids were howling with laughter. Parents had started to show up to collect their children and they acted as if the scene wasn't unusual at all.

"Those are Savannah's glasses. She never goes anywhere without them. He's sure got a silly side," Michelle said, chuckling. "But you'd never know it at first glance."

No, you wouldn't. Not with that frown and the serious gaze. As if he could feel her looking at him, Grant glanced up and she saw the smile slip from his face. Calista felt her heart sink. Then again, she wasn't here to get a boyfriend or find true love. She was here because her life had become a self-centered whirlpool of ambition, with her swirling around at the bottom like a piece of driftwood.

Grant seemed to come to some kind of decision. He waded through the kids until he was standing next to them. "Miss Sheffield, it's almost lunchtime. Why don't you come in for something to eat and then I can introduce you to the kitchen staff?"

Calista darted a glance at Lissa. The teen probably thought Calista had been angling for an invitation all along. But she couldn't resist jumping at the chance to get to know this man better. She nodded quickly and he turned toward the far side of the lobby.

"Is there a kid version of catnip? If there is, you must be stuffing your pockets with it."

"Nope, I just listen to them. It's funny how many

people forget that kids need someone to hear them," he said, his words serious, but a grin spread over his features.

At that moment, as they stood smiling at each other, the other side of the cafeteria door swung open and nearly knocked Calista off her feet.

"Watch out! You shouldn't stand in front of the door," an old man shouted at her as she stumbled, struggling to regain her balance.

"Duane, please keep your voice down." Calista could tell Grant was angry, maybe by the way his voice had gone very quiet and dropped an octave or two. "Are you all right?" He reached out and rubbed her left shoulder, which had taken the brunt of the impact.

She nodded slowly, distracted less by the pain than by the warmth of his hand. "Fine, not a problem." Meeting the old man's eyes, she was surprised to see such animosity reflected there. "I'm sorry I was standing behind the door." When both sides were at fault, it was always best to be the first to offer an apology.

But if she was hoping for reciprocation, it didn't come. He blinked, one eye milky white while the other was a hazy blue, and sniffed. "You're still standing here and I gotta get through."

Calista moved to the side immediately and let him pass. As they walked through the doors into the full dining hall, she glanced back at Grant. "Off to a good start, don't you think?"

Again that warm chuckle. She could get used to hearing that sound, even if she couldn't get used to the way it ran shivers up her spine.

"I think we're off to a great start," he said, and something in his tone made her look up. His smile made her heart jump into her throat and he stepped near. Although she knew the whole cafeteria was watching behind them, she couldn't tear her gaze from his.

Calista watched those blue eyes come closer, her heart pounding in her chest. Her brain seemed to have shorted out somewhere between the shoulder rub and the chuckle.

Grant leaned forward, his gaze locked on hers, and then he looked directly behind her. "Scan it twice, please. She doesn't have her guest pass yet."

Calista blinked and turned to see him holding out a security badge with a small photo in the middle. A pretty young woman sitting at a small table took the badge without comment and passed it twice through a card reader. Her dark eyes flicked up and down Calista's outfit, then handed Grant the security badge.

"We use visitor passes to keep track of how many meals are served," he explained.

"I see," she said in a bright tone, but clenched her jaw at her own stupidity. Was she so lonely that any good-looking man caused her brain to shut down? Did she think he was leaning over to kiss her, in the doorway of the mission dining hall? She was so angry at herself that she wanted to stomp out the door. Except she had vowed to do something useful. Which did not include mooning over the director.

She stood for a moment and gazed around at the dining hall. It was much bigger than the lobby and had an assortment of elderly, teens, women, men and what seemed like a hundred babies crying in unison. The noise was horrible but the smell wasn't bad, not even close to what she remembered from "mystery casserole" day in grade school. The rich scent of coffee, buttery rolls, eggs, sausages and something sweet she couldn't identify made her mouth water.

"I haven't eaten with this many people since college." She peered around. "Is there a cool kids' table?"

He grinned. "Sure there is, but I don't sit there." He led her forward to the long line of glass-fronted serving areas. "Here are the hot dishes. We try to keep it as low-fat as possible. Over there—" he pointed to a wall that held row after row of cereal dispensers "—are the cold cereals and bowls. The drinks are self-serve, at the end of the row. Milk, juice, coffee, tea, hot chocolate. We don't serve soda anymore."

Calista nodded. "I see that trend a lot."

"In schools? I'm sorry. I didn't catch what you do."

"I'm the CEO of VitaWow." She felt her cheeks heat a little at the words and was surprised. She was proud of her job, of how she'd turned the company into a national brand. But standing here, in this place, it didn't seem as important.

She watched his eyes widen a little. "I've heard good things about your company. Didn't the city honor VitaWow with a business award?"

"Best of the best." She liked saying the words and couldn't help the small smile. "I'm proud of our product and our commitment to health. But I also care about our employees. We have excellent benefits and give every employee a free pass to Denver's biggest fitness center."

He smiled, and she was struck once more by the difference it made. He seemed like a friend, the kind she wished she had.

Calista nodded.

"Our main goal is to provide a safe place where people can fill their spiritual needs. But we also want to make sure the people have healthy food that gives them a good start to the day."

He lifted a tray from the stack and handed it to her. "I don't recommend the hash browns but the breakfast burritos aren't too bad."

"I like having a food guide." A quick peek at the hash browns supported his opinion. They were soggy and limp. The metal serving dish was full, proving the rest of the cafeteria avoided them, too.

He moved down the line behind her, sliding his tray along the counter. "If that's a job offer, I have to warn you that I have great benefits here. Unlimited overtime, my own coffee machine, a corner office with a wonderful view of the parking lot."

Calista couldn't help laughing as she spooned a bit of scrambled egg onto her tray. "Sounds like my job, except I have a view of the roof of the building next door. And lots of pigeons to keep me company."

A short, wiry woman smiled at him as he reached for a biscuit. "Mr. Monohan, it's good to see you having breakfast. You have to eat and keep strong." Her softly curling hair was covered by a hairnet and she wore a brightly colored apron that was missing one large pocket in the front.

"Marisol, this is Calista Sheffield. She's a new volunteer."

Calista hoped the emotion that flickered over the lined face was curiosity, and not skepticism. "We can always use more of those, eh, Mr. Monohan?" The thick accent was a bit like Jose's but more lyrical, as if she was more used to singing than speaking.

"We sure can. When are you going to cook me some

of your arroz con pollo? I've been dreaming of it all week."

Marisol beamed with pleasure. "Anytime, Mr. Monohan, anytime. You tell me and I cook you a big dinner. Maybe you bring a friend, too? How 'bout that nice Jennie girl?"

Calista studied the biscuit on her tray, wishing she couldn't hear this conversation.

"Sadly, Mari, I don't think there's much future for us," Grant said, sounding not at all sad about it.

"Oh, no." She wagged her finger over the glass case at him. "You let her get away. I told you, she's a nice girl and you work too much." She seemed honestly grieved by this new development.

"You wouldn't want me to be with the wrong girl, would you, Marisol? And she wasn't right for me." Calista glanced at him and could tell Grant was trying not to laugh, his lips quirked up on one side.

"But how you know that when you only see her once or twice? You work all the time and the girl decides you don't like her. That's what happened." She was giving him a glare that any kid would recognize from the "mom look."

"No, I made time for her. But it just didn't work out." He smiled, trying to convey his sincerity but Marisol was not budging. Finally, he sighed. "I don't want to gossip, but I'll tell you something she said."

"Go ahead," Marisol dared him, frowning. Calista couldn't imagine how long it was going to take to convince this little Hispanic woman that Grant hadn't done Jennie wrong.

"She said I was too religious."

Calista felt her eyes widen, a perfect mirror to Marisol's own expression. They both stared at Grant, disbelieving.

"Oh, Mr. Monohan. That's bad. Very bad." Her eyes were sad as she shrugged. "Because you don't drink? Did you tell that girl your mama drink herself to death?"

"It wasn't that. And I never told her about my mother." His words were light, with no hint of anger. He could have told Marisol to zip it, but he looked more amused than anything.

"Well, good thing she's gone. You tell me when you want me to cook. Maybe I bring my niece, that pretty one? She's in college and wants to be a social worker!"

Calista bit back a laugh at how quickly Marisol had let go of Jennie as Grant's future wife.

"Thanks, I will." Grant nodded at Calista and she figured it was safe to move on.

They got glasses of orange juice and he chose a table near the entrance. As they settled on either side of the long table, he extended his hand to her, palm up.

She stared for a moment, uncomprehending, then remembered how her sister, Elaine, always held hands with her husband as they said grace before meals. It had made Calista uncomfortable a few years ago but she felt her heart warm in her chest now. She placed her hand in his and bowed her head. The steady strength of his fingers sent a thrill of joy through her. He spoke simple words of thanks and asked God's blessing on their day.

He let go of her hand and she put it in her lap, feeling strangely lonely without the pressure of his hand.

"Did she really say you were too religious?"

"I wouldn't lie about that," Grant said, grinning. He paused, as if choosing his words. "And I'm sorry about Marisol. Too much information on your first day, right?

But she doesn't mean any harm. She thinks everyone will accept people for who they are, not holding the sins of their parents against them."

Calista dropped her gaze to her tray. She'd worked hard to reinvent herself from a poor girl from a tiny Southern town, the one with a mean father and a dead mother, into a polished and beautiful businesswoman. But there was only so far you could run from yourself. Then it was all about facing your fears and being bigger than your past. She was ready to be what God intended her to be, no matter how crazy it seemed to everyone else.

Chapter Two

"You don't seem very upset about losing your girlfriend."

He took a sip of his orange juice and paused, a small line between his brows. "You know that moment, when you're not sure exactly which way to go, when opposite choices are equally attractive?"

"Of course." She hated that moment. The indecision nearly killed her.

"That was how I felt about Jennie. She was smart, caring, made good conversation. Everybody thought we'd be a great couple."

Calista groaned and he raised his eyebrows in question. "Every time a friend tells me that I'd be great with someone, I know it's doomed." Jackie, her assistant, never tired of setting her up. It was always a disaster and Jackie always enjoyed the dramatic story the day after. Which made Calista wonder if she picked the men for her own amusement.

Grant laughed out loud and nodded. "Maybe I should have known, but my best friend, Eric, set us up. Well, he brought her in to volunteer and he knew we'd hit it off."

Calista took a bite of her biscuit and chewed thoughtfully. Eric thought they'd hit it off because they were so alike, or because Grant went for pretty volunteers? The idea that she was sitting in a spot where twenty other girls had been made her heart sink.

"She's an attorney and spends most of her time as a prosecutor for the city's worst abuse cases. She also handles some family law, but mostly fights for the weakest of our residents. He knew I'd appreciate her passion for protecting vulnerable kids."

The buttery biscuit turned to ashes in her mouth. Grant would certainly not appreciate her own passion for building a vitamin-water empire. There was nothing admirable about getting folks to pay a lot of money for something that didn't really make them any healthier.

"And I really did—I mean, I do—think she does a great job. But we just didn't seem to connect." His voice trailed off and he took a bite of scrambled egg. "But I knew that before she told me I was too religious, so it only made it easier to leave it at being friends."

Calista took a sip of her juice and pondered his words. Elaine told her once that if a man wasn't in contact with any of his ex-girlfriends, then he was a bitter and spiteful person. So, maybe staying friends with Jennie was good.

"I'm just wondering..." She shook her head, trying to formulate her thoughts. He watched her, waiting. "Why did she say that? Was it something you did? Or said? I don't want to pry, but it's an odd comment. Don't you think?"

He grinned at her and she felt her brain go fuzzy around the edges. "Not odd at all. Most people consider anything more than a passing gesture to be too much. Sunday service is okay. Giving up a big promotion because God is calling you in another direction is not. Saying a blessing before eating is fine. Praying for your future spouse is not."

Calista paused, her fork halfway to her mouth. "Future spouse? What does that kind of prayer sound like, if I can ask?"

He shrugged a little. "Uh, I don't usually focus on that, since I have bigger fish to fry. But let me think. I usually pray for her health and safety, for her to grow in God's grace."

Her fork was still poised above her tray. She hadn't spent much time praying in the past ten years, but if she had, it wouldn't have been for anyone else. It would have been for herself. Was there a man praying for her right now? One she'd never met, but who cared for her already? She dropped her gaze as the thought brought sudden tears to her eyes. Could she be loved and not even know it yet?

"That sounds weird to you," he said lightly, but she heard the hint of something in his voice, maybe disappointment.

"No, not weird." She looked up at him. "It's beautiful. I'd never thought of it before, praying for your future spouse."

"Really?" He sounded surprised.

"Really. I'm pretty new to this." She waved a hand between their trays, meaning the blessing. He frowned, trying to understand. "Blessing your food, asking for direction in your life."

He nodded. "How new? Like, today new?"

She laughed. "Not that new!"

He grinned back at her, his broad shoulders relaxing

a little. She wished she could tell him that there were years of prayer behind her, that she was a seasoned Christian. But she was practically a newborn, trying to understand what God's will was in her life.

"New enough." She sighed. "It's a long story but I grew up in a place that was less about the truth and more about what made a good show."

His eyes were sad as he searched her face. "That could be anywhere. I think once pride gets center stage, God's truth is hard to hear over the noise."

She nodded, thinking it through. "You're right. It's probably a pretty common thing. But I let it get between me and God for a long time."

"But not anymore." Grant's eyes were soft, his biscuit forgotten in his hand.

"No," she said, unable to keep her smile from spreading as she gazed back. "Not anymore."

Calista slipped out the mission's door into the mid-November chill. She had been so nervous about volunteering that she had forgotten her coat and gloves in the car, but now she felt the wind whip through her expensive sweater. Tucking her hands in her pockets with a shiver, Calista glanced up at the snow-covered Rocky Mountains. It was hard enough to be homeless in the winter, but it was downright deadly in Denver.

She walked to the secure parking behind the mission, hardly noticing the people passing her on the sidewalk. Her mind was full to bursting and she struggled to squelch the feelings Grant brought to the surface. She'd told Lissa the truth: she was way too busy to date and it never worked out anyway. No guy wanted to be known as "Calista Sheffield's boyfriend" instead of by his own name. There were very few men her age who earned more than her or had more power. The ones who were eager to take on the role were only interested in the boost it gave their own business reputations.

Her mind flashed back to Grant's face, his apprais-ing glance. He hadn't seemed interested in her job so he probably didn't care. That would be a good thing. Her life had become so consumed by her success that she had let her soul wither away. She felt as if she was just a husk, dried up and empty inside. Where there should be something vibrant, something connected to God, there was a pitifully weak, underfed shadow.

But she was ready to change, to let God call the shots for a while. She wanted to feel joy, like the look on Grant's face when the little girl had practically tack-led him with her hug. She pressed the button on her key ring and her Mercedes beeped in response. Sliding into the leather seat and reaching for the buckle, Calista felt her whole self yearn for purpose in her life. Her God was a God of second chances so she didn't have to wal-low around in her sad and lonely life.

Now, if she could just get everybody else to give her a second chance at being a decent human being, then she'd be all set.

Her cell phone trilled in her pocket. And she an-swered it automatically.

"I'm sending you the report on the new building sites and you have four urgent messages." The voice on the phone belonged to Jackie, her personal assistant, who sounded calm and collected as usual. She rattled off the messages in rapid-fire.

Calista tucked the cell phone into her shoulder and turned onto the freeway. "Tell Jim Bishop that Branchout Corporation's new commercial is encroaching on the VitaWow brand and we need to send them a cease and desist letter. Also, get Alicia down to tech support and make them promise not to wipe the hard drive on my laptop ever again. They said they were cleaning it, but all my temporary files disappeared into thin air." She could hear Jackie typing at a frantic pace.

"How was the appointment?"

"What appointment?" Calista asked, before remembering that she'd told Jackie she had a toothache and was going to the dentist. "Right. The dentist was great. All fixed."

The sound of Jackie's laughter made Calista glare at the freeway in front of her.

"This is why I have complete faith in VitaWow's CEO. You can't tell a lie to save your life."

"Why do you think I'm lying?"

"You never forget details, but more importantly, nobody ever says their dental appointment was *great*."

Calista let out a sigh. "Fine. I wasn't at the dentist. But I'll tell you about it later. This traffic is just crazy in the afternoon." Cars were slowing to a crawl in front of her. "Good thing I'm always at the office until late. I completely miss rush hour."

"Are you using your headset?" Jackie asked suddenly.

Calista already had one ticket for cell use while driving. "I was, but I dropped it when I got out of the car and it shattered."

"New headset," Jackie mumbled into Calista's ear as she typed another note. "Okay, I'm hanging up now because it would be extra bad for the company image if you racked up another ticket."

"All right," Calista said. "See you on Monday."

Jackie snorted. "And talk to you tomorrow, you mean. You don't take weekends off. Which means I don't, either."

She frowned, easing into another lane of slow-moving traffic. "Well, that might have been true before. But I'm determined to make it a priority to enjoy some free time. I don't want to wake up at eighty and realize I worked my life away."

"I never thought I'd hear you say that. How surprising."

"Realizing your only friends are people who get paid to talk to you will do that to a girl."

Jackie laughed and her infectious giggle made Calista grin long-distance. "I thought it was your biological clock ticking away."

"I'm not that old! I just need to expand my horizons," she said huffily. But the thought had crossed her mind, right about the time her sister, Elaine, had given birth and Calista had seen the pictures of all her friends gathered to meet the new baby. Calista wanted a family, but she wanted the whole picture. She wanted the faith that brought fullness to life, and the friends to experience it all with her.

"And I mean it about the weekends. I might pop into the office on Saturdays but no more Sunday work. I want to get a real life."

"Hey, as a card-carrying member of your current life, I don't appreciate you getting a new one unless I'm in it. But this is sounding stranger and stranger." Jackie's voice was still light, but Calista knew her words concealed real worry. And she had cause to be worried because Calista had made no secret of how her hypocritical father had ruined her life.

"It's a long story."

"Then Monday it is, and be careful driving in that traffic," Jackie said, sounding uncharacteristically maternal before she hung up.

Calista focused on the road in front of her and tried not to think of the horror stories she had told Jackie. None of them had been exaggerated.

Her father had been the most respected man in their dusty, Southern town, but he ruled their little house like a dictator. He acted loving and gentle in front of their church family, but told his own family when to eat, sleep and pray.

The blaze that burned her house to the ground and took her mama's life told her for certain that God couldn't be trusted. So, she would have to make her own way in the world, without His help. Her choices were either go to college or settle down with Ray Collier, the football coach's son. Ray was a good guy, but he would never have been happy with her. She had too many opinions and didn't like football. Her sophomore year in college she heard he'd married Tina Bowdy, a pretty girl whose father owned the gas station. She hoped they were a lot happier than she had been the past fifteen years. But her unhappiness was her own fault. There was ambition, and then there was insanity.

As Calista turned the car into the private parking garage under her condo, she felt hope rising in her chest. The mission was going to be a good place to spread her wings. She could be wealthy and successful, and have a few friends, too. As Grant's face crossed her mind, she willed it away. She wasn't volunteering so she could meet a nice guy. Even if she never saw him again, she knew this was the beginning of something…something real, something she'd been missing so far. It was time to stop hiding who she was. She had been born for a purpose, and she was ready to find out what it was, even if it meant admitting to the world that she wasn't the perfect woman they all knew as the VitaWow CEO.

Chapter Three

"You haven't cashed my check." The low growl on the other end of the phone set Grant's teeth on edge.

"I tore it up. Don't send another because I don't want your money." He worked to keep his voice steady and even, but his heart was pounding in his chest.

"You're a fool. Or a liar. I've heard the mission is in big trouble. I know you need the cash." A thick, mucusy cough followed the last word, and Grant flinched as the sound echoed in his ear.

"I do what's best for the mission and that would never be accepting your money. You'd always be there, trying to worm your way into every decision I make." His voice had risen higher as anger threatened to choke him. They'd had this conversation ten, twenty times. He was sick of it.

"You're right. I'll always be here, whether you take the money or not. But thanks for letting me know I need to have my accountant send another. This time, to the board." Then there was silence.

Grant stared into space, then slowly replaced the receiver. The board consisted of nine very respected and dedicated professionals, from bankers to business owners to pastors. All good people who would wonder why Grant wouldn't take money the mission desperately needed for repairs and upgrades. Especially from the state's richest man. But he couldn't. It was tainted, stained. It was money made off the backs of the poorest of the poor. Taking money from a man who wouldn't even provide his workers with decent health insurance was like making a deal with the devil.

He dropped his head in his hands and groaned. *Lord, I'm not asking for You to stop the sun from rising. I just want him to go away. He had his chance and blew it. Isn't it enough that I forgive him?*

The sudden sound of a throat being cleared, loudly, brought Grant's head up with a snap. Jose was standing in the doorway, shifting his weight from foot to foot, his thick arms folded over his chest. "What's up?"

"Nothing," Grant answered tersely. Jose had the habit of appearing and disappearing without a sound. He should put a cowbell on that kid.

"Alrighty then," he said lightly, but his face was creased with concern. "Just wondering what you thought about the new chick."

Grant struggled to regain his composure, feeling like a gorilla at the zoo who just had his cage rattled. He stood up and stretched. "She's not a chick. And she seems all right. Should be good for office help, at least. She wanted to work in the cafeteria."

Jose chuckled. "Yeah, that would have been a disaster. She's so pretty the line would have taken forever. She's like, more than the usual pretty."

Grant didn't want to discuss the "new chick" but he nodded. "Yup, certainly got blessed in that department.

But she seemed sort of…" His mind thought back to the tapping foot, the arms wrapped around her middle.

"Nervous?"

"Right. Or sad. I don't know." He shrugged and checked his watch. "But then again, it was probably because her car might get broken into out in the parking lot."

Jose's eyebrows went up. "She has a sweet ride, for sure. But, boss…"

"Sorry." Grant couldn't shake off the irritation that wrapped itself around his neck like a scarf. He rubbed a hand against the base of his skull. "I'm just on edge. True, everyone carries a burden. We'll probably never know the whole story because after Christmas, she'll be gone."

"She said that?"

"No, but you know how it goes. Guilt sets in, they come sign up for a few meals, then January hits and they feel better about themselves so they never come back. Until next November."

Jose nodded. "Well, probably a good thing anyway."

"Why? You know something I don't?" No matter how careful or protective he was of the people here, there would always be those who came to prey on the weaker ones. He had set up several lines of defense with background checks, personal references and lots of observant employees. But there were cracks in every fortress.

"Nope. Just thinking she's definitely your type." Jose grinned and waggled his thick eyebrows.

"That's unprofessional," he said, frowning. Unprofessional and unsettling. She wasn't anything like his type. He felt comfortable with women who were reserved, even a little distant. The woman who came here today was a bundle of emotions; they flickered across her face like pictures on a screen.

"Yeah, it is, but it's still true. Plus, how would this place survive if you actually got a life?"

"I do have a life. It's just very quiet."

"You mean, boring." And with that Jose popped back out.

Grant sighed and pushed back his chair, stretching his long legs out under the old wooden desk. He was busy. He didn't have time for a girlfriend. At least, that's what he told himself.

He rubbed a hand over his face. Sometimes, when it was just a little too quiet, he thought about his mother. A beautiful woman ruined by her addictions, heartbroken when she trusted the wrong person. She never stopped reminiscing over how rich his father was, how successful. It almost seemed as if she didn't remember that he'd left her with nothing but a baby to raise. The memory of the fast cars, wads of cash and fancy parties blurred her focus, polluted her heart. The love of money was the root of all evil, right? Grant straightened his shoulders. He was never going to be sucked into that fantasy world. He was happy, right where he was.

His mind flicked toward the image of Calista's face, her large green eyes sparkling with hope. He wished her well. He really did. But people like that didn't stick around places like a homeless shelter. The pull of money was too strong. And money was one thing the mission didn't have.

If God didn't nudge somebody to donate really soon, and in a big way, they might not even have to worry about Christmas preparations. The mission would have to close. But he would do everything in his power to make sure that didn't happen.

Calista slid her car into the open space at the parking garage behind the mission and tried to calm her pounding heart. She allowed a small smile to touch her lips as she thought of the irony of the situation. Just that morning she had brokered a huge deal with a company in Northern California. It had been months in the making and if it succeeded, their production and distribution would be on the fast track to making VitaWow a nationwide phenomenon. Before ten this morning, she was CEO to a company that was a regional star. After ten, she was CEO to a company that could be as widely recognized as Coca-Cola in just a few years.

The irony of her anxiety now was that she hadn't felt a bit uncomfortable going into a meeting that could decide the fate of her company. She knew business and marketing, she understood the language and the terms. More than all of that, she had a gift for business. Calista took another deep breath and shook her head.

But this mission gig had her stomach in knots. Definitely out of the comfort zone, right where God wanted her.

The short walk to the front doors of the lobby seemed to take forever but finally Calista stepped into the warmth. She headed for Lana's desk, unbuttoning her bright red wool peacoat on the way.

The secretary glanced up and raised a hand. "Glad to see you. You're early. I just love early people."

Calista felt her heart lift. Lana sounded like she really was glad to see her. "I was raised in a family of chronically late people so I rebel by arriving just a bit early," Calista said, trying not to look toward Grant's office. She wondered if he was at the mission, or if he was in a meeting somewhere, and then was irritated at herself for wondering.

"Just a bit early is perfect. Then there are those people who come twenty minutes early for everything." Lana rubbed the spiky ends of her hair, and Calista recognized the gesture from her last visit.

"What do you need me to do today?"

"Thanksgiving is a really busy time for us. Not just for meals. There's lots of paperwork. It would be a relief to have someone do a little filing. We have a skeleton crew for the office right now, since two of our part-timers left for other positions."

"You're at the front desk a lot of the time?"

"Right, so when I'm out here, I can't be in there," she said, waving a hand toward the locked door on the right.

Calista's mouth went dry and she cleared her throat. "So, I'll be working with you at the desk, or back in the offices?" She added hastily, "I can answer phones, too. If you show me your system." She actually hadn't worked a switchboard since college but the thought of working in close quarters with Grant sent a thrill of alarm through her.

"Because of privacy issues, you should probably work in the office area. We can have you organize files into specific cabinets, without having to look at the papers, since they're all color coded."

Calista nodded, resigned to the fact she was going to bump into the man. She would just have to get a grip. "I'm ready," she chirped, hoping she was convincing enough.

Lana must have thought so, because she pushed a button on her phone and said, "Grant, Calista's here."

"Be right out." The answering voice was familiar, in a tinny way.

Lana let go of the button. "Thanks again for the help. You're saving me a headache."

She smiled automatically but her mind was whirling. "Jose's not here? I would think Grant's way too busy to show me the filing system."

"He's here, but the director asked to be the one to show you around the offices." Lana's words were followed by the appearance of the man himself.

Calista heard the door and turned her head in time to see him open the door with speed. He looked a little harried, his red tie crooked and crisp white shirtsleeves rolled halfway up his forearms.

He was happy to see her. At least, his expression changed from something like worry to pleasure. His lips quirked up and his eyes radiated warmth. She couldn't stop herself from responding. It had been so long since anyone had looked happy to see her. She let her eyes drift over him for the briefest moment and then clamped down hard on any desire to give a closer examination.

"Glad you're back. Come on in," he said, motioning her through the door.

It was just a common phrase, but her smile only got bigger. It was like she'd swallowed a happy pill.

"I'll show you the offices first, then the general meeting rooms and the break room." He strode down a carpeted hallway and stopped at the first door, knocking lightly.

The affirmative answer from the inside sounded muffled, and she saw why when Grant pushed open the door. Jose was crouched near the desk, piles of power cords in his hands.

"This power strip is dead. I'll have to get another from the supply closet. Maybe they only last a few—" His sentence trailed off as he finally caught a glimpse of his audience. "Hey, Calista. Glad to see you back."

"Hi there," she responded, grinning. Three people had welcomed her in less than ten minutes. She felt all warm and fuzzy inside. It had been a very long time since anybody had said "hey" to her. People didn't say "hey" to the CEO.

"Jose's office. He oversees the group that works with the food boxes distributed to needy families. He also organizes social activities for the residents."

"Yup. And I say we spring for a real Santa this year. The kids are starting to suspect the truth when Santa has a Tex-Mex accent." He grabbed his stomach and tried a few "ho ho ho" sounds.

Grant laughed and waved a hand. "You know you love it. All right, on to the next stop."

The next door was an empty office that had a high window with a pulled shade. "One of our three empty offices. Soon to be filled, God willing. The person here handles class scheduling and addiction support. The main counselors and teachers are doing well right now, but it helps to have a manager type to handle any conflicts."

Another short walk to the next door and Grant pushed it open without knocking. "My office. Lana started calling it my 'man cave' after Jose brought in a small fridge."

"Got it stocked with beer for those slow afternoons?" She chuckled to herself the split second before she realized her mistake. "Oh, Grant. Sorry. That was stupid." His mother was an alcoholic, Grant didn't drink, and she'd just made a beer joke. She wanted to fall through the floor.

To her relief he seemed to shrug off the insensitive comment. "No big deal. And no beer."

Calista gazed around the space and wondered why Grant didn't have a nicer office. As the director, he needed to give the impression that he was the head of a thriving organization. People donated to the cause they thought would succeed—it was human nature. Maybe it was because the donors always met in the conference rooms. Or maybe with nonprofits, it might not work as well to flash too much wealth. In her world, understated luxury was the only way to go.

His office was more than understated; it was shabby. An older-than-Methuselah desk, a battered chair, a few framed photos, his diplomas and the small fridge.

"How long have you been here?"

"Five years as director, about eight altogether."

"And you don't even have a plant?" She turned to him with a curious look.

To her surprise, he flushed. "I should make it a little homier, considering all the time I spend in here."

Calista nodded. "I don't know much about charities, but if you're bringing donors through this hallway to get to the boardroom, you had better keep this door closed."

He let out a sound that was more of a startled cough. "I don't think it's all that bad, personally."

"It's not bad. But it doesn't look good. And donors will judge the entire mission on you and your space." She surveyed the room once more. "Maybe a nice framed photo of the staff, right here, that you could see when you passed down the hallway."

Grant frowned. Putting money into furnishings when there were people who didn't even have shoes was unthinkable. And a photo? He hated anything done for show. It smacked of insincerity to have a photo taken of his staff, even though they were his friends, just to show it off to donors. But he tried to take a mental step back and look at her advice with a cool head. He knew better than anybody that donors saw him and the mission as inseparable. He was the human face they could put on the problems of hunger and homelessness in their community.

"I suppose I can see your point. I'll look for something that might go in that spot. I appreciate the advice."

People didn't usually thank her for the advice she handed out. Probably because she made it a habit to break the cardinal rule of giving advice: wait for someone to ask. She turned, surprised and ready with a quick retort if she saw the faintest suggestion of sarcasm.

Their eyes met. Time seemed to slow as he stood very still. His gaze wandered down to her mouth. It had been so long since any man had looked at her like that and she read in his blue eyes exactly what was going through his mind.

He moved a half inch forward. Calista felt a thrill course through her and couldn't stop her breath from catching in her throat. The tiny noise she made seemed to remind him where they were and what they were doing. He blinked, and his gaze flashed back to the empty spot on the wall.

He cleared his throat and stepped back into the hallway. “I’ll show you the filing room so you can see the mess we have in there.” His voice was rough.

Calista nodded, following his lead without comment. She really needed to get a grip. All of this talk about purpose and change, but here she was ogling the director. Of course, there were some major sparks flying, but the poor man had enough on his plate without adding a woman like herself to it. She trudged behind him down the hallway, barely listening while making appropriately interested sounds. Everything about Grant Monohan made her want to be a better person, and that meant learning not to indulge every wish and whim. Not something she was really used to, but she was determined to make herself useful at the mission…and stay out of his way.

Grant struggled to put words together as he led Calista down the hallway toward the file room. His mind churned as he pointed out stacks of loose files, gave her a quick tutorial and then made as quick an exit as was humanly possible.

He reentered his office and shut the door, leaning heavily against it. What on earth had just happened there? One minute she was giving him sound business advice, and then next he was about to make a move on the pretty new volunteer. He felt a shiver of fear run through him. Maybe all the stress of making their low funds stretch through the holidays was messing with his head. Maybe he needed to get some counseling to make sure he was staying on track.

And being seconds from kissing a woman in his office was about as offtrack as he could get.

He didn’t even really know much about her, except

she was smart, bossy and emotionally vulnerable in a way that made him want to protect her from the world. But she didn't need him to do that. Rich people just hired someone to protect them. Grant rubbed his temples and tried to corral his thoughts.

In a job like this, you had to understand the danger of becoming too emotionally close to the people who needed your help. It was okay to make friends, to give support and encouragement; it wasn't okay to let attraction lead to actions. To be fair, it was definitely a mutual attraction. The way her eyes looked at him told him that.

And she wasn't a resident or someone in need of counseling. But she had already said she was working her way back from some kind of traumatic past. Her faith was new, untested. He had no right to get in the way of what God was working in her heart. It was too much, too soon. The "new chick" was going to have to find her way without any of his attention. Plus, he had bigger problems on his plate, starting with a leaky roof and a Thanksgiving dinner for five hundred. After that, he had to take another look at the financials. If anything else went wrong, anything at all, their reserves would be tapped out.

Chapter Four

Calista's usual morning routine began with two pieces of seven-grain toast, some orange juice and a long run on her treadmill. This Wednesday was no different, except that she pounded out a solid five miles with an overwhelming feeling of happiness. The awesome view of the Rocky Mountains never got old. She couldn't wait for the next snowfall, a few days from now, if the forecast was right. Last year she'd been too busy to enjoy any of it, practically living at the office. But this year would be different.

It would be the perfect winter moment: watching big flakes drifting past her tenth-floor windows as she read in her favorite chair, wrapped in a cozy blanket and sipping hot chocolate. In her mind's eye, there was someone new in the picture. Someone tall, handsome, caring. Calista shook her head and turned off the treadmill. Grant was never going to end up in her condo, sipping hot chocolate or not. To him, the luxury high-rise would be a disgusting waste of money.

Mimi wandered into the kitchen and surveyed her

domain from the end of her squashed and furry nose. Cruella De Vil could have learned a thing or two from Mimi. The cat was bad to the core. Deceptively sweet on the outside, Mimi would wait for Calista to leave before she took her revenge, usually by chewing on her nicest pumps.

Calista put out a tentative hand, hoping for the hundredth time that they could be friends. The Siamese cat waited for her to get closer, then darted forward with lightning speed to nip Calista's fingers with her tiny, sharp teeth. She yelped and snatched her hand back. Mimi made a slow-motion about-face and presented her fluffy behind before she sidled out of the kitchen.

Calista sighed and headed for the master bathroom.

After her shower, she decided on a simple tailored white shirt and khaki pants. She let her blond hair dry naturally so it curled a bit and swiped on a light pink lipstick.

Calista took a long look in the mirror. She tilted her head and squinted, watching little crow's-feet appear at the corners of her large green eyes. She had always taken care of her skin and watched her weight, but no more than most women. Calista knew she had a lot of spiritual work to do but at least she wasn't obsessed with her appearance.

It was a strange feeling, looking at her own personality under the microscope. She'd spent so many years gliding by on power and position that she wasn't even sure what her weaknesses were.

She closed her eyes for a moment, praying that God would reveal her faults to her. *Just not all at once, please,* she thought hastily. Maybe she could tackle one issue a month. And this month would be…being a better friend. She opened her eyes and grinned at her reflection. This would be the ultimate makeover, from the heart on out.

"Glad to see you this morning," Grant said.

Calista knew it was just words, but she couldn't help grinning every time he said it. "Thanks, I can't seem to stay away."

He reached out a hand and she responded, feeling the warmth and strength that she had missed ever since the first time they'd met. She struggled to sort her feelings, to narrow down the whirl of conflicting emotions. But all she could feel was the touch of his hand, and hear the steady beat of her heart against her ribs. As he let go, she noticed dark shadows under his eyes and there was a persistent frown line between his brows.

"Everything all right? You look tired."

His shoulders straightened a bit and he glanced out the lobby window behind her, watching the residents filing in from the halls. "Fine. Just the busy season."

"Does your family live around here?" As she asked the question, she wished she could snag back the words. He probably thought she wanted to know more about his alcoholic mother. Her cheeks went hot.

His gaze traveled back to her and he frowned, thinking. "My family…is here. At the mission."

Well, that was clear enough. He could have waved a sign that said, "None of your business. Stop prying." Calista nodded, biting her bottom lip.

"Mr. Monohan?" A young man with a long, lean face approached them. He was wearing one of the red polo shirts that identified him as a mission worker and it hung from his thin frame.

"Hi, Jorge." Grant turned his attention to the mission worker. "What's up?"

Deep brown eyes flitted to Calista and then away. He cleared his throat, his Adam's apple bobbing. "Your girlfriend is on the phone."

Calista's stomach suddenly fell to her feet. There was no reason on God's green earth that she should feel anything at those words. She looked around desperately for Lana and pretended she couldn't hear the conversation only a foot away.

"My *what*?"

"Jennie Close, that lawyer? She said to tell you that your girlfriend was on the phone." His eyes flickered nervously between Calista and Grant again.

Grant opened his mouth, then seemed to think better of what he was going to say. "Tell her I'll be right there."

Jorge nodded and slipped back through the door to the offices.

"Lana should be here in just a bit. She has some projects she wanted to show you."

Calista forced a bright smile. "Great. I'll wait right here."

As Grant walked away, Calista felt her face grow hot. No wonder she was at her best in the boardroom. She was a total failure at normal conversation.

"Hey, Calista, did you want to grab some coffee with me in the cafeteria? Then I can show you the filing system." Calista turned her head in surprise, then readjusted her gaze downward.

"Lana, that sounds great, actually."

Lana wheeled past her, leading the way to the cafeteria. She handed Calista her badge on the way. "Here's your ID. Go ahead and slip it on. You should have it visible at all times, especially since you don't have a uniform."

Calista took the square badge and slipped the lanyard over her neck. She was thankful she didn't have to wear that awful uniform. Then she squashed the feeling down, irritated with her own shallowness. At least the shirts weren't yellow. She looked awful in yellow.

They swiped the badges at the front and went to the coffee bar. Lana balanced her cup on a tray settled on her knees. Calista hovered, undecided, then said nothing. Lana had lots of practice carrying her own cup. She should probably just back up and let her do it.

Lana stopped at a table, scooted a chair to the side, then wheeled into place. "You're a godsend for the mission, you know."

Calista choked, the bitter liquid burning its way up her throat. She took a few seconds to clear her airway, her mind spinning. Of all the things she had expected Lana to say, this was close to last on a very long list. "Why do you say that?"

"Your business background. We're in big trouble here and I think someone with your experience could get us back on track."

Calista stared into her cup, watching the overhead lights shimmer on the black surface. "I hadn't heard that. I don't know anything about nonprofits. I wish I did, truly, but—"

"How different can it be? We need money, you know how to make money." Lana leaned forward, her usually pleasant expression now serious. "Grant doesn't want to alarm anyone, but this is the worst situation we've been in for years. Our funds have been low, but this is scraping the barrel."

"What's the problem? Did you have a big donor back out?"

Lana sighed. "The day care area needed to be updated to keep in line with federal standards. Then we had to widen all the doorways and bathrooms for handicapped access." She glanced up. "Don't get me wrong. I'm all for being able to get to the bathroom. But the board thought we should widen everything, not just have one designated exit or bathroom on each floor. That was early this year. Right after that, the classrooms had to have all the electrical redone to be up to code. Then the state recommended every public space have an emergency contact system put in, so we had to put in a PA system."

Calista nodded. Sometimes things snowballed and there wasn't anything you could do about it. "So, how bad is it? The financial situation, I mean."

"Bad. The roof is leaking, so it has to be fixed, and soon. We've got another four months of snow. We'll have to close that building if we can't fix the roof. Thanksgiving is a huge expense, and then winter comes right on top, so we'll be full to the brim. If it was June, we could probably make it through. But as it is right now..." Lana's light blue eyes dropped to her cup, her lips thinned out in a line. "Even with Christmas donations on the way, we won't make it into December at this rate."

A woman appeared behind Lana, her round face pocked with acne scars but her dark eyes were bright. "Lana? Jose needs you at the desk. There's some question about the switchboard. They can't transfer a call."

Lana nodded. "I'm coming." She motioned to her cup. "Finish your coffee. Come on back when you're done."

"Thanks," Calista said and watched Lana push herself with powerful arms toward the doorway. She couldn't shake the sense of alarm that threaded through her at Lana's news. The mission had serious money issues and they thought she could help? How? A for-profit company sold stock or got investors and promised some kind of return. What kind of return was there in giving cash to a homeless shelter? No wealthy person she knew would be willing to donate the kind of money they needed. There was nothing in it for them.

Calista's shoulders straightened. She would just have to figure something out. But first she needed to get a specific idea of what kind of numbers they were talking about. She glanced around, feeling like the new kid in junior high who had to eat lunch alone. The cafeteria had emptied considerably in the few minutes they'd been talking and the kitchen staff had come out to wipe down the tables and collect trays.

Marisol directed several groups in aprons as they cleared the food trays out of the warming areas. The small Hispanic woman was a blur of movement as she bustled between workers. She spotted Calista sitting alone at the table and paused, frowning. Seconds later she was standing before her, hands on hips, lined face creasing with displeasure.

"Did they go and leave you alone?"

Calista considered her options. She could rat out Grant and feel a little satisfaction after being dumped for Jennie-the-lawyer-but-not-girlfriend. Or she could be honest.

"Lana was here, but they needed her back at the desk." She tried a placating tone, hoping for an undercurrent of nonchalance.

"That's no excuse. Where Mr. Monohan?" If anything, Calista's explanation made the frown even deeper.

"He got a phone call. It was Jennie, the girl you were asking about." She had no idea if that would be helpful, but she felt as if she'd been called to the principal's office.

The noise that came out of Marisol's mouth made her think of an angry goose. An angry mama goose. "So! He leave you to go talk to the girl who says he love Jesus too much!"

Calista felt her face start to flush. The cafeteria crowd was sparse, but there were still a few curious looks being cast in her direction. "It's fine, really. I don't mind."

Her dark head was cocked slightly, eyes appraising Calista. "Oh? You think he is too religious, like that crazy girl?"

Calista's gaze swept the cafeteria for any sign of rescue in the form of Jose. "No, he's perfect the way he is. And I don't mind eating by myself." Or she didn't until the cafeteria matron came to give her a hard time.

As if someone had flipped a switch, Marisol dropped her fists from her hips and slid into the seat across from her. "I'm sorry if I make you feel upset. I want him to have a family, a wife who love him, but he is so busy."

At least she knew when to back down. Her cheeks still felt hot but Calista said, "That's all right. I can tell you care about him."

"Oh, yes. Mr. Monohan save my life." She said this as if she was simply giving the time of day.

Grant laid the phone in its cradle and dropped his head in his hands. What an awkward conversation. He never wanted to repeat anything like it, ever. Jennie wanted to give it—them—another shot and well, he didn't.

Jose peeked in the door and gave him a sympathetic glance. "Looks like that went about as well as I thought it would."

"Yeah, you called it." Grant stared at the desktop, shoulders slumped. "I'll have to call Eric and tell him he's banned from setting me up with anyone, ever again."

"It's not his fault. You have to admit, she's pretty good-looking."

Grant frowned. "So, how did you know that she…?"

"Wasn't your type?" Jose sidled a glance at him and then chuckled at his boss's irritated expression.

"Right. Did you give her a personality test when I wasn't watching?"

"She wasn't interested in the mission. Just you. And that was never going to work."

"Not interested? Why else would she be here? I'm pretty good at spotting the fakers and the takers." He'd spent close to ten years at the mission, on and off, and after a while he could smell a user at fifty yards. Not a drug user, but a people user. Although he'd gotten pretty good at spotting the addicts, as well.

"Simple." Jose's black eyes were restless, like a bird's, as he glanced around the lobby. "She never tried to talk to anybody else but you. Not the kids, not the staff, not Lana or Michelle or Lissa, or the residents."

"I can't believe that she never talked to anybody. There are hundreds of people here every day."

"I didn't say she didn't talk to them. I said she didn't try."

Grant frowned, trying to remember. "Well, make sure you use your superpowers the next time, okay? You can save me some time."

He turned to see a huge grin spread over Jose's face. "Now what?"

"You sure you want me to put on my cape and tell you who to ask out?"

Grant rolled his eyes. "Sure, why not? Just don't make the list too long. I'm not made of money, you know."

"How about the new volunteer?"

"Oh, right." Grant paused, struggling to come up with a reason that Calista was not his type. He decided not to argue with the type just yet. "Well, I don't think it's a great idea to be using the new volunteers as my personal dating pool. Eric introduced Jennie and me, so it was all right for us to go out socially."

Jose continued to grin. He stuck his hands in the pockets of his slacks and rocked back on his heels, looking like a man who knew more than was good for him.

"And then there's the matter of faith." Grant wouldn't normally share that kind of conversation, but Jose was killing him with that smug expression. "She just said that she's new to all of this. That's how she said it. *All of this.*" Grant waved a hand, indicating the cross on the wall, the lobby, everything.

"That's a bad thing? I'd rather have a fiery convert than a lukewarm cradle Christian."

Grant had to admit he agreed with him there. He tried a new tack. "I really don't think someone who wears Ralph Lauren to a homeless mission is my type."

The smile slipped from Jose's face. He crossed his arms over his chest and said, "Lana and I were talking about that. What? We weren't gossiping." Grant had opened his mouth to remind Jose that the mission was a "no gossip" zone. There was too much real drama without creating any of their own. "She was wondering if she should mention it to her, just ask her if she could dress down a bit since some of the residents might feel uncomfortable."

Grant nodded. That was one of the reasons they wore the red-polos-and-khaki-pants outfit. Of course, they were easy to identify, but it also took some of the pressure off the staff. It was hard to wear nice office clothes when you worked with people who only had one pair of pants to their name. He should know, because he'd been on both sides of that fence.

"She makes me think of myself, when I first came to Denver." Jose's jaw tensed as he spoke those last words and Grant remembered clearly how troubled the young man had been. "All I knew was how to be tough and I dressed the part. Almost everybody I knew back in El Paso dressed like that, even my family. I knew it made people think twice about messing with me, but I didn't know it made them think twice about giving me a job or being friendly."

Grant had thought more than twice about being friendly. Jose had been positively lethal looking. He had been fighting his way out of alcohol dependency and he'd radiated anger.

"What I wore didn't mean the same thing to me as it did to everyone who knew me here. But I gradually learned to let the gang clothes go."

"So, you think she doesn't realize that wearing a hundred-dollar shirt is a bit offensive in a homeless shelter?" Grant couldn't hide the skepticism in his voice.

Jose uncrossed his arms and gave him a steady look. "I'm not sure what's going through her head. Maybe she doesn't think anyone will recognize the brand. Maybe she's so rich that these *are* her casual clothes. But I know she'll figure it out and she'll care when she does. And I'm telling you, she's your type."

Grant threw up his hands at the last words and started to laugh. "Okay, I give up. No more talk about dating because I'm probably going to end up a bachelor forever at the rate I'm going. What's so wrong with being single, anyway?"

"Nothing, if you want to be, if you're supposed to be. There's room for everybody, right? But see, Cassandra showed me how happy I can be. I just don't want you to miss out on something good."

There was no way to argue with that. Jose had never been so happy, or so determined to stay sober, as he was now. Cassandra was a small woman with a huge laugh. She'd grown up in the roughest part of LA and was part of the day care staff. Their wedding a few months ago was one of the highlights of the year, in Grant's mind. Two incredibly happy people, making a lifetime commitment before God, inspired them all to be a little gentler to each other.

"Cassandra is a direct message from God to you."

Jose grinned and nodded. "You got it. Anyway, where's the new recruit?"

"I think Lana's showing her what to do."

"Why not you? There's nothing on the schedule this morning, and Lana's busy enough as it is. She asked me to do it but I've got a meeting in ten minutes."

Grant shoved his hands in his slacks' pockets and stared at the floor. He knew he was being ridiculous, but he was afraid if he spent too much time with Calista then his life was going to get a whole lot more complicated. And he liked it simple. Or as simple as it could get at this point.

"Take a chance, boss. You never know what good things are planned for you today." Jose's voice was teasing but Grant got his meaning loud and clear.

"All right, but I'm not saying anything to her about her clothes." Grant stood up with a frown and brushed past Jose, who was struggling to suppress a very broad smile.

He pushed open the dining-room door, feeling a wave of warm air against his face. The smell of casseroles mixed with overcooked vegetables was as familiar as his mother's perfume. Calista probably thought sitting in this place was the worst possible way to spend a Wednesday but it felt like home to him.

He turned toward the table where Calista sat and halted midstep. Her back was to him but she might not have seen him even if she was facing him. Her bright blond head was bent toward a familiar dark one. Marisol had one hand on Calista's arm and the two women looked like they had known each other forever.

"Oh, yes. Mr. Monohan save my life. Is a very long story." The woman waved a hand like she was swatting flies.

"I know you're busy, but I'd like to hear it." Calista glanced back at the groups wiping tables and clearing dishes.

"Well, I tell you a little." She paused, staring at her hands that were clasped together, dark fingers intertwined. "I came to Denver for my son. He come over to work. His papa died many years ago, it was just us. He sent me an address and money but when I get here, he was gone." Her eyes settled on the wall behind Calista, as if she was seeing something very far away. "I was so scared. I run out of money, not knowing where I can go, what I can do to get home. Then I see the mission sign."

It sounded like Calista's worst nightmare, being stranded, penniless. A horrible dilemma. To stay and search for her son while trying to keep off the streets, or go home and always wonder what happened. She shivered, rubbing her arms through the expensive cotton shirt. Calista tried to swallow past the lump in her throat. "So what did you do?"

"I spend my day looking, hoping. But I need a job and Mr. Monohan asks me if I can cook." She grinned, bright teeth shining again in her dark face. "And that is the end of the story."

Except for Marisol's son. Calista was afraid to ask, but couldn't help herself. "Did you—did you ever find out…?"

Tears welled in her brown eyes but her voice was strong. "I think my Gabriel is gone from this life and he is with *Nuestro Señor*, Jesus. He would have found me by now."

Calista nodded, blinking back her own tears. What would it be like to be loved so deeply? To have someone sleep on the street, to live in a shelter, to refuse to leave a foreign land, just to find you again? "That's a mother's love," she said, almost to herself.

Marisol regarded her for a moment. "*Sí.* Your mother is close to you?"

"My mother died when I was young."

"Ah, *mija*." The older woman sighed out the words

and reached over to pat Calista's arm. "There is nothing sadder than a girl without a mother. Nothing."

She didn't know if that was true, even as her heart was aching in her chest. "Even sadder than a mother without a son?"

To her surprise, Marisol nodded. "*Sí.* I miss my son, it's true. I am sad that he did not have a wife or *niños*. I will never be called *abuela*." She wiped her eyes with the edge of her apron. "But I have everything I learned from my mother. Her cooking and her stories, how to rock a baby and how to feed a man."

Calista squeezed her eyes shut for a moment, feeling the loss of her mother acutely. "But Mr. Monohan has no mother and he looks like he's doing perfectly fine." She didn't know why she wanted to argue about it.

"Oh, *Dios*," the woman exclaimed, clapping her hands together in grief. "Poor man, he is an orphan. Worse than an orphan! But he is strong, he works hard and his faith will keep him on the right path. He is busy making the world better."

And that was the difference between them.

Grant had put all of his heart into helping others and he was surrounded by people who respected him, loved him. *I'm sure when he walks into the mission Christmas party, the room doesn't fall completely silent.* No, he was swarmed by kids, beloved by bossy old ladies, protected by friends. Calista felt self-pity well up in her and wondered if it was too late for her to get a real life, one like Grant's.

"Don't look so sad, *mija*." There was that word again, whatever it meant. And the comforting pat on the arm. "There is room in his life for a woman. He works a lot, but I know he is lonely, too. I think if you show him what you feel, there is a chance for you and Mr. Monohan."

Calista shook her head, trying not to laugh as she tried to make sense of such an odd comment. Then there was the ominous sound of someone clearing his throat a little too loudly. She turned her head, knowing before she saw his face that Grant Monohan had heard the last few sentences and was coming to a very awkward conclusion.

Chapter Five

Grant cleared his throat and waited to be noticed. His mind was reeling from the words that had just come from Marisol's mouth. He was busy but was he lonely? And the new volunteer had feelings for him?

Calista turned toward him, her face the color of fresh beets.

His thoughts stuttered as he tried to make sense of what he'd heard. Did she care for him? But they hardly knew each other. He took a deep breath and gave them both a steady gaze. Whatever was going on, he needed to be as professional as possible.

"Mari, thanks for keeping Calista company."

"My pleasure, but you should be ashamed of yourself. You leave this beautiful girl to talk to the crazy woman? No wonder you still not married." This all came out in a rapid-fire, heavily accented stream. The words were a little unkind, but Marisol softened the blow by standing up and placing a loud kiss on Grant's cheek. "And you need a haircut. Is getting too long. Soon, no one will know whether you are a resident or the director. You come over next week and I trim it for you."

Grant felt heat creep up his neck but he nodded. He'd never get used to being treated like a kid, because he'd always taken care of himself. If his hair started to curl over his collar, then he was the only one who ever noticed, until he met Marisol. There was no halfway with her. Once he'd been adopted by the fierce little woman, she got full rights to his grooming, love life and nutrition, in no particular order.

"I got to go make sure they don't break all my dishes." Marisol swept up the tray from the table and turned to Calista. "You come back next weekend and I'll give you some tamales to take home. It's a tradition. Tamales at Christmas." With that last bit of bossiness, she turned and disappeared into the kitchen.

There was a moment's pause while Grant wondered what to say and how to say it.

Calista stood up, grabbing her coat off the back of the chair, and brushed back a wavy curl from her face. Grant wondered what she looked like when she laughed, then felt irritation at wondering.

"I need to go find out what Lana needs me to do," she said, her smile a perfect balance of friendliness and distance.

He knew she was being helpful, being flexible about all the upheaval around the mission, but somehow he felt disappointed. Part of him wished she would seek him out, make an effort to be around him. He realized that even though they'd only known each other a few days, he felt absurdly relaxed around her. Except for when he stood a little too close or looked too deeply into her eyes, and then he felt the very opposite. "I let Lana know I was coming in here. I'd like to show you the rest of the complex, if that's all right."

Her eyes crinkled with pleasure. "Lead the way." Her whole figure seemed to exude high energy.

As they walked through the almost-empty cafeteria toward the double doors at the far end, he glanced at her. "Are you a runner?"

She almost stopped in surprise. "How did you know that?"

"Because of the way you move." The words were out of his mouth before he really thought through them. He hurried to elaborate. "Runners have a confident stride. My friend Eric ran in a marathon last month and he walks like you do."

"I'm no marathoner," she said, laughing. "Those people are nuts. I've done a 10K and a half marathon, but the real deal is way beyond me. I started running when I was in college to relieve stress."

"I hear you. I swim every morning at the Y. When I don't get in my laps in the pool, I feel out of sorts."

She turned to him as he opened the door and motioned for her to pass through. "Earth and water. Those two elements don't mix, do they?"

For a moment, their eyes locked and he felt his brain shift from small talk to something deeper. Her smile faltered as she waited for him to say something, anything. His gaze slipped down to her lips. He struggled to find the thread of the conversation. "Um, I think that's fire and water."

"Right. I don't know why I said that."

Again, that long, loping stride. He grinned, thinking of how many times he'd had to slow down because his long legs left friends behind. Their strides were well matched, in tune.

"We'll start with the recreation areas so you can

get an idea of the different buildings." He pushed the long handle of an exit door and they came out into the mid-November sunshine. The snow-filled courtyard was empty except for two men talking at the far end. Buildings rose on every side, warm-colored bricks offset against the cool blue of the sky. The snow sparkled in the bright sun and the air smelled like it had blown straight down from Mt. Evans.

"We have five separate but connected buildings. The largest is the residence hall, which can house up to two hundred men, and has one hundred cots for emergency overflow. The women and children are housed here—" he pointed across the grass "—and we have family housing on Ninth Street, in an apartment block. The lobby, offices and cafeteria are behind us, of course, in the main entrance areas. In the cafeteria they serve almost three hundred people, three meals every day.

"To your right we have the old classrooms, which we use for addiction counseling and parenting classes and anger-management classes. Then over here we have the recreation areas and the day care rooms. We have a small library that's stocked with children's books, thanks to a community reading program."

"A library? Now that's a good thing. I think books were my best friends when I was little. Maybe they still are." She glanced around, sizing up the buildings. "Which one has the roof that needs replacing?"

He glanced at her in surprise. He opened his mouth to ask, but she was already talking, eyes fixed on the building ahead.

"Lana mentioned it. She also says the mission is running on fumes, financially." She sidled a look at him. "Running a business isn't easy, to say the least."

Grant didn't know whether to be irritated or relieved. Part of him wanted to impress her with how well the mission was doing, but it was true they were in serious trouble.

"What's the fund-raising like here? Do you have a special board? Is there a general fund or are there building funds and program funds? Is the money accessible or is it in trust?" Calista was frowning slightly, a hand over her eyes as she surveyed the building, one hand tucked in her jacket pocket.

"The board handles most of the financial decisions. The money is in a general fund unless a donor asks for it to be earmarked for a certain area, like the children's playground. We have a charity drive twice a year, once in December and once in July." He had to admire her questions; they were thorough and intelligent.

"Have you ever had a fund-raising for a specific cause?"

Grant shook his head. "You mean, like when they have the big thermometer with the red line pointing out how much more needs to be donated?"

Calista's broad grin flashed in the sunlight. "Exactly. And everybody fights to be the one to move the arrow every time the money gets recounted."

The thought of Lana and Jose wrestling over the red arrow made him chuckle. She glanced back at the building, her smile turning serious. Grant dropped his gaze, wishing that he could say something to make her laugh again. The two men who had been talking near the far end of the courtyard disappeared through the doors to the recreation building.

"Grant, it really shouldn't be hard to raise that kind of cash."

He opened his mouth to argue, to tell her how hard they worked for the donations, then thought better of it. He had a business degree, but most of his concerns were wrapped up in the health and safety of his residents. "You have any ideas?"

She nodded, still surveying the area. "Absolutely. You need to involve some bigger sponsors than the neighborhood grocer or carpet-cleaning service." She turned, green eyes serious. "You know what I mean? Big sponsors. Like Denver Bank or the big chain stores or even my company, VitaWow."

"That's not going to be a conflict of interest?"

Grant wanted to smooth the tiny wrinkle that appeared between her brows.

"Why would it be? We partner with charities, especially during the holidays. If I make up a list, you'll need to start reaching out to them right away. Like, tomorrow. Before all their holiday charity funds are snapped up by the bigger places."

"I suppose I can manage that," he said. He laughed and realized with a shock that he didn't mind some wealthy volunteer giving him orders. How did she do that? How did she boss him around and tell him what to do, and make it feel good? The only other person who could tell him what to do was Marisol.

Which brought back the words he'd heard when he'd entered the cafeteria. *He works a lot, but I know he is lonely, too. I think if you show him what you feel, there is a chance for you and Mr. Monohan.*

He cleared his throat and thrust his hands in his pockets, shifting his feet in the snow. He really didn't want to bring it up, but living with an alcoholic had made him allergic to secrets and lies. He didn't have time to wonder what she was thinking, or what Marisol was trying to tell her.

"Calista, do you mind if I ask you a personal question?"

He watched a look of wariness settle in her eyes. She lifted her chin and straightened her shoulders, as if she was waiting for him to say something awful. For the first time, he wondered what, exactly, she was hiding. How anyone could top the burden of shame he carried around, day and night, he couldn't imagine. But something about the fear and courage that battled in her eyes told him Calista Sheffield just might have bigger secrets than he did.

Chapter Six

Calista's heart pounded in her chest. The look on his face was so grave, it sent her warning sirens blaring. Had he heard something about the horrible CEO of VitaWow, the one who made the secretaries cry? That was all in the past. She was a kinder, gentler person. The kind who would let everyone decorate their cubicles and chew gum and cook nasty frozen entrees in the microwaves. Of course, she'd have to put all the microwaves back in the break rooms, but that was a small step.

"What exactly did Marisol tell you today? When I came back from the lobby, I heard something and I—"

Relieved laughter bubbled up and she cut him off midsentence. "Oh, Grant! That woman is priceless! Promise me you never, ever let her leave." She clutched her middle and struggled to catch her breath. "She's just the greatest. And the way she was fussing over your hair." Another wave of laughter rocked her. She was so thankful his question was about Marisol's silly advice that she wanted to turn a cartwheel.

He was grinning right along with her, although his blue eyes remained shadowed with curiosity. "She's a keeper. And I suppose I shouldn't have wondered, but what I heard was so strange…" He shrugged sheepishly.

Calista felt a tiny bit of irritation at the word "strange," but shoved it down inside. Of course she didn't have a chance with Grant. "I know, right? We were just talking about, I don't know, everything." She struggled to remember the entire conversation. "She told me how she got to Denver, about Gabriel, about how you and the former director tried to help her."

"She told you all of that?" His tone was a little sharp. For the first time Calista noticed a dimple in his chin that must only show up when he was frowning.

"I'm sorry, I didn't mean to bring up bad feelings for her. But she said that you'd saved her life and I asked her to tell me her story. If I shouldn't have done that, I apologize." She felt as if the sun had cooled a little and she rubbed her arms through her jacket.

"No, not at all. It's just that she doesn't usually share her story. It's very painful for her, even after all these years."

Calista nodded, remembering Marisol's tear-filled eyes. "She seems resigned to never seeing her son again. And then we were talking about whether it was better to be an orphan or to lose a child."

Grant made a sound of surprise, somewhere between a cough and an exclamation.

She felt heat creep up her neck and squinted out toward the snowy square. "I didn't ask her that. It just sort of came up." She darted a glance at him and was surprised to see his lips quirked up in a half smile.

"It's nice to hear. That she was talking, I mean. Marisol is a good supervisor, friend and grandmother type. But she doesn't open up to a lot of people."

Calista mulled that over. She decided to take it as a compliment. "I'm glad she felt safe with me. Anyway, we were talking about losing parents and—"

"Are your parents living?"

The question startled her, although it was a natural one. "My mother died when I was in high school, and my father and I don't really get along. Too much bitter history." She watched his eyebrows rise but didn't care. Better to have the truth out as soon as possible.

"I'm sorry for your loss. And does he have anything to do with the faith you mentioned, the one that puts the show before the truth?"

She was surprised he remembered her exact words. "Right. So, Marisol was saying you were like an orphan but your faith would see you through and I was feeling a little sad that I had spent so much time building a life that didn't have anything worthwhile in it, and she completely misunderstood my expression and thought I was upset that you were too busy for a girlfriend. And then you came in."

Calista hauled in a breath. She desperately wanted the conversation to veer back into something safe, like planning for the new roofing fund. But his blue eyes were locked on hers. The emotions that flickered over his face were unreadable.

The sudden sound of the door slamming open behind them interrupted whatever thought he had been forming.

A young couple with a small child waved as soon as they caught sight of Grant. They changed their trajectory across the snowy courtyard to meet Calista and the director. The girl had shoulder-length hair with a strip of bright pink on one side and her dark brown eyes were heavily rimmed with liner. She had dark circles under her eyes but walked quickly, holding the baby on one slim hip like a bag of flour. The little girl's curly brown hair bounced with every step her mother took. The young man's shoulders were hunched under his thick, oversize sweatshirt and the hood was pulled over his head. As they got closer, Calista noticed a large tattoo covered the area from his collarbone to his jaw.

"Hey, Aliya, Josh." Grant put out a hand to Josh but was pulled into a bear hug. Aliya grinned and stepped forward to give Grant a squeeze. The little girl reached out for Grant and he took her in his arms. Calista felt a tug around her heart at the ease of his gesture. She couldn't remember the last time she had held a child, let alone had a child reach for her like that.

"Miss McKenzie, you look happy today." The little girl beamed in response and said something that might or might not have been English. Grant looked to Aliya for help and the young mom shrugged, laughing.

"She talks like that all the time. We have no idea what she means, either."

"Calista, this is Aliya and Josh, and their daughter McKenzie." Grant made the introductions and Calista felt the couple's curious gazes. She smiled and held out a hand, which they both shook without comment.

"You guys come for breakfast? Or are you heading for the recreation rooms?"

"Naw. We're gonna go to a class. McKenzie will be in the day care for a few hours." Josh looked dangerous, but his voice was quiet, almost childlike.

"Which class? We've got a great list this month."

"The job-prep class. I think Miss Borne is teaching it. I like the way she gives lots of examples and we read articles from *Newsweek*." Aliya brushed back the pink shock of hair and said, "I don't want to work in fast food forever."

"Glad to hear you like her teaching style. Some people think she's mean." Just yesterday there was a middle-aged woman who had come directly to him to complain about the homework load. But if they were going to give credits for the classes, they had to keep track of the homework, he'd told her.

"Well, if you're dumb enough to give a presentation without doing your work, yeah, she can be pretty mean." Josh ducked his head, as if he knew exactly how that felt.

McKenzie let out a stream of syllables and poked her finger into Grant's ear. He winced, laughing. "All right, missy. Back to your mom before you stick that finger in my eye." He passed the chattering toddler back to Aliya and waved as the couple headed across the courtyard and to the door that led to the classrooms.

Calista watched them walk away, her mind turning on the young couple. "That's really encouraging."

"That they're taking classes?"

"I mean, they could just get on welfare, right?"

Grant was silent for a moment. He seemed to be considering his words carefully. "After a while, if you stick around, you'll realize that many of these people are very proud in their own way. Those two were street kids and are trying to work their way back from some serious mistakes. Josh doesn't look like much, but he's gentle and wants to provide for his kid."

Calista felt shame slice through her. She turned to face him, noting how the bright winter light brought out tiny gold flecks in his blue eyes. "I didn't mean…

I wasn't trying to say..." Her voice trailed off, wanting to defend herself but knowing he was right.

"I know. There are the ones like Duane who will take everything you offer without any gratitude, but he's not the norm." His eyes were troubled, almost sad. "Anyway, let's get started on this tour. I want to make sure you've got a good idea of where everything is in case we need you to volunteer in different sections."

Calista nodded and tried to cover her shame. "I'm ready." As he headed for the dormitories, she sneaked a glance in his direction. The strong shoulders, the slightly wavy black hair, even those startlingly blue eyes were nothing compared to what was inside. His dedication to the mission and his faith in the people shone like a beacon.

As they passed from room to room and into other buildings there were more introductions and more warm greetings for Grant. Calista had an eerie knack for remembering names and faces, and she absorbed the small details of the tour. But half an hour later, her heart was fuller than her mind. Every time she saw him shake a homeless man's hand, touch the shoulder of a teenage boy, kneel down to talk to a little child, the scene dropped into her heart like something warm and substantial. She could feel the weight of it pressing against her ribs, like a hug from the inside.

Calista exited the elevator at full speed and narrowly missed the building's snack cart. Mrs. Benjamin let out a yelp of warning but they were both saved only by Calista's last-second dodge to the left.

"I'm so sorry, Miss Sheffield," the older woman said while picking up the snack-size potato-chip bags that had been jolted off their hooks when the cart stopped on a dime.

A surge of irritation flared in her chest. She didn't have time to be dodging old ladies pushing food carts today. *Love is patient, love is kind.* The verse came out of nowhere and all the words she wanted to say, about not standing in front of the elevator, of moving more quickly, died in her throat.

"It's my fault. I shouldn't have been running out of the door like that." Calista bent down and retrieved one small bag from under the cart's front wheels. "This one looks a little squashed. Let me buy it." She dug in her shoulder bag for a dollar and deposited it on the tray. "Have a good day."

Now the proud owner of a seriously smashed pile of chips in a cellophane bag, Calista continued toward the glossy black desk that designated the waiting area for the top floor of VitaWow. Renee sat motionless, her almond-shaped eyes fixed on Calista. Her shiny, flame-colored bob was lacquered in place and accentuated her sharp cheekbones. Calista had hired Renee for her speed and professionalism, but the woman would have looked at home in the biggest corporations in the country. She was beautiful, educated and had just the right mix of charm and aloofness.

"Morning, Renee." She didn't usually interact much with Renee, since Jackie was her go-to girl, the ultimate personal assistant. But maybe it was time to start reaching out. She stopped in front of the desk and admired an arrangement of exotic flowers. The deep red blooms were striking against the shiny black desk and the scent was strong and sweet. "These are pretty. Did you order them?"

Renee slowly nodded, her eyes still fixed on Calista. "Yes, I order the flowers for the main desk downstairs, the departmental secretaries and your reception area every week."

"Oh." Calista felt her cheeks grow warm. It was not as if that was something she should have known. Deciding who ordered the flowers was not her job. But still she felt a niggle of embarrassment. She'd never even noticed any flowers before. She usually flew right past the desk while yelling instructions. Well, she might slow down just a mite to snag her phone messages out of Renee's outstretched hand. She cleared her throat. "Any messages?"

Renee held several small pink slips of paper and Calista took them, grateful to have something to distract herself. "Thank you," she called on her way into her office.

The reception area of the top floor was empty but the hallways were bustling with employees. Calista stood for a moment, watching the movement of the staff. She felt her brows draw down. Long aisles were bound on each side with half-walled cubicles, but most of the staff seemed to be walking around. Walking wasn't really the word. They seemed almost frantic. In fact, she was sure that one man had just entered and left the same cube twice in one minute.

"What's wrong?" Jackie's voice cut into her thoughts and she turned to see her personal assistant wandering toward her, a stack of collated brochures in her arms. Her hair was brushed back from her face but fell in small ringlets to her shoulders. As she came nearer, Calista saw dark circles under her deep brown eyes. Competent, capable Jackie. Of course, she had her own life, probably filled to the brim with friends and family but Calista couldn't name a single one.

"Nothing." She turned back to the hustling crowd. "It just seems like everyone's on red alert. What's with the running around? See, that guy there with the green striped tie, I swear he just went to check the fax machine for the third time."

A snort of laughter came from behind her and Jackie shook her head, curls bouncing every which way. "Are you serious? Of *course* they're all on red alert. The boss is standing there with a face like thunder and they want to look busy."

Calista whirled to face her. "I'm not some whip-cracking taskmaster. Plus, I come through here all the time."

A single, well-groomed eyebrow lifted in response. "All the time?"

She felt her face grow warm. "At least once a day. Just to hang out."

Now both eyebrows had gone up. "Just…to hang out." Jackie could really pack a lot of meaning into four little words.

Calista frowned furiously and went back to studying the wide-open office space. Could the twenty-five employees who worked on the top floor of VitaWow really have that much dislike for their boss? She tried to think of the other departments. She'd always been warmly welcomed when she visited the lower six levels. Of course, there was usually a reason she was there. A meeting or an announcement. Or to find out who had dropped the ball on some project. Now that she thought of it, those warm welcomes were just a bit tense.

"Okay, not to hang out. To survey my domain.

Happy?" Bitterness crept into her voice. "But that's my job, isn't it? Not to make friends with everybody."

"Right." She could see Jackie nodding out of the corner of her eye. "But it wouldn't hurt to make friends with, say…one or two."

And there it was, out for all to hear. She had no friends. She felt her heart sink in her chest.

"Are you going out for dinner after work?" Jackie sounded contrite and rushed to change the subject. "You sure look nice."

Calista crossed her arms over her light blue linen dress. After the mission she'd made a special effort to choose something that wasn't a slacks-and-jacket set. Now she felt plain silly.

"No, not going to dinner. I just felt like wearing something pretty." She'd had enough of surveying. Time to let the employees relax. She turned back toward her office and Jackie followed beside her.

"So, how was the dentist?" Again that sly note in her voice spoke volumes.

"It wasn't the dentist, as you know. Come in and I'll tell you all about it." Calista led the way into her office and closed the door behind them. She crossed to the small coffeepot in the corner and dumped in some French vanilla. But decaf, since she'd had enough excitement this morning, thank you.

The bright light streamed through the floor-to-ceiling windows and she began to pull the shades on the four windows that flanked her desk. Calista liked her corner office for the stunning 180-degree views of the Colorado Rockies, but directly below the mountain range and too close to ignore there was the mass of air-conditioning units on the building next door. Plus, afternoon sun could really heat up the room and when she used the pull-down shades, the whole room took on a sepia tinge. But all of that would change when they built the new VitaWow headquarters. State-of-the-art glass would adjust to the direct light. The plans had been revised about ten times, but her top-floor corner office was set in stone. Or so the architects had said.

She pulled the last long acrylic shade down over the view, blocking out the sun and the ugly sight of the AC units. By this time next year, her view would be about twenty floors higher up and duct-free. They hadn't picked a location, but the board was fielding offers and counteroffers. Within months, she would be helping break ground on a brand-new building. The thought filled her with satisfaction. She'd grown this company from the very beginning so it was sort of like expecting a baby. A twenty-story, smoked-glass-and-steel baby.

"So, spill it." Jackie perched on the edge of a leather plum-colored armchair and gave her best "I'm listening" look.

Calista plopped into her chair and planted her hands on the top of her mahogany desk. "I'm volunteering at the Downtown Denver Mission. Probably once a week, maybe more if they decide they need me to help them with fund-raising."

There was a beat of silence that became two, then three. Jackie blinked and cleared her throat. "And why would the CEO of this fine company be volunteering at a homeless shelter?"

"Because I woke up one morning and realized I was a terrible human being."

"Just like that?"

Calista sighed. "No, not quite. And it would have been nice if you'd argued just a little with that statement."

Jackie had the heart to look sheepish. "You're not a terrible human being. You're just not very approachable. Or sympathetic. Or caring about anybody's personal life. Or—"

"All right! I got it." Calista stood up and paced back and forth in front of the shaded windows. The watery, muted sunlight made the room look especially monochromatic.

"But I think you could be helpful there."

She turned, hope making her voice rise. "You think so?"

"Definitely. Especially the fund-raising. They can give you the figures and you can whip up some marketing scheme. You probably won't even have to go into the shelter after the first day."

Calista felt her insides tighten with anxiety. Jackie didn't think she could do anything other than make some money. "See, I don't want to just fax over papers or visit with the board. I want to do something real." That sounded ridiculous. They both understood that money was as real as it got.

Jackie looked at her hard for a moment. "You mean, you want to make a difference in someone's life." Her voice had a cautious tone.

"Exactly."

"Don't you think spending time at a homeless shelter is a bit…ambitious? You could always mentor some business majors or even build some relationships here at the company. I'm sure they would appreciate your mentoring a few pegs down on the totem pole."

"You know, that's a great idea." Calista stopped pacing for a moment and put a finger on her lips. "I'll bring that up to Human Resources and see what they say. But I'm still going to volunteer. This morning I took a tour and met most of the staff."

Jackie seemed like she was still struggling to grasp the concept of her boss spending time out of the office, with people who weren't rich or powerful.

"The director is very inspiring, too." Calista left this last comment hanging in the air as she fiddled with the large leaves of the potted banana tree near the window. She tried to make her voice light, but every time she thought of Grant, her stomach did a little jump.

"Inspiring how? The shave-your-head-wear-a-sheet-give-all-your-money kind of inspiring?"

Calista snorted. "Not quite." But she had to admit, it was pretty close. And that was a scary thought. Because if there was one thing Calista Sheffield did not do, it was play "follow the leader." She stared out at the snowy peaks of the Rocky Mountains, letting Jackie's light conversation wind around her. There was nothing else to do except make sure her focus stayed on the mission and not on the director. That gorgeous smile could turn anybody's head but he didn't need another groupie. He needed someone who could raise some cash. And that was what she was going to do.

Chapter Seven

"Hello, *mijo*," Marisol said, loading a giant aluminum pot into one of the three commercial-grade dishwashers. Grant reached over the petite woman and positioned the pot. The steam from the last batch of dishes snaked out of the metal machine in tiny wisps. He slid the door closed and flipped the switch, careful to avoid the hot metal of the utensils in a small green basket she had just removed.

"Looks like you have experience. You want to be the new dishwasher?" Marisol's teasing tone helped the knot ease at the back of Grant's neck.

"Anytime. At least this doesn't include any long meetings."

Marisol laughed, a light, carefree sound that seemed to belong to a much younger person. "No, *gracias a Dios*, no meetings." Tucking one dark brown hand into the pocket of her apron, she waited for him to speak. He rarely came into the kitchen unless he had a purpose there.

He cleared his throat, looking for the right words.

He'd heard Calista's version, now he wanted to hear what Marisol had to say.

"Why did you tell Calista I was busy, but she had a chance with me if she showed her feelings?" He didn't know if he was asking out of insanity or sheer curiosity. Part of him wanted her to give a perfectly normal explanation and another part—the part that had him thinking about Calista nonstop since the moment he'd seen her—wanted Marisol to tell him Calista cared for him.

"She said you were perfect. I was just making her feel better because she look so sad." Marisol shrugged, as if that statement hadn't knocked Grant's world for a loop.

He felt his eyes go wide. "She said those words, those exact words?"

Marisol beamed again. "She did. I knew you would like that."

"No, Mari, I'm not perfect. You know I'm not. I'm so far from it that I should come with a warning sign. I get wrapped up in my work, I care way too much, I have a temper." He ticked off his faults in rapid-fire, while holding up one finger at a time.

To his surprise, Marisol laughed, the sound mingling with the clanks and clatter of the busy kitchen. "*I* know that, *you* know that, but *she* doesn't know that."

"And lying to her is okay with you?" He couldn't stop the bitter note of accusation that accompanied his words.

She sighed and reached out a hand to touch his arm. "*Mijo*, I would not lie to the girl. And she is not one to believe a lie. But when the heart first loves, it only sees perfection. With time, the love remains but the heart knows the truth—no one is perfect. Only God. That is what I mean." Her brown eyes were wide with earnestness. "So, when she says you are perfect, and those were her words, it made me happy. That is always how it is in the beginning."

Grant wanted to tell her that she had no right to discuss his personal life, especially with a woman he barely knew. He wanted to be angry that she could laugh about Calista thinking he was perfect, when he was so far from it. But he couldn't. A strange sensation had crept over him while she spoke. It was a mix of yearning and dread, of excitement and fear. He felt as if he were standing on the edge of a cliff.

"Let's not get ahead of ourselves." He worked to get his voice under control. "A lot of people throw that word around."

Marisol nodded in a way that didn't fool him in the least. Her eyes were still bright as she turned to accept another large pot coming from a worker. "You are right. We cannot jump ahead. Let us go one step at a time."

Which made his stomach drop again, as if he really had just jumped off a cliff. Because the next step was going to be seeing more of Calista. Maybe he should ask Lana to assign her some scheduled hours when he was sure to be out of the building. If they never saw each other, then their friendship would never turn into something else. And she would never know he was anything less than perfect, which might be what he really wanted, a small voice reminded him. He heaved a sigh and resigned himself to the fact that he had to trust God. He knew what He was doing. Even if it looked like He was trying to throw Grant off a cliff.

* * *

Jackie poked at her iPad, tapping and scrolling through screens. Another crazy Tuesday morning. But Calista didn't mind because she had tomorrow morning at the mission, which was absolutely the best part of her week.

"I'm assuming you're not attending this year's Christmas party," Jackie said, not bothering to glance away from her glowing screen.

"Actually, I think I will."

If Jackie had been the excitable type, she would have bolted from her perch on the armchair and let out a screech. But all she did was raise both eyebrows and let her mouth fall open a little in surprise.

"And stay for a while." Calista dropped the words into the space between them as casually as if she had been present for every single VitaWow party for the past five years. Which she hadn't. Well, not really. She would show up for fifteen minutes, shake some hands, watch the party fizzle out to almost nothing, then make her exit. Last year, she swore she could hear sighs of relief on her way out. She was the original wet blanket.

"Is it because it's being held at the Grant-Humphreys Mansion? You said you didn't really care, so I thought it was time to make a change from the Ritz."

"Now you're making me feel unwelcome."

"No, I think it's a great idea." Jackie nibbled a nail, still focusing on her boss. "Are you bringing a date?"

She pasted a noncommittal look on her face and shrugged. "I'm sure someone will pop up."

"Right." And with that, her assistant dropped her gaze to her lap and continued jotting notes.

Calista swiveled in her office chair and gazed at the

scenery outside. Little fluffs of white snow were falling lazily from the sky and the peaks in the distance were almost obscured by the low, heavy clouds. Was it possible that she could combine work and play? Just once? If she brought Grant to the party, he could really make some contacts. Enough with the fifty-dollar-a-month donations from old ladies down the block. The man needed to find some serious donors. The guest list had some very influential business owners, and she could certainly pull in a few more. A very small part of her insisted that she wasn't being completely honest. *To thine own self be true.* She sighed and admitted that, just for a moment, it would be nice to go to a party and have a good time. Maybe dress up and dance a little.

The corners of her mouth tugged up. She would ask him today. Her stomach gave a shiver of nerves but she straightened her shoulders. She was done investing time and effort into projects that didn't make her happy. The mission made her feel useful, and she'd made friends there. And Grant… She didn't quite know if the feeling she got around him could be contained in that one word, but happy was definitely part of it.

Grant stared at his desk calendar and counted back the days. Almost Thanksgiving already. It had been three weeks since Calista Sheffield had walked into the mission. She was coming more than once a week now. Even though she spent a lot of time in the filing room at the end of the hall, there was a standing need in the nursery on Friday evenings, when the women's Bible study was held in one of the classrooms. Thursday evening was the grant-writing team meeting and they worked side by side perfecting the applications.

And Saturday morning was Marisol's cooking class and Calista had been thrilled to find out there was still a place for one more.

At first, he tried to ignore her. Impossible. He found himself staring into those bottomless green eyes, just seconds after he had decided to ignore her, again. The days when she wore her hair soft and loose, he swore he could smell the delicate scent of her shampoo when she passed his door.

Avoiding her worked a bit better, except that he never saw Marisol when Calista was around because the two had become fast friends. And he could never quite seem to forget she was here, in the building, somewhere close by.

So, finally he decided he would treat the situation like a twelve-step program. *The first step is to admit you are powerless.* He couldn't control his emotions when she was around. It was useless to try. He would just turn it all over to God.

Of course, that didn't mean he was luring her into his office for another near-miss kiss. It just meant he couldn't fight what he was feeling. It was a huge relief. Now all he had to do was battle the insane impulse to follow her around, just to be in her presence.

And he wasn't going to let himself go there, because she was going to leave. Maybe not today, maybe not after Thanksgiving, but for sure when the Christmas tinsel came down and reality set in. If the mission could stay open that long. He might not even have to worry about Calista leaving if he didn't get some big donations real soon.

What if they had met at some sort of business function, not as director and volunteer? Would they have had a chance? There was that edge-of-the-cliff feeling again. He grimaced and tried to calm his breathing. But nothing would be able to get past the fact that she believed in the power of the almighty buck and he didn't. He didn't think he could be with someone who spent all their time making money.

He rubbed a spot in the middle of his chest, a dull ache. Was it stress or something else? He chuckled at the question and then a knock on the door made him nearly jump out of his skin.

Lana rolled her chair toward his desk, an envelope in one hand.

"This came in the mail today and I wanted you to see it before the board does," she said, her blue eyes narrowing with anxiety.

Grant frowned and took the plain manila envelope. The paper inside was folded in thirds and as he spread it against his desk, the first thing he noticed was the crude handwriting. The next was the message scrawled in black ink.

I know who you are, Grant Monohan.

Under that was a line that made the hair on the back of his neck prickle.

Time to make Daddy's little boy pay.

Lana waited, watching Grant with worry etched in every line of her face.

"I guess it's time, then," he said. "This is the fourth one this month and now there's a threat attached."

She nodded and reached for the paper. "It was bound

to come out sooner or later." She folded the paper back into its envelope. "There's nothing for you to be ashamed of, you know."

He rubbed a hand over his face, feeling the stubble that appeared right around this time of day. "I know, but it doesn't make it any easier. People will come to their own conclusions, no matter how I spin it."

"Then let God handle it, no spin required." Lana was unshakable in her faith and Grant loved that. He felt as if he was holding on to his by a thread most of the time. No, he had plenty of faith, but the doubts were constant reminders of how far he had to go.

"Right. Will you help me craft the statement? I'll give this to the board tonight. We can set up a media announcement for Friday morning. Then we have to turn it over to the police." Standard procedure when there was a threat of any kind. And a big place like this attracted a lot of crazy stuff. Good thing their financial statement was up to speed. Last year's audit was ready if the press started slinging mud.

Lana ran a hand through her short gray-purple hair. He felt himself relax at the sight of the familiar gesture. The secretary had been a good friend these past years, like a steady rock in the storm. "The day after Thanksgiving? Well, that will be a way to avoid Black Friday sales, for sure. I'll get right on it. Short and sweet?"

"Probably better that way, don't you think? It's going to cause enough publicity as it is." His stomach twisted at the thought of making a public statement about his personal life, the past he'd been hiding. No, not hiding but avoiding.

"Grant, you know we all love you." She fixed him with a steady gaze and Grant felt affection for her well up inside, his anxiety replaced with gratitude. His throat closed a bit and he said huskily, "I know, Lana, and I won't forget it."

She smiled a little sadly and swiveled the chair toward the door. She turned back for a moment and said, "You're used to expecting the worst out of the world. You just might be surprised about how this all turns out."

Grant nodded and she wheeled out the door, strong arms propelling the metal chair across the threshold. He stared for a moment at the space she'd left behind. Maybe she was right, but years of seeing the worst in humanity had trained him to prepare for disaster.

When he announced to the world that he was the only child of the wealthiest businessman in the state, his life would never be the same. He gazed around the small, plain office and shuddered at the thought of paparazzi camped out in the lobby, harassing the homeless people. The preschoolers would be frightened and confused by the camera crews. The everyday folks who came here for addiction counseling and spiritual support would feel too intimidated by the cameras to get near the door. He dropped his head in his hands and tried to slow his breathing. Maybe it would be best for everybody if he resigned. Maybe he could continue to work in some other capacity, like board members did.

But the thought of leaving the only place he had ever felt at home made him sick to his stomach. The father who had abandoned him to an alcoholic mother, who'd never sent a penny in support, who'd jetted around the world while his own kid had dug in Dumpsters for food, was not going to run Grant's life.

Grant straightened up and took a deep breath. *Lord,*

You've been with me every step of the way. Help me to remember You're the only father who matters. Wherever You want me to go, I'll go. He closed his eyes and waited in silence, feeling as if words had failed him but knowing God read what was unfinished in his heart.

The file room at the Downtown Denver Mission was a little gray box with scratchy carpet and a window too high to let in much light. After twenty minutes that first day, Calista started to sympathize with the VitaWow employees who worked in the basement. She would never again complain about the fact that her office got a blinding dose of afternoon sun. As soon as she'd returned to her office, she'd authorized some very nice coffeemakers and a new set of leather couches to give their break room some extra perks. For the past three weeks, she'd also thrown in movie tickets for every basement-level employee, to sweeten the deal.

But no matter how nice VitaWow's basement was now, this little file room was still a claustrophobia-inducing box. She'd never liked small spaces, especially after the house fire. Her mind flashed on the old wooden porch, blackened and listing to one side. Before she could stop it, images flickered of the living-room floor burned through, the basement where the fire broke out, where her mother had been doing laundry. Finally, where her mother had been trapped when the old wooden steps into the low-ceilinged basement had collapsed.

Calista took a breath and closed her eyes. *Lord, I trust in You.* That was all she could pray when the images began to flash before her, especially in the middle of the night. There was no way she could try to explain why her mama had to die like that. She was a gracious and kind woman, who brought dinner to sick folk and took in stray dogs. How could it ever be made right? But her faith told her to trust that it would be made clear someday. Right now, all she could do was trust.

Eric knocked and opened Grant's office door at the same time. He stood there looking exceptionally grouchy. His best friend's bright red hair stuck up in tufts like it always did when he'd been clutching his head. It would have been funny except for the frosty glare underneath.

"Hey, what's up?" Grant waved him toward a seat and grabbed two sodas from the mini fridge. Maybe a cold drink would buy him some mercy. He was pretty certain he knew what prompted Eric's visit.

"So, you dumped Jennie and now you won't even talk to her?" He didn't make a move to sit down or take the soda.

Grant winced. "Happy Thanksgiving to you, too. I told you that she wanted—we both wanted—to be friends."

"She just paid me a visit to complain that you weren't answering her phone calls."

"I'm not."

Eric's frown intensified. "Well, must be a story there because you're not usually the type to freeze someone out. Spill it." He plopped his lean runner's body into a chair.

"Well, she said I was too religious, decided we should be friends. Then she called here, saying she was my girlfriend. I think she knows there's something more to be gained by dating a poverty-stricken shelter director after all."

Eric sighed. "Wow. So you think she knows about your father? She seemed so wounded this morning, she was almost crying."

Grant almost snorted soda up his nose as he thought of how many tears would be shed when he made that announcement. "I have no doubt she was." He straightened his shoulders and rolled his neck, trying to ease some of the stress in his muscles. "I'm holding a press conference tomorrow."

Eric's eyebrows shot up. "Time to get it out in the open?"

"I suppose so. There was another threatening letter today…" His voice trailed off as he remembered the awkward scrawl.

Eric shook his head, staring into his can. "I'm sorry. What a mess. And to think I've always envied you."

Grant looked up in surprise. "Me?" He was speechless for a few seconds as he processed that information. "Because I'm the heir to a fortune made by barely legal activities? Because my father just recently decided that I exist and he wants me to pretend we're best buds? Now, you, you have more talent than anyone I know, a beautiful wife who loves you, a baby on the way and an extended family that makes the mob look disloyal."

He nodded. "Thanks, and she does and they do. But I always thought you had it better because of… Well, everybody loves you on sight. You never have to work to make friends. If you had five minutes alone with him, you could get the Grinch to give this place a donation."

Eric continued. "I had to work for every date. I'm

still shocked that Marla even gave me a second glance. But you just smile, and women fall all over themselves."

Grant knew where this was going and got a sinking feeling in his stomach.

"But now, you're way worse off than I ever was. After you tell the world that you're Kurt Daniels's son, it'll be like you've got the relationship version of the Midas touch. Every girl you meet is going to want to date you and you'll never know for sure if they really care. That just stinks."

He couldn't help laughing. It was all so awful, and so painfully true, that it was more than a little funny. "You've nailed it, as usual."

Eric shook his head and took a sip. "I guess I can stop trying to fix you up."

Grant nodded, chuckling. "That would be a welcome change. I don't think it's a good time to be dating anybody right now."

Another knock at the door, and Jose poked his head in. "Michelle wanted to know if the new chick could help her in the day care."

Grant sighed. "Her name is not 'the new chick.'" Maybe it was time for some sensitivity training. The mission was a safe zone, for all people.

"Okay, the new girl. Is she stashed back here somewhere?" Jose jerked his head toward the offices.

"Yeah, she's in the filing room, but let me get her." Grant stood up and took a slug from his cold soda. It felt as though he was getting ready to face some unknown danger, the way his heart started pounding. He could feel his body temperature rise about ten degrees.

"I want you to meet our new volunteer. She's been

helping with fund-raising. And no smart comments, got it?" He ignored Eric's expression of open curiosity.

His oldest friend flashed him a grin. "Scout's honor."

They headed out the door and Eric paused, his head cocked to one side.

"This is new, this picture here."

Grant nodded. "Calista thought I should make my office more personable."

Eric raised his eyebrows. "I take it that's the new girl. And this was your solution?"

"I think it's perfect." He regarded the crayon drawing of a fluffy cat wearing pink sunglasses. Savannah was an excellent little artist.

"Better than one of those awful head shots with the fake trees in the background. Plus, the kitty is way better looking than you are."

Responding to the gibe with a good-natured punch to Eric's arm, Grant headed out the door. Halfway down the hallway he had misgivings. Introducing Calista to Eric wasn't something he should do. He should keep her separate from his personal friendships. She wouldn't be just a volunteer anymore if she made friends with Eric. And if he wasn't wrong, that was exactly what was going to happen.

Calista wondered if Grant was still at the mission. She hadn't seen him at all today. Not much at all last week, in fact. But he'd been downright friendly on Saturday, helping Marisol with her kitchen class. The man could definitely cook. One more point in his favor, as if he needed any more.

It must be the Thanksgiving spirit. She almost wished he'd go back to staying out of her way. She'd wondered about him all day if she didn't force herself to concentrate on something else. Which was staying on task and having a purpose. And it was going very well, so far. She opened her eyes and decided she'd been sitting for too long in one spot, plunking folders in color-coded file boxes. Reaching high above her head, she laced her fingers together and felt the pleasant strain on her muscles. Her light blue linen jacket had wrinkled at the elbows and the matching pants were looking a little worse for wear. Calista leaned over, arms outstretched, eyes closed and a blissful feeling spreading through her body. Until she smacked into a pile of folders she had just placed on the edge of the desk and several slipped out of sight into the crack against the wall.

Very smooth. She heaved a sigh and glanced around. The metal desk was about five feet long and weighed a ton. Beyond old-school, this thing must have been around when the mission was founded. Calista tried to tug an edge, but realized all her other carefully sorted piles would have to be moved before the desk budged an inch. Nothing to do but crawl underneath. She wasn't a big girl by any means, but it took a bit of maneuvering to get her body wedged into the small space between the built-in drawers.

As Calista pried the stiff manila folder from the crack, there was a light tapping on the half-open door. She froze, hoping against hope it was Marisol. Or Jose. Or even Lissa.

There was no way to see who it was without backing out, so she did an awkward reverse crawl that seemed to have a lot more wiggling involved than it did on the way in. She refused to imagine what she must look like from the door, but all the same, her cheeks were scorching by the time she got turned all the way around.

Of course it was Grant. His face was a mixture of surprise and something that might have been barely concealed laughter. Oh, that gorgeous smile… And he'd brought a friend, who seemed to find the whole thing very interesting.

Calista popped to her feet and brushed off the knees of her pants.

"Sorry. Some files fell behind the desk." She brushed the hair back from her face and wished she had an excuse to turn her back until her face lost what must be a lovely shade of pink.

"Calista Sheffield, this is my friend, Eric Young. He works over at MusiComp as a composer." Grant's voice was steady but his eyes were crinkled as if he were still laughing inside.

Calista forced herself to look away, hoping her face didn't betray anything of the warm glow that flared inside. She dragged her gaze from Grant's and reached out a hand to Eric, surprised at the genuine warmth in his grip. "Nice to meet you. Do you volunteer here, as well?"

Eric snorted. "Are you kidding? I can't stand listening to Grant boss everybody around."

She felt her mouth drop open a little. Grant didn't really boss anybody, ever. He had a quiet kind of authority that most people responded to without argument.

Grant rushed in to fill the awkward pause. "You'll have to excuse him. He's hardly ever serious."

"True," he said, grinning. "My wife takes about a tenth of what I say at face value."

"But how does she know when you're serious?"

Eric laughed outright. "Practice."

Calista shook her head, bemused. She couldn't imagine a relationship with that much teasing and goofing around. It sounded like fun. His laughter sparked an idea in her, an image of Grant, relaxed and grinning. How would it be to spend time with him, just getting to know what was behind the quick smile and the sad eyes?

"Do you work here in the city? I think Grant said you were helping him with fund-raising."

"I'm the CEO of VitaWow." Calista felt her face warm just a little. It was nothing to be ashamed of, but she was pretty sure it was the first time she had said the words in front of Grant. She sidled a glance at him and his expression was inscrutable.

"The vitamin-water company? That stuff's great." Eric nodded his head. "And it's encouraging to see new volunteers around this place. Will you be here for Thanksgiving? You can meet my wife, Marla."

"Wouldn't miss it for the world." And she meant it. For the first time in years she actually had someplace to go.

Eric seemed to weigh her words, a gentleness in his eyes. "Excellent. It's a total madhouse. We always need the extra hands. Will you be here for Christmas, too?"

The innocent question threw Calista for a moment. Of course she was staying for Christmas. And the next. And the next, if she had her way.

She finally opened her mouth to respond but Grant spoke first, his tone brisk, almost cold. "Let's not plan too far ahead."

Eric blinked, then shrugged.

Right, the mission was way behind on funds. Maybe it was still touch and go. But she had a plan and she was going to put it in motion just as soon as she got the chance. "Well, I better get back to work. Lana wants this last pile cleared up before the new office recruit comes in tomorrow."

See, easy peasy. Calista felt satisfaction with her businesslike attitude. That was always something she could fall back on, professional distance. And with Grant, any distance was a good thing.

Grant suppressed an urge to slap his forehead as he remembered why they'd come down there in the first place. "Actually, I was wondering if you could go help Michelle in the day care. She's short staffed this morning and they finger paint on Wednesdays."

He glanced at her light blue linen jacket and the cream silk blouse underneath and hoped they had enough aprons. Then he jerked his gaze away as he realized she might not understand his concern. His face went hot.

"I'd be glad to," she said, eyes widening with surprise, sounding genuinely happy about being given finger-painting duty.

"Don't worry about the files. We'll get to them later today. You've really cut down the stacks in the past few weeks."

She flashed him a bright smile and gave another quick dusting to the knees of her pants. "I'll head right over. Nice to meet you, Eric."

They both moved out of the doorway as she slipped by and headed down the hallway. A light fragrance followed her and he resisted the urge to take a deep breath. The view from the back brought the sudden image of her wiggling back out from under that desk. He ran a finger under his collar and frowned. "They must have the heat on high in this room."

Eric let out a laugh. "No, buddy, it's just you. Not that I'm blaming you, you understand."

Grant glared at his oldest friend and refused to take the bait. "Whatever. And what was that about staying for Christmas?"

Eric threw up his hands, as if to ward off Grant's unhappiness. "A perfectly reasonable question! And don't worry. She's not going anywhere. She's so into you."

He had turned back toward his office but he swiveled to face Eric. "Why do you say that?"

A huge sigh escaped Eric's lips as he shook his head. "Are you saying you just can't tell, or are you saying you're not sure if she's sincere?"

Grant blinked. "Well, if she did feel something for me, then I think she's sincere. She seems that type. Honest, straightforward, doesn't play games."

"I agree. And to answer the first question for you, I say there's a whole lot of something going on there. I don't think she was blushing for me."

Grant continued down the hallway, letting Eric carry the conversation alone. He held open the door to his office and was glad of the momentary pause to collect his thoughts. He wanted to lean his head out the little office window and shout to the world that Calista—sharp, clever, sweet Calista—felt something for *him*. It was almost unbelievable. What did she even see in him? His whole life was wrapped up in the mission, in these people who were struggling just to survive.

But then he thought of the one thing they could never conquer, and slumped against the desk, legs outstretched. *You can't live your life for making money and be able to let it go at the same time.* And working at the mission was all about letting it go.

"Is she Christian?" Eric settled back in his chair and Grant snapped back to the moment. He'd asked the one question that made Grant want to give him a high five. That was why he was a good friend, a best friend. He knew where the bottom line was in Grant's life.

He leaned against his desk, smiling. "Yes, but she's sort of making her way back from a rough childhood."

"That can be awkward, if one of you is farther along on your faith journey." Eric's tone was cautionary. He had been in love before he met Marla. And the woman just never could make up her mind. In the end, he broke his own heart rather than marry a girl who didn't even believe in God. It was a horrible time and Grant remembered the sadness that shadowed Eric's eyes.

Grant nodded. "I know. But…" He stared at his shoes for a moment, frowning. "There's something about her, the way she makes friends. She listens to the old people and the kids. And Marisol." He rubbed a hand over his face. "I can't explain it. She seems to have this *joy* about her." He shook his head, frustrated with his inability to nail it down, whatever it was.

"Whatever it is, don't worry so much. God's will comes first. Everything and everybody else falls in line. Or not." Eric's expression hardened, probably thinking back on his own wasted attempt to convince God that he knew better. "And if she's on the same page, then there's nothing to worry about. She'll be searching for His will, too."

Grant hesitated, contemplating the strange new idea that there was more to his future than leading this mission. He felt at home here herding kids, counseling parents and raising funds. But God knew his needs, knew his heart inside and out.

He rubbed his jaw and voiced his doubts. “I don’t want it to take away from my work here, to be a distraction.”

“I know. That’s why you’re great at what you do. You really care about keeping your commitment to these people. But remember that verse in John, the one that says Jesus came so that we might have life and live it more abundantly? If it’s right, you won’t be carving out a piece from a pie, diverting your attention away from this place. Your life will be more abundant because of her.”

Grant nodded, feeling the tension in his neck ease at the reassurance. Eric was an excellent sounding board. For years, he’d been bouncing doubts off his red-haired friend.

“You’re a good man, you know that, right?”

“Yup. But ten years from now, when your house is overrun with little kids, just remember I had nothing to do with it,” Eric said, his voice full of laughter.

Chapter Eight

"Do you have any experience with children?" Michelle shot Calista a dubious look as they set out the pots of finger paints. Lissa and two helpers were leading the preschoolers in a rousing game of "duck, duck, goose" while the craft tables were readied for the onslaught of small artists. A CD of Christmas music played softly on a stereo. Nobody seemed to mind that they'd started the season just shy of Thanksgiving.

"Um, well…" Calista didn't quite know how to answer the question. She had done a little babysitting in high school. It wasn't exactly rocket science. "A little."

"I guess I'm trying to ask whether you know what you're getting into here." Michelle stood up and put her hands on her hips, eyeing Calista as if she was applying for a position at the FDIC.

She nodded, lining up small tubs of primary colors next to large sheets of glossy white paper. "Kids don't bother me. I know they can be noisy, have snotty noses, cry a lot. But I'm made of tougher stuff than you might think." She looked up at Michelle and flashed a bright smile, but only got silence in return. "How hard can it be to keep a bunch of little kids occupied for a few hours?"

Michelle let out what sounded suspiciously like a laugh disguised at the last minute as a cough. "Exactly. How hard can it be?"

Calista went back to setting out finger-paint pots and paper, trying to squelch the fear that was rising in her chest. She had nerves of steel. She brokered deals with huge corporations, oversaw hundreds of employees. A group of preschoolers wasn't going to be a problem. Was it?

Grant stood in the open classroom door and fought to keep his expression neutral. Michelle was holding her own at a long table of squirming children dripping with paint. Most of the color was getting onto the paper and the rest was dabbed on the oversize smocks the kids were wearing. Michelle's helper looked like a Ping-Pong player, balancing on the balls of her feet as she waited for the next semiemergency and her chance to swoop in for the save.

Lissa's table was about the same, maybe a little noisier with mostly little boys. They bounced in their chairs like jumping beans, constantly in motion. There was one small child who had smeared paint in his hair and all the way up both arms, but Lissa didn't bother to wipe him clean. As soon as the paint was put away they would have to hose him down.

But the next table was a disaster. Calista was lost. As thoroughly lost as if God had plunked her down in the Gobi Desert without any water. And she didn't even seem to know it.

She met his eyes and smiled hugely, blue paint

smeared over one cheek, waving to him with a hand covered in green paint. He raised a hand in greeting, wishing he could take a picture, just for posterity. Her face was pure joy, as if she had waited her whole life to finger paint with a group of four-year-olds. The dark-haired teenage girl at the end of the table was shooting exasperated glances at Calista and the rowdy bunch of children as they splattered paint on each other and the table. She urged them to stay seated, reminding the worst offenders that they were going to have to wash the table if they didn't behave. At any one time, half of the children were out of their seats, borrowing more paint or wiping their hands on their neighbor's smock, or even their neighbor's hair.

Grant stared as Calista carefully removed a little boy's sock and painted his bare foot a bright green. The blond-haired toddler shrieked with laughter as she worked, then he stood up unsteadily, still grinning. Calista slid a piece of paper under his foot and he pressed his foot onto the paper. As he proudly showed off his work, most of Calista's crew started to take off their shoes and socks, ready to follow suit. The assistant waved her arms in the air, eyes wide at this alarming development.

He figured he better lend a hand and strode toward the group. Savannah stood up from Calista's table and waved energetically. "Mr. Monohan! I made another picture for your office and it has a kitty."

He caught Calista's look, her eyes bright with surprise.

"Beautiful, Savannah," he responded enthusiastically. The little girl held up her new masterpiece, the paint glistening wetly. A blue cat with red sunglasses stared back at him. Of course it was a kitty. Savannah swore she was going to have her own someday, when she was in a real home.

"Isn't she talented? Aren't they so creative? Look at this one!" Calista pointed out a little boy's rocket ship. And there were Christmas trees and orange lions and lots of turkeys and all manner of blobs and squiggles. The chatter was deafening but he hardly noticed as he patted shoulders and complimented the artwork. Calista's happiness was infectious. He wanted to sit down and join their table, take off his shoe and paint the bottom of his foot. But that's not what you did when you were trying to keep kids under control. You had to keep a kind but stern demeanor. Calista looked like she followed an "if you can't beat 'em, join 'em" motto.

"Very creative, but let's keep our shoes on, okay?" He laid a hand on the shoulder of a curly-haired little boy who was struggling to untie his laces. The boy frowned but turned back to his paper, his fingers covered in brown paint.

He glanced over at Calista, who was carefully wiping off the boy's foot with a wet paper towel. Her light blue linen suit had more paint on it than a lot of the papers. "I think your suit is a lost cause."

"Oh, for sure." She grinned up at him, brushing the hair away from her clear green eyes with one forearm. She was so happy, she was shining with it.

Something about that gesture, and the light in her expression, caught at his heart. Eric had asked him why Calista was different and he hadn't been able to say. But he knew now, watching her in this room. She wasn't afraid to grab every opportunity and wring something good from it. He flashed back to how she had looked that first day, arms wrapped around her middle, fear hovering behind her eyes. She'd reached out to Marisol and Lana, become friends with Jose and Lissa, worked side by side with recovering addicts and teen parents clearing tables in the cafeteria. He'd heard her laughing this morning when she walked into the janitor's closet by accident. *I come that they may have life and have it more abundantly.* That's what she had, like the verse said, life abundant.

Grant felt his heart contract with the sudden realization that he cared for her in a way he had never cared for anyone before. A surprised smile spread over his face. He wanted to stand up and holler that he finally got it.

"Did you…want to paint?" Calista's hesitant voice brought him back down to earth. Her eyes were watching him steadily. Yeah, he got it, but he sure wasn't going to yell about it here and now. Calista would be off and running the moment the words came out of his mouth. She would think he was crazy.

"No, thanks." He cleared his throat. "I was just thinking how great this is for the kids. They go through a lot of upheaval and a little finger painting goes a long way toward making them feel normal."

"It's true, everyone should try it. When I think of all the years I paid for therapy when I could have just been making footprints…" She shook her head, laughing.

Lissa walked over, arms full of empty paint pots. "We've got about five more minutes and then we'll need to clean up. If any of your kids are finished, try to get them to slip off their smocks by the sink and wash up." She flicked a glance toward the disaster that was Calista's table and rolled her eyes. "Or maybe we can just declare this a national emergency and call in the troops."

"I'm sorry. I don't know how you get them to stay in one place." Calista stood up to start clearing the table, her voice registering the admiration she felt for the day care staff.

"It's a gift. And I can look really serious when I have to," Lissa said, her face relaxing. She seemed relieved that Calista wasn't going to skip out on the hardest part of the activity: the cleanup.

"All right, kiddos, put your hands in the air." Grant demonstrated by putting his palms up high. "Walk with your helper to the sinks. We're going to get cleaned up so we can have snack time."

The response was a burst of excitement, followed by the assistant helping the group line up for the sink. He winked at Calista as they filed past. "The key is to give them a little incentive."

"That's just what Michelle said," she responded, stacking lids and gathering up papers. "I guess I need to write that tip down somewhere."

"Planning on another stint in the day care?"

She frowned up at him, green eyes clouding over with confusion. "I'd like to come back here again. Unless Michelle thinks I wasn't up to spec today."

"I'm sure you were fine." He hesitated, wanting to say so much more, but knowing the time wasn't right. Not just yet. "I'm glad you had fun."

"More fun than I've had all week. Thanks for letting me help out."

"So, if you had to choose, it would be little-kid chaos over filing?"

She laughed again, that sweet sound that drew him toward her like she was pulling on a string. "This beats filing any day."

"I can name a few people off the top of my head who would rather have teeth pulled than spend the morning in here." Like Jose. If he ever wanted the young guy to quit, he could have him transferred to day care. Jose thought little kids were germ factories.

"There's nothing like tidy paperwork. But this—" she waved a green-colored hand at the room "—is beautiful. These kids are a treat after spending the day with businesspeople." She turned serious for a moment, weighing her words. "They're honest. You don't have to wonder what they're thinking. And they don't care what you're wearing or what kind of car you drive or how big your company is."

He wanted to say something, but he couldn't seem to form words. His fingers itched to reach out and brush back that strand of hair that kept falling into her eyes. Her face shone with that fragile sweetness he'd seen the first day she came to the mission.

"And they don't care who your parents are," he added, his voice sounding huskier than he'd intended.

"Exactly." She nodded, her gaze locked on his. "I always thought that verse about being like little children meant we were supposed to be gullible. But that's not what Jesus meant at all." She watched a little girl run toward the door, excitedly waving her art project in the air as her father grinned in greeting. "He meant that we needed to believe first, and doubt later. Not the other way around."

"Sort of the way that little kids love you first and ask questions later?"

Her face lit up at his words. "That's just what I mean."

Love first, and ask questions later. Great for kids,

but it was the very worst advice he'd heard for adults. And still, that was what was happening in his heart. It was almost enough to make him open his mouth and blurt it all out, tell her how thankful he was that God brought her through the mission doors.

Instead, he managed to look away, his heart pounding. "Kids. You gotta love 'em." Probably the dumbest rejoinder in history, but it was either end the conversation or ask her out to dinner. She'd probably appreciate not being covered in paint when he took a step in that direction. "I better help Janice."

"Janice?" Calista's brow furrowed in confusion.

"Your assistant. She's got about ten kids left to scrub down."

"Oh, right. And I'd better clean this area or I won't be invited back." She grabbed another handful of paper towels and started to swab off the tiny chairs.

He stood there for a moment, debating. Lana had set the time for the media announcement. He should probably say something now, before Calista saw it on the news.

"I know you won't be here on Friday morning, but I wanted—"

"Actually, I'm filling in for Lissa for an hour." Calista smiled up at him, hands full of soggy towels.

Grant paused, struggling to find his place again. This shouldn't be that hard. No harder than telling the whole nation. But what did he say? *Hi, you know the guy who owns half of this fine state? Well, he's my dad. But not really, because he abandoned me and my mother when I was born. He really wants to know me now, so I guess I get to be his son whether I like it or not.*

Calista was watching him, a frown appearing between her brows, green eyes turning serious.

A wave of shame flooded him. He couldn't do it. "Great. Michelle needs the help."

Grant ducked his head and crossed the room to where toddlers stood in line for the sink. Janicc helped them stand on the stool, soap up and rinse off. Some were spick-and-span in no time. Some would need a thorough dunking. Thcy chattered and giggled, chubby fingers leaving colored prints along the sides of the white porcelain sink. Grant grabbed the dispenser and delivered dollops of soap into waiting palms, all the while replaying their conversation.

He wished he could just blurt it out. But she was going to hear the ugly news the same way everybody else would: on the news. *Love first.* He felt the words echoing around in his brain, in his heart. He was used to being careful, wary, never taking anyone at face value. Was it possible he should trust that Calista was going to stick around? He wanted it so badly that his teeth ached with it.

But before he could build any kind of life with her, he had to bring his ugly little secret out into the light. Tomorrow would be his last Thanksgiving—no, his last *day*—as Grant Monohan, mission director, and not Grant Monohan, Kurt Daniels's illegitimate son.

Calista wiped down the table and gave herself a quick pep talk. It was now or never. She knew she should probably wait until she was looking her best, or even just a little less colorful, but he seemed so friendly, so open.

She kept glancing back at him, watching the line

get shorter and shorter at the sink. Finally, he was almost done. Janice led a little girl toward the door and her waiting mother. Calista took a deep breath. It was just a Christmas party, not a wedding. She marched up behind him and cleared her throat.

He looked back, tilting his head down at her, dark hair just a bit mussed as usual. She picked up a faint woodsy smell, his cologne, and for some reason it was her undoing.

"Grant-Humphreys," she started, then slapped a hand over her mouth.

He blinked. "Excuse me?"

Calista felt heat creep up her neck and wanted to press the rewind and delete buttons. "Sorry. That came out wrong. I was wondering if you wanted to come to the VitaWow Christmas party in a few weeks." There it was. Out, for better or worse.

He turned, helping a little boy with jet-black hair down from the step stool. "Let me guess. It's at the Grant-Humphreys Mansion?"

Calista couldn't help the snort of laughter that answered him. "Sorry. I haven't asked anybody to a dance since my Sadie Hawkins days."

"I'm sure you haven't." He leveled a gaze at her, something in his eyes she couldn't quite define. "And I'd be honored to go."

"You don't even know the date yet," she protested, feeling unreasonably happy, her voice losing its anxious tone.

"Don't need to, but you can tell me anyway. I'll just make sure I'm free." Then there was that smile again, the one that made her brain take a leave of absence.

"It's the fifteenth," she said briskly, working hard

to keep herself from puddling at his feet. *Get a grip. You're not a teenager!*

Grant said nothing, just inclined his head a little, as if that smile was just between the two of them. As if there weren't thirty small children still rocketing around the room. "Yup, definitely free."

She stood there half a second too long, her gaze locked on his. "I thought it would be a great opportunity to meet some really big donors. I've already made sure the guest list has a few considering a sponsorship of the roof project and the classroom remodels."

His eyes went dark as if someone had hit a switch. "Gotcha."

Something about that one word rang a warning bell in her mind. But she couldn't figure out why. The mission needed money, right?

"We can talk specifics later." And he turned back to the sink, running the water and washing the sides of the porcelain with a sponge.

Calista nodded, to herself, since he wasn't even looking, and wandered to the door. She had done something wrong, but she couldn't figure out what.

"Calista, can you be here in ten minutes?" Jackie's rapid-fire speech interrupted Calista's vivid daydream. Something about Grant and kids and lots of laughter. She adjusted her Bluetooth and glanced at her car's dashboard clock.

"I can't. I have to get home and change. Isn't my schedule cleared until one?"

"It was, but then the PR director from Genesis Drinks decided we needed to approve some paperwork ASAP.

I didn't think it would be a problem to tell him to come on over. Can't you leave early?"

"I'm already on the road. But I can't come straight back to the office, so he'll have to wait until I get there."

"You got a hot lunch date?" The curiosity in Jackie's voice should have made Calista smile, but part of her wanted to keep Grant safely away from her other life. Which was how she was starting to think of VitaWow.

"No, but thanks for asking. There was a little mishap and I need to change. I'll be quick."

There was a pause, long enough for Calista to imagine that Jackie had disconnected the call. "A mishap." She repeated the words carefully, as if debating whether she really wanted to hear the details.

Calista peeked in her rearview mirror and changed lanes without dropping her speed. "Nothing too awful. Just paint."

"You were painting? Couldn't they hire some of the homeless people to do that?"

She squashed the niggle of irritation at Jackie's tone. "Not that kind of painting. It was finger-painting day at the day care."

"The day care?"

Calista heaved a sigh. "You know what I've always loved about you? You're so quick on the uptake that I hardly ever have to repeat myself." She pulled onto the exit ramp and tapped her brakes. A long line of cars were queued at the intersection leading to her condominium.

Her sarcasm startled a laugh out of Jackie. "Sorry. You've just always been work first, play later. This new you takes some getting used to."

She pulled through the intersection and took a quick

right. "I'm almost home. Give me about fifteen minutes and I'll be back on my way to work. We can conference call while I drive over, if he really can't wait."

"I'll try and stall until you get back. We've got some cookies around here somewhere."

"Okay. And you can always try the basement break room. They get a shipment of bakery goodies from Les Amis every few days."

"They do? No wonder everybody's trying to get transferred down there. When did you start that?"

"About a month ago. It's a long story," Calista said shortly, sliding her car into the parking spot in front of her condo.

Calista hung up and jumped from the car. If she didn't take too long, she might even get there before the press people. She pushed open her apartment door and kicked off her shoes. Probably better to throw the clothes away than try to dry-clean the fine linen. She paused, fingering the sleeve of her jacket, a smile tugging up one corner of her mouth. Streaks of red paint slashed from her elbow to her wrist. She remembered a little boy tugging her sleeve, wanting her to see his creation. There had been so many little hands and chattering voices, she couldn't even keep up with them all. But Grant was a natural, the way he crouched down to talk to them and let a hand on their small shoulders speak volumes. She ran her hand along the dry paint, smiling at the visible memento of a perfect morning.

Grant's words echoed in her head, about loving like children. She allowed herself to wonder, just for a moment, how Grant loved. Was he someone who fell in love at first sight? Or did he have to warm up to a woman? Any woman he loved would be amazing. She'd certainly have a rock-hard faith, a real purpose in life and a clear calling.

Calista sure had the rock-hard, clear and real part down. But the faith, life and calling was still a work in progress.

She needed to get her priorities straight before she ended up going to the mission just to see Grant. It was so easy to get wrapped up in his purpose, his joy. But she was trying to help other people, not satisfy her own needs.

She'd spent years focusing on herself and now it was time to let God use her for something important, which did not include daydreaming about Grant Monohan.

"*Mija*, take this pan to the front line, please." Marisol passed a large tray to Calista and pointed to the far right, her bright eyes flashing with energy. "The smashed potatoes are almost gone. We cannot have a good Thanksgiving without the smashed potatoes."

Calista bit back a smile and carried the metal serving dish as quickly as she could out into the serving area. The noise of the packed cafeteria was almost deafening, lessened only by the high-ceilinged room. Everywhere she looked there were tables of people, talking and laughing. It might have been a big party, if not for the number of old men in shabby coats and hollow-cheeked women. If you didn't look too closely, it was a happy gathering. If you focused on each person, you started to see the tiredness in their faces, the discouragement in the set of their shoulders.

There was a traffic jam near the end of the serving area. Calista stopped, feeling the muscles in her arms start to protest. Twenty pounds of potatoes must multiply exponentially when you added butter and milk.

"Can I take that?"

Calista felt her cheeks grow hot before she could even register the words. All she knew was the voice, and the man it belonged to. She turned her head and smiled, hoping her face wasn't as sweaty as it felt. Her light cream sweater was uncomfortably warm. "You miss your weight training today? Because a few reps with this pan and you'd be good to go."

Grant chuckled, already lifting the heavy dish from her hands. She could see the darkness where he'd shaved, how his tan skin contrasted against his white shirt collar. His cologne was woodsy, virile. She wanted to lean in and inhale.

"Marisol takes this day very, very seriously," he said, indicating the long rows of serving dishes. "If we run out of something, she thinks she'll be barred from heaven."

"Especially the 'smashed' potatoes," Calista said, lips twitching.

"And the 'corns' and the bread 'balls' and the 'staffing.'"

She couldn't help laughing out loud, and then put a guilty hand to her lips. "Is that rude? She's learned a lot in two years. I don't think I could learn that much Spanish if you gave me ten years."

"She doesn't mind. It's not personal for her. But the food is. We make fun of the cooking and we're all in trouble."

Calista nodded, vividly imagining how the fierce Hispanic woman would shrug off her mispronunciation, but be horrified if the potatoes were lumpy. The woman in front of them moved to the side and a place opened up for Grant to rest the dish against the long countertop. Calista deftly lifted the empty tray from its resting spot, careful not to burn herself with the hot steam underneath.

Grant slid the full tray in place and Calista took the spoon. The line was moving steadily, even though the dinner had been going on for more than an hour already. A young woman with two small children glanced up and smiled tentatively. Calista served a portion on each plate and watched the smallest child's eyes light up. "Some! Some!"

Calista giggled and the mother shushed the little boy, her face going pink. "He loves mashed potatoes," she said, her voice a half whisper.

"Don't we all," Grant agreed, smiling. The little family moved on, the baby still shouting "some" at the top of his lungs.

"Are you going somewhere for dinner after this?"

Calista should have been prepared for the question, but she wasn't. Surprise lanced through her and she focused on the tray in front of her. *No, because I don't have any friends and no one invited me. Thanksgiving stinks when you're all alone.* Probably not the best response.

He waved a hand, the one holding a large serving spoon. "Sorry. I wasn't trying to pry. Just making conversation." His voice was light but his back seemed to stiffen as he spoke.

"I don't care if you ask me personal questions," Calista started to say, pausing to serve another spoonful of potatoes and give a warm smile to the old man holding the plate.

"Really?" He packed so much disbelief into that one word that she had to grin.

"Really. At least, I don't mind the way you think I mind."

"Ah. So, you're saying that you do mind, but I'm mistaken in the exact manner in which you mind my asking."

"Exactly."

His deep laugh kindled something in her chest, and the warmth spread outward, making her fingers tingle. She sidled a glance his way. How she loved that smile. The deep creases around his mouth, the way it transformed his face from almost severe to incredibly warm, the way his eyes crinkled at the edges. She watched his grin slowly fade into something softer, something more like wonder. He cleared his throat and indicated the potatoes. "Someone's waiting."

Calista snapped back to her task, face going hot, plopping the creamy side dish on a plate with a little more force than necessary. Yeah, definitely wonder. *He's wondering why I'm staring at him with my mouth hanging open.* She would have given up her Mercedes to be able to erase the last minute and a half. It was like junior high all over again. And she knew better than to try to be cooler than she really was. It never worked out. You were always caught out in the end.

"I'm not going to another dinner. I haven't been to a Thanksgiving dinner in years."

He paused, scraping corn into a pile in his silver serving tray, waiting for the next customer. "Why? Not your favorite holiday?"

She shrugged, suddenly tired. "Because I haven't been invited."

He didn't respond to that and they worked in silence for a few minutes. Calista chewed the inside of her lip, wishing she could lie and say she was rejecting offers every holiday. Then she was angry at wishing it, then finally sighed under the confusion of it all.

"But you're right here, at my Thanksgiving dinner."

Calista turned to him, ready to roll her eyes, and then hesitated. He looked serious, solemn. "I'm a volunteer."

"And you're my guest." He playfully bumped her with an elbow. "I always make my friends work for their keep. You didn't know what you were signing up for, but you've got years of this ahead of you."

Calista scooped up another spoonful of potatoes for the next plate that slid into view, a goofy smile plastered to her face. She knew he was just being kind to her, making conversation, acting like the concerned shepherd to the lost sheep, but she couldn't help it. Those sweet words made her heart full to bursting. She was a friend, a guest, someone who was welcome. *Years of this ahead of you.* Oh, how she wished it was true.

Chapter Nine

The media descended on the mission before the sun had risen above the snow-covered peaks of the Rocky Mountains. Vans plastered with channel numbers lined the streets and camera crews jostled for position on the sidewalk. The mission doors wouldn't unlock to the public until six o'clock but that didn't keep the reporters from tugging at the handle every few minutes. Last night's press release had caused a frenzy. The man who owned a business empire had fathered a child by a drug-addicted C-list actress and then refused to acknowledge his paternity. Then the actress drank herself to death and the kid had lived on the streets. Definitely newsworthy by itself, but add in the enormous fortune that awaited the only child of Kurt Daniels and the fact that this child was now running the area's biggest homeless shelter, and the story couldn't get any bigger. Everyone was desperate to know everything about Grant Monohan, from his love life right down to what he ate for breakfast.

On the other side of the glass door, across the lobby and down a carpeted hallway, the city's newest celebrity sat with his head in his hands. He slumped in his chair at the long conference table, which was empty except for two other silent individuals. Jose took a gulp of steaming hot coffee and set his mug back on the table, face solemn. Lana sat next to Grant, one hand gently kneading his shoulder. There was nothing she could say that would make this any easier, but she couldn't bear to see him sitting there so alone. Grant raised his head and gave her a tentative smile that he hoped looked stronger than it felt. Lana had been through some rough times herself after her abusive husband sent a bullet through her spine and left her a paraplegic. She'd found her way to the mission the same way he had, wanting to make a difference in a world that could be heartless and cruel.

"Almost time, boss," Jose said, breaking the silence. He looked like he was swallowing glass. His thickly muscled arms strained his polo shirt yet his expression of anxiety made him look like a vulnerable child.

Grant nodded. "Well, let's pray, then go get this done." They bowed their heads as he spoke simple words of praise, because even in this moment Grant was thankful. God had never let him down and never would.

As they stood up, Grant felt as if he was heading to his own execution. His palms were sweaty, his heart was racing. He had never had such an urge to flee in his entire life. The years he'd spent on the street had been rough, but this was worse. He couldn't suppress the twist of his lips at the irony. Announcing that he was the heir to an enormous fortune was worse than sleeping in doorways and begging for handouts.

"Showtime," whispered Grant and they headed for the lobby. Lana asked the residents to clear the space as they prepared for the media to flood into the mission.

Most of the homeless were more than eager to get out of the way. Old Conchita refused to budge from her spot on the last couch, rocking and mumbling, so Jose let her be. A few curious stragglers huddled by the double doors that led to the cafeteria. Breakfast had been served an hour ago and the clang of dishes being loaded into the enormous dishwashers echoed dimly in the silent lobby.

The moment he unlocked the front door would stay with Grant forever. Flashbulbs blinded him as he stood in the entryway, grimly waving in the reporters and cameramen. He hated the way they swarmed into the lobby and invaded this place of refuge.

"As soon as you can arrange yourselves, I will make a prepared statement and answer a few questions." Grant's voice felt uncertain but he cleared his throat and waited for the reporters to stop jockeying for position. He glanced at Lana, who gave him a thumbs-up sign, and Jose, who nodded encouragingly.

Taking a deep breath, he read from a paper he clutched in his hand. "My name is Grant Monohan and I am Kurt Daniels's son." He paused as the cameras flashed like strobe lights. "I have always been aware that he was my biological father. My mother, Annie Monohan, struggled with drugs and alcohol before passing away ten years ago. As a teenager, I spent several years living on the streets of Denver. I came to know the good people who ran the Denver mission and they encouraged me to finish my education. The previous director, Edward Thompson, helped me apply for scholarships, and I earned a degree in business from UC Davis. I returned to the mission to take a position as assistant director, and then was hired as director five years ago." Grant paused, hoping against hope that the frantic scribbling from the horde of reporters would include actual words from his mouth.

"I understand the fascination with celebrities but I am asking you to respect my privacy and the privacy of the mission residents. This is a place of refuge and solace for many people struggling in difficult circumstances. Do not film or record any area of the mission without permission, and do not approach the residents. After I am done answering questions, I will ask you to leave. If you have further questions, I can be reached through the main phone number."

He put the paper away in his pocket and lifted his head, waiting for the onslaught. "Now I will answer a few questions."

The resulting din was deafening as every reporter shouted to be heard above the others.

Grant pointed toward the newscaster for a major Denver news channel. The dignified-looking man lifted his microphone and said in his best dramatic tone, "Is it true you drive a Ferrari while pretending to the homeless population that you aren't wealthy?"

It took several seconds for the question to make sense. Grant's mouth hung open in surprise before he snapped it shut and glared. "No, that is false. Are there any serious questions here?"

Another wave of shouting assaulted his ears and he pointed to a narrow-faced woman in a bright green jacket. She stepped forward. "Can you tell us why you refused to accept any money from your father, when the mission could use the funds for a new roof?"

Again, Grant stood speechless, eyes narrowed. How did she know that he wouldn't cash the check, and that the roof was in need of replacing? He searched around for an answer. "The policy of the mission is to rely on the generosity of the many, rather than depend on large gifts from a few. We also adhere to federal standards for nonprofit organizations, which prohibits some types of donations."

The woman spoke again before he could turn to another reporter. "Surely accepting one gift from Mr. Daniels wouldn't hurt."

The words left Grant's mouth before he thought them through. "My father tends to spoil everything he touches."

The resulting chaos was impossible to calm. Grant waved his hands for quiet but the reporters yelled questions over each other. Finally the mob subsided into restlessness, waiting for him to choose another reporter. But he had had enough.

"That's all I have to say at this time. Please exit the lobby and clear the sidewalk in front of the mission. This is private property and we will call in police assistance if necessary. Thank you for understanding." He pointed to the front doors and his eyes swept over a familiar face at the edge of the surging crowd.

Calista stood to the side, her brow creased with worry, hands up to her mouth and eyes wide in shock. His gut twisted in response as they locked eyes. He wanted to take it all back: the whole morning, the board's approval of the media statement, the threatening letters. He wanted to go back to before she left Thanksgiving night. He felt steel bands tighten around his chest and he struggled to look away from her face. She slowly dropped her hands and gave him a slight smile.

He struggled to look as if nothing much had changed.

But if there was anything that Grant Monohan knew, it was that there was no erasing the past.

Calista watched Grant Monohan face a room of screaming reporters and thought she had never witnessed a braver act in her life. He was tall and straight, head held high as he read from a small piece of paper in his left hand. She knew what it was like to have a painful past. Her throat ached in anguish as he gave the briefest description of his teen years. It sent shock waves through her system to hear him say he was Kurt Daniels's son. He was as recognizable as the president, like Colorado royalty.

Grant's life was never going to be the same after this moment. She watched him plead for privacy for the residents and visitors. And then he had made the fatal mistake of answering a few questions. The first rule of a press conference was control, and in a madhouse like this, control meant no questions.

The first question was the sort of ridiculous gossip she was prepared to hear. Calista could tell that Grant wasn't, because his mouth dropped open a little. She could see the emotions flitting over his face: disbelief, anger, frustration. She wanted to walk in there and grab his microphone. He was going to be chewed up and spit out on national television.

The next question was strange, but Grant's response was even stranger. He didn't deny that his father had offered support or that he had refused help. And then he spoke from his gut, which broke rule number two of press conferences: if you can't keep your emotions in check, don't answer the question. Calista felt her hands go up to her mouth and stifled a groan. It was like watching the proverbial train wreck and knowing it was going to replay in a constant loop for the next week.

Grant looked up at her, right after he'd refused to answer more questions, and she tried to give him an encouraging smile. At least he'd stopped them at two, instead of twenty. She didn't think she could have watched another five minutes of this. The look on his face was difficult to interpret. He turned and strode through the door to the offices.

She knew how it felt to have a past that was beyond your control, and a family that you did not care to own up to. What happened when they came out of the shadows to interfere with your life? Her stomach turned icy at the thought. But Grant's bombshell was delicious for the gossip hounds because he was so *good.* People just loved to see a fall from grace. And pretending to be a normal guy who cared about the homeless while being a millionaire was a pretty big bombshell.

Several large men wearing the mission's signature red polo shirt directed the crowd of reporters to the door. Calista wound her way through the throng, dodging enormous cameras and trying not to trip on long cords strewn over the lobby floor. It sounded as if most of them would be content to park across the street and wait for another opportunity.

Lana rolled into her spot behind the desk, her face pale, dark shadows under her eyes. "Hi, Calista," she said in a friendly tone. Her gaze darted behind Calista, and she said more loudly, "I will not answer any questions."

There were two paparazzi standing a few feet away, apparently hoping for some kind of statement. A tall, thin young man with a baseball cap on backward smirked and said, "You probably will, for the right price."

Calista sucked in a breath and felt anger spread through her limbs. But Lana spoke first, and her voice was controlled. "You can't put a price on friendship. I'm sure you understand."

The man rolled his eyes and turned to his friend, laughing. But the other man shook his head, dark eyes gazing at the ground, and replaced the lens on his camera. His tan face was somber, even sad. Calista wondered if he had seen that friendship almost always had an asking price.

"Very nice. You should have made the statement to the press." Calista hoped Lana would take the compliment the right way, not as a criticism of Grant.

The secretary ran a hand through her short gray hair so that the purple ends stood up straight. "I told him that. But he didn't want to look like he was running away."

"Well, it certainly didn't look like he was running." Calista couldn't keep the admiration from her voice. "How is he? I mean, with all of this?" She didn't know why those words came out of her mouth but she didn't want to take them back, either.

Lana shrugged. "He's tough. He's been through a lot worse than a press conference with some silly reporters."

She nodded. It sounded like Grant was made of steel to survive that kind of abandonment and not be bitter. "He seems so..." Her voice trailed off as she struggled to grasp the word. Hopeful? At peace? "I'm sorry, I guess I'm in awe of his ability to forgive his dad."

Lana's eyes narrowed. "I don't know if he has forgiven him, but I do know he doesn't consider him his *dad*."

Jose came through the office door, his usually mild expression gone. His brows were drawn down, lips pressed together. A coffee mug gently steamed in his hand. He held the door open behind him and Grant followed. His powerful frame seemed to swallow up the space as he came toward the desk. The dark blue suit coat was gone and his dress shirt was rolled up at the elbows. His red tie was still on, but the knot seemed looser. His face was calm, but Calista saw sadness in his eyes.

"That wasn't enough to scare you away?" Grant stopped a few feet from her and his tone was teasing, but his face said that he thought she should run while she could.

"Nothing scary about it except that it was done all wrong," she replied, sneaking a glance at Grant's face. She was taking a chance, but from what she'd seen, Grant was the type to put his ego on the back burner and take help if it was offered.

"Oh, so you know how to do it right?" Jose leaned against the desk and set his coffee cup on the smooth wooden surface.

Grant said nothing, but his eyes were bright with laughter. Calista sucked in a breath at the sight. She could see his star pedigree in the strong jaw and the high cheekbones. But she was right that his ego wasn't bruised by her honesty.

"Grant probably had a few media classes with that UC Davis business degree. He can tell you what he did wrong." She could feel Lana's gaze on her and Jose made a sound in the back of his throat.

"She's right. It was a total disaster and it didn't have to be," Grant said, nodding. "I shouldn't have taken any questions. As soon as I saw the crowd, I knew this wasn't a normal news conference. Most of them were from the tabloids."

Calista said nothing, hoping her face showed the sympathy she felt. Jose looked from his boss to the new girl and back.

"And then I lost my cool." He shook his head, as if he still couldn't believe he'd let a reporter get the best of him.

"It happens. Have you always handled the press for the mission? Maybe it's time to assign that to another staff member." She looked at Lana, who had taken the paparazzo's gibe and turned it around.

"Are you saying you'd be willing to take that role?" His words were light, but Calista could tell Grant was more than half-serious.

"Not me, I have a quick temper," she said, laughing. "I'd just make it worse. But Lana seems like she'd do a great job."

To her surprise the secretary shook her head. "Now, that should be some rule of working with the press. Don't choose the middle-aged woman with purple hair in a wheelchair."

Calista couldn't keep surprised laughter from bubbling out of her throat. "Whatever you all do, just choose somebody who can keep calm and—"

"Avoid insulting Kurt Daniels?" Grant's voice was cool. The smile had slipped from his face.

"How about not giving them anything to make into a headline," she shot back. She was on his side, whether he believed it or not.

Jose took a sip from his mug. The smell of fresh coffee made Calista's mouth water. She'd had enough espresso, but it was definitely time for a real breakfast. As if in response to her thoughts, her stomach let out a rumble that seemed to echo in the high-ceilinged lobby. Her cheeks went hot.

Grant grinned. "Sounds like it's breakfast time. I didn't eat before the press got here because I was too nervous, but I'm starving now. Want to join me in the cafeteria?"

The idea of spending some one-on-one time with Grant was tempting. "Sure, I'll join you."

"Well, I'll see you two later," Jose called as they headed for the double doors on the far end of the lobby. They both lifted a hand in response.

"He has a mild form of obsessive-compulsive disorder and can't handle the crowd in here," Grant said in a quiet tone.

Calista looked up, surprised. "Would he mind you telling me that?"

"It's better if you know. He's learning coping mechanisms, but he still would feel very uncomfortable if you touched his mug or his food." He reached for the door and looked her in the eye. "You seemed the type of person that's sensitive to others' feelings and would appreciate the heads-up."

She didn't know what to say. She wanted to agree, to say she cared enough to avoid hurting people or offending them. But all that came to mind was Liz Albrecht, the new secretary in Human Resources at VitaWow. She had been sent up to take Jackie's place for a few hours last week. The girl was not the brightest bulb in the firmament and Calista had made it clear that she would not be making another trip to the top floor. Her cheeks flushed a little as she remembered how Liz's eyes had filled with tears as she corrected her again and again. She could have been gentler. Calista dropped her gaze and waited for Grant to open the door.

"And thanks again." His voice was still quiet.

"For what?"

"For being honest. When you're the boss, people have a hard time telling you the truth."

She nodded, knowing exactly how that was. It made her paranoid some days, just thinking of the things she could do without a single employee speaking up. She wanted them to think for themselves, not just their paycheck.

"I have a feeling that's going to be a much bigger issue, now that you've let the cat out of the bag."

Grant laughed out loud, his blue eyes crinkling up. "Great, I feel tons better."

"Lana, I was wondering if I could ask you a personal question." Grant stuffed his hands in his pockets and tried to stop fidgeting. It had been a tough weekend, dodging reporters outside his apartment. But there was a more pressing issue than paparazzi. He'd spent an hour browsing online flower shops, not the greatest way to spend a Monday morning. He'd visited two flower boutiques over the weekend. None of it had felt right. Especially not the little glass doodads he'd seen on the festively decorated shop shelves.

Behind the lobby desk, Lana lifted her head and grinned hugely. "Well, that took long enough."

"What did?"

"I thought you were never going to ask my opinion about whether Calista's a good catch."

Grant choked back his surprise. "I'm not."

Lana's wide blue eyes blinked in confusion. "Oh, sorry. Go ahead."

He shuffled his feet and leaned against the desk. The lobby was bustling with residents on their way to dinner. But if he waited for perfect privacy, that moment would never come. Plus, he needed an answer before Calista showed up for the fund-raising meeting in an hour.

"I was wondering, if you wanted a man to show interest in you, what would you want him to do? Give you flowers? Or maybe a little gift?"

Lana's brows drew down. "I thought you said this wasn't about Calista."

He could feel the warmth spreading up his neck. "I just wanted your opinion. As a woman."

Now Lana's eyes were wide, and a look of alarm crossed her face. "Okay, let's just be clear here. You're not asking me what I would want a man to give me because *you're* the man, right?"

"No! I mean, not because you're not attractive or a nice person—"

"Oh, Grant." Lana started to laugh. "You almost gave me a heart attack. But can we just be honest with each other? We're friends, and friends can tell each other things in confidence. So, talk to me before you do something crazy, like follow Eric's advice." She blinked innocently up at him, a sly grin crossing her face.

"Did he talk to you?" Surprise made his voice rise.

"Nope, Eric is as good as gold that way. Not a peep to me. But I figured you would ask him for advice before me or Jose or Marisol—"

"I get the picture." Grant rubbed a hand over his face and wondered how many people in this mission had noticed his feelings for Calista.

"Look, I saw this coming a long time ago and it's a good thing. She's got a strong faith and a soft heart, but she's as tough as nails when she needs to be. You can't beat that combination."

Grant interrupted her with a groan. "See, I agree with all that. I'm not asking for your opinion on *her* exactly." He paused, trying to speak past the sudden tightness in his chest. "Honestly, I have a lot more reservations about myself than her, if we're talking about relationships."

"I'm not following you." Lana frowned up at him, then let out a low whistle. "Oh. You think because your father's a jerk, you've got some inherited flaw? You think you're going to walk out as soon as the going gets rough?"

He didn't answer, just tried to compose his expression into something other than fear. "I know that loyalty and faithfulness are choices we make. But I don't want to mess up. I don't want to hurt anybody."

"Oh, Grant. You won't. You're not that type of man." Her eyes were soft with sympathy.

"Thanks, Lana." But he couldn't take all the credit for the kind of man he was. God had more to do with it than anyone. "Anyway, what I was going to ask you, before we got sidetracked, is about flowers. Do you think…?"

Lana opened her mouth to answer, but then her eyes flicked behind Grant and widened. "Um, well, let me see. I think most women like flowers. But let's ask Calista what she thinks."

Grant felt as if someone had dumped a cold bucket of water over his head. He steeled himself to turn slowly. Had she heard his doubts and Lana's advice? He was caught between hoping she still thought he was perfect, like Marisol had said, and understanding he came from a man who couldn't stay faithful if his life depended on it.

"The fund-raising meeting isn't for another hour." He frowned toward her, trying to cover his discomfort.

"Two of our board members are stuck out of town, no flights in or out of Denver, so my schedule got cleared for the morning. I decided to come in early." She was brushing snow out of her blond hair, loose to her shoulders, and her nose was pink with the cold. Bright yellow mittens were a new addition to her red peacoat.

Lana grinned at her. "And how I love you early types." She peered over the desk. "Those are pretty mittens."

"Thanks. I made them myself." Calista held up both hands and beamed. "I've been trying to learn how to knit. This one is a little bigger than the other because I got distracted and added too many rows."

"They're supercute. Anyway, we were debating and maybe you could settle the argument."

Calista's eyes were bright with curiosity, her tone light. "I can try. What are you all arguing about?"

Grant's noted the "you all" and filed it away. "Do women really like flowers?"

Calista nodded. "Lots of women do."

"What about you?" Grant hoped his voice was extra casual.

She hesitated.

"And those little cut crystal figurines, like teddy bears or roses?"

Her grimace was all the answer he needed. "You mean, for a Christmas gift?"

"No, more of a romantic thing." Lana's words seemed to startle Calista, who glanced between them before answering.

"I would say I'd rather have a man offer me something that he can't buy. Like time. It's easy to buy something and have it wrapped up nicely. But to let someone into your life, to introduce them to your family and friends, take them to church with you… That's a commitment of yourself. I would find that very romantic."

Lana was nodding as she spoke, but Grant couldn't tear his gaze from Calista's face. *That you might have life and live it more abundantly.* He'd never needed anything more than this place and his friends. His life was full, complete. But now he felt God nudging him toward something more.

"Calista, would you like to come to church with me this Sunday?" The words came out a little quicker than he would have liked, but they felt so right he couldn't help the huge smile that spread over his face.

There was a beat of silence, then another, as Calista looked from Grant to Lana, and back again. She took a breath and said, "I would really like that." Twin spots of pink appeared on her cheeks by the time she finished the sentence.

He wanted to pump his fist in the air but settled for a more sedate response. "Good." He couldn't seem to stop grinning.

Lana sighed and swiped a finger under each eye. "I love the Christmas season. I just love it."

Chapter Ten

Calista slipped on another dress and gave her reflection a critical eye. The pale pink wool shift dress showed off her trim figure. Too girlie? The last one had been too dark. The one before it had been a sweater dress and was too clingy. The one before that was from last year's Christmas party and was really too fancy.

She dropped onto the edge of the bed and stared morosely at the pile of clothing on the floor. It had never been a problem to grab an outfit for church before, especially since she didn't know that many people. She had more trouble finding the hymns than anything else.

A glance at the clock reminded her that she had just a few minutes before Grant showed up. She felt her stomach knot unpleasantly. What would he think when he saw where she lived, how she lived?

Lord, You know my heart. I'm learning to be more like You every day but I know how far I have to go. Calista sighed and went to pick out a pair of shoes. As she swung open the separate closet for her shoes, Mimi darted in, tail held high.

"No, you don't!" She swatted at the Siamese shoe terror and managed to reverse her trajectory.

Just as she picked out a pair of pale pink pumps, the doorbell rang. Calista jumped as if she'd been electrocuted. She slammed the shoe closet closed and ran to open the front door barefoot.

Her heart almost stuttered to a stop as Grant flashed her that perfect smile. Nice suit, check. Fresh shave, check. Delicious smell of soap and aftershave, check and check. She could have stood there and cataloged his attributes all day.

"Hi, come on in." She stepped back and waved him inside.

"Nice place." He took a few steps into the room and gazed around.

Calista couldn't help seeing everything new through his eyes. The wall of glass emphasized the cool steel accent points at the ceiling and the avant-garde table with minimalist modern art above it. It all looked so cold and…expensive.

"I think we share a fondness for a certain artist." Grant's lips twitched as he nodded toward her latest acquisitions. A wall full of Savannah's crayon drawings might be a bit much but she couldn't bear to throw them away. And for every picture she accepted, there was another one a few hours later. They were all kitties with pink sunglasses, most of them by a Christmas tree.

"She told me they were limited edition, but apparently I've been conned."

He reached out to the delicate side table and picked up a silver-framed photo of Elaine's new family. "She looks like you."

"My sister. That's her husband and their new baby."

Calista loved that photo of the three of them, lost in love with their new baby, wrapped up in themselves.

"They live near here?"

"No. I wish they did. But they might be coming to visit in the spring, when the baby's a little bigger."

"You'll certainly have enough room for them." Again his gaze swept the apartment. High ceiling, track lighting, minimal furniture, wide-open space bordered only by the sheer glass wall. The living room alone could hold a family.

"I probably won't be here when they visit, though."

For a moment, she thought he hadn't heard her. Grant was motionless, his head turned toward the awesome view of the mountains. Clouds were moving in over the peaks. He frowned into the distance. "You're leaving Denver?"

"No, no, I mean the condo." She watched him visibly relax, his expression turning to curiosity.

A little sound near the couch made them both turn their heads. Mimi stood, her fluffy head cocked to one side.

"Is that the evil cat?"

"Yup. I better get my shoes on before she takes her chance."

Grant let out a laugh that made even a shoe-destroying cat seem like a wonderful thing.

Calista beamed in his direction as he helped her into her red peacoat and they made their way out the door, but her stomach dropped. How could orchestrating a corporate merger be easier than Sunday services with Grant? She felt like an impostor.

She was barely beyond thinking she was the center of

the universe. She swallowed the lump in her throat and lifted her chin. Well, everybody had to start somewhere.

She sneaked a glance at him as they walked. A lock of dark hair fell over his forehead and Calista realized with a jolt how very much he looked like his famous father, right down to the same perfect mouth. A mouth that was tugged up a bit at one corner.

He reached out and took her hand, the pressure of it short-circuiting her thoughts. Calista felt the tension ease in the pit of her stomach, loving the warmth of his touch.

At that moment, as if they were in an old-time Hollywood movie, fat snowflakes began to drift down around them. Calista's eyes widened and she held out her free hand to catch a falling clump. "Perfect," she whispered.

Grant lifted a hand to her cheek, running his warm thumb across her cheekbone. "Yes, it is." And the look in his eyes made her want to believe it was possible. That a man like him could love a woman like her. Was God that good, that forgiving, to give her such a gift when she hadn't done anything to deserve it? Sudden doubt coursed through her. Grant didn't even really know her yet.

"We don't want to be late," she said softly.

He dropped his hand and grinned. "Definitely not. Especially if you're one of those early people."

She shot him an amused glance and let him lead the way.

Calista had always heard that phrase "church family" but had never really known what it meant. Maybe because her own had been so twisted by her father's need for control and her own fear. Whatever it was, she got it now.

Grant held the hymnbook for them both and she sang along with the familiar stately tune, but inside she was anything but sedate. She had never felt so at home since her mother died. From the moment they stepped through the doors, they'd been greeted and hugged. Grant had already fielded three offers of lunch by the time they'd made it to a pew halfway up the sanctuary.

The little church was filled to the brim and after an hour all the bodies had made it pleasantly warm. She glanced around as the organist paused, then started another verse. Old people, families, singles, teens, everybody was here. A little boy directly in front of them sat sideways on the pew and ran a tiny toy car up and down the wood. His mother, without pausing from her song, reached down a hand and rubbed it through his soft black hair. They all seemed so at ease, so *happy*. She never remembered church this way. Her father had always parked them in the front row and they were bound for a whipping if they even twitched during the service.

As the last notes faded away, Grant turned toward her and said, "I forgot to tell you, we usually go to the parish hall for doughnuts. Is that okay?"

Calista blinked. Doughnuts, too? This was definitely not the church of her youth. "If you knew me better, you wouldn't even have to ask that question."

He let out a soft chuckle and helped her into her coat again. "Someone has a doughnut problem? But I thought you were a runner."

"That's *why* I'm a runner," she said, giving him a quick wink. "On the other hand, maybe we should skip the after-church social because you just might see a side of me that's better off hidden."

"I'll take my chances." He shook hands with an older man whose white mustache bristled as he smiled.

They walked the ten yards to the parish hall and joined the after-church crowd. It seemed as if everyone had stayed for coffee. A giant poster was taped to the front door announcing a spaghetti dinner and silent auction to benefit the Downtown Denver Mission next Sunday. The kids shed their coats and ran through a pair of doors into a modern-looking gym.

"Hi, Eric." Calista didn't know why she was surprised to see Grant's best friend here.

"Hi there, new girl." His wild red hair had been tamed a bit, probably by the dark-haired woman next to him. As she came around her husband to give Grant a hug, Calista saw her rounded tummy. Eric introduced her, with a flourish. "This is my wife, Marla. And our baby."

Marla took Calista's arm, steering her toward one of the tables. "Don't mind him, he's never serious."

Eric was certainly a lighthearted guy.

"Let's park it here while the men get us some sustenance." Marla gestured to the chair across from her and they sat down, leaving Grant and Eric to wait in line.

"When is your baby due?"

"Three weeks. Right in time for Christmas." Marla flipped her long dark hair over one shoulder and rubbed her tummy.

Something in that gesture touched her heart. How would it feel to have such a tiny person to hold for the first time? "I guess you can't wait."

"I feel like I've been waiting for this baby my whole

life." Her smile was tender, then wry. "And at this point, I swear I really have been. It's hard to waddle around with twenty pounds strapped to your front."

Calista laughed. No wonder women felt so off-kilter. She felt a pressure on her shoulder and turned her head to see a very old woman standing next to her. She was tiny, with curling steel-gray hair. Her brown eyes were fixed on Calista, and although her mouth was smiling, nothing was getting past those eyes.

"Are you Grant's new girlfriend?" Her tone was light, conversational.

Calista shook her head, struggling to marshal her thoughts. Out of the corner of her eye she could see Marla laughing into her hand.

"Well, if you've got plans for the boy, I want you to know we're all very fond of him. We want the best for him, especially now after all that trouble with his father."

Calista's face went hot. Did this little old lady think she was a gold digger? She watched the woman's eyes travel over Calista's outfit, stopping at the hem of her dress, right at the knee.

"I understand." That was all she could manage. Her voice seemed to have become stuck somewhere in her throat.

"Mrs. Herne, how are you this fine morning?" Grant's deep voice behind them cut through the chatter in the parish hall. Calista wanted to bolt from the scene but instead she turned and met his laughing gaze. His smile faltered at her subdued expression and he looked from Mrs. Herne to Calista and back again. He laid the small paper plates of doughnuts on the table and cocked his head.

"Now, see here. I won't bring her back if you're going to give her a hard time."

"I wasn't! Not at all." To Calista's surprise, the old woman's lined face turned pink and her eyes widened. "I was just letting her know how fond we are of you."

"Uh-huh." Grant folded his arms over his chest and pretended to fix a beady eye on Mrs. Herne. "I bet you were. I can take care of myself, you know. I'm a big boy."

By this point Marla was wiping tears from under her eyes and her shoulders were shaking with suppressed laughter. Eric dropped into a chair across from them and bit into a doughnut.

The old woman stood her ground. "Yes, Grant, dear, but even big boys get their hearts broken." And with that she gave his arm a little squeeze and walked away.

"I just love her," Eric mumbled through his doughnut. "I could have used her five years ago when I was dating the wrong girl."

Marla wrapped her arm around his shoulders and gave him a tender kiss on the cheek. "But you've never been on the other side. She scared me silly when I first met her. And plus, your broken heart was very attractive to a shy girl like me."

Eric glanced up into his wife's eyes and frowned. "Broken heart? Did I have a broken heart? I can't seem to recall…" He leaned in and pressed his lips to her forehead, dropping a hand to her tummy.

Calista watched them, her throat feeling tight. Her life was so empty of anything that truly mattered. She shot a glance at Grant, and met his eyes. He was studying her face, wondering. It probably wasn't hard to tell what she was feeling. She suddenly felt like the poor cousin at the family reunion, the one everybody felt sorry for.

"Hey, I saw the poster for the spaghetti dinner next Sunday." It wasn't a great transition, but it would have to do. Anything except broken hearts and babies and true love.

Grant nodded, taking a sip of his coffee. "We can pull in three or four hundred dollars in a day."

"But the roof will cost a whole lot more than that."

Eric shrugged. "It probably doesn't sound like much to a CEO like you."

Calista put down her half-eaten maple bar. "I do think it's a lousy way to make money, but not because I'm a CEO. It's basic business. You're on a deadline, you know your target and you're doing a church dinner?"

"And what do you suggest?" Grant's voice was light but there was steel in his eyes. "Ask my father to pay for it all?"

Grant's heart was pounding. Did Calista really think he would take the easy route and ask his father for money? Money that was probably made less than legally?

Her eyes widened, then narrowed. "I can see you're too proud to take that route."

"Proud? Because I won't accept money from Kurt Daniels?" Just saying the name made him angry.

"No." She sat back, choosing her words. "There are other deep pockets in this city. But you're too proud to go where the money is, and ask for it."

Grant almost stood up, he was so surprised. "I'm asking! I spend all day on the phone, calling donors. I send out fliers and do news pieces. I'm practically the poster boy for begging."

She was shaking her head, blond hair falling around her shoulders, green eyes deadly serious. If he wasn't so mad, he would have stopped to enjoy how close she was, how great she smelled.

"You're begging where you feel comfortable." She waved a hand. "Here, your friends. It's a lot easier to ask your favorite brother to loan you ten dollars than to ask a rich stranger for much more."

Grant gripped his head, running his hands through his hair. "Why would I ask a rich stranger for money, when I have close friends and family?" This conversation was so crazy, so unbelievable, that he felt as though all the logic had fallen out of it.

She laid a hand on his arm, leveled her gaze. "Grant, listen to yourself. It's not about *you*, is it?"

Grant stared at her, their gazes locked. Understanding flooded through him, followed by a healthy dose of shame. He'd been proud. Too proud to beg for himself. But it wasn't about him; it was about the people who didn't have a voice.

He nodded slowly. "I see your point." He watched her hand drop from his arm, and immediately wished they were still arguing. She picked up her maple bar and took a satisfied bite.

"Good," she mumbled. "Because that roof was never going to get fixed on spaghetti dinners."

Grant glanced across the table, remembering for the first time in several minutes that Eric and Marla were there. They wore matching expressions. And he knew exactly what they were thinking. He had met more than his match. This beautiful girl with the sharp mind and the bright green eyes, the quick blush and the fighting spirit, she was the one he'd been waiting for.

And she loved doughnuts, to boot.

"How did the visit to Grant's church go?" Lana's bright glance added to the friendly tone of her question.

"Amazing." Calista paused on her way back to the offices, handing over a double-shot caramel mocha and a large plate of homemade cookies. It had felt wonderful to hold the steaming drink on her trek down the snowy sidewalk, dodging foot-high drifts. Another Wednesday morning in her favorite place on earth.

"Ooh, thanks. You sure know how to get on my good side." Lana accepted the hot coffee and took a careful sip. "So, elaborate on amazing," she said and bit the head off a gingerbread man.

"Well, everyone was welcoming, the music was beautiful, the sermon was inspiring and nobody gave me the third degree except one little old lady. I think she has appointed herself Grant's personal protector against women."

Lana snorted, nodding her head. "That would be Mrs. Herne. When my son and I visited Grant's church last year for a special concert, she spent ten minutes asking me about my romantic history."

"Yikes." Calista couldn't help laughing, imagining the tiny elderly woman badgering Lana. "But it's kind of sweet that she's watching out for him."

"Did you pass inspection?"

"Not on your life. I think my dress was too short for her liking."

Lana grinned over her coffee. "I just love that nosy old lady. She'll keep you in line for sure."

"Well, it's not like I'll be seeing a lot of her."

Lana waggled her eyebrows. "We'll see about that. I heard a rumor about a Christmas party at the Grant-Humphreys Mansion."

Calista felt her cheeks flush and was annoyed at her own reactions. "Oh, that. It's nothing—"

Lana burst out laughing. "It's hard to take someone seriously when they're blushing and glaring. I would say it's definitely something."

Before Calista could do more than shrug sheepishly, the office door swung open and Jose wandered over. "Hey, ladies. Who's up for some filing?"

The two women glanced at each other and laughed.

"When you say it like that, it almost sounds exciting." Calista waved to Lana and headed for the office door.

"Like a lamb to slaughter," Lana said, laughing.

Another day, another list of phone calls to make. Grant raked his fingers through his hair and stared down at the page. Most of these people should have sent in their Christmas donation by now. Maybe they thought Kurt Daniels's son didn't need their hard-earned money this year. The idea made his gut twist in anger. He felt as though his father was circling like a vulture, getting closer and closer to cornering him.

He hadn't called since their last conversation, but he was sure Kurt Daniels was going to send the next check straight to the board. And Grant would rather leave the mission than watch it become one more trophy for his father. When he wanted something, he got it. Companies, homes, political influence—it seemed like there was no end to his father's desperate grabs for power.

On the surface, he looked like a man who was active in his community. Underneath, Grant knew that taking money from him was like making a deal with the devil. He had watched political careers soar, then falter when Kurt Daniels decided he wanted the candidate to flip-flop on a campaign promise. Whatever his father touched withered and spoiled. End of discussion.

Grant shook the disturbing thoughts away and refocused on his long list. Calista had given him a list of corporations and by the middle of the week, he'd begged enough corporate sponsorships to get the roof replaced. It wasn't hard at all, once he got his head around the fact that he wasn't as humble as he'd thought.

But they were still behind where they'd been last year. He rubbed his eyes, wishing that he could stop worrying. God provided; He always had. But it was an uphill battle to have faith when he saw numbers like these.

He needed to try on his tuxedo and make sure it still fit. Not that he'd changed since the last time he'd worn it at his cousin's fancy wedding. He was sort of looking forward to the party. It was strange because he hated functions like that, with women so overly glamorous you couldn't recognize them from their everyday selves. He wondered what Calista would wear, couldn't even wager a guess. Black-tie parties were carte blanche to layer on the jewels and the fur. Whatever she did, she would look amazing, that he knew for a fact. A corner of his mouth tugged up as he thought of her with the finger-painting crowd. The girl glowed, whether she had blue paint in her hair or was dressed to the nines.

A tap on the half-open door announced Jose…or rather Jose's head. "Marisol wants to know if the new chick can work in the kitchen."

Grant opened his mouth to correct Jose and then decided against it. He was going to save his energy for a real battle, and he was tired of reminding him that "new chick" wasn't Calista's name.

"She's in the filing room. I can go get her." It would be a welcome distraction from his morning's work. But then, Calista was a welcome distraction at any time, he thought with a grin.

The small room was almost completely clear of files, with only a few boxes left on a long desk near the door. Calista looked up at his quiet knock, a smile spreading over her face.

"Hey, you." The warmth in her voice was like a physical touch.

"Hey, yourself." Not the most brilliant response, but his brain had gone blank at the sight of her.

"Have you come to observe me in my purgatory?"

"I've come to release you." He couldn't help taking a step closer. She smelled wonderful, like vanilla and cinnamon.

"Excellent! What's the plan, Mr. Director?"

"Marisol needs an extra kitchen helper, if you're willing."

"Really? I've been dying to get in some kitchen time. It's like a private club and no one will share the secret handshake." She tucked a file into its place and grinned up at him.

"Today's your lucky day." His fingers itched to tuck the blond lock of hair behind her ear but he had to remind himself that they were at work, and professionalism was key. He cleared his throat. "I really enjoyed Sunday."

"I did, too." Her cheeks turned pink and she paused,

chewing her lip. "And Mrs. Herne was very interested in my past. We had a long conversation. Well, she asked questions and I answered them."

Grant couldn't suppress the laugh that rose up in him. "I should put her on a retainer. She's as good as a private investigator. Between the questions and the fear, I can weed out all the weak candidates."

Calista's happy grin slipped a little. "She's good. You definitely need her."

Grant regarded her for a second, trying to decipher the emotions that flitted over her face. When he figured it out, he stepped forward and lifted her chin with his fingers. Professionalism would have to wait. "There have never been a lot of candidates, and there's only one right now."

A smile played around her lips. "And what did Mrs. Herne decide?"

"She told me we'd make beautiful babies."

Calista's eyes widened in shock, and her face flushed a deep pink. "She did not!"

"I'm telling you the truth. Those old ladies have only one thing on their minds." He shook his head in dismay. "Grandchildren."

She snorted and swatted his arm. "I better get to the kitchen."

"Tell Marisol I'm dying for some tamales."

"Will do." And she flashed him one last lingering smile that deepened as she slipped out the door.

Chapter Eleven

"There you are," called Marisol from the other side of the kitchen. She waved cheerily and beckoned Calista to the long metal table that took up most of the far wall. Calista snagged a burgundy apron from the hooks by the door, careful to choose one that didn't have a name embroidered on it. Before she slipped the halter over her head, she removed her jacket and hung it up. Her short-sleeved silk shirt underneath was a bright red, for the Christmas holiday, just days away. The apron wouldn't save her clothes if she dropped a pot of chili, but if she was just chopping vegetables it was probably going to be all right. She washed her hands at the sink near the door and headed for the rest of the group.

She came to stand beside the short Hispanic woman. She noted once more the worn apron, the leathery hands and the familiar smell of chili powder. Her quick glance was paired with a wide smile. Marisol's quiet joy was visible in everything she did. Calista's heart rate slowed to a comfortable rate as she took in the pleasant chatter around her. The kitchen was hopping today. Not like the filing room. She was so glad to be out of there she could have skipped down the hallway. Except that Grant had been watching. She felt her cheeks warm at the thought of his fingers tipping her chin, his assurance that she was the only one he was interested in right now. She struggled to refocus on the task ahead.

"What do you need me to do? I'm ready and willing."

"I'm making vegetable beef stew for dinner and the big chopper broke." She waved a hand toward a large appliance that looked like a mixer, but much more dangerous. Sharp blades showed where a brushed metal hood had been removed. A middle-aged man peered into the innards, a scowl on his face. There was a cart underneath that was half-filled with potato pieces.

"I've never seen anything like that," Calista said, then jumped as the man flipped a red switch and the food processor roared to life. The kitchen workers paused collectively to watch, but then turned back to their tasks as the motor coughed and died.

"It also does french fries and carrot sticks, shreds lettuce, all sorts of things. I sure hope Jim can get it going." Marisol was chopping furiously while she talked.

Calista grabbed a large knife and a potato. "Is it very old? It might still be under warranty."

"No, is too old for the company to come fix. Maybe we can call a mechanic if he can't make it work."

"How much does it cost to replace?" The knife was making quick work of her small stack of potatoes, and Calista made a mental note to sharpen her own kitchen knives.

"That one cost about ten thousand, but that was a while ago."

She gasped, startled, and her knife narrowly missed her own index finger. "Ten thousand *dollars*?"

Marisol nodded, her brown eyes fixed on her work. "Kitchen equipment is very expensive. And costs to run, too. Lots of electricity for the hot water, the stoves, the dishwashers."

Calista stared around the kitchen, suddenly seeing it in a whole new light. The enormous side-by-side refrigerators, the pots that looked as though they could hold a whole turkey, the two large stoves, metal cart after metal cart. Grant needed to have major funds just to keep the kitchen going, let alone the rest of the mission. She started to wonder just what kind of budget a homeless shelter needed.

"I always thought the food was the most expensive part."

Marisol chuckled. "No, we get lots of food donations. Two big bakeries downtown give us all their day-old bread. In the summertime, the local growers bring us fruit. Christmas is a big day, lots of people, but we already have the turkeys ready in the freezer. It is the machinery that is so hard to get." She shook her head, her brow furrowing. "Poor Mr. Monohan. He has too many things to fix."

Calista was silent. A place as famous as the Downtown Denver Mission shouldn't be hurting for support. Times were hard in Denver, just like they were everywhere because of the economy, but people still tended to give at this time of year.

"Christmas is a good time for donations, right?"

Marisol reached for another potato and shrugged. "It can be. But Lana says the donations are down this month. Probably because of Mr. Monohan's father."

Calista felt a wave of pure anger sweep through her. They were holding it against him, and Grant had never asked to be recognized as Kurt Daniels's son. Plus, it was unfair that he had to bow to the pressure and give up his privacy. She couldn't imagine how it felt to be exposed that way.

The pile of whole potatoes was almost finished and Calista felt satisfaction at their quick work. Then Marisol reached under the metal table and tugged a fifty-pound sack into the light. Calista peeked under the table and almost groaned. Four more sacks lay side by side. This was going to be a long morning. But it was still better than the little filing room.

Marisol called a worker to come collect the sack of potatoes for washing.

"Okay, I am going to get the stew meat. Is all chopped and ready." Marisol pointed to a large metal door with a long, flat handle. "You can come with me so you see the inside."

Putting down her knife, Calista dutifully followed Marisol to the door, then gasped as it swung open to reveal a full-size room. The walls were lined with floor-to-ceiling shelves and buckets were tidily lined up on the lowest areas.

"This is a refrigerator?" She should have known that the fridges out in the main area couldn't contain enough food for several hundred people.

"Yes, and we have two walk-in freezers. Always take your coat in when you go."

Calista shivered, partly at the chill and partly at the thought of being stuck in a freezer without coat. As the door eased closed behind them, she resisted the urge to push it back open. The handle on the inside was reassuring, but it was still unnerving to be standing in a steel fridge with only one way out.

Marisol lifted a long packet of stew meat and handed it to Calista. Then she hefted the other into her arms. "Oh, now, see here." She nodded her head in the direction of the shelf.

She was no weakling, but there was at least forty pounds of beef cubes in her arms. Calista leaned over, feeling the strain in her biceps. Light red puddles rested on the floor. Beef blood had dripped from the packages, through the wire shelving and pooled on the concrete.

"We will bring these out and then I have to clean. I tell the workers to always have a drip pan under the meat but sometimes they do not listen."

"Do you want me to clean it? You can keep supervising the stew." Beef blood was on her list of things to avoid, but Calista shrugged off the thought. She wanted to be useful.

"No, *mija*, but thank you." Marisol beamed at her as they reentered the warm kitchen. "I have to wash down the floor with the hose, then spray it with bleach, then scrub. I have a thick coat so I will not be cold." She set the tray near the stove and turned to eye Calista's outfit. "You always look so pretty."

For some reason, Marisol's compliment lightened her heart. Maybe because she was sure it was sincere. At work, compliments flowed freely, but were rarely worth more than the breath they took.

"Thank you. I'll keep working on the potatoes, then?"

Shrugging into a heavy work jacket that was much too big for her short frame, Marisol nodded and headed toward the refrigerator, stopping to grab a hose from where it was neatly coiled on the floor.

Her table was covered with freshly washed potatoes

and Calista wondered if this was what it was like to get kitchen duty in the army. The sound of the power hose washing down the cement floor echoed faintly through the crack left in the closed door. She worked in silence, glancing up every now and then to watch the workers in the kitchen. Marisol pushed the door open and recoiled the bright yellow hose, then twisted the faucet closed with sharp movements. She disappeared back into the refrigerator, this time closing the door with a firm thud.

Calista shivered at the sight. It looked like a bank vault from the outside.

At that moment, a large squeal sounded above the stove. She dropped her potato in surprise, then saw the source of the noise. A ceiling fan, several feet square, had decided to stop working. Grant really had to make a list of items that needed to be replaced. She would talk to him about the ideas she'd been working on for fund-raising.

That was the last thing that went through Calista's mind before she saw the flames. Flickering orange, the fire licked along the edges of grating that covered the fan and grew several feet in just seconds.

"Thank you for your generous support of the mission. As a long-time donor—" Grant's attempt to connect with one of the many people who had not given their usual Christmastime donation was interrupted by the piercing wail of the fire alarm.

Just peachy. He gave an internal sigh and hurriedly finished leaving the message.

But this wasn't a drill. Lana always let him know when she was going to have a drill and which building it was in. Grant jumped to his feet, feeling a sudden contraction of fear in his chest.

The hallway was empty but he jogged to the filing room, just in case Calista had come back. His heart was beating so loudly the fire alarm was hardly noticeable. The room was empty. He closed it and hung the All Clear sign that was previously hanging on the inside, then did the same for the other offices. Probably it was nothing. Most likely it was just a false alarm.

Out in the lobby, Lana was giving directions to the residents who were filing by the decorated fir tree, toward the front doors. She caught his eye and called, "Kitchen fire! The meeting rooms on this side are cleared. We're heading out the front."

"Offices are clear," he called back.

Calista. His mind flashed on horrible scenarios of flaming grease or exploding stoves and then he shoved the images away. Marisol would never let her handle anything dangerous without training. And Marisol would make sure everyone was out safely. Every worker was trained in fire exits and procedures. Each supervisor would help clear the building, and herd other workers out. The other buildings would evacuate to the parking lot and the sidewalks. He should be following Lana to the street since he was in the office area but Grant had to look. It was probably just a dish of something going up in flames.

The cafeteria was empty except for the last of the workers trooping out the back exit. Grant ducked into the kitchen, holding his breath against the thick smoke. Bright flames were all too visible as they shot from the ceiling and licked along the edge where the ceiling met the wall. An industrial-size fire extinguisher lay spent on the floor and Grant felt his heart drop into his shoes. This fire was too big to put out. He peered through the black smoke, crouching low to get a better look. He reassured himself the kitchen was truly empty.

Everyone was out. The rest was in God's hands.

He jogged through the cafeteria, letting out a deep breath he'd been holding in the smoky kitchen. The outside door swung open at his touch and he sucked in the fresh air. The mission's fire protocol stated kitchen workers would gather on the far side of the courtyard, which was their rendezvous point. The snow reflected the sun and he squinted toward the workers, searching. They huddled together, some with their arms around the shoulders of friends. He scanned the group for Calista's blond hair, trying to recall her outfit. With the mass of red polos and khaki pants, it only took a second to realize Calista was not there.

Fear gripped him like steel bands tightening around his ribs. He strode over, determined to be calm. His eyes searched the group for Marisol and what had been fear turned to outright dread.

"Mr. Monohan!" A young woman rushed up to him, her red hair escaping from the standard-issue hairnet. Her eyes were streaming tears, but whether from the smoke or the shock of the fire, he wasn't sure.

"That new girl, she was with us but then she went back!"

Grant felt his limbs go numb. He wanted to move, wanted to ask her a question, but for several seconds his mind shut down completely. Went back in? But he hadn't seen anyone, and the offices were clear.

He spun on his heel, staring at the closed cafeteria door. Was it possible she had made it back to the kitchen by the time he had crouched down in the doorway to make sure it was clear? Could she be in there now?

"Did she say anything?" He said the words calmly but his voice broke on the last word. "And where is Marisol?"

The young woman started to sob in earnest. "I don't know. She wasn't in the kitchen with us when the fire started. The new girl got the fire extinguisher and tried to put it out, but it was already burning through the ceiling."

Grant stared at the roof of what was the kitchen. Smoke billowed from the vents and long red flames appeared in the northwest corner. His heart thudded in his throat. He knew the very worst thing was to go back into a fire, for any reason. Everything could be replaced except for human life.

Lord, show me what to do!

In answer to his prayer, the pieces of the puzzle clicked into place. "Were they working together, before the fire?"

She coughed, struggling to suppress her sobs. "I think so. They were chopping potatoes at the long prep table."

Marisol was in there. And Calista knew where. The wail of the fire trucks sounded in the distance and Grant was already moving toward the cafeteria door. He heard several voices calling him back but he ignored them. Within seconds he reached the door, pulled it open and entered the cafeteria. Only it wasn't a cafeteria any longer. It was as black as night with acrid smoke and the heat buffeted against him in waves. He crouched down but could see only marginally better.

"Marisol! Calista!" He called out as loudly as he

could, then sucked in a breath. That was a mistake. The coughs that racked his body made it impossible to call out again. He stumbled forward, squinting against the smoke, and ran directly into Marisol's soft, familiar form. He barely recognized her face, blackened with smoke, eyes wide with fear. Calista supported her on one side and her eyes were streaming. He grabbed hold of Marisol's other arm and sped her toward the outside door.

The clear sky above them and the crunch of the snow underfoot were like heaven as they burst out of the cafeteria. Grant supported Marisol and was relieved to notice that she was uninjured, as much as he could ascertain in the few seconds before they reached the kitchen workers huddled in the far corner. She was enveloped by the group and hugged over and over. Calista stood still, panting slightly, streaks of soot on her face. Grant looked over at her, a question on his lips, his fear finally ebbing at the sight of them. He wanted to ask, but before he did he simply held out his arms.

Calista walked into them as naturally as if she had been born to rest there against his chest. He could feel her trembling, her arms locked around his waist. Squeezing his eyes shut, he spoke a prayer of thanks into her hair.

He could have stayed that way for hours, feeling the beat of his heart slowly return to normal.

The sound of water being sprayed at full force onto the roof brought him back to reality. The fire trucks had unrolled the long ladders and were directing water to the hole in the kitchen where flames were still emerging.

"She was in the fridge," Calista choked out. Her

green eyes were bloodshot and soot was smeared along one cheek.

Grant stepped back, struggling to make sense of her words. “The walk-in refrigerator?”

Calista nodded, swallowing hard. One arm was still around his waist, under his jacket, and he could feel her shaking. “I panicked when the fan caught on fire. I tried to put it out but then I just ran out with everybody else.” Her face collapsed with the weight of her tears and she pressed a fist against her mouth.

“You did what you were supposed to do,” he said, pulling her against him again.

“I forgot she was there, trapped in that place,” she said and began to sob.

Grant could feel the hysteria rising in her and lifted her face to his. Her tears were hot under his fingers. “Calista, you saved her life. There’s a light that flashes in the fridge when the alarm goes off. She should have seen it. You did the right thing, and more.”

“When I opened the door, she was on her hands and knees scrubbing the floor. She didn’t see it flashing.” She shook her head and squeezed her eyes shut, tears leaking out from under her lids. “It felt just like last time.”

Grant frowned and moved his hands from her face to her shoulders. “Last time?”

“My mother died when our house caught fire. She was in the basement. Doing laundry.” Her eyes were still closed, face tight with fear and pain.

He felt the blood rushing to his head. He couldn’t fathom that she had gone back inside, in the face of all her fears.

"Grant, can I sit down?" She opened her eyes and swayed a little as she spoke.

He cursed himself for letting her talk when she needed to be wrapped in a blanket and checked out for burns. He slipped out of his jacket and wrapped it around her shoulders.

Marisol was still cocooned in several pairs of arms, her heavy coat hardly visible. Grant gently led them away from the group, his arm around Marisol's shoulders, Calista's hand firmly in his, and the three of them made their way down the sidewalk. Marisol mumbled a few words and Grant wondered if she was in shock.

The ambulance crew gave them both a thorough examination, thankful there were only two victims of the smoke. Grant hovered, his heart torn between watching the progress on the fire and making sure they were okay.

Savannah ran toward him from across the parking lot, her pink sunglasses slipping down her nose. Her mother trailed behind, a hand to her mouth in shock.

"Mr. Monohan! There was a fire and everything burnded! Even the pretty Christmas tree!"

He stooped down and caught Savannah's small figure in his arms. There were rules about hugging the residents, especially children. An arm across the shoulders was fine, a handshake was better. But today, he didn't feel like following the recommendations. The little girl was frightened and a hug was really all he had to give. That, and his assurance that everything was going to be okay.

"Savannah, don't worry. It was a kitchen fire and the firemen got it under control."

She tipped back her dark head and searched his face. "Is that a lie, Mr. Monohan?"

He tried to smile at the question, but his sadness got in the way. She was used to adults saying one thing and meaning another. "Nope, not a lie."

"'Cause it looks like everything got burnded up."

"Burned, not burnded. And no, it was just the kitchen. The tree is fine. Everybody is okay." His gaze went straight to Calista, then Marisol.

"Then why is Miss Calista in the ambulance?" Savannah pointed toward Calista, tears threatening to spill over onto her round cheeks.

"They're just making sure she's not hurt. It was scary, but the firemen came and are putting it out."

Savannah rested her head on his shoulder for a moment, her small body relaxing against him. Her mother stood off to the side, transfixed by the smoke that streamed from the kitchen roof.

"Okay, I believe you."

Grant felt his heart constrict with the power of those words. There were so many people who needed reassurance. *Lord, help me show them Your faithfulness.*

"But what are we gonna eat now if the food is all gone?"

"I promise that no one will be hungry."

"Good. I hate being hungry." The little girl shoved her sunglasses back up her nose.

"Why don't you go say hi to Miss Calista?"

Savannah nodded and went over to her mother, slipping her small hand into hers and tugging her toward Calista. Grant watched them with a heavy heart. So many people depended on this mission, on him.

The fire raged on, the hoses poured thousands of gallons of water on the flames, and through it all, Grant had a running conversation with God about Calista, the mission, his future, his father. *Why, Lord? Why now?* And then he would glance back at Marisol resting on the ambulance table and gratitude would sweep over him again. *Thank You for keeping them safe.*

"Are you the director?" A slight man in a fireman-captain's uniform appeared at the side of the emergency vehicle.

"I am." Grant stood up, his body tensing with the news he knew was just seconds away.

"Well, you're really lucky no one was seriously injured because electrical fires spread quickly. We've got it contained now. But the kitchen is a total loss."

Chapter Twelve

Calista sat huddled in a blanket, taking tiny sips of coffee and watching flames shoot through the roof of the Downtown Denver Mission. Marisol was a few feet away, staring blankly into the smoky sky. Calista didn't know if she was praying or in shock. She hadn't said much of anything since Calista had led her out of the refrigerator and through scorching flames.

She was aware of the bitter smell of burned hair and for the first time Calista put up a hand to her head. Sure enough, clumps of hair came away when she ran her fingers through it. She sighed. How many days had she gone to work with her hair down? Two, maybe three? But she had wanted to look nice for Grant and left off her usual French chignon or softly made bun. The irony of it was almost laughable. She would have to call her hairdresser and have some sort of stylishly short 'do for a while.

Calista shook the hair off her fingers and went back to watching the fire. Or watching Grant watching the fire. He stuffed his hands in his pockets and paced for a few minutes. Then he ran his hands through his hair, looked over at Marisol and back at the fire. Then he started with the pocket stuffing and pacing again. She knew what it was like to watch your home burn to the ground. But she had no idea what it was like to watch your home burn, and know hundreds of people depended on you for survival. Their Christmas was ruined.

Lissa and Michelle weren't too far away, surrounded by kids, waiting for parents to come. A few of the little ones were crying but most were jumping up and down in excitement. Two firemen walked over to hand out stickers and show the kids the gear.

Lissa caught Calista's gaze and wandered over, her arms wrapped around her thin waist.

Calista blinked up at the teen, and forced a smile. "How are the kids?" She couldn't imagine herding dozens of small children out of a building with the fire alarms wailing.

Lissa bent down and gave Calista a fierce hug, then stood back. The expression on her face was a mixture Calista couldn't quite decipher.

"And that was for…?"

"For asking about the kids when you're the one who's sitting in the back of the ambulance."

"I'm actually on the bumper, but I see your point." Calista grinned, wondering how Lissa managed to be so defensive and endearing all at the same time. "And thank you for the hug. I needed it."

Lissa nodded, her gaze fixed on the man who paced the sidewalk. She flipped her dark braid back over one shoulder and said, "I wish a hug fixed everything, but it doesn't."

Calista sighed. "Truer words were never spoken."

"I've got to get back to the kids. Michelle says this

is the very first class we've ever run in the parking lot, with firemen as assistants."

She laughed, and raised a hand to Lissa's coworker, who looked ready to hand out kids as party favors. Lissa went back to her group and the kids surrounded her. She was sarcastic and tense, but something in that girl touched Calista and reminded her of her own teen years.

Her gaze was jerked back to the scene in front of her as the fire chief interrupted Grant's twentieth tour of the sidewalk and delivered what must have been the bad news. Calista wasn't near enough to hear the words, but she was near enough to see his shoulders slump. He nodded, his features stiff, and shook the chief's hand before the fireman went back to his crew.

Calista wanted to run to Grant and throw her arms around him, as if that would shield him from what had already happened. She knew there was no use in trying to pretend it was all right, or put a positive spin on the situation. The mission was crippled, maybe permanently.

She raised her eyes and saw him regarding her steadily. She slowly lifted a hand, maybe in greeting or in goodbye since she wasn't sure where he would go from here. Maybe this would be one of the last times they saw each other. He was going to have way more on his mind than getting to know her. She felt as though someone had grabbed her by the throat, the feeling of loss was so sudden. Tears sprang to her eyes and she furiously blinked them away. How ridiculous to cry over Grant, when hundreds of vulnerable people in poverty were in a truly terrible situation. But it was no use yelling at herself; the tears continued to flow down her cheeks. She ducked her head and swiped at her face.

"You need to go home and get some rest," he said, suddenly a few feet away.

Calista frowned, mopping her face one last time with the edge of the blanket. "I'm okay," she said, trying for confident but sounding argumentative.

He sat down next to her and was silent for a moment. They watched the firemen winding their hoses back on to the trucks. Most of the workers had gone home, but Jose hovered near the fire trucks and Lana remained near the corner, giving periodic statements to reporters when needed. Calista felt a surge of gratitude for the middle-aged secretary.

"I can give you a ride home."

Calista glanced up, surprised. Did he think she wasn't able to drive herself? She must look worse than she'd thought.

"I'm really okay. It was pretty darn scary, I admit. But everything worked out..." The words trailed away. It didn't work out for the people who relied on the mission for meals. She jumped back in before Grant could speak. "Is there anything I can do? What's the plan for providing meals? I'm sure you've notified the board and there's probably an emergency backup plan."

He turned to look her full in the face and she struggled not to let another tear slip away from her. His expression was so raw, his despair so clear, that it took her breath away.

"The board has been notified. The residents may stay in the unaffected buildings, so they'll be able to sleep here and have classes. Our paperwork and computers survived, which is a blessing. But the kitchen..." Grant turned back toward the smoking corner of the main building. "The kitchen is the heart and soul of this mission's outreach. A lot of people would never come through these doors if they weren't hungry. Once they have a hot meal, they can face a lot of their other issues."

Calista stared at Grant's profile, finally understanding. "It all started with the kitchen, didn't it? When it was founded?"

He nodded.

"So…" Calista hated to say anything that might bring back that look of despair. But what was the plan? Did they all just go on without a kitchen?

"So," he repeated, sounding a little stronger. "We'll be assessing the damage and probably have some smoke issues with the lobby. I think the offices were spared any smoke damage because the main door was closed."

She felt a burst of relief, hoping that meant she was supposed to come back. He moved to sit down next to her on the ambulance bumper and stared at the smoking kitchen.

"You never did tell me how much of the funding is earmarked for repairs. How long would the board take to authorize construction on a new kitchen?"

He turned to face her, bright blue gaze soft on hers. "You're right. I forgot to outline all of that." He paused. "You know, Calista, I wanted to thank you for being here. Not just what happened with Marisol." He paused, swallowing audibly and glancing away for a moment. Calista waited, scanning his face for the little flickers of emotion that hinted at everything he held inside.

"I wanted to thank you for taking an interest in the mission. A lot of people don't want to be bothered with the paperwork or the dirty details of fund-raising."

Calista let out a breath she didn't know she'd been holding. What did she think he was going to say? That he was glad for her sparkling personality? She swallowed back her disappointment and nodded brightly. "Well, that's what I do best, Grant. Some people lead the sing-alongs or wipe noses. I like the paperwork. And I'm more than willing to help organize the fundraising for the new kitchen project."

"I've seen you wipe a few noses." He contradicted her, his tone teasing.

"True, but if it's a choice between paperwork and wiping a nose, I choose paperwork any day."

He laughed. "We're two of a kind there, I guess."

She glanced at the smoking ruins and continued in a softer tone. "I know it must be so hard to see all your work ruined, but the faster you start rebuilding, the better it will be for the mission."

"And that's what I'm talking about, right there. Someone else might say that a disaster like this is a huge setback and we should take our time, maybe even close down for a while."

Calista shook her head, struggling to keep her thoughts straight under threat of that smile. "Sure, that would make sense if we weren't talking about *people*. Buildings can wait, stores can open months later than planned, but hungry people can't wait."

He didn't answer, just kept smiling. Then he slowly reached out a hand and ran a thumb along her jaw.

Calista felt as if her whole body had been thrown into a pot of hot water. Her cheeks flushed and she wanted to say something, anything. But her voice was gone, along with any ability to form a complete thought.

"You have soot on your face," he said, very softly.

"Oh."

His eyes crinkled with laughter. "Yes, oh." And then

he was leaning closer, one arm resting lightly behind her back. For a fleeting moment, Calista flashed back to the first time he had been this close. She had thought he was going to kiss her and he was actually giving his security badge to the cafeteria girl. Maybe she should turn and look behind her, just in case he was reaching for something in the back of the ambulance?

The next moment she knew for sure. Grant's lips pressed softly against hers and she couldn't keep her eyes open one second longer. She was lost; his arm against her back and his lips against hers were the only important things in the entire universe.

He sat back a few inches, still close enough for her to see the rough stubble on his jaw and the thick dark lashes that rimmed his bright blue eyes. "Now I know."

"Know what?" Her voice came out all breathless.

"That you won't run away if I try that."

The idea of turning tail at the sight of an impending kiss from Grant startled a laugh out of her. "Why would you ever think I'd run?"

His lips curved up, even as sadness flared behind his eyes. "Plenty of reasons. This isn't a nine-to-five job. And a lot of times I get wrapped up in the problems the residents are having. I should be more distant, but I just can't be."

Calista lifted her hand to his cheek and whispered, "That's what I like about you. Of all the people I've met, you would have the best excuse for being distant. But you're not."

He shook his head, the movement insistent against her palm. "Because I'm not bitter that things haven't always gone the way I've wanted?"

Calista waved her hand at the smoldering ruins of

the kitchen. "This is a little more than not getting what you want. This is watching hard work, effort, hopes and dreams…" Just the words made the reality of the situation so much more real, Calista felt overwhelmed. She struggled to speak past the lump in her throat. "I've been here two months and this fire breaks my heart. It makes me wonder what God is thinking."

Grant sighed and wrapped an arm around her shoulders. "I know. But in Jeremiah it says that God wants to show us great and marvelous things. So, maybe He has to burn down a kitchen or two in the process."

Calista stared out toward the smoking lobby area, the firemen sorting their gear into piles and wrapping up hoses. The snowdrifts were black and dirty, puddles of water mixed with slush. She thought of her mother, and the fire that took her life. What great and marvelous things came from that? Pain rose up in her chest like a wave of icy water. She struggled to take a breath. *I trust in You, Jesus. I trust in You.* Calista rested her head on Grant's shoulder and closed her eyes, fighting back the fear. Fear that she was all alone in the universe, that God was a myth made by fragile, human minds.

"Mija?" Marisol's trembling voice shook Calista out of her thoughts. The older woman walked toward them, still wrapped in a brown emergency blanket.

She stood up and hugged Marisol for all she was worth. "I'm so sorry," she said, her voice catching. "I'm so sorry for leaving you in there."

"But *mija*, you did not leave me! You saved me." Marisol's tone was indignant.

Calista just shook her head and hugged harder. Finally, she stepped back and wiped the fresh tears from her face.

"And we are all safe, that is what matters," Marisol declared, her brown eyes flashing. "And plus, it seems some good has come out of this already." She nodded her head at Grant and gave Calista a huge wink.

She felt the heat rise in her cheeks but couldn't suppress the grin that spread over her face.

"I knew it would take something very big to get Mr. Monohan to show his feelings to you. And for you, too, Calista." She shook a finger at the two of them, each in turn.

Grant made a choking sound and started to protest. "It wasn't the fire, really…"

But Calista never heard the rest because the fire chief came over then.

"We're heading out, Mr. Monohan. Again, I'm sorry about what happened to the mission. If there's anything we can do, let me know. Maybe we can help with fund-raising."

Grant thanked the chief for the team's efforts. "I'll be sure to give you a call when we get a plan."

As they watched him walk away, Marisol said, "Mr. Monohan, I better get home and wash these smoky clothes. Jose said he'd give me a ride home." She gave them both one last hug and walked over to Jose, who gave them a sad-looking wave before heading home.

Calista sighed. "Me, too. And call my hairdresser."

For the first time, Grant seemed to notice Calista's damaged hair. His mouth dropped open in shock and he gently ran his fingers through one side of the sooty mess. Broken and singed strands came away with his hand.

"Oh, Calista," he whispered. "I'm so sorry."

She couldn't help laughing. "You're sorry about my hair? The mission kitchen just burned down and you're worried about my hair?" The more she thought about it, the funnier it was. Soon, she was doubled over, tears leaking from her eyes. Grant watched her, bemused.

"Let me take you home," he said, concern edging his voice even though his expression was light.

Calista took a deep breath, and straightened up, struggling to keep her face straight. "Sorry, maybe it wasn't that funny. I definitely need a hot bath and some calm music." She handed her blanket back to the ambulance crew and turned just in time to see Jackie running toward them.

"Calista! I've been calling you for hours." Her voice was high-pitched with panic, eyes sweeping over the scene and Calista's ruined clothes.

"Jackie, everything's okay, we're fine." She rushed to reassure her friend, reaching out with one sooty hand. "Did you see the fire on the news?"

Jackie stepped back from her touch, careful not to get her pale violet suit smudged. "No, I didn't. But you missed the big board meeting at one and since no one could reach you, the directors were having fits."

Grant watched Calista's eyes change as if a door had slammed shut inside. Where there had been softness and vulnerability, there was only icy silence.

"It's time to get back to your real life, boss, because the office is falling apart." The pretty girl flicked a curl over her shoulder as if she was talking about the weather.

When Calista found her voice, the tone was impersonal. "My phone is in my purse, which is in the file room." She turned to Grant, face expressionless. "Is it all right if I go back inside?"

He nodded, but held up a hand. "You two can talk while I go get it." And he walked away without waiting for an answer.

The door was propped open and he stepped carefully through the flooded patches in the lobby. His heart was pounding, but not in anticipation this time. He was angry, and he needed a few minutes to compose himself or he was going to give that woman a piece of his mind. Calista had been in a fire, saved a friend, confronted her worst fears, and all she could say was that Calista missed a big meeting? He felt the blood rushing in his ears and shook his head.

What was all that about her "real life"? He pushed back a whisper of fear. She had a job, a high-powered position that she didn't make any effort to hide. He was just reacting to the stew of lies his father concocted. It was an offhand comment and nothing more.

The hallway to the offices was a little hazy, but otherwise there was no smoke damage. He stopped to open a few windows at the end of the hall then headed for the file room. Calista's small black purse was sitting on the desk by the door. Grant grabbed it and her coat, and walked back toward the lobby. His head was still whirling with relief and anger and disbelief when he walked through the lobby door, straight into his father.

Kurt Daniels stood at the front of the Downtown Denver Mission as if he owned the place, but that's how he looked wherever he went. With thick, wavy hair that was more silver than black and a stature that made other men feel small, the powerful businessman didn't have to work for respect. It just came to him naturally, whether he had earned it or not. A suit that must cost as much as the average mortgage payment was the final touch.

He was awesome to behold. As long as you didn't know what kind of person was on the inside.

Grant planted himself a few feet away, waiting for his father to speak. Those dark blue eyes were exactly like his own, except for the calculating look.

"I have to talk to you." The gravelly voice was utterly familiar and it set Grant's teeth on edge.

"So you can force me to do everything your way? You're absolutely predictable." He was too tired to argue about this, not now.

"Please." Kurt Daniels held up a long, elegant hand.

Grant waited, eyebrows raised, not trusting for a moment that his father actually had a valid reason to be here, at this moment.

"I made a mistake."

Grant couldn't keep from shaking his head and taking a step toward the parking lot.

"Grant, you need to hear this, no matter what's between us." The intensity of his tone, the set of his jaw, slowed Grant's steps.

After a short debate, he said, "Five seconds. Which is more than you ever gave me until this year."

His father sighed, closed his eyes for a moment and then said, "I hired someone to convince you to see things my way, to make sure you let me get involved in your life. I didn't know what he was doing." He stopped, looking up, pain in his eyes. "No, I made sure not to know. Which is different."

Grant's mind was stuck, spinning like car wheels in the snow. "You…hired someone to write me threatening letters?"

Kurt Daniels glanced at the parking lot, the reporters with camera equipment. "I thought it would hurry things along, if you thought you had to admit to the world we were related."

Grant heaved a sigh. "I don't even know what to say. I'm glad to know who was behind it all. But this is a bad time to be having this conversation. As you can see—" he swept a hand behind him at the smoking shell of the mission "—we've had a fire."

His father stepped forward and grabbed his arm, eyes flashing. "That's why I'm here," he hissed.

Grant jerked his arm away. "What are you talking about?"

"I think the man I hired started that fire."

He felt the words drop one by one, like ice cubes down his spine. "You…did this?" Even after all he knew about his father, he could never have imagined this. It was too horrible, too evil.

"I didn't know, I swear. I thought he was trying to scare you with anonymous threats. When I saw the fire on the news, it occurred to me for the first time that he might do something more."

Grant shook his head, hardly able to form words. He looked over at Calista, standing near the ambulance. How could she ever want to be part of this soap opera? People could have been hurt; Marisol could have died. Fury choked him and Grant struggled to speak calmly.

"If you're here to beg forgiveness, that's not for me to decide. The police will be involved if this was arson, and I'm not going to jail for you." With those words he stalked past him into the parking lot.

Calista stood with her arms folded across her waist, while Jackie paced a few feet away, speaking urgently into her cell phone.

"I'm sorry for the delay." He handed over her purse, hoping he didn't sound as furious as he felt.

Calista accepted her purse without comment, but she shot a dubious look behind him.

"You don't want to know," he said, trying for black humor and ending up somewhere near bitterness.

"Grant, I'm going to go home and get cleaned up, then head back to work so I can handle the crisis that erupted there today. But..." She fixed him with a steady look. "I'm hoping we can talk tomorrow. I don't understand why you can't take his money."

He felt her words like a slap to the face. Of course, everyone wanted him to take the money. That was all that really mattered, unless you knew the truth.

She seemed to read his thoughts because she said, "It just doesn't make sense and I want to understand, if you'll trust me."

Her look gripped his heart and he hauled in a deep breath. He did trust her. As much as he trusted Marisol or Eric, friends he'd known for years. There was a powerful ache to tell her the whole story right here and now, but not because he thought she wasn't going to come back. His heart told him Calista was here to stay. He glanced behind him and wasn't surprised to see Kurt Daniels had already disappeared. He was good at that.

"All right. But it's not a pretty story."

"I wasn't hoping for a fairy tale." Calista's lips twitched for a moment and Grant felt his heart lighten at the sight. This woman could lead him anywhere with one word, one look. It would be sort of scary, if it didn't feel so right.

Jackie snapped her cell phone closed and strode over to them. "We've got to get moving. The board has called a meeting for this evening. I told them what happened and that you needed a few hours to get ready." She nodded at Grant, her eyes taking in his appearance from his head to his shoes, then flickering past him to where his father had been just minutes before.

Calista nodded, her expression all business. "Let's go." She hesitated, and Grant wished he could give her a kiss goodbye. But Jackie was waiting and Calista reached out a hand to touch his sleeve, then turned away and walked toward the far parking lot.

He watched them until they had turned the corner. *Please keep her safe.* Because whatever had gone wrong today at VitaWow, her expression showed that it was a bigger threat to her peace of mind than a raging fire.

Calista flipped the switch inside that took her from normal girl to CEO. It wasn't a hard move, considering she had spent the past decade being fearlessly in control. But this time there was a piece of her, her mind or even her heart, that seemed stuck back in the Downtown Denver Mission parking lot. She could almost feel Grant's thumb moving along her jaw, his warm lips on hers. She struggled to focus on Jackie's fast-paced chatter.

"The board received a last-minute offer on a new location for the headquarters. It's better than the last by a long shot. It's so good I thought it was a joke. As soon as I heard this morning, I tried to call you about twenty times to give you a heads-up before the meeting but you must have had your phone turned off."

Calista frowned, shaking her head. They were standing in front of her car, Jackie's sports car pulled up at an angle to hers. A testament of how panicked she'd been when she'd arrived. Not for her safety, of course, but because of the meeting. Calista swallowed the hurt that swamped her and focused on what seemed like the palest details in a dramatic day.

"I never turn my phone off, but I did go to the kitchen around ten because they needed help in there. I forgot to take it with me." Forgot because she'd been rattled at having a sweet conversation with Grant about babies. Instead of smiling at the memory, she felt her jaw clench. Grant's presence had thrown her into a blushing frenzy, like a teenager. She couldn't even trust herself to keep track of minor things like her phone when he was around.

"Then when the kitchen caught fire, I panicked and got out." Calista left the rest of the story for another time. Or maybe never. She was so tired her teeth ached but she still needed to get cleaned up and head to VitaWow.

For the first time Jackie seemed to consider the implications of finding Calista sitting in the ambulance. "Are you sure you're okay to meet with the board this evening? I could try to get them all rescheduled for tomorrow morning."

Calista almost snorted. Of course she wasn't, but she didn't really have a choice. "It's fine, but see if you can get my hairdresser to meet me at my apartment in thirty minutes. Tell her it's an emergency."

Jackie nodded, eyes wide. "Oh, wow. Your hair is really…going to need some help."

She sighed, hating to admit how shallow Jackie was, if her hair got a bigger reaction than the mission losing a major part of its operation.

Chapter Thirteen

Grant felt a buzz in his pocket for the tenth time that hour. He resisted the urge to throw the cell phone out the open window of his office and answered it like the good director he was. But if today got any longer, he didn't know how much goodness was left in him.

"I saw it on the news. I'm on my way over."

Eric's statement, instead of a greeting, made Grant smile in spite of himself.

"You were just here. There's not much difference except the big black, smokin' hole where the kitchen used to be."

"Be there in ten." And with a click, Grant was reminded why Eric was his best friend. He closed his own phone and laid it on the desk, wanting to lay his head in his arms and close his eyes. The few minutes of quiet in his office was supposed to give him energy to get through the day, but all it seemed to do was remind him how very tired he was. And smoky. And wishing Calista was still here.

Instead she was on her way back to VitaWow, which wasn't fair because she needed to go home and rest.

Jackie's lack of compassion to Calista irked him every time he thought about it. She was supposed to run off to a meeting after what had happened here? Poor woman, no wonder she felt as though she had no real friends if that was as close as she got to friendship. But somehow Calista showed compassion, loyalty, generosity, when she was at the mission…and amazing bravery today. *Give her strength, Lord, for what she needs to do today. Whatever it is.*

His father jumped to mind and he shoved the image away. He just didn't have time to even consider the implications. Was his father really so unhinged he would hire someone to burn the mission down? Just to get attention?

His desk phone rang and he stared at it. What he wouldn't give to pretend he wasn't sitting six inches away. He rubbed a hand over his face and picked it up.

"Mr. Monohan, this is Chief Andrew Neilly of the Denver Police."

That got his attention.

The chief continued. "Just wanted to confirm the fire chief's finding of an accidental fire. Since you've had trouble with the threatening letters, we want to be doubly sure."

"As far as I know, it was a fan that shorted out. A kitchen worker also witnessed the fire start. But I need to tell you something about those letters."

"Go ahead." Grant could hear the chief tearing a sheet of paper off a notepad.

He took a steadying breath and gave the chief as much information as he had, about his father and the man he'd hired.

"Oh, boy."

Grant smiled a little at Chief Neilly's comment. "Oh, boy" didn't really cover it, but what else was there to say? "If the fire is accidental, then I don't want to press charges. I'm going to try and talk to him, see if we can reach some kind of understanding."

There was a pause. "I understand. But Mr. Monohan? Be careful. And if you ever need help, be sure to call."

Careful. He wished he knew if it was wise to even speak to his father again. But something in the old man's face today was different. He seemed to realize, for the first time, that he couldn't always get his way. Grant thanked him and hung up the phone. Another knock at the door announced Lana.

"I know you're taking a break, but I thought you'd want to know about the call I just got from Janet Jeffrey at Seventh Street Mission."

He came around the side of his desk and leaned against it, stuffing his hands in his pockets. "Janet's probably wondering how many people to expect over there."

To his surprise, Lana grinned. "Not exactly. She's been on the phone as soon as they heard about the fire. They've got some meals lined up, dinner for starters."

"Dinner?"

"Yeah. They pulled in some favors and dinner will be coming to the mission at six, right on the dot. A full, balanced meal for two hundred and fifty."

So his residents didn't have to find somewhere else, at least for the immediate future. He felt as if an enormous weight just lifted from his shoulders. "Well, that's some seriously good news. I guess we'll worry about breakfast later."

Lana ran her fingers through her hair and stared

innocently at the ceiling. "Maybe we will, maybe we won't."

"What does that mean?"

She laughed outright, glee written on her features. "Calista sent out a petition and they've already got donors scheduled for the next two weeks. Every meal is covered at least that far, maybe farther if they keep at it."

Grant felt his mouth drop open. He leaned heavily back against the desk, his mind spinning. "How? She's back at work."

"You've got to hand it to the girl. She knows her stuff." Lana shook her head, eyes bright.

"What do you mean by donors?"

"Hospitals, a few sports teams, banks, corporations, you name it!" She was laughing as she ticked off the places on her fingers. "Isn't God amazing, Grant? I could hardly believe it when that assistant of hers called. I asked if she wanted to tell you, but she said she was supposed to keep working and see if they can get the whole month covered."

"Unbelievable. We can set up the classrooms as meal rooms. Maybe use some of the bigger cafeteria tables, if they'll fit. Some of them might have to go in the lobby." He frowned, working the logistics in his head. So many people, so little space.

"Outdoor Rentals called and said they had some all-purpose tents that can be used with a wooden floor for outdoor seating if we need it. It comes with a few heaters. They'll be over later to set it up, just in case we need it for overflow."

It was so much to take in, he had to sit down. Grant went back behind his desk and carefully lowered his long frame into the chair. His legs felt numb. Maybe he was having a delayed reaction from the fire. "Why would they do this? I've never even heard of Outdoor Rentals."

Lana wheeled closer to the desk and reached out for his hand. "Grant, they've heard of *you*. And not because you're famous now. Every phone call I've taken since the fire, and I've taken dozens, has been someone asking to help, wanting to give back to the mission, the same way this place has fed and sheltered people in need."

As if a warm blanket had settled around his shoulders, Grant felt the truth of her words. Calista had told him that there were so many good corporations out there, wanting to help. But every year he had watched downtown businesses call for the city to close the mission and to "clean up" the area. What they really wanted was to hide the problems of homelessness, abuse, addiction and hunger. Every year the city refused to bow to the megacorporations. But he had wondered how many were on the side of the mission. A few? A handful?

He didn't try to hide the moistness in his eyes. "I feel like Jimmy Stewart in *It's a Wonderful Life*. You know, the part where everybody starts throwing money into a big pot?"

Lana chuckled. "Does that make me the goofy angel, Clarence?"

"No, no, you're definitely Uncle Billy," Grant teased, lacing his fingers behind his head.

"And we all know who plays Mary in this version. I saw a little lip-on-lip action this afternoon." She gave him a wink, then started to laugh. "I don't think I've ever really seen you turn that color, boss."

He shrugged, wishing he could force the grin from

his face. But with the immediate needs of the residents taken care of, his mind was free to wander back to Calista…and that kiss. "It was the world's worst timing but it somehow felt right. And she didn't run."

"Always a good sign," Lana agreed. Her eyes were bright with happiness. "Forget about her superhero powers and lining up all these donors. I knew you were meant for each other from the very beginning. Remember the day she told you not to handle the PR for the mission?"

Grant groaned. "How could I forget?"

"A woman who can be that honest is a treasure. I just prayed that everything else would fall into place."

He nodded, feeling the certainty of her words and the faith of her prayers. As soon as he could, he needed to return the favor and be as honest as possible about his past. He didn't want anything to stand in the way of their future, least of all a man like Kurt Daniels.

"That's a great style. Trying something new?" Catherine Banks peeked over her bifocals to get a better glimpse of Calista's hair. The fiftyish woman was not a rabid fan of fashion but the atmosphere in the boardroom was as tense as a war zone and she seemed desperate to lighten the mood.

"I was in a fire. My hairdresser did the best she could with what was left." She ran her fingers through the sleek style that fell to her collarbone and kept her expression affable, enjoying the look of shock on Catherine's face. She understood the woman was elected to the board because she was one of the top shareholders but she sure didn't contribute much. When things got tough, Catherine was the first to change her vote to side with the loudest complainer and Calista didn't respect a woman who couldn't make up her mind.

Brett Caldwell cleared his throat and stacked a pile of papers on the surface of the long mahogany table. "Let's get started. We've got everyone here, finally."

Calista suppressed a retort and pasted an easy smile on her face. As CEO, she had always gotten along well with the twelve board members. They'd hired her, after all. She made VitaWow profitable, and they made sure the profits were dispersed fairly to the stockholders. Not hard to get along, usually. But right now she was sensing wariness from most, and downright hostility from a few. Choosing the site for the new building wasn't in their purview, and they knew it, but somehow it was coming through the board first. Her stomach gave an uncomfortable wriggle of foreboding.

She glanced around the long table at the ten men and two women. Something serious was happening and she was the last to know.

"There's been a new development in the search for a building site. Calista, this is a copy of the formal offer given to us by the board of the Downtown Denver Mission." Brett passed a folder to his right and Calista flipped it open before he'd even finished speaking.

He continued. "They have accepted a generous donation that includes a brand-new facility on private land. The donor wishes to remain anonymous. There are several unusual stipulations to this donation and one is that they offer the current site of the Downtown Denver Mission to VitaWow at a steep discount."

The mission? Why did the mission board want to sell now? Was the money situation worse than she'd thought? Calista scanned the document as swiftly as she could, her mind filing away facts and figures. Something was very wrong with this offer but she couldn't point to a single major problem.

"The anonymous donor wishes the transaction to be agreed on by Christmas Eve. That is why we are here, why some of us have delayed departing on a ski vacation with our family." He straightened his tie with a jerk. At least one member didn't appreciate the donor's need for a speedy resolution.

"The mission site was on our list of possible land options but the board refused to sell at the time we approached them in the spring. We asked only about the north end of the block, which is some sort of a community garden, but this offer includes all the mission property. It seems with the sudden appearance of this very generous mystery donor, they've changed their minds."

Calista sat shaking her head. Page after page of legal documents had already been drafted, waiting for signatures. She didn't see Grant's name anywhere yet. How had this all been prepared so quickly? "When did you first hear from the mission board?"

Brett glanced around, waiting for someone to answer. He shrugged. "I received a call this afternoon at one."

Her mind was spinning but she forced herself to take a slow breath. "So, the fire happened around ten. By one, the mission board had been approached by this donor, who also wants VitaWow to buy the property. Why?" She tapped a pen on the desk.

Alan Johnson groaned and said, "If the mission board agreed, then why should we concern ourselves?"

Several members nodded. "If it works out well for everyone involved, why not?" asked Gerald Manley.

He wiped his balding head with a hankie and tucked it back in his pocket.

Helen Bonnet pursed her bright orange lips and wagged a finger at the group. "Calista is right to ask the question. We can't afford to be involved in a shady deal."

Gerald snorted. "Shady? What makes you think there's anything other than good business going on here?"

Helen leaned forward and glared across the table. "I know good business. I built a company from the bottom up and sold it for millions. Nobody gives that kind of donation and demands the papers be signed in a deadline. Something stinks."

"Now, now, Helen. Let's not be dramatic." Brett adjusted his tie again and Calista saw drops of sweat appear at his temples.

"I have a few questions." Calista kept her tone light, but her heart was pounding. The board could decide whatever they wanted without her approval. And she had a feeling that her usual hard-line tactics were not going to serve her well here.

"Did the donor make a similar offer to the mission before, but was refused? Does the mission board feel that they have no choice to accept because of the fire today?"

Brett sighed. "Does it matter?"

"It might." And now for the biggest question. Calista searched each of their faces, wondering which of them knew who was behind this fiasco. It was someone powerful, well connected and immensely wealthy. Grant's face flashed into her mind and she felt a pulse pounding at her temples. "Why VitaWow? How did this donor know that VitaWow approached the mission back in the spring?"

"Again, I don't think these are serious issues." Brett huffed out the words.

"Maybe not by themselves. But if we add the fact that Grant Monohan has been refusing significant monetary assistance from his father, Kurt Daniels, then things get more complicated." Calista was taking a risk.

"Wait, we don't know for sure that Kurt Daniels is the donor." Gerald waved a hand in the air as if to dispel the entire argument.

There was a silence and Calista almost laughed as the members exchanged glances. Of course it was Kurt Daniels. These men and women may be willing to overlook a questionable deal, but they weren't stupid.

"Fine, let's just assume it is. That's not really a problem, is it?"

Helen leaned forward. "How do you know Grant Monohan refused his money, dear?" Her pale gray eyes sparked with curiosity.

"He said as much at the press conference. And today, after the fire, I saw Kurt Daniels at the mission."

Brett shrugged and said, "He's obviously holding a grudge against his father for having a less-than-perfect childhood."

Calista wanted to slap her hand against the table and shout that *less-than-perfect* did not describe what Grant lived through. But she took a breath and smiled calmly. "I'm not sure what his reservations are, exactly, but I can guarantee they're more serious than being estranged from a wealthy businessman."

Calista closed her eyes for just a moment and breathed a prayer. Now was the moment she needed to convince them that they had to look beyond a generous land transaction. The people needed food and a place to stay today and tomorrow and the next day. They couldn't wait years for a new site to be built.

"This company has thrived because of dedication, focus and drive. But we're also active in the community, support local charities and are working to reduce our carbon footprint. So, maybe we should look at all the angles here. Even the ones that don't directly concern VitaWow."

Helen nodded, listening intently. Brett stared at his papers and didn't respond. Calista continued, hoping her words would make them think, just for a moment, about the people that didn't get a vote in this decision.

"If the mission sells to VitaWow, the demolition would start immediately to keep our own building project on time. That leaves at least two years without any place for the homeless to go. Although the new mission site will be state-of-the-art buildings with extra security and a playground—" she held up the pages, pointing at paragraphs "—it is also situated five miles outside the city. The residents need the central location for school and jobs." But from a business owner's viewpoint, it was a win-win. No more poor people wandering about, disrupting the beautiful views.

"There are other missions. Some of them are just a few blocks away," Catherine interjected.

"Seventh Street Mission is a quarter the size and has no classrooms or day care."

"What is your relationship with the director?" Brett's question came out of nowhere and Calista felt as though the air was driven from her lungs.

"I'm a volunteer."

"Is that all?"

Calista stared, wondering where Brett was headed with his interrogation. Admitting that she was in love with Grant wasn't going to help her argument. "If we're more than friends, won't it look even worse for Vita-Wow to buy the mission property at a huge price cut?"

Silence pulsed in the room and Calista could hear her heart thudding in her chest.

"Like I said, something stinks here." Helen sat back in her chair with a decisive motion. "Why would Kurt Daniels force the sale of the mission and build a new one against his son's wishes?"

There was no good answer. Calista wished she had taken the time to get the whole story from Grant right after the fire.

"I'm not sure. Now, you all know that in business we have to take risks." She paused, looking each one of the board members in the eye. "I don't think this is one of those times. There are too many unanswered questions, too many potential negatives. Whatever ugly war is brewing between Kurt Daniels and his son, it shouldn't involve VitaWow."

Chapter Fourteen

A week. That was all the time the board would give her before they made a decision. Calista dropped her head in her hands and stared at the top of her desk. It was covered with little slips of paper, messages that needed to be answered. Jackie was out calling the donors, getting the month of meals covered.

Lord, I'm so confused. I don't know what You want me to do. She knew that closing the mission for twenty-four months would be devastating for the residents. She knew that VitaWow needed to make smart business decisions. But everything else was a fog, a blur of conflicting advice. She wanted to talk to Grant about it, but he wasn't just her friend. He was the director of the mission and would be absolutely livid when he heard the VitaWow plan. Maybe he already had.

The idea that he was sitting in exactly the same posture, miles away, made her groan. What a mess. It would be awkward enough if she was just a volunteer, but she was more than that. Wasn't she? Calista sat up, trying to shake the confusion from her mind. There didn't seem any way out of it. If she stopped volunteering, the mission wouldn't be a conflict of interest for her. But she didn't want to leave them, or Grant. Not now. If she resigned her position as CEO, the board was much more likely to take the offer. She laid her hands on the table, startled. Was she even considering that? Her whole life was wrapped up in this company. Would she walk away if it meant saving the mission?

There was a knock on the door and Jackie came in, carrying a large clothing bag. "I think your dress is here."

If Calista could have let out a scream of frustration and gotten away with it, she would have. She had completely forgotten about the party, just days away…the party she was attending with Grant.

"Right. Let me take a look. The boutique had to make a few alterations." She tried to be calm and act naturally as her fingers fumbled at the garment-bag zipper.

Jackie let out a low whistle. "Well, now. This isn't your usual little black dress." She cocked her head, surveying the fabric as she lifted it from the bag. "When you got that new red coat, I wondered if you were on a red kick. This proves it."

Calista smiled, hoping it didn't look as brittle as it felt. "Do you like it? I just wanted more color."

"Put it on, I have to see."

It was the last thing she wanted to do at the moment, but Calista shrugged. She might not even get a chance to wear it. No harm in playing dress up now.

A few minutes later, she emerged from the bathroom and had to smile at Jackie's expression. The formfitting bodice gently followed her curves to the hip, where the bright red silk fell in a full skirt, gathered every so often in a draping effect. A large black velvet ribbon was wrapped around her waist, and the ends trailed to the hem. It might have made a woman look like a giant Christmas present, but the creative genius of the designer only made it seem charming. It looked sweet. Young. *Joyful.*

Calista smoothed her hands down the dress and felt her eyes fill with sudden tears. She wanted one evening of magic with Grant. One evening when he was just a man and she was just a woman. She came to a decision, standing there in her party dress, wishing life was different than it really was.

"I think it fits. Now, I better get out of this dress and get cracking. We've got a lot of work to catch up on today."

Jackie grinned, reaching out a hand to touch the black velvet sash. "If you say so. But I'm so into the Christmas spirit now, I'll need some cookies to get me through the day."

"It's a done deal." Ralph Maricort leaned back in his chair. The older man's face was deeply lined but his dark eyes were like a robin's, bright and quick. Only a day after the fire, the smell of smoke was still thick in Grant's office.

"Ralph, I'm stunned. When did this happen? How could the board make this kind of decision without even consulting me?" Grant was struggling to keep his voice even but it seemed like all his breath had been driven from his body with Ralph's news. "If it's about the fire, we've already got the next two weeks' worth of meals planned, and the other buildings weren't even touched." His voice was rising in anger. "There's no legal reason to close the mission. The fire was an accident and everything was up to code. The fire chief said it was an electrical issue, a faulty wire."

"Grant, I knew you were dealing with a lot here, so the board just decided to wait a bit before telling you. And I know this is hard, but it's a temporary closure. The new complex will be built within twenty-four months. We've been deeded the land, seen the plans, and the company is thrilled to get this spot. They approached us back in April about the empty lot by the parking area, but we didn't want to lose any more space, in case we had to expand."

Nothing was making sense. He felt ambushed. Grant shook his head, his mind racing to catch up with the older man's words. "I remembered something about an offer for the community garden area." The board fielded a lot of inquiries about the mission land, since it was a prime downtown spot.

"They've outgrown their building on Plymouth Avenue and have plans for a pretty nice high-rise, complete with a new corner office for the CEO. And she deserves it. Calista Sheffield has worked wonders for that water company." Ralph smirked at his weak play on words.

"Excuse me?" The question seemed to be dragged from somewhere deep in his chest, pulling his heart up into his throat.

"The CEO. She's a real dragon lady. I heard she brokered a deal last month that had the Genesis board quaking in their boots."

If he hadn't been sitting down, Grant would have sunk to the floor. He felt his legs go numb, his mind stutter. Of course. It couldn't be just any company; it had to be VitaWow. What were the odds?

"When did you say this offer came through?"

Ralph wrinkled his brow, thinking. "The day of the fire, and then the VitaWow board met that evening. The CEO asked them to wait a few days, I think, to make sure the papers were in order."

His head pounded as he tried to understand the situation. The mission would close. These people who were struggling with unemployment, hunger, abuse and addiction would be forced to start over. And all because Calista Sheffield wanted a new building.

Something awful occurred to him and he dropped his head into his hands, not caring that Ralph was still speaking. Maybe she knew all along. Maybe she didn't just walk in off the street because she needed a life outside her work. His hopes and dreams of a life with her turned to ashes. A woman who cared so little for the poor and the vulnerable had nothing in common with him. It made no sense to fall back on the defense of how wonderful the new mission would be, when the people here *now* would suffer. People like Savannah and her mother. And the employees. Marisol's face popped into his head and he groaned audibly.

"The staff. They can't wait around for the new building. They'll have to find other work."

Ralph nodded. "True. But you'll keep your position, and maybe the secretary, so that you can oversee the new project."

Grant felt sick. They were a dedicated crew. He couldn't imagine how it would be to break the news that their jobs were gone.

"Where is this new site?" He struggled to ask questions, to fight through the shock and disappointment.

"Out near Landry. Very nice views." The older man steepled his fingers.

"Landry...the neighborhood? Isn't that about five miles from here?"

He nodded. "Right. Not residential, of course, since city ordinances wouldn't allow it, but some strip malls and big-box stores."

Grant stood up and walked around the desk. He clenched his fists, fighting for control. "You're telling me the mission will close. Everyone will have to find new lodgings, won't finish their classes or training. My employees will lose their jobs. And the new site is near a strip mall in Landry? How will the inner-city homeless find their way out to Landry? On the bus? And how will they get to their jobs, and get their kids to school?"

Ralph held up his hands, eyes showing alarm. "Just hold on. You've got to look at the big picture, Grant. We can't turn this down because it's not the perfect location. A brand-new facility is something we've needed for years. That fire was long overdue, if you ask me. And I'm tired of hearing about how the mission is bad for the downtown area. This way, we're farther away from the fancy businesses and we have a great new location. Everybody is happy."

"No," Grant choked out. "Everybody is *not* happy. The people who need these services will suffer."

"We've got to do what's best in the long run." Ralph's black eyes turned serious, and he chose his words carefully. "We would hate to lose you, Grant. But the board has made its decision. We're accepting the donor's land and his offer to build a new mission."

He shook his head, trying in vain to wrap his mind

around the past few hours. "Who is this donor, anyway?"

Ralph dropped his gaze. In the next half second of silence, Grant knew. Kurt Daniels had orchestrated another coup. He swore he would get Grant to take his money and he had succeeded. Could Calista have been in on this plan with his father, plotting and lying all along? He sat back against the edge of the desk, his hands limp at his sides.

"He wants to remain anonymous." Ralph had the decency to look ashamed.

"I'm sure he does," Grant murmured.

"He's not what you think, Grant. He's changed. He really thinks this will be good for the mission, and for you." His voice was quiet, as if he was worried Kurt Daniels would hear him. He stood up and headed for the door.

"I don't know what he is, honestly. But I do know that this is wrong on so many different levels." He felt his shoulders sag. He thought he'd gotten used to lies and betrayals, been hardened to them, but he must still have a soft spot because it felt as though someone had just kicked it.

"It's for the best. You'll see," he said, and with those words Ralph walked out the door.

The sharp trill of his office phone broke into Grant's shock. He moved to lift the receiver, and his greeting felt sluggish and awkward.

She could hear by his voice that he already knew, but she asked anyway. "Grant, have you seen the offer?"

There was a pause that was so long, she wondered if they'd been disconnected. "Yes."

Another beat of silence, then Calista rushed in to fill the void. "I've asked the board to wait a few days to make their decision, but it seems like the majority is in favor."

"I'm sure they are."

Calista chewed her lip and clutched the phone tighter. She had to make him understand. "At the Christmas party on Saturday, I think—"

She was interrupted by a sound that could only signal shock and disgust, something sharp and guttural. Then he said, as if the words were spilling out, "I may not have made this clear, but one thing I have had my fill of is lies. I've had a lifetime's worth, and I don't need any more. I'm not going to your Christmas party, Calista, because I avoid people who can't be honest. And don't try to say something like 'I didn't lie, I just didn't tell the whole truth' because we both know that's not true."

Calista's jaw had dropped after his first few words and her fingers had gone numb from gripping the phone. She swallowed. "Grant, I have a lot of faults, but dishonesty is not one of them."

"And how do I know for sure? Should I ask my father for a character reference?"

"Your—" Did he think she and Kurt Daniels were in league? She squeezed her eyes closed. There was no one to vouch for her; she had no advocates. "I don't know him. I'm as surprised as you are. I heard the news yesterday evening."

There was no response. She thought she heard him exhale.

"Anyway, I don't think I'll be up for a Christmas party this weekend. I have a lot to do."

Calista's throat closed shut and she struggled to take

a breath. She didn't care about the party, the dress, the elegant evening. If she hung up now, she might never see him again. He would always think she had schemed her way into owning the mission property.

"Grant, listen to me." Her voice shook on the last word and she stopped to swallow again. "Whatever you believe—about me and this deal and your father—just listen."

Silence. But there wasn't a click, either.

"This party will be full of people that I invited just for you to meet. The Genesis Drinks president will be there. And Terrence Brewer, the head of Alton Banking; and Jenn Blackrite, who runs Cimulus, the software giant; and the governor, Dennis Michael." She paused for a breath. He didn't interrupt. So maybe he was still listening. "Whatever you think—" she could hardly speak the words "—of me, I'm asking you to come meet these people. I think this is your best chance to save the mission. Your board is accepting the offer because of the fire. I'm almost sure of it."

"I don't see how it can possibly make that much difference." His tone was flat, colorless.

"You don't, but I do. I've seen how deep these corporate pockets can be. I know the kinds of donations they give. We're talking hundreds of thousands of dollars."

"Wouldn't it be better to approach their representatives, the traditional way? Nobody wants to be bothered at a party."

"Trust me, Grant. Just this once." Her heart was in her throat. "After the party, you can never speak to me again, if you want, but for the mission, I'm asking you..." She couldn't finish. The room blurred and Calista blinked furiously.

"Well, like you said at church, maybe I'm being too proud. I'm thinking of myself, and not the mission." He said it lightly, but his words cut her so sharply, Calista was surprised that she wasn't bleeding. He didn't want to be around her, it was clear.

"Right." She was proud the word came out clearly, not wavering or breathless.

"Then I'll see you Saturday. Can we meet there?"

He wanted to spend as little time as possible with her alone. Calista shrugged off the biting pain and agreed. As she hung up the phone, she dropped her face into her hands. Hot tears slipped between her fingers, and the grief she'd kept in check for the past several minutes spilled over her in waves. Yet again, in the end, all she had left was her job.

Lord, take this situation and everything in it. Help me to know what to do.

Grant stood on the steps of the Grant-Humphreys Mansion and tried to look pleasant. His face felt frozen, unyielding, but he forced the corners of his mouth into a smile. The elite of Denver business and society streamed out of luxury vehicles and up the steps, diamonds glittering in the darkness, white tuxedo fronts glowing. Golden light shone from the long window panes and off the oversize balconies. The sound of a string quartet and holiday cheer spilled out the door and mingled with the slam of car doors. He paced a few steps, from one giant pillar to the next, then checked his watch again. She was always early. Or so she said. He wasn't sure what to believe anymore.

The wide expanse of the stone steps had been cleared of the snow that fell earlier in the day. Tonight there would be more. Grant had always loved the snow, but now he felt empty, cold. That was about all he could manage and he hoped it was enough. God knew what he was feeling. He couldn't put any of the rest of it into words, anyway.

A silver car caught his eye and he straightened his shoulders. Calista got out, handed her keys to the valet and strode toward the front steps. He had told himself to be distant but friendly, focused on business. He was here for the mission. But one glimpse of her and his heart felt as though it was being squeezed in a steel trap. One with teeth. His mind seemed to take in every detail and catalog it for the future, without his permission.

Her eyes were darker, dramatically shadowed, and her lips were a shade lighter than her dress, a red that was purely Christmas. No plum or burgundy or demure wine color. The color reminded him of the very best Christmas memories he had. She was halfway up the steps, still focused on the front door, holding her ankle-length dress in one hand. A matching jacket covered her shoulders and her bright blond hair was up in a soft chignon, dotted with sparkling pins. On her jacket was a snowflake brooch that caught the light and shimmered against the soft skin of her neck. When she was just feet from him, she looked up, caught his gaze and tripped.

Chapter Fifteen

Calista rehearsed the words in her head, willing herself to remember. She had spent hours working on the right phrases, the right tones. He couldn't leave this party thinking she was a liar and a cheat. It felt as though her whole life depended on it.

She handed off her keys to the valet and started up the stone steps. The mansion looked as gorgeous as always, strong and sturdy, built to show the wealth and prosperity of turn-of-the-century Denver. Every time she visited, she felt another wave of awe. It looked like the party was in full swing and people milled everywhere. She glanced up at the balconies and noted the figures huddled in groups. It was a great party if people braved the freezing temperatures for a breather in the night air.

One hand went to her mama's pin on her jacket. It calmed her just a bit, and she whispered a prayer. *Please, Lord, be with us.*

She dodged a slow-moving couple and glanced up, one hand holding her dress so she didn't step on the hem. And she saw him just a foot away, standing cold and aloof in the shadow of a pillar. His handsome face bore some expression she couldn't define. His eyes were locked on hers. Tuxedos always made her feel as if the man was wearing a disguise, but he seemed achingly familiar. She dropped the fold of fabric in her hand to wave, and the next moment she was pitching forward. Strong hands gripped her elbows and he used the momentum to propel her clear of the last step. An abrupt stop, and she dragged in a breath, her heart pounding. They were only inches apart. His hands still gripping her arms, she couldn't seem to look away, even though his eyes had a hollow look to them that made her stomach clench.

"Well, that's what I get for being late." What a stupid thing to say, but for some reason it made him smile. A real smile that reached those bright blue eyes.

"Are you all right?"

"Of course, just not used to the long dress. And probably shouldn't be running in heels."

"I think that's a rule, isn't it?" He took her hand and tucked it into the curve of his arm.

"It can't be. Women run in heels all the time in the movies. Usually when they're dodging bombs or running from assassins."

He laughed a bit, a soft sound that made hope spring up in her chest. They were almost at the front door, crowds already visible inside.

"Grant, I'm glad you came. I really think this can work." So much for all the fancy phrases she was going to use. When she looked into his face, noted the set of his jaw and the line of his lips, she couldn't remember a thing she'd thought to say. Oh, well, it seemed to cover it.

His smile faded away and he nodded. “I hope you’re right. You look beautiful. In case I don’t tell you that when we get going inside.”

Calista’s heart jumped to her throat and she felt her cheeks burn. She wanted to be beautiful for him, wanted this party to be something special. If only they could fall into some other life, or start fresh. But that wasn’t going to happen. They had people relying on them to keep the mission open. She swallowed. “Thank you. And you should wear a tux at least once a month. Just for fun.” She gave him a saucy wink that had more confidence than she felt.

He snorted. “Don’t get any ideas.”

They stepped into the large ballroom and Grant could feel the gaze of every person there on him. The chatter of party guests grew quiet and eventually, it was nearly silent except for the string quartet. The marble floors and tall ceilings made the mournful tones echo. Calista glanced at him, her expression rueful. “Sorry, I tend to have that effect on parties. I suck the life right out of them.”

He scanned the room, looking for familiar faces. Not a one. And the faces he saw didn’t look exactly thrilled to see them.

“Come on.” Calista held her head high, walking confidently toward a lanky gentleman with fine gray hair and a weak chin. As they crossed the room, the conversation seemed to pick up again, strand by strand, until the party was back in full swing.

“Brett, this is Grant Monohan, the director of the Downtown Denver Mission. Brett Caldwell, the head of our board of directors.”

Grant reached out a hand, pasting a pleasant smile to his face. He could see the surprise flicker across Brett's face and wondered if the board even knew Calista volunteered at the mission.

"A pleasure, for sure. We're very happy with the mission's offer to sell. This will be a good move for all of us." Brett's tone was slightly condescending, as if he were thanking Grant for trading lunches.

"We'll see, Brett. Nothing has been decided yet." Calista's voice was light, but Grant felt her hand right on his arm. "Enjoy the party. We're off to make the rounds."

She guided him away, leaning her head toward his shoulder. He could smell a light floral perfume and something like vanilla. "Ignore him. He knows nothing is signed yet."

"And he also knows I can't force the board to do what I want."

She glanced up at him, her green eyes made deeper by the dramatic shadow. She reminded him of the old film stars, beautiful and elegant. He thought he would be happy to stare at her all night. Thankfully that wasn't an option. "Your snowflake pin is pretty. It looks like an antique."

She put a hand to the pin, touching it lightly with her fingers. A soft smile touched her lips. "It was my mother's. The only thing of hers that survived the fire. She loaned it to me for senior pictures…that day."

He turned her to face him, pausing in the middle of the crowd. "I didn't get a chance to tell you how sorry I am about your mother. And how very brave you were during the mission fire."

In an instant, she wasn't the CEO of a company that held its Christmas party in a mansion. She was a young girl, facing her fears. "I can't imagine the mission without Marisol."

He nodded. He couldn't imagine his *life* without Marisol. "Sometimes I think she holds the place together."

A woman approached them from the side, her dark hair dramatically streaked with white on one side. The gold column gown she wore showcased a lithe figure. Her eyes flitted from one to another, but her smile was bright. "Calista, dear! You've brought a date this year."

Calista introduced them, and he shook hands with Jenn Blackrite. He had always figured millionaires to be aloof, critical, like his father. But Jenn was witty and warm, asking questions about the mission and the fire.

"They're going to close if they can't raise the funds to repair the kitchen." Calista's words caught him by surprise. It was true. Mostly.

Jenn put a hand to her mouth, her large topaz ring winking in the light. "No! That can't happen. There are so many people who need the mission, especially now, in the wintertime."

"I agree. But what can they do?"

Jenn leaned forward, gripping Grant's arm. "We give to Universal Charity every year. This year we can give our donation to the mission. And more. We can't let it close."

Grant opened his mouth to thank her, when they were interrupted by a slim young woman. Jenn handed him her card, scribbling something on the back, with instructions to call on Monday. Then she walked away with the young woman, deep in conversation.

"See?" The glee in Calista's voice was infectious.

"But does she mean it? Or is it like 'let's do lunch' and then nothing ever happens?"

"Jenn has a great reputation and if she says she will, she will."

He couldn't help chuckling a bit. Was there hope after all?

"And there are so many more. Oh, Grant! I know this will work!" She fairly bounced on her toes, face alight.

"Where next? I feel like I should be using some sort of title for you, like 'Most Magnificent One.' You have a gift. I'm glad you use it for good and not evil." He was teasing, the success letting his words slip away without any thought.

Her eyes turned somber. "I haven't always. I made money to make money, with no purpose to it."

There was such a sadness in her tone, it was hard for him to resist reaching out and gathering her to him. He was barely aware of the guests milling around them. Her face was tilted up to him and he could see tiny flecks of gold in her green eyes. "That was then."

"And this is now." Her lips tugged up at the corners. "Let's get cracking, Mr. Director."

"I've got to take a break. My jaw hurts from smiling so much." Calista rubbed her cheeks and groaned. She almost wished she could go back to the days when she popped into a party for five minutes and then left.

"Agreed. I'm going to go over and drink the entire punch bowl."

Calista giggled, and then groaned again. "Please don't make me laugh. I don't think my face can take it."

"Knock, knock," he said, then broke off as she poked him in the side.

"Here, let's get some spiced cider and take it out on the balcony. I need some air."

Grant poured her a cup of the steaming, fragrant liquid and then took one for himself. She glanced at him, wondering if he was enjoying himself at all. He was certainly not as distant as he'd been on the phone.

The balcony was occupied with one other couple, an older man and woman holding hands, and they exchanged smiles. Grant led her to the edge and peered out into the night. "They said there would be more snow."

"Smells like it." Calista took a sip and let the spices tingle her tongue. She looked out into the darkness, struggling to find the right words. She knew better than to leave anything unsaid. This might be their only chance. "Thank you for coming tonight. I know the offer came as a shock."

"Calista." He set his hot cider on the balcony ledge and turned to her, expression all business. "I need to tell you something."

Her heart pounded in her chest and she searched for a clue in his face. Was this where he told her that he would never see her again? Is this the moment her heart would break?

She nodded. "Go ahead."

He looked out into the darkness, his profile half in shadow, and seemed to be having trouble finding the words. "I held the media announcement because I was receiving threatening letters. And it's true my father sent me checks that I never cashed."

Calista blinked, struggling to switch gears. After the fire, she wanted to hear the whole story. But this was an odd moment to tell it.

"There are rumors that my father's wealth is from illegal enterprises." He looked her in the eyes, gauging her reaction. "They're all true. So I refused to have any kind of relationship with him."

Calista nodded, but inside she was confused. Letters, money, broken laws. Was there anything here she didn't know or hadn't heard?

"When he showed up after the fire, he admitted he was the one sending the letters. Well, he was paying someone to do it."

She couldn't restrain a gasp. Her hand went to her throat, and she felt her eyes go wide with shock.

His face was rigid, eyes narrowed. "It's an ugly situation. And you deserve to know the truth."

"Oh, Grant. I'm so sorry." She reached out a hand and touched his arm. Her eyes started to burn and she blinked tears away. "You can't be held accountable for your father's deeds."

He let out a breath, his shoulders slumping. "But when image is everything, these things matter. I wanted you to know, probably should have told you sooner." He met her gaze. "You deserved the chance to step away from the situation, to consider your own reputation."

Calista wanted to deny it, but he was right. Sometimes image *was* everything. But she didn't care about image as much as she did a few months ago. Maybe that was a bad thing, but it didn't feel bad. It felt very, very good. She stepped closer, lifting her hand to his cheek, feeling the slight stubble on his jaw. His eyes were hot, searching her face. "I think my reputation can withstand a few rumors."

She felt his smile under her fingers, and he turned his head and pressed a kiss to the palm of her hand. "Let me know when it gets to be too much."

"I will." Her words were barely audible but his lips

twitched moments before they met hers. Her lids drifted closed, reveling in the warmth of him, the familiar smell of aftershave and soap. One arm slipped around her waist and she let herself forget she was a CEO, forget that her life had been completely empty until a few months ago. She let herself be just a woman who was in love with a man. Something wet and cold touched her face and she opened her eyes with a gasp.

"It's snowing." She glanced up and grinned at the fat flakes falling thickly from the sky.

Grant's arms were still wrapped around her. The softness in his eyes made her breath catch. "This is the best Christmas ever." His voice was full of wonder.

She laughed, leaning back to look into his face. "I was just thinking the same thing."

He planted a kiss on her cheek and grabbed her hand. "What do you say we get back in there and raise some money?"

"Lead the way." She let him pull her back into the ballroom, heart filled with the sort of joy she had never had before.

Christmas Eve dawned bright and sunny, completely contrary to Calista's mood. After spending the night staring at the ceiling, she gave up at dawn and padded to the kitchen. Maybe making a few dozen sugar cookies would make it seem like Christmas. An hour later, her condominium smelled absolutely edible but she didn't feel an ounce of joy.

She checked her phone for messages for the tenth time that hour. No word from Grant since the party. She knew he was busy keeping the residents fed, but how hard was it to pick up the phone? Heck, he could even text a few lines. She would take anything at this point. She glared at the plate of perfect little cookies, trees and stars and bells with colored sprinkles. It had been shaping up to be the best Christmas in recent memory and now… Her chest tightened at the thought of spending Christmas without Grant. How many Christmas Days had she spent alone? But not like this, not missing someone so badly it felt as though a hole had been torn in her heart.

Calista straightened her shoulders. Maybe he was angry that VitaWow had turned down the mission's offer. Maybe he thought she had volunteered, trying to get inside information. Maybe he thought she'd started the fire. She just couldn't guess what was going through his mind. And if he wasn't going to tell her, there was no other choice but to go to the mission and ask.

She swung open the lobby door to the mission and strode inside.

"Hey, Lana, is Grant somewhere around here?"

Lana took several seconds to respond, her blue eyes wide. "Uh, he sure is. Let me call him out."

Calista put the cookies on the desktop. "Don't bother. I can go back, if he's not busy." Calista headed for the security door, waving away Lana's protests. "Have a cookie. They're fresh," she called and punched in the code with shaking fingers.

She was a modern woman. She knew that a little hand-holding and a couple of brief kisses didn't make a relationship. But that line he'd thrown out about how she was the only woman he was interested in right now? Somehow she had grabbed that one line and run with it. In her head they had been practically raising a brood of kids already. Until the fire, and the building offer. Calista gritted her teeth and tried to make her expression pleasant, when she felt only pain at how easily she had fallen in love with Grant. And how easily her heart was breaking. She should have known better. How many times had he said he was too busy for love? Five? Ten? And she had said the same thing.

But her doubts ran deeper than that. Calista paused outside his door and finally faced the possibility that Grant wasn't too busy to call. He knew who she was and how she spent her time. She poured all her energy into making money and selling a product that didn't really make anyone healthier. He would never want a woman like her. She closed her eyes and whispered a prayer. *Please give me strength to face him, Lord. I want to make sure he's okay and that Marisol is okay and the mission will go on. Then I can leave.*

She knocked loudly on his closed office door and waited for some kind of response. There was the muted sound of footsteps and the door swung inward, revealing the man who had changed everything about the way she saw the world.

"Come on in." His tone was subdued, and she caught a glimpse of dark shadows under his eyes before he turned away. His suit looked a little rumpled, as if he had slept at his desk. He definitely looked the worse for wear.

"I got worried. You haven't called me back." She wrapped her arms around her middle, feeling like she was trying to hold herself together. All her anger was turning to fear. He looked like a man who had lost everything.

"It's been pretty busy around here. You want to take off your coat?" He settled into his office chair and his gaze flicked past her. She saw how his usually freshly shaved jaw was rough with stubble.

Calista hesitated, then hung up her red wool coat on the hook. Clumps of fresh snow on the shoulders and hood were melting into nothingness. It was the same feeling she had in the pit of her stomach.

“Grant, are you okay? You look exhausted. And pale.” She took a step forward, wishing she could take his face in her hands and wipe the frown from his brow.

“I’m fine.” With those last words, he looked up at her. The expression made her breath catch in her throat. It was sadness, pity, resolve, pain. He shrugged, as if switching gears. “But your party plan worked. We’ve had half a million dollars in pledges already this week. The board agreed to reject the VitaWow offer. But when Ralph called over, he heard they had already voted against it. I’m glad your company decided it wasn’t in its best interests to buy the mission site.”

Calista frowned. They’d already been over this. “Grant, it was a great deal. No doubt about it. But what about the people here? What about the staff? They can’t wait for some big complex to be built. Especially if it’s way out of town.”

His deep blue eyes settled on her, his gaze intense. “You’re saying VitaWow board voted against acquiring the land because it would close the mission.”

Calista paused and wished she could say the board was so compassionate. “No. I tried that argument. I also tried to say it would look bad for VitaWow to buy this place right after the fire. In the end I tried a little scare tactic.”

“Which was?”

“I told them we couldn’t afford to get tangled up with

whatever struggle was happening between you and Kurt Daniels." She shrugged. "I don't know what convinced them, but I was praying my heart out the whole time."

Grant stood up and crossed the room in a few steps. Calista felt her mouth drop open a little at the speed of his approach. His jaw was set; intensity radiated from him.

"That's what they told me. VitaWow backed out because nobody wants to be in the middle of the drama that is Kurt Daniels and his son. Reputations are valuable. Once tarnished, there's no restoring them. And what about you? Can you afford to get tangled up in this mess?"

Calista lifted her chin and said quietly, "I already am, aren't I?"

He stood inches away, expressions crossing his face faster than she could track them. "I'm sorry."

"Please, don't be..." And she meant to finish the sentence, to tell him how she understood what it was like to run from your past. How she wasn't sorry she came to the mission and met Marisol. How she'd learned to love something much bigger than herself for once. But there was a lump in her throat that made the words impossible.

He nodded and turned toward the window, his voice soft but steady. "I never should have gotten involved with you. It's not fair to drag anybody into my family's drama. But we haven't known each other very long and this city has a short memory. By next year, no one will even remember."

It was obvious he'd changed his mind about her. Them. Whatever they were. *No one will even remember.* He was going to forget her as soon as she was out of sight. She hauled in a breath and steeled herself to make a graceful exit.

"Grant, I want to thank you for letting me volunteer. I've learned so much about the needs of the people here. I've made friends..." Her voice trailed away into nothingness. How did you say goodbye when your heart was shattering?

He nodded, still not meeting her eyes. "Thank you, Calista. You're welcome back anytime."

She stood, not wanting to move away but not able to bridge the space between them. In the end, she slipped on her coat and walked out, wishing she was somewhere, anywhere, but in her own life.

As she pushed open the lobby door, Calista hoped her face showed calm, and not the raw pain that twisted through her.

Lana looked up from the desk and called out to her. "Come here, Calista."

It was the last thing in the world she wanted to do but she moved her leaden feet away from the front door and toward the desk. The Christmas tree winked and sparkled with colored lights. A group of kids gathered by the cafeteria doors, chattering and laughing.

Jose came over to the desk, watching Calista's face with a wary expression.

"Where are you going?" Lana seemed almost accusatory.

She coughed, trying to clear the lump from her throat. "I was going to head home."

"It's Christmas Eve and we're going to sing some carols with the kids. Savannah was asking for you yesterday."

How could she stay and sing carols when all her hopes were gone? She wanted to crawl into bed and never come out. "Thanks, but I need to go home."

"No, you should join us. It'll be fun." Jose nodded agreement.

"*Mija*, you are leaving?" Now Marisol had joined them, her dark eyes wide with surprise.

She could hardly lift her eyes. Of course they would all want her to stay and be festive. But she was barely keeping herself together for the few minutes it would take to get to her car. There was no way she could sing carols. "Yes, I need to go. I just stopped…to make sure everybody was okay."

"But everybody is not okay! Mr. Monohan is thinking that—and you are leaving without—and how will we—" Marisol broke down in tears at the last word. Her face crumpled with grief and her chin dropped to her chest as she began to sob noisily.

Calista felt her face go slack and she shot a glance at Lana, only to see the same shock on her face. Jose looked as if someone was pounding a nail through his hand.

"Don't cry, Mari. Don't cry. I'll fix this." Jose patted her awkwardly on the shoulder.

"No, it cannot be fixed! It is all ruined and now they will never—"

"No, Marisol, just wait. I can fix this." Jose grabbed Calista's arm and steered her back toward the office door.

"What are you doing?" she gasped in surprise.

"Fixing," he responded, his face set in a grim mask. He punched in the code and marched her back down the carpeted hallway to Grant's office. The door was open, just as Calista had left it.

"Mr. Monohan." Jose's tone brought Grant's head up with a snap. His eyes widened as he took in the scene before him: Jose gripping Calista's elbow, her expression probably furious and embarrassed.

"You need to know something." Jose paused, his chin jutting out. "Marisol is crying because Calista is leaving."

Grant studied his hands, jaw clenched. Finally, he said, "I don't understand. What does this have to do with me?"

Jose sighed. "You know what. If you want to be stubborn, then you go out and tell Marisol that you would rather break her heart than swallow your pride."

Calista felt anger boil up inside. Break Marisol's heart? What about hers? "Just wait a minute."

Jose turned and said fiercely, "No, you two wait a minute. We live in a place where dreams die, families are broken, kids are placed in foster care, sons are lost, parents leave. And you two are willing to let this good thing God has planned for you just…just fall apart because you're too proud to actually have a conversation."

Calista felt heat creep up her neck and into her face. *This good thing God has planned?* She shot a glance at Grant.

"So, you two stand here and think about it for a while. I'm going back out to see if I can get Marisol to stop crying so we can sing some Christmas carols." He said the last sentence in such a threatening tone that Calista almost burst out laughing at the incongruity. Jose was like a mother hen, scolding her chicks.

He turned and left the room, leaving Calista to stare after him, her mouth twitching.

The sound of a warm chuckle made her knees weak and she could hardly raise her eyes to meet Grant's gaze.

Chapter Sixteen

"Who knew Jose was so afraid of Marisol?" Grant asked, shaking his head.

"Or Marisol's tears." Calista closed her eyes briefly, as if gathering strength. "Look, Grant, she's a sweet woman but we can't let her expectations decide our futures."

Grant crossed the room and stood before her. He'd never felt more afraid, or more hopeful. He was jumping off the cliff and not even checking to see if there was a parachute. "I agree. It doesn't matter what Marisol thought was happening here. It doesn't matter what Jose will do to us if we don't make Marisol happy. What matters is you and me."

"Is there a you and me?" Her voice was almost all breath, her green eyes shining with tears.

"I want there to be. I know how awkward this is, with my father and the media—"

"I don't care. I love you."

Those sweet words coming from her mouth were more than he could bear. He opened his arms and she walked right into them, as if she had been made to live next to his heart. She smelled like warm cookies. Her voice was muffled as she spoke into his shirt. "He's right. I was too proud to come in here and ask to be part of your life."

He kissed her hair, her temple, feeling her arms wrap around his waist under his jacket. "You shouldn't have had to ask. I'm sorry, Calista. I was so sure you wouldn't want to be with a man like me."

She raised her head in surprise. "A man like you? You mean, a man who works at a homeless mission? Grant, the joy and purpose you have in your work has changed my life. I'm a different person because of you."

He searched her face, not able to believe that God could be so good to him. "I meant the situation with Kurt Daniels. We're trying to get to know each other. But he's got a serious past. Someday, there'll be a huge scandal. It will touch me, and this mission, just because we're related."

He watched her eyes narrow, appreciating his words. She said, "If God is with us, we'll be okay. And that future scandal? Bring it on."

A huge grin spread over his face and he shook his head. "I love you. You're scary sometimes, but I love you." And he dropped his head to hers, meeting her lips halfway. He lost himself in the joy of holding her close, of glimpsing a future he never could have imagined.

She broke off their kiss and tilted her head. "Listen," she whispered.

Out in the lobby the caroling had begun. The sweet sound of children's voices filtered through the office door and down the hallway, bringing a message of faith and hope.

He hated to let her go, but there would be time. Days

and weeks and years left to talk and revel in the blessings God had in store. "We'd better get out there and make sure Marisol hasn't flooded the lobby with tears."

She stood up on her tiptoes and feathered one last kiss on his lips. "Lead the way."

"That's what you said the first day we met. Do you remember?"

"Did I?" Her lips tilted up, eyes bright with love. "Well, I'm so glad you did. It's what you do best."

Live more abundantly. He paused, knowing that timing was everything. And he had a great feeling that it was the right time to say what was in his heart. "With you by my side, I'll lead even better. Will you marry me? Share your life with me? Be a part of this mission?"

A wonder that words so softly spoken could hold his entire future. "Yes, oh, yes."

He tugged her back into his arms, her tears blending into their kisses.

"But, Calista, I have to say something," he murmured as he trailed kisses along her cheek.

"Anything."

"You've got to give away that cat."

She pulled back from him, laughter creasing her face. "With pleasure."

Epilogue

"The photographer is wearing a path in the floor," Lissa said, popping her head into the room. "I don't think he's used to this kind of crowd." She slipped into the room and stood uncertainly behind Calista. "And you look totally gorgeous. In case no one has told you that."

"Tell him to keep his hat on." Marisol fussed with Calista's veil and frowned.

Calista met Lissa's gaze in the mirror and mouthed, "Thank you."

Jackie cleared her throat and stood up, smoothing down her elegant green satin dress. "I'm headed out. Lana's got all the groomsmen corralled." She waved her bouquet in the air and the scent of fresh baby roses filled the room. "Don't be late." She dropped a kiss on Calista's cheek.

"Never." If only she could get Marisol to stop fluffing her veil. The gauzy material was dotted with tiny freshwater pearls. It fell in stiff cascades down her back to her waist, accenting the simplicity of the satin bodice and cap sleeves.

"Mari," Calista whispered, gently catching the old woman's hand in hers. "It's not going to be a winter wedding if I wait any longer," she said, her tone teasing.

"Ah, *mija*!" Marisol shook her head forlornly. "I feel as if my children are growing up. But I suppose it is God's will. Just promise me that I can be *abuelita* to all your babies."

For the first time that day, Calista felt tears well up in her eyes. To be called *mija* with such fierce love, to be called family by this faithful woman, was almost too much. She rose swiftly, and reached out to hug Marisol tight, inhaling the familiar smell of chili powder and clean soap.

"Gracias, por todo," she whispered in her ear. Then with one final squeeze, she turned to the door.

"Are you ready?" Lissa bounced on her toes, the bridesmaid dress shimmering darkly with the movement. The sight of the young woman who preferred rips and tears in her clothes wearing something so girlie made Calista's heart swell with affection.

"Never been more ready," Calista said, taking a last sweeping glance around the old room. In all her daydreams she had never imagined prepping for her wedding in second-hand chairs, on ugly orange carpet, in front of a shadowy mirror. But how she had come to love this place and these people!

Marisol took a white handkerchief from her sleeve and waved it. "Now I'm ready."

Calista laughed out loud and took her arm. "Then let's go show them how it's done, Marisol."

Walking slowly to accommodate the older woman's halting steps, they moved to the entranceway as the music began. Lissa, Lana and Jackie progressed at a dignified pace, handsome escorts at their sides.

The change of music signaled the bride's approach and Calista smiled at the sedate notes of Pachelbel's *Canon in D.* Jorge lifted a hand in greeting, his head bobbing as he worked his magic with the stereo equipment. Grant was the one who'd asked him to play DJ for the day and Calista had half expected her walk down the aisle to be to a thumping hip-hop beat.

They stepped onto the green-carpeted aisle and Calista gasped at the transformation of the old cafeteria. A green velvet curtain blocked off the view of the kitchen construction. Trailing ivy and fairy lights lined the doors and the aisle. Tea lights and white satin bows decorated the sills along each frosty window, with generous boughs of holly every few feet. Her gaze swept the crowd, seeing so many friends and family. Her sister Elaine's husband stood near the back row, bouncing their baby boy as he fussed, smiling apologetically at the baby's contribution to the ceremony. Aliya, Josh and McKenzie grinned from the front row while little Savannah, pink sunglasses in place, waved like a metronome set on high.

At the very front stood Grant, impossibly handsome in a tuxedo, tiny white rose in his lapel. Eric stood a little to his left, red hair smoothed down for once. Elaine stood to the right of the minister. The two sisters locked eyes for a moment and Calista forced herself to glance away as her throat squeezed shut. The joy on Elaine's face spoke of healing and new beginnings, a family learning to love each other again.

The details of the room faded away as Calista looked into Grant's eyes. His face was alight with hope and the promise of years to love each other, of the family they wanted to make together. She wanted to sprint down the aisle but managed to keep a steady pace with Marisol.

With just a few more steps she stood at his side, unable to tear her gaze from his.

He leaned forward, dark hair falling over his forehead, and whispered in her ear, "I've decided to throw in a corner office to sweeten the deal. What do you say?"

She couldn't help laughing. "Just not the filing room?" she whispered back.

As they turned as one to face the minister, he spoke out of the corner of his mouth. "Nope. And it comes with some great art."

Calista blinked back sudden tears and gripped Grant's hand. God had moved heaven and earth, and the board of directors, to bring them to this point. She answered Grant's radiant smile with one of her own and knew that God's timing had never been more perfect.

* * * * *

SPECIAL EXCERPT FROM

LOVE INSPIRED

INSPIRATIONAL ROMANCE

When a therapy dog trainer must work with her high school crush, can she focus on her mission instead of her heart?

Read on for a sneak preview of Their Unbreakable Bond *by Deb Kastner.*

“Are you okay?” Stone asked, tightening his hold around her waist and gripping one of her hands.

“I— Yes.” She didn’t have time to explain to Stone why this had nothing to do with her sore ankle, nor why avalanches were her worst nightmare and that was the real reason why she’d suddenly swayed in his arms.

Not when there was work to be done. There were people in Holden Springs who needed help, and she knew she should be there.

Tugger whined and pressed against her leg as he’d been taught to do as a therapy dog. He could tell her heart rate had increased and her pulse was pounding in her ears, even if she didn’t show it in her expression, although there was probably that, too. The dog was responding to cues most humans couldn’t see, and Felicity reached out and absently ran a hand between Tugger’s ears to steady her insides.

“Have they set up a temporary disaster shelter yet?” she asked.

“Yes. At Holden High School,” her sister said. “They’re using the cafeteria and the gym, I think. I’d go myself except I have clients in the middle of service dog

LIEXP1221

training back at the center. Do you mind taking Tugger and heading out there?"

Felicity did mind. More than anyone would ever know, because she never talked about it, not even to her siblings. But now was not the time to give in to those feelings. She could cry into her pillow later when she was alone and the people of Holden Springs were safe.

"I'll take Tugger." She nodded. "And Dandy, too," she said, referring to a young black Labrador retriever who was part of the therapy dog program.

"I can tag along, if there's anything I can do to assist," Stone said. "That way you'll have an extra person for the dogs."

Felicity was going to decline, but Ruby spoke up first. "Thank you, Stone. They need all the help they can get. From what I hear, there are a lot of families who were suddenly evacuated from their homes."

"It's settled, then," Stone said. "I'm going with you."

Felicity didn't feel settled. The last thing she needed was Stone alongside her. It would distract her from her real work.

She sighed deeply.

A bruised ankle.

Stone's unnerving presence.

And now an avalanche.

Could things get any worse?

Don't miss
Their Unbreakable Bond *by Deb Kastner,*
available January 2022 wherever
Love Inspired books and ebooks are sold.

LoveInspired.com

LIEXP1221